Invisible Borders

a novel

POLLY KOCH

SIMON & SCHUSTER

New York   London   Toronto   Sydney   Tokyo   Singapore

Simon & Schuster
Simon & Schuster Building
Rockefeller Center
1230 Avenue of the Americas
New York, New York 10020

This book is a work of fiction. Names, characters, places and incidents are either the product of the author's imagination or are used fictitiously. Any resemblance to actual events or locales or persons, living or dead, is entirely coincidental.

Library of Congress Cataloging-in-Publication Data

Koch, Polly.
Invisible Borders/Polly Koch.
p.   cm.
I. Title.
PS3561.0285E45   1991
813'.54—dc20   90-45183
CIP
ISBN 0-671-72477-0

*Excerpts from The Tooth of Crime are from
Seven Plays by Sam Shepard, © 1974 by Sam Shepard,
Bantam Books, a division of Bantam, Doubleday,
Dell Publishing Group, Inc.*

for
Marion Stocking

Contents

ONE

Prologue

2015

THE COMMUNAL LIFE IN THE HOUSE BY THE RIVER, COMING together by slow degrees in the opening years of the twenty-first century, had Elise as its unwilling pivot. A microbiologist in her early fifties, Elise was indifferent to the political scene, at that time populated by everybody now living along the river, and had reacted to their hero worship by adopting an ironic stance. This included an abrupt and edgy celibacy. Ramona had fumed, *expedient* the mildest of the words she used. Still, the loss of certainty as the century turned had made everyone cling that much more to the expected, and Elise presenting the implacable front of her sexual abstinence had been the Elise the others wanted preserved—an embodiment of the cool, passionless authority they had lost inside. Ramona, of course, even in her fury at being seduced and then wantonly dropped, was right about the expediency. What the others wanted could not in any sense matter to Elise, but the love affair with Ramona was too deeply fraught with unexpected variables to last, and it was a simple enough matter for Elise to anchor that free-floating nouveau-fin-de-siècle angst to herself, to become the absent presence the others wanted. And they *did* want it. However much they moved into and out of each other's bedrooms—the light-filled upstairs rooms with their white paint and paper shades, and the darker odd-shaped rooms below fitted around stairwells and latter-day plumbing and an eccentric arrangement of closets—the collective left Elise in her downstairs room at the river end of the hall alone.

This was fine with her, accustomed to her own company since the summers she spent from age four at her grandmother's house in the small southern town where her father grew up. The memories were unused and fleeting, primarily of heat and how the glare had vanished into green-shaded yard, grass thick and spiky underfoot, a hedge at the side hazy with insects, all the trees too big to climb. Stories were scant, cautionary tales, some about her grandfather slipping and falling as he hung a swing from the largest tree, breaking his neck years before she was born. The beveled edges of Nana's house had reached up to deep eaves with a cocked hat where the roof split apart onto screened vents for the attic. Propped open, the small-paned windows from below looked like casements in a castle, and inside on the kitchen table a cut-glass vase held fifty silver spoons. It had been one of three houses, all of them full of terrible old women.

Great-aunt Helen's house, on the other side of the hedge and past an overgrown drive, had been surrounded by lawns and ornamental gardens, which Elise regularly crossed in the late afternoons, coming for supper vegetables, usually things Helen didn't want—a mess of stringy pole beans or oversized okra or tomatoes that split in Elise's palms no matter how lightly she held them. She had liked walking through the banks of flowers and down the shadowy lawn to the pond with its wooden pump shed propping up the long silvery skimmer, though she didn't care for the two dogs, aging Weimeraners who would sniff her fingertips and, after a cursory look, turn their bored yellow eyes away. Helen talked to the dogs as she picked through the vegetables under the shed, and once as Elise started back she had seen her pull one of those heavy heads into the crook of her arm to kiss its muzzle, her bright gold hair slipping suddenly down over one eye.

The intervening drive led back under the trees to a third house, empty and falling away, the weeds in the field between Nana's back hedge and the brick-edged flower beds of that other house reaching higher than Elise's head. Nana had told her the field used to be a long sweeping lawn marked with flowering shrubs and a path of white paving stones that went from Nana's back steps all the way up to her daddy's front porch. There had been stone benches and sheep to crop the grass.

Surveying the collapsing house by the river that January morning some fifteen years ago, everyone suddenly inhabiting a brand-new century, Elise had wasted an impatient thought on the tiresome symmetry of pegging her life at either end to an empty house in provisional ruin. Ramona, a good twenty years younger and in possession of deeds to house and land, had laughed at Elise's sour expression and looped one arm around her neck, kissing her cheek then the side of her mouth then the hollow inside her open collar, finally making love to Elise on the dirty boards that smelled of dry rot, the sun's faint warmth coming through the broken windows. Now, as Elise entered her mid-sixties, she slept with Hale, having embraced chastity only as long as it served her purposes. Though conceptually at a loss as Hale made his unexpected appearance in their midst, the others in the collective agreed that the two matched in an unlikely way —Elise broad-beamed and heavy with her loosely muscled arms, white skin, the darkened silver of her hair, and Hale shorter, slim in the hips, his eyes a catlike green to her variable amber. And while the fact they were lovers, despite the forty-year difference between them, may have restored Elise as a sexual possibility to the others, she remained a possibility the commune was reluctant to entertain, certainly not approach in actuality. They waited only for her to make the first move, which was something Elise might well never do—in fact, she could have told them, almost certainly would not do.

Walking down to the river, towel in hand, Elise couldn't have said what set her so neatly off, the others held at arm's length by her half-smiling silence, unless it was a consequence of the privileged place granted her or merely of time—the stiff-backed weight that age gave Elise finding a corollary in her formal distance. Picking her way through the rocks, Elise discounted as she always did their cautious deference to her supposedly unassailable intelligence. Her reputation as a bright iconoclast in biotechnology was a minor one, largely keyed to the seventeen-year-old scandal that erupted from her cross-border field test of a microbe she had created in the lab—a simple bacterium, Stone Age–like next to the higher cells. That the collective should look to her as an authority who could insist on intellectual truisms for them was not, Elise decided, wading into the water, her bloody fault. The symbolic process could break down like anything else in the psyche, and for everyone living in the renovated farmhouse sprawled above a slope that dropped to the tree-crowded river, the loss of both "real" fears and internal authority had left them prey to an unpredictable moodiness.

The surrounding hills were precipitous, rocky, threaded with dry gullies, although a silvery grass softened the curves, blowing on hillsides above the live oaks ranged in dark olive creases down tracks of water. Beside the river and on the smooth saddlebacks between hills, peach trees tangled together in rows while pastures thickened to a bright green. It was at the top of one of those plush, baizelike pastures, half-circled in a bow of the river, that the farmhouse stood beneath its windbreak—a big two-story wooden annex cobbled to one end and over the original house, stores and washrooms tacked to the other, cellars dug into the side of the hill. A wide deck at the back running nearly the length of the house was set on cinderblock pillars with a partial lattice, wood stacked below among a jumble of tools. Surfacing, shaking the water from her eyes, Elise scarcely remembered the trashed, door-banging wreck it had been when she first saw it, before she even knew Ramona, roughly thirty years ago. Back then everything had been dwarfed by the sky and the hills, by Nick, by the clear, punishing light.

Now the collective found itself dwarfed by events, feeling less liberated than lost—abandoned perhaps. Nothing they did was sufficiently out of the ordinary to merit that sense of social dislocation, but they felt sometimes like colonists who had disembarked on the wrong planet. Much remained the same. The cities had come through the millennium roughly intact, government and corporate entities indifferent to their invisible corruption by the drug lords they thought they had neutralized— nothing new there or in the futile quasi-leftist opposition. What was new was the evanescence of things, a breakdown going on below. Whenever Elise worked in the makeshift lab beyond the paddock, it amused her to imagine the scavenged equipment as slowly losing its meaning, becoming more alien by the moment, until some day recognition would cease—all the machines used to magnify, to spin, to measure, to record, rendered comical or curious, vaguely perverse. Outside, trees scraped the tarpaper roof and birds sang. Elise had seen a sculptor once put twenty pipettes inside a cartridge belt, the slender glass tubes winking and turning, infinitely fragile. The world had paled, social conventions now without objective existence. Even the idea of a market economy had been subverted by its anarchist shadow in the deal-making Channel, whence Elise had plucked Hale like a plum from a tree, a youth maddening and sweet by turns, less afflicted than the others by the memory of loss.

Most of them had joined the collective in a kind of shock, dismayed by the speed with which events had unraveled, by the smooth rightist machinery that stopped it, by the general hysteria that had caught everyone in the shrinking space between the immediate present and the next millennium. Elise had not ignored that sudden accumulation of social potential at the end, but her premillennial optimism had retained at all times a dry doubt. Elise, born in 1950, claimed to be intimate with the aging population and its nervous neoconservatism, despite Rita, a longtime friend from college, who resented Elise's desire to dragoon them both into early old age. That Max was dying, Rita said, was enough—the stiff-jointed Great Dane, who had come into Rita's house as a pup about the time that Elise moved there, leaning his heavy head against her thigh. Afterward Elise and Rita were never able to recall those times of impending so-called apocalypse without the seriocomic weight of Max coming between, the given object materializing in the effort not to think about it. Demographics, at any rate, prevailed as the cutting edge of the baby boom, faced with a bankrupt social-security trust and nonexistent safety net, chose to shore up the status quo—Max, with head slightly cocked, ears askance, eyes focused on some interior dial tone, the frazzled and stupefied dog let lie.

What was left was a world that teemed with oddly empty universals. A fundamentalist theocracy took over everywhere except in the cities, regimenting the rural towns, the empty land all around them indistinguishable, fallow or range, refuge or slag. Elise heard the others make up mocking names for the elusive landmarks they imagined existed, Stillwater or Slough of Despond, but only those from a different language and so simply the sound of their disparate syllables took hold—the rough camp to the north they called Archuleyta or places like Cibolo Creek. All else was God's country, grief, goodness and mercy, clinical despair. Ramona was the only one of them to move as more than a chance visitor in the generalized landscape.

In the course of the 1998 hearings on Elise's quasi-legal field test, Ramona had performed technical feats of elegant reportage, oblivious to the surrounding hysteria, the grandstanding by ecologists and the CIA, the likelihood of jail. The succession of brilliant examples she unfolded on the witness stand to illustrate Elise's theory on what the engineered microbe could do in the field, or not do, was a virtuoso diversion. In her mid-twenties Ramona had possessed startling good looks—angular, her gaze intense, a river of brown hair in waves down her back, mouth flexible, sexy in the rare instants she smiled. Elise did not seduce her. Elise did not think you could seduce anyone who was that consistently angry, that smart, and indeed, Ramona in bed was shy as a colt. The twenties for her generation had replaced the

14

teens in rebellious pain, or extended it, the props of adulthood unattainable, Ramona no different for all her brains.

Or Elise, who had finessed adulthood much of her life, so peripherally linked to the adult acts of marriage and divorce and career and aunthood as to make them somehow self-negating. The years married to Michael in eastern Oregon had been both monastic and suffused with a male adolescence of pickups and guns, cowboy boots and bars, not "marriage," and their casual goodbye, in the room with his microscopes and centrifuge, not a real divorce. Not like her sister Laura, two years younger than Elise, who did it right, or who suffered at least recognizable grief. Elise found the present communal life, with its loose appropriations from a dozen different traditions, familiar only in its unhinged approach, its pastiche, a comedy of alien quotations. Everything was open to challenge, to a quick loss of interest— who would do what, who would sleep with whom, who would make the deeper philosophical decisions, who would pick the petty quarrels, who would stay. Hale, their resident odalisque and advocate of one-pointed thinking, said they lacked discrimination, and they were, absolutely, intellectual whores, but everything went to deny convention—the more bizarre the collision, the better.

Elise recognized little, thank God, from the youthful ferment of her own generation. As she sat in the sweet-smelling night with wicker digging into the backs of her thighs, Elise felt immobilized among the others sprawled out on the deck, sleepy from the day's work, haloed in the peppery-sweet smell of dope. The river clucking across the gravel bar at the foot of the hill was a sotto voce constant to the ringing static of insects that intensified then faded away, to the low staccato of conversation. Everything was allowed to drift except her, the ostensible figurehead, materfamilias—Elise lifted her eyes briefly upward to where stars crowded the sky, thick as dusted sugar. Even the children, half asleep inside on the floor, were at greater liberty. Rita and Hollis had once argued about how idealization became a trap, Hollis a classic beauty, a classic tart, always acting onstage, to a degree, against type. Elise had sat with her back against the screen door, listening as she drank another beer, the neighborhood noisy with *conjunto* blaring from backyard radios and barking dogs and sirens—now a silent no-man's-land of Jamaican dealers, or it was the last time Elise was there.

Elise had learned to distrust the words people gave things, the collective itself a useful embodiment of Satan for the farmer-ranchers, the old retirees. Even they could be spooked, however, a town girl in the queue for coffee telling Elise how her prayer group had once healed a cow, a healing that had driven the petitioners into a mutually nervous, tight-lipped silence. The old reprobates, drinking in the cinderblock bar, a lot of them women, kept their own austere counsel. The place was full of close-mouthed women, left in the countryside to the traditionally debased work of provision and caretaking—nothing new again—but their subversive power was unexpected. No one would let a commune member past the church doors, but they could imagine that bare wooden cube full of weathered women in the fierce grip of unintelligible speech, something to make even a deacon think twice. Elise did not look for God but for a larger intelligence, a clear and palpable emptiness. During the time she was driving south to the test field once a month, she had entertained the notion of absence. She imagined rationalizing through the small, lucid space of her modest microbe in its mechanical dance to come out at a signal-pathway model applicable to the dense black box of the cell, moving into a venue already absent, already without referential anchors.

The commune seemed sometimes like an outpost on an invisible border, each lit window tiny, swallowed by the night, where Elise stood watching across the ridge and above the river, knee-deep in a muddle of sleeping sheep. She moved her loose fists in her pockets, listening with the dog for the soft movement of bands of illegal travelers, the hemorrhage north by now a superstitious gesture, the north as deadly as anywhere else. Everybody seemed poised at the outer edge of a collapsed star, Elise amused by the conceit, smiling as she watched the distant farmhouse, the black canopy of trees, the star-washed sky. The dog whined and trotted into the dark. Anything pulled past the event horizon of a burnt-out star disappeared forever, squeezed out of existence at the singularity just beyond where laws of space-time broke down. Elise followed the dog a few steps and caught a glint of water from the river below. They would all stop, though, the way she had stopped, despite her amalgam of esoteric technology, her deeply ironic will to subvert what seemed ridiculous strictures. Pure science still cycled separate from the massive absurdities of life as lived, its archaic organization, no one knowing how to move past that particular force of gravity. The collective was stuck for now, like everyone else, in the same overextended and unending pregnancy.

They knew they would stay to the end, and when it didn't end, they would stay for that too, waiting until there was nothing left but them, the multifaceted being of them, shifting personae around a vanished core, postwar, post-Bomb, post-apocalyptic, poised at the brink, withdrawing from loss. Memory diffused, ran together, until everyone there remembered themselves as children digging up the dead bird again and again to check on its imminent flight to heaven, or lying under the sullen neighborhood boy as he took a dozen shaky breaths, or promising their duty to God and their country, or throwing up sweet wine, or peeing for the police into a paper cup, or shouting threats at those they loved, or looking into X-rays for cancer, or crying, palms dug hard into their eye sockets, crying, all of them reflections of reflections of reflections, crying together. Elise rolled over in bed. Hale breathed beside her, the window across the room an empty gray square. They would make one hell of a final witness, in their boots and wool and worn-out denim, smartass jokers with a secret depression, vocally adept in the oh-oh-oh of carnal bliss, in the long, repeatedly gasped sustain at the light-rimmed peak of their inner black planet, and adept as well at postcoital sadness. They were stuck with the part of not dying while everyone else onstage fell prey to a bright, definitive, preordained doom. They would stay, they knew, circling, to the bitter end, and after.

TWO

Rita

1984

CARS WERE ALWAYS PARKED IN THE YARD OFF THE ALLEY THAT from Decker Avenue looked like a driveway going up to the biker bar. Rita, who had worked at Redbone's, knew the bikers as universals, constants, the way she knew the cars in front of her house on a given morning, already hot, the spokes of her bicycle flicking weeds in what was once the side yard of the house. Elise's Fiat was pulled up under the trees with Sloan's Oldsmobile, the ones that belonged there, the house looming flat and angular beside them. Rita had hated like hell putting burglar bars on, but after the last rip-off, Sloan had kicked through the mess, yelling at her. "You *like* getting screwed? You *like* sweeping up shit?" The windows on Elise's side were narrow rectangles, pseudo–French Quarter behind wrought-iron bars.

Ducking under the oleanders, pack catching on the leaves, Rita walked the bike toward the cluttered front porch, which faced toward Decker, hard up against the fence of Carmen's backyard. The television was on just inside the screen door, and the air held its usual faint aroma of dope. Each evening Sloan would stand on the porch and wave genially to Carmen, to the men playing horseshoes under the lights, and smile at Rita. He resented the way the house faced. "A quarter turn," he would say softly to her, as if it were a simple request for a house. A turn either way—he wasn't particular.

Sloan should talk, the ultimate immovable object. When Rita thought about Sloan it was always of his heavy arms, his pianist hands, how when he worked outside the fine hair on his back and chest stuck flat in the sweat. Rita dropped the bike and walked by the porch and around the house to the backyard. Sloan was building a fence from scrap lumber for Max, the Great Dane puppy, an apparently endless project. The fence looked piss-poor, each board a different length and width, a mix of raw and weathered pine with planks here and there of turquoise, yellowed white.

"It's theatrical, creative," Sloan had said, eating mushrooms yesterday as he worked on the fence, Rita waiting to do her share inside. When she came back from her shower, the yard had turned a vibrant amber, weeds curling green around Sloan where he still nailed boards, the hammer a hot silver arc above his hand. Shirtless, he had looked solid and buttery, the light making his skin glow, the round glasses flash. When he started toward her, Rita felt a sudden distaste. "Come on, Sloan, I just got clean." He grinned. He had a small mouth and heavy eyelids, everything—flesh, garden, fence—more than they should be in the flickering light, his sweaty face coming closer. She turned, genuinely annoyed. "Sloan, dammit." His arm across her breasts was damp. Still mad, she fell against him and the warmth of his chest, his black curls wild against the pulsing sky as he pulled her in toward him and she tasted first salt then the warm familiar thrust of his tongue in her mouth.

The cucumbers needed water. Rita slid the pack onto one

shoulder and poked at the vines, dirt crumbling against her knuckles as she twisted two zucchini free then thumbed the curled blossoms off the ends. It was too hot during the day to garden and she spent all her evenings now down at the theater. Not a bad space for what used to be a wallpaper store, crowded in by all those upscale bars, once pinochle joints and shoe-repair shops until the local drug money bought them up. The bars were pretty damn depressing, as was the ever-younger crowd, boys and girls growing backwards into replicas of her own generation's conservative parents. When she started, she had bums with bottles in paper bags falling in to watch *The Balcony* and *Ubu Roi.* Ten years later and the place was full of regulars, critical and clubby. "Sam Shepard . . . ?" The voice had been polite and bemused. "Doesn't he write the same thing over and over?"

Squatting in her garden midmorning, Rita doubted you could even do that, never managing the same thing twice herself. The lettuce had gone to seed, turned frowsy. The new designer that morning had looked as bad. "Fucking queens," was all he would say, lighting his second cigarette and staring moodily up at the homemade grid. His light plots, though, were meticulous, inspired.

"They think Shepard writes the same thing over and over," Rita had told Elise, whose production it was. "Is that possible?" Elise said vaguely. After a long moment she added, "This is early Shepard, anyway."

The step to the back door sagged under Rita's weight as she elbowed open the screen, the kitchen dark inside. Max came wagging around the table, a blacker shadow, and slammed his flank into her legs as Elise's voice said, "Hey," then "Max. Bad." Rita could just see her turning in the shadows at the end of the room, her bare arms luminous in the half-light. On the shelf beside her was a row of empty jars.

Rita dropped the pack onto the counter and rolled the two zucchini across the kitchen table, dizzy from the sudden dark, Max's tail smacking her knees. The sun was beating against the window shade above the sink, and the square of light made her skin look flushed, sunburned. Elise, walking to the table, gave

Rita a lazy, contemplative smile, her gaze sliding away to some pleasant middle distance. Bits of maroon hair curled around her forehead. She was in another one of her boring life-is-sweet-nothing moods. "What's up?" said Rita, shoving Max to the side and opening the refrigerator door.

Elise selected the larger zucchini and weighed it solemnly in her fist. " 'Alas, poor Yorick.' " She looked at Rita with regret.

Rita gazed back at her, popping the Coke tab. Max nosed her arm. Elise's awkward clowning was a pain in the butt, something secretly manipulative lying behind all that protean unhappiness. When they graduated a year after everyone else and left for Alaska in a secondhand truck, they had shared at least a mutual cynicism, an upfront rage. Rita kept the faith even after she inherited the house, but Elise, going on to marry and divorce somewhere the hell in Oregon, had not. Trying to connect after close to ten years was tough, Rita falling into Elise's silence; she missed Elise's hard rise after the dangled bait. In six months still nothing Rita said made it through.

Elise brought her eyes around to Rita's face, smile dreamy. " 'Oh, that this too too solid flesh would melt, thaw, and resolve itself into a dew.' " She slapped the zucchini into her palm. Rita took a long swallow of Coke.

The line seemed to remind Elise of something else. Looking down, she frowned at Max and lowered her voice. "Bad," she said with reproach. "Are you a bad dog?" Max sidled his eyes toward the door.

Rita glanced along the floor and found the puddle by the stove. Housebreaking Max was taking forever, mainly because Sloan didn't do a damn thing to help. "What is *this?*" Rita walked to the stove and pointed. Max was sneaking out of the room. *"Max."*

Elise gazed at the dog, who had stopped. "We could jump him," she said. One book had advised them to throw Max on his back and shout at him, simulating the lead wolf of a pack, but with a dog that size it was a lot of work. Rita sighed. She couldn't do everything around there.

Elise turned toward the end of the kitchen. For all her height, she could come across small and vulnerable, the oversized shirt with the sleeves cut off falling to her knees. When she stopped, looking for the mop, the line of jars reflected her in wavery streaks. Rita had come into the kitchen one night to find the nervous kid with the bad skin pushing Elise up against the jars, his mouth on her neck as he kneaded the front of her shirt. Chin turned, Elise was peeling off first one hand then the other, shoving his head away with her arm, as if she had walked into a web and were picking the invisible gossamer from her skin, irritated and resigned. The boy had only pressed closer, pumping against her, making the jars chime.

"I shouldn't smoke," Elise said to herself.

She probably shouldn't, not that it would make that much difference, Elise already buffered from here to Tuesday. Rita made herself move, picking up the paper towels. "Sloan took the mop; don't ask me why," she said and crouched to wipe up. The floor was amazingly filthy. God knows when someone had last swept up. She added over her shoulder, "You would not believe the dirt down here."

When Elise didn't answer, Rita looked around to see her just standing there, one hand on her hip, looking at the floor. Rita watched her for a minute. "You're right," she finally said. "If you don't toke up, the dog doesn't piss on the floor. It's called the Zen of housebreaking." Elise smiled faintly.

Sloan was calling from the living room, and Rita swiveled to look down the hall. At the far end she could see the edge of the sofa, half of the oscillating fan set on the floor, but no Sloan. She waited then picked up the wad of towels.

In the places where she and Elise had stayed, from the duplex in Louisville's inner city to the bus set on blocks in Indiana, always room opened on room, shotgun style. Late at night, everyone hot and high, they would turn off all the lights but the overhead in the last room and watch from the dark how the simple gesture of anyone standing in the lit doorway was instantly dramatized, turned to cinematic art. Elise would wave from the door then step with elaborate grace off the screen and into the darkened room.

22

"The fourth wall," said Elise behind her, remembering the same thing.

Sloan was in the doorway, the phone dangling from one hand, receiver wedged to his ear. He gestured at them, clearly irked. Then he was gone and Max appeared. A noise behind him made him turn, ears flipped back, rear end starting to wag. As he lowered his head and disappeared from the doorway, the fan fell over.

A one-dog demolition team, though why laughing at Max made her want to cry was completely beyond Rita. She stood up and stuffed the towels in the trash. Elise at the table reached for the pack on the counter and pulled the rolled light plot out. "So where did you find this guy, this light designer, Devo or Darvon or whatever his name is?" Rita said.

"Devon." Elise bent over the drawing, laying the zucchini on top of the curled corners to hold it flat. She smiled at the stenciled shapes of Lekos and Fresnels. "My dentist told me. Devon's his lover."

"Right. Your dentist."

"The romance is on the skids, a mutual disenchantment as far as I could tell; that little suction thing was making too much noise." Elise caught Rita's stare and arched her eyebrows. "Come on, Ree, I *did* check him out."

Sloan yelled again, and Rita took one last swallow of her Coke and left. Elise *would* have checked, making half a dozen separate inquiries, pinning DaVida in less than two hours. When she put her mind to it, Elise was good, the only one of them gainfully employed. Only slightly more improbable than the fact she had deigned to come back at all was Elise as a broker of breeding stock, she of the simple off-base smile, drama major, swimming jock.

Elise could play dumb like no one else. While it clearly annoyed Rita's second cousins that their aunt, her great-aunt, gave Rita the house, she couldn't get a straight reaction from Elise. Fall in Minnesota meant the air off the lake turned cold and smoky. The phone woke Rita up in the trailer belonging to a blond and trusting musician who had handed off his trailer keys

23

and a job tending bar in some backwoods joint so he could take a two-month gig in St. Paul. The trailer came with dogs, junked appliances, and a lake, the sun bouncing off the waves when Rita went looking for Elise to tell her about the house.

"Door." Sloan pointed, shifting the phone to his other ear. "For Elise." Rita looked through the screen. She didn't recognize the man on the porch, whistling between his teeth as he looked down at the canvas bases. Max stood, his nose inches from the screen, watching. The man had a small mustache and wore white running shorts with a polo shirt; his thighs were big, muscled from cycling. It was anybody's guess where Elise had met him. He touched his upper lip.

On the set the Red Sox were playing somebody, second inning (Rita looked closer), one man on base. The sound of the announcer was soporific. The room glowed sepia behind the pulled-down shades, torn and taped in half a dozen places. The kid who had pinned Elise against the kitchen shelves was bent over the dope tray, carding out seeds with a matchbook cover; the soft rush and ping was another stupefyingly familiar sound. Three guys from Sloan's softball team lay sprawled on the floor, the shortstop slowly pedaling his feet in the air.

The man outside was trying to peer politely into the room, and Sloan, phone against his chest, glared at Rita. Swinging backwards, one hand gripping the edge of the door, she looked behind her toward the kitchen. Elise was staring at the window and, as Rita watched, tilted her head back slightly and yawned. "Elise," Rita said. "Company."

Elise had a way of walking that made her look simple-minded, somehow sexy. She had come up from the lake that way, arms reaching a little, her boots caked with mud. "You what?" she said. While Rita explained how her great-aunt left her the house, Elise yawned, looking back at the water. "Smell that?" she said when Rita stopped. "Fall's coming." Rita didn't give a shit about the seasons. "Would you listen? It's a *place*, Elise. It's mine." When Elise lifted an eyebrow and said something about property is theft, Rita slowed down, started to take cautious stock. Birds were chirping overhead in the trees. "Come on,

Elise," she finally said. "It'll be fun. We can fix it up." The air stank of cowshit, the ground soaking a chill all the way to Rita's knees. One of the dogs shoved its snout into a tangle of roots, waited a moment, and sneezed. Then Elise smiled softly at nothing, her eyes still as glass, the lake reflecting off her face. "I don't want to go back," she said.

"Oh, yeah." Elise was looking past Rita's shoulder at the man waiting on the porch. "The guy from Colorado."

"Right." Rita kept her face blank. The men were an increasingly tired joke; they seemed to follow Elise home from everywhere.

"Give me a break, Ree. He's homesick." Elise went out, hand holding the latch so the door groaned as it closed. The man was smiling and turned self-consciously when she waved behind him toward her door. Then they were gone.

Sloan had hung up and was starting to dial again. "Who's he?" he said. Rita shrugged. The kid was licking the joint, his tongue sharp and unhealthy-looking. When Sloan started to say something more, Rita cut him off. "So what, we get three times the traffic over here." Sloan said that he at least knew their friends, and Rita looked across at the kid now striking a match and walked back into the bedroom.

The bed had a striped spread. Her T-shirt tightened across her breasts as Rita lay down, pulled under her arms, muscles hard from lifting weights at the Y, swinging lights one-handed up a ladder. The dog bent around the corner as if built on hinges and lay down on the floor then stretched out onto his side and sighed. Rita flexed one foot then the other, pressing her lower back down against the mattress.

Sloan had come out of the icy dark of the downtown bar like some kind of Botticelli angel, itchy, high as a kite. "I've seen you," he told her. "I've seen you." His hand played along the bar beside her arm, making invisible chords, the fingers muscular, pale against the wet wood. "I've seen you," he whispered. "No," she said and held onto her drink. "You sing?" his hand picking out notes, "bluesy, country, full of heartache? A little Patsy Cline?" "No." "But I've seen you, seen you singing," and

25

his eyes under the heavy lids had some kind of crazy wind blowing through.

Rita shifted her hips. The announcer's voice in the next room rose, singsonged rapidly, fell; the crowd noise pattered. Still on the phone, Sloan grunted. He had walked into Redbone's kitchen a week later, two minutes before closing time, slapping through the door into the skim-milk light where Rita was spraying the last tray of glasses with water. Redbone caught the door in one big hand and came inside like a cat, the light purpling his black skin. He took Sloan by the shoulder, his thumb in a smooth line against Sloan's throat. "You get some manners on you, boy. You ask *polite* like before you set foot inside my kitchen." "May I please," Sloan said, smiling nicely, "fraternize with your help?"

He had a good supplier with quality dope. Stopping with him halfway up the dark alley, Rita took a hit. She watched the tip sizzle and run toward her fingers, the hot cloud funneling into her mouth, and swayed slightly. Something glittered at the edges of her eyes and she stumbled. "Whoa," said Sloan, and his hands circled her upper arms. She could not see.

"Sloan?" Redbone knifed open the case of tequila. "I got no real trouble with him. What you might call your middleweight, your soft-core dealer. Never been out there to hear him play?" Redbone grinned and marked something on a piece of paper. "Shoo-ee, puts tears in your eyes. I just wouldn't cross him is all. You don't want to cross those sweet-looking boys."

Rita opened her eyes and drew one leg up. A trickle of air moved cool against the sweat along her calf, the back of her thigh. After all the years with Sloan in her house, she still had to lightly pull her punches. She closed her eyes again, tented the T-shirt above her stomach and let it fall, let her hand fall.

Stop, start—the steam always had a mild bleachy smell, the spray nozzle loose in her fingers. As he let Sloan go, Redbone had shrugged. The kitchen was fifteen degrees hotter than the bar, where she could be racking the balls, cool and smooth under her fingers, Redbone scrutinizing her break as the sirens wailed outside. Do that or take a walk with Sloan, of the heavy arms, of the sweet-looking smile. She bounced the spray off the metal sink.

The leaves were falling in Minnesota. Elise, hitting the surface of the lake in a shallow dive, shouted as she came up and pedaled furiously, hair plastered to her cheeks: shit, shit, shit, coming in gasps. "All right, already," Rita said from the shore, "you win the macho contest." Elise rolled onto her stomach and stroked away. They had flipped to see who got the truck and Elise had won; Rita was catching the evening bus. The haze across the water hurt her eyes.

She couldn't see Sloan in the alley, only felt his hands shift around her arms, the thumbs moving across her breasts. There. His head was a black silhouette against the night, lights across his rimless glasses a stream shattering into a nimbus she couldn't blink away, the slow circling thumbs, his lips coming down soft and open. No. He slipped his tongue inside the circle of her mouthed refusal. No. The night hummed.

Rita loved watching Elise drive, loved that total self-absorption, muscles flexing as she shifted gears, her elbow hanging out the window, sometimes her whole arm as she beat her palm on the door in time to the music. She would cram her hair up under the strap of the visor, shoved down on the curls that whipped in the wind around her shiny reflector shades. Her mouth moved as she sang to herself beneath the rattle of the truck. Farmland outside would be flat as a plate, dense and green, rows of soybeans flying past like the spokes of a wheel.

"So where are you going?" Rita had asked Elise, who was flipping the dime again in the darkened trailer, up through a bar of light from the window. The musician, back from St. Paul, his bass fiddle tipped alongside the couch, was in the kitchen. "Where are you going?" Rita asked again. The trailer was small. The bass seemed to fill the room, Rubenesque curves in scuffed black leather. In the kitchen oil popped and sputtered over the sudden ching of the toaster. "Elise?" Elise's stoicism with that blank half-smile of hers made Rita crazy. The dime spun, gray, silver, gray, and Rita stood up suddenly, a box of blankets, Elise's black waders on top, in her way. Pissed, she kicked it then felt

27

the dime hit her cheek. "I'm going swimming," said Elise, already stepping around the packs, onto the sofa and over the back, out the door. A hot smell of dirt and pine needles came in with the blast of light as the door hung open. The blond bass player, spatula in hand, watched Rita pick her way through. "You got trouble?" he asked. "The only thing I've *got*, apparently," Rita said through gritted teeth, "is a house."

Max whimpered in his sleep. He had his back pressed against the door that led to what Sloan called the billiards room, a big windowless space at the center of the house. Rita had put her bed there when she first moved in, her great-aunt's bed: tall semicircles of bronze bars, two lumpy mattresses, no box springs. It was a great bed, heavier than it looked, stationed in the middle of the varnished floor.

"Christ," Sloan had said, staring inside, "do you burn black candles at midnight?" Framed by the light from the room behind them, their shadows stretched toward the bed. The uneven floor looked glossy, like river water, moving. Rita held onto the edge of the door. She watched Sloan's shirt glow in the dark of the room, dipping and swaying. He clicked on the tensor lamp she had tied to a bar, lighting up rumpled sheets, a scarlet bedspread. His face was pale and sweaty, lost in glass and ebony ringlets. "Turn it off," Rita said. She was walking on water, suddenly furious, frantic, then everything was dark again. She reached out and touched the curve at the foot of the bed.

"It's okay." Sloan stood in front of her, stroking her shoulders, but there was water to her knees, swimming in the back of her throat. "Shh," and he brushed his fingers along the nape of her neck, lifting the heavy braid. He bent closer, his voice musing next to her ear. "Do you ever undo it?" He was working the rubber band off. After a minute she felt her hair hot on her back. "This room," he said, "you know what this room needs?" His hands were moving through her hair, then along her back, pressing her toward him. "One of those big hanging lights, you know? With the colored edges?" He slid his hand under her shirt and started to push it up along her back. "And a billiards table, with inlaid mahogany and green baize." His hands came around

28

to her sides, lifting the shirt over her breasts. He moved against her. "And you bent over, lining up a shot, in a red velvet dress." He ran his palm along her spine. "Cut low," he whispered, sliding his hand down. He pushed at the waistband of her cut-offs. "Very, very low," and his fingers dipped inside, probed deeper. "Down to there," he said.

"Do you want to kiss me?" Elise had said to the kid she had picked up at the Dairy Queen. Even in the dim glow of the two flashlights, Rita could see him flush. The tent flaps were open, but it was still hot inside. The kid looked over at his friend. "Well?" said Elise, happily drunk. Nothing stopped her when she got like that. Rita unzipped the mesh and crawled out, the friend stumbling after her. The tent looked spooky from the outside, a silver dome lit up in a corner of the campground. Rita walked to the truck and boosted herself onto the tailgate. Some people laughed outside an Airstream trailer four sites away, their lawn chairs set around a dwindling fire. The trees pressed over-head, leaves still. "He's got a real nice girlfriend," the boy said as Rita swung her legs up and stuffed a pack behind her head. "Works at the Winn Dixie till nine." The light inside the tent went out.

The light from Redbone's kitchen seemed to vanish at once, swallowed up in the overgrown fences and shrubs. Redbone was happy to shoot pool by himself in the empty bar, a Fats Waller record spitting and crackling on the old hi-fi. He had been whistling inside as he slapped a wet rag down the counter before the sound of crickets drowned him out, then even the light was gone. Forlorn, Rita tried to bring up the neighborhood, all the poor working-class couples sleeping in the heat on top of their sheets, but nothing worked—she could have been on the moon. "This just came in," said Sloan, striking a match.

The afternoon breeze had been cold. Rita frowned as she watched Elise swim, the white flash of her arms against the water, her head a sleek dot. She counted the strokes, nine, ten, and still Elise didn't turn. Come on, she thought, come on. Leaves stirred at her feet, dry and yellow. After watching a minute more, Rita turned and jogged back to the trailer. The bass player looked up from his plate as Rita climbed over the couch. "Is there a boat?" she said, scooping up two blankets and the rubber boots. "What?" he said. "A boat, a boat." He shook his head. Rita was out the door, skidding on the pine needles then running downhill. The chill air was golden. When she got to the water's edge, Elise had started back.

Elise was a good swimmer, but she hadn't trained in months, a year, maybe more. She stopped once and treaded water, staring at the shore. Rita didn't know whether to wave. Then Elise arrowed both hands forward and started to breaststroke, her head bobbing, face lifted. For something to do, Rita pulled on the boots and took a careful step into the water. Muck swirled around her ankle.

Trees lined the lake except where a long graveled bluff rose up near the road and a stretch of bottomland bloomed with yellow flowers. A Corvair crunched into the picnic area far to the right and two people got out. Rita heard the faint music from their radio, somewhere else a dog barking. She could now see Elise's face, pale and intent, the glistening line of her shoulders. Rita stepped deeper in. Elise was less than a dozen yards away. When she got close enough to stand, she grimaced and tried to kick the sludge off her foot, splashing forward, sinking. Her eyes were shadowed, her lips without color. Rita reached for her hand. "Don't touch me," Elise said. She lunged, stroking with her hands, and Rita took her arm anyway. When Elise jerked back, Rita swayed off balance, water pouring into one boot. Damn it, damn it—Rita tightened her grip and pulled as Elise fell forward, legs kicking weakly. Two more steps and they were on the bank and Rita had reached down for a blanket.

Elise, who had three inches on Rita and longer arms, caught Rita backhanded in the jaw and nearly knocked her down. The blanket slid off Elise's shoulder, the skin along her ribs and flank goose-pimpled a mottled white. "You're going to freeze," Rita said, stumbling in the waterlogged boots as she reached for another blanket. Her jaw hurt like hell. Elise hit her again but this time almost fell, and Rita caught her, wrapping the blanket around her shoulders. Crying now, Elise bucked in Rita's grip as

30

she tried to wiggle her arms free. "Shh," said Rita, "it's okay." Elise cried harder. "It's okay," Rita said, her face in Elise's wet hair, eyes closing, exhausted. After a while, she crouched then sat in the leaves and drew the second blanket toward her across Elise's mud-streaked legs.

Rita touched the wet spot on the bed next to her mouth. Her eyelids were heavy and the backs of her legs ached. The bed sank slightly as Sloan sat beside her and ran his fingertips around the outline of her face against the bedspread. "Drool," he said. "How lovely."

Rita rolled onto her stomach and stuck her face in the crook of her arm. "I also stink."

"Man, I just don't know." Sloan traced his thumb down her backbone. "The romance of it all could be killing us." His palm was warm on the back of her thigh. The phone rang and rang again. "Yo," said someone in the other room and after a short pause, "Sloan." The television was still on. Rita felt the bed lighten, her thigh cool. She tightened her butt, pushing down into the mattress, stretched each leg, and sighed.

Two weeks after she slept with him, Sloan and a friend moved her bed out of the middle room. The pool table that took its place was old, balding, obnoxious, worse than one of Redbone's. That was *her* room, where *she* slept. Staring, Rita could hear Sloan whistling down the hall in the kitchen. She turned off the light then went through the house turning off all the lights until she got to the kitchen. She saw him, stirring spaghetti in a skillet on the stove, then he was gone. "Shit, Rita," he said. The floor creaked. When he hit the switch by the back door, Rita flicked hers off again. In the silence that followed, a bird suddenly chirped outside the window. She could feel her ribs jerking, her breath tight with anger. "There's a store downtown, three blocks from the freeway," she said. "The guy's old and he's selling out. It's the right size and shape for a theater." The spaghetti made a slow popping noise, the blue gas flame like a penciled ring. "I want you to buy it for me," Rita said. The house was still for a moment then "You got it, babe," said Sloan out of the dark.

"What do you know about theaters?" Redbone put the accent

on the *a*, made it long, gold molar winking as he set up his shot. "All I need to know," she said. The needle ticked at the end of the record.

She and Elise had directed themselves in Ursule Molinaro's *Breakfast Past Noon* as their undergraduate thesis, sitting on the two harp cases and taking turns listening to each other's lines, Mother and Daughter. The audiences thought it was dogshit, but Elise had loved the ending, mashing the cigarette into Rita's mouth. " 'I couldn't help myself,' " her voice sweet and clear, eyes narrowed to amber slits, " 'my hands were stuffing the burn-ing cigarette into her mouth.' " Lying in the closed harp case, smelling sweat and sawdust and painted canvas, Rita would hiss at Elise pressed down on top, their legs tangled, until Elise gig-gled and touched the wet nail polish on Rita's cheek, squirming around to kiss her hard on the lips.

"Where is it?" Sloan had said softly in the alley, moving his mouth away. His thumbs brushed the T-shirt over her nipples. Rita tried to shift her brain into thought. He was laughing, teasing her lips with his tongue. "Rita?" The gravel crunched under his feet. "Lovely Rita, meetah maid." His breath smelled like dope. "Where is what," she finally said. "The house." Christ, she thought, closing her eyes.

Elise had described her grandmother Nana's house and the racetrack for horses, then greyhounds, laid out back by the river with public swimming from platforms that Nana's brother Gar had made. Nana's house was nothing special, one story with an L-shaped porch, while through the hedge and across the road Uncle Gar and Aunt Helen's house lay dwarfed by gardens and lawn. It was the *old* house, though, the house behind the others on the bluff above the river, that Elise really liked. She said in pictures there were beds of roses and a low white wall and deco-rative clumps of prickly pear and two sheep tethered to keep the grass smooth. "I probably," she said later, "made up the sheep." But not Linnie, appearing pale as dust in her heavy shoes, her hair falling down, then as suddenly gone. Elise's sister Laura never saw the ghost. Elise said that Laura wouldn't stay at Nana's without the whole family and Linnie never showed when the family was there.

"The worms crawl in, the worms crawl out," Rita sang. "Fuck you," said Elise. The worms play pinochle on your snout. Rita, at the edge of the yard, wanted to spin, toe touching for balance, across to her house, a pale gray shadow against the night. ("Fuck you, Rita.") The house always seemed to Rita to clench its jaw in profile, patient as the day is long. ("And fuck your mother too.") Sloan ran his hand along her shoulders and Rita moved away. Her great-aunt had played a mean game of cribbage, her rings dangling on her big-knuckled fingers; she could add in her head like lightning. Rita was now deeply sorry she had sung about the worms. When Sloan put his mouth on her neck, she walked into the yard. Without speaking, he followed her around to the porch then stopped to balance the roach lightly between his lips. The crack of the match, Rita thought, sounded like the last little piece of her heart breaking.

"So what's the matter with *you?*" said Redbone. Rita shrugged and spun listlessly on the bar stool. A Harley guttered up outside, roared, and was choked off. Redbone gave her a look. "How you fixed for money these days?" The door opened, a sharp wedge of daylight, then wheezed shut behind the biker. "Stony broke," Rita said cheerfully, her back to Redbone, elbows on the bar. She felt him walk behind her, then his voice floated out to her left, asking What'll it be. The cap came off the bottle with an icy pop. "I miss her," Rita said softly and jumped when Redbone spoke at her elbow. "Of course you do," he said.

Sloan moved his hand against her stomach and unsnapped her cutoffs then eased the zipper down with two fingers. The cutoffs hung loose on her hips until he pushed a little, worked his hand inside, then they were falling gradually down her legs, over her knees, into warm hollows around her feet. He took in a breath on a light groan, held her hard against him, half bending his legs. "Oh yeah," he whispered. Still holding onto the bed, Rita opened her eyes as he suddenly pulled her around, her fingers jerked loose. She made a dizzy circle in the dark, then the mattress was thudding under her back. The bed bounced. As she groped above, Sloan slid her shirt the rest of the way up, pulling it over her head. She worked her hands free and reached up again, fingers grazing a pillow. She couldn't tell which way they were lying. When Sloan leaned up and away to pull his own shirt off, she squirmed around and saw they were on a slight diagonal. He put his mouth around her nipple just as she touched the bars and tightened her fingers. The rush of warmth from breast to groin ached, and she tried to push his head away with her free hand. He sucked harder then moved to the other breast, one hand fumbling with his belt. Cloth bunched and slid against her, the buckle scraping her thigh, the touch of his bare leg a shock.

Feeling her stiffen, he slowed down, his finger flicking her breast lightly as he kissed her around her mouth. "You okay?" he said softly, his knee easing between her legs. "This okay?" he murmured, his cock pressed along her thigh, a hard curve in the knit of his underwear. He rubbed it against her. Elise, thought Rita, turning her head. She thought she could see Elise waving slowly in the doorway, shirt blowing around her, one hand tocking back and forth like a beauty queen on a float. Feeling the bed shift, Rita looked away. Sloan had slid her underpants down and, half up on his elbows, was pulling his own off. Rita watched him hold his cock for a second then turn, rolling toward her. I miss her, she had said. Sloan slid his tongue deep into her mouth and moved on top. Elise had twisted around inside the blanket, elbows caught awkwardly in front, trying to work an arm free, crying. Sloan lay between her legs, part the way inside, and Rita lifted one foot over his back, curving her hips up toward him, breath jerking in her throat. Of course you do. Braced above her on his arms, his face bent into her neck, Sloan pushed. Of course you do. All the way in now, he moved slowly at first, then faster; the bed rocked. Rita dug one heel into the mattress and arched her back as he touched and vanished, touched and vanished, deeper inside. "Oh baby," he panted, and Rita rolled her cheek into the sheets, eyes shut. God *damn* you, Elise. She tried then to pull back, to stop, but it was too late; she was already sliding over the curve, blooming, her leg tight against his back as she pressed herself out into the vacant dark where nothing else lived and someone far away could be heard, with dispassion, calling this the saddest fuck in the world.

Rita opened her eyes. The shadows were higher on the wall. The house was quiet. In the yard another car door slammed, then the engine whined a second or two before it caught. Tires were already crunching down the alley. Yawning, Rita wondered whether Elise had gone. Everyone met for the games at the lakeside park—the lawyers Sloan knew from painting their renovated Victorians and moving their Colombian snow, the theater crowd of actors and regulars, even Elise's breeder friends. Laura still showed up, more than eight months pregnant, coming in a separate car from Milos so she could leave if she wanted.

"Has Milos directed before?" Rita had rested her chin in her palm, wondering what exactly Elise thought this would do, backing the play for her brother-in-law—make Laura happy, Rita rich? Besides, Shepard wasn't the theater's style, too macho American, rock-and-roll, plus the summer schedule was already soft. Air-conditioning alone would be a bitch. Elise swung her legs, sitting on the desk. "He's Ukrainian," she said. Rita gazed down as she doodled on an electrician's estimate. "Laura said he's a natural. Meyerhold in the blood. Or Eisenstein. One of those. Or somebody else." Rita nodded, thinking about the pick-up band required, whether that would draw a newer crowd, punks, skinheads, whether they even had money. Elise leaned closer, the lamp turning one side of her head ruby red. "I weel give to you a-one a-thousand dollars een unmarked beels," she whispered. Still looking down, knowing she would give Elise the moon on a silver chain if she asked for it, Rita started to laugh.

The billiards room was airless. Rita walked across to Elise's door, listened for a moment, and tapped.

Elise opened the door. "Hi. I thought you had gone."

"I was sleeping." Rita looked past her to the bicyclist sitting cross-legged on the floor.

"This is Charles."

Charles nodded. Rita hadn't noticed his forehead before, how it bulged a little over his eyes. He sat hunched forward slightly as if he were listening intently to music or making a low-voiced confession. Across the room Elise had raised the shades halfway. Her Fiat was the only car left in the yard.

"So I guess we need to get going?" Elise sat back on the floor, stretching her legs straight in front.

Through the gaping armholes of the workshirt, Rita could see the undercurve where her breast began. Charles looked then slid his eyes toward the window. Lots of luck, loser, Rita thought, running her tongue along the corner of her mouth with its dried saliva. Elise didn't sleep with anyone these days. A fan turned back and forth in the doorway to the bedroom.

"Rita?" Elise was looking at her. "Yo, Rita."

"What?"

"Softball." She smiled, her eyelids still a bit flushed.

Hands on his knees, Charles cleared his throat. "You need to go somewheres?"

Elise shrugged. "Softball game."

"Well, I need to get going myself." He rolled to one side, knelt, and stood, nearly graceful. He had a pleasant smile. "Nice to meet you," he said to Rita.

When the front door shut behind him, Rita closed her eyes. Next door Carmen was browning hamburger, the smell drifting across the yard and through the window. A screen door banged, someone yelling for her kids. When the bicycle gritted by, gears clicking into place, Rita opened her eyes. Elise was watching him from the window. "Come on," she had said once to Rita, "I mean, look at them. Don't they just break your heart?"

The team was in the field when they drove up, Elise spinning the wheel so the rear end slewed sideways in the dirt as she stopped. Getting out, Rita saw Sloan sitting at the end of the bench, staring at the outfield. When she came up behind him, he leaned back without moving his eyes and reached overhead to touch her fingers through the fence. "You were sleeping hard," he said.

"You should have got me up."

"But you looked so peaceful . . . all right, come *on*." A pop fly arched slowly up. The shortstop drifted underneath it, face tilted back, and caught it easily. The stands applauded.

Rita squinted behind her through the haze of dust raised by the batter's sprint for first and scanned the crowd on the bleachers. "Small crowd."

36

"It's too hot." The pitcher sent the ball in and the batter whiffed it. Sloan bent forward and started writing something on his clipboard.

Rita yawned, hooked her fingers through the fence. She watched Milos at first base, moving from foot to foot like a dancer; he radiated a muscled energy. His English had that sure-fire foreign charm, faintly Slavic, Old World, or maybe it wasn't the accent but the turn of the head, that display of finely honed jaw. Milos, half-smile curled slightly into his cheek, was saying something to the coach hovering beside him. The man grinned just as the batter struck out.

As the team jogged in, Rita turned away. The plank seats of the stands were so buckled, when the actor who played Cheyenne stepped down in front of her, two rows bounced. Rita smiled. "How'd you get burned?" She touched the red skin along his shoulder.

He turned his chest to edge by and shrugged, rueful. "Rowing," he said. She smelled hot pressed cotton. The ribbed tank top fit like a second skin, his own skin so silky smooth it looked oiled. Elise had told Rita that when he walked onstage the band played a two-bar Beach Boys signature.

Rita stepped up on a rise and balanced. The man who gave her his hand was a royal jerk, a lawyer in real estate. His grip was hard, turning her fingers as if the two of them swung on a dance floor. "Tell Sloan to come by," he said.

Rita saw an opening two feet over and tugged at her hand. "You tell him."

"Rita, sweetheart." He stood and tightened his hold. "Why hassle over such a simple request?"

"It's not my business."

"But it *is*, I think, your house, am I right?"

"Hey, hey, what's the keen for the Gypsy scene?" Rita worked her hand loose just as Gale's arm snaked in and swung her off the seat. A line drive went into right field and everyone stood up, the tall black actor tightroping her down the bench. "A shootin' star, baby. High flyin' and no jivin'. You is off to number nine." Gale stayed in character all the time—the Method In Extremis, he called it; Redbone didn't let him shoot pool anymore, he was so sick of hearing the lines. "No need to doubt. No need to pout. The course is clear." He jumped down. The spectators had thinned at the bleachers' edges. Looking east, Rita could see the long narrow shape of the lake, cars winking across the bridge. The applause scattered behind them, a runner out on third.

"Nineteenth-century." Rita turned and saw Devon, leg crossed neatly at the knee. He flicked his fingers at the light. "That sepia wash. The public sees pure Victoriana. The fashion is all wrong, of course."

Gale looked down at him. "You just got the buggered blues, man," he said. "You been talkin' to the wrong visions. You gotta get a head set. Put yer ears on straight. Zoot yourself down, boy."

Devon glanced at Rita. "Meet Gale," she said. "A.k.a. Galactic Jack."

Devon turned slightly. "An actor," he said.

"That's me, Jim. Heavy duty and on the whim. Back flappin', side trackin', finger poppin', reelin' rockin'."

"You have an interesting face," Devon said. He turned back to the game. Milos was up, crouched over the plate, bat cocked at a peculiar angle. Rita saw Elise come around the edge of the stands with Laura. Elise poked her sister lightly in her rounded belly then held her palms on either side, swiveling a little, head moving, as if she spotted players, looked for the hand off, ready to dribble. The great sister act, ladies and gentlemen, if anyone believed it. Elise's laughter came clearly over the people between them. Milos hit a foul ball. "Was that gentleman down there," Devon said, "accosting you?"

"Making a deal." Rita rubbed her T-shirt under her breasts.

Milos socked the next ball hard. It skipped off the pitcher's mitt and rolled by the second baseman. Dust hanging in the air around him, Milos ran around first and halfway to second then stopped, dancing. Distracted, the second baseman missed an easy toss, scrambled for the ball, and Milos dove. The people in the stands next to Rita cheered. The umpire shouted him safe then jumped in to keep the shortstop from

38

taking a swing. Sloan and most of the bench started out around the fence.

"Get that." Laura's voice had a soft twang, out of breath from the climb. "How does Milos start those fucking things?"

Rita shrugged, moving over to make room, thinking already how to make her escape, Laura's softened face and curved stomach, her tiredness, her resemblance to Elise too much for Rita. "What's Elise doing?"

"Getting the ice chest out of my car."

"I'll help her. You met Devon?" Rita, starting down, heard Devon say his full name politely behind her. Laura's head turned as Rita passed. The flurry on the field was over, Sloan waving the team back, wiping his glasses on his shirt.

As Rita walked by, the man waiting to bat wandered toward the fence. "Coming to haul your old man off the field?" he said.

Rita ignored him. He still had those boyish movie-star looks even with faint creases showing around his eyes. The first of the returning team slammed back onto the bench, panting. "Saving your face?" someone said to the batter, and he walked back to the plate. He was playing Doc and Star-man as a favor for Rita, but he didn't fit in—too many years on local television. Rita wiped her upper lip.

"Don't be shy, I tell no lie." Gale patted her on the head. "Catch ya on the re-bop. Say bye and keep the slide greased down." He walked toward the parking lot, elbows swinging. When Rita looked back up into the bleachers, she could see Laura and Devon laughing. When Laura talked, she pushed her hair off her face and behind her ear with a quick flip of one hand then a moment later would repeat the movement and again. She had the same slender arms as Elise but hunched her shoulders together, crossing her arms over her belly when she listened, trying to make herself small. She laughed a lot while she talked. Devon seemed amused.

Elise had called out of the blue when she learned Laura was pregnant, in January sometime. Rita remembered the air as freezing, early dusk filling the rooms. She had listened to the sound of Elise's voice after six years' silence then heard herself

39

answer, her breath in a pale swirl against the dusk, saying yes, saying yes, half the house is yours, saying only the smallest words possible because the cold might make her teeth ache, her throat hurt worse than it already did.

The thud of bat against ball sounded solid, sweet. From where Rita stood, the outfield looked dreamy, sun-kissed green, the men running in slow motion. The crowd was screaming, the catcher jumped in front of her then back, the team off the bench yelling, then Milos was pumping closer, leaping, sliding in an explosion of dirt as the catcher reached and the ball bounded off the fence a foot from her face. Rita could hear the catcher grunt, swearing, and past him saw Doc/Star-man stop, trot back to third, stand bent forward slightly, hands on his hips. Milos smacked the fence as he passed, eyes fierce.

"Did you know Laura was there?" Elise had said on the phone. "She's married. She's going to have a baby." Laura had been a skinny high-school kid, a closet speed-freak always good for white crosses, who had surprised everyone by going to college in the east. Elise's voice dropped almost too low to hear. "I miss her," she said.

Elise appeared, leaning out against the weight of the ice chest hanging from her left hand; she had found someone to help her. Walking toward them, Rita felt herself tense.

"Oomph." Seeing Rita, Elise dropped her side of the cooler. "What has she *got* in here?"

"Gourmet food for twelve would be my bet." Rita moved around to test the weight herself. "Hello, Nick," she said.

"Rita, my sweet."

"Hardly that, thank you."

Nick smiled. He had an angular, oddly androgynous face with quirky eyebrows, green eyes. He kept his sand-colored hair clipped short to make an easier blend with the G.I.'s he worked, selling them high-grade Asian pot. He and Sloan had a slippery relationship. It was over Rita's protests that Milos had asked Nick to play Crow in the play, while Milos himself played Hoss. "Shall we?" He lifted up his end.

The cooler came up easily, but Rita was shorter, her stride three-quarters as long. Nick was wearing tight, narrow-cut jeans

40

that made him look even taller, his boots digging into the dirt. As they reached the bleachers, Rita two-stepped in front and swung her end onto the riser first, twisting Nick off balance. She was barely breathing hard.

"Been working out, Ree?" Nick flexed his hand, face unmoving, the faintest of freckles showing in a mist of sweat under his eyes.

"Just making a living." Rita smiled her dislike.

Elise was looking at the scoreboard without interest. "Well, way to go, huh?" she said.

A man pulled Nick toward the fence and started talking in his ear. Rita studied the field. Someone stopped beside her, asked her something about the fall schedule, a plug for Ibsen. The ball thumped into the mitt. When she looked back, Elise was listening to a heavyset man in thongs, her face polite. It was too hot, too many people, everyone moving in a long dance between Rita and Elise, Nick like some cowboy angel of death, Laura flipping her hand through that coppery hair, men with muscled little-boy thighs. Rita wiped the side of her face on her shoulder. "Elise," she said.

Elise heard and smiled, started to move, but to Rita it seemed too slow. Someone had struck out; they were changing positions, and she could hear Sloan yelling something. Nick, she could see from the corner of her eye, was almost through. Come on, come on, come on, damn it. "Yo," said Elise.

"You want to go swimming? I'm hot."

"All the way to the spring?" Elise opened the cooler. "Just have a beer."

"I don't want a beer."

"But the game's almost over, Rita."

"Say you don't want to then. Jesus."

"What's the matter?" Elise gave Rita a wary look. A man touched her on the arm as he passed and said something. Once Elise knew what Rita was thinking almost before she spoke. There had been a time when Elise wanted nothing more than Rita's mutually hell-raising company. Now Rita felt a million years too old, stupid. The guy was asking Elise about clones.

Rita interrupted. "You mind lending me the keys then?"

"No." Elise looked over and dug in her back pocket. "You going to rehearsal?"

"I'll be working in the back. You want me to pick you up here in an hour?"

"I can get a ride." Elise glanced around as Nick walked up then looked back at Rita. "Come on, watch the rehearsal for once."

"I'm saving myself."

"Milos thinks you're afraid it's a disaster."

"Milos is paranoid." Rita took the keys and turned.

"You afraid of anything?" This was Nick.

"I sweat the big stuff, Nick—incontinence, or maybe nuclear war." Rita didn't see the point of more conversation.

The quarter-mile, spring-fed pool was open until nine. Rita changed into one of the suits Elise kept in the car, then clanged through the gate and walked across the grass. The serious lappers were already at work under angled light that through the trees looked golden. Rita's first plunge into that cold green water shocked her mind into welcome silence.

Redbone had eased himself carefully down onto the kitchen floor beside Rita, who was sitting against the metal sinks, the bottle between her legs. "You finished?" he said. She had just spent an hour leaning over the bar being brilliant. Her nose now felt raw and the linoleum under her legs was freezing.

"Elise is coming home," she said, and Redbone grunted. Rita managed a smile and swayed the bottle over to him. "But not for me," she said. "Not for me."

Rita's office was in the back corner of the building, but she could hear the band onstage anyway. She pushed away the books and tilted the lamp slightly as she put her feet on the desk, closing her eyes. Hollis was singing "Becky's Song," a lilting rock ballad that she gave a bluesy undertone. Wild woman Hollis, with her ruffled black hair and gorgeous looks, someone straight-talking Elise could get drunk with, no complications. Someone tapped at the door.

"Yeah?" Rita opened her eyes as Devon stuck his head inside. "Hi. You getting what you need to set cues?"

"Enough. He's got a good eye, your Milos-Eisenstein. I was wondering, though, if you would help me."

"How?"

"Elise says Milos wants some atmospherics for 'Crow's Song,' which they have moved to the end of the first act. Nick's up with the band on the scaffold in those stunning platform shoes of his, vamping into a mike. I need to think out angles and levels for him *and* Milos downstage—the song goes fast. I wanted you to take cues."

"Elise can't?"

"She's doing director stuff."

"Run the scene twice."

"It's already after one. My understanding is that Nick can't blast the stratosphere but once a night."

"Did you check the greenroom?"

"They *act,* my dear; that's all they do." Hollis' song was long over. Onstage the Hoss soliloquies were starting, Milos' voice rising and falling, indistinct.

Rita rubbed her eyes. "It's Elise's play."

"So if you look you turn to salt?"

Rita was already lowering her feet. She found her keys then glanced at Devon. When he wasn't smiling, the lines around his mouth showed disappointment, a faint resignation. "Is that what I'll see?" she said, holding her hand out for the clipboard. "Sodom and Gomorrah burning?"

What she saw, sitting in the house bent over the pencil flash with Devon's voice murmuring in her ear, was Nick standing stock-still, high above the stage, microphone canted back in one clenched hand, ripping the face off the night. The music pounded around him as he sang, tall, skinny, three inches added to his legs by the shoes, his ribs jerking under the open shirt. " 'But I believe in my mask. The man I made up is me.' " The lead guitar swayed in the shadows just behind him, and the drummer hunched forward, slamming out the beat. Nick's face was set, mouth stretched open, eyes narrowed. He had pushed his hair up into ruffled spikes. Sweat ran down his face. " 'And I believe in my dance.' " His hips moved slightly, voice sliding down a note. " 'And my destiny.' "

He tilted the mike back an inch as the band shot the music higher then damped down for the second verse—weirdly poetic lines, folk lyrics wrapped around the sizzling thrum of an electric bass. As he sang, the momentary lilt in his voice was eerie, self-mocking. Rita glanced down the row of seats at Elise. Devon spoke and Rita automatically coded the lines, her eyes slipping back to Elise. She was watching Nick, the pencil loose in her fingers, her eyes almost as narrowed as his, lips moving. She didn't stir a muscle until the band crashed through the last chord, then she relaxed slowly in the reverberating aftershock, as if she came somehow back from drowning. The actors offstage whooped.

"Rita," said Devon.

Elise was still watching Nick, now slouched on one hip, twirling the mike around by its cord as he talked to Milos standing below. Her lips tightened a little with the old skepticism Rita remembered then relaxed. She looked sad and bemused. Milos stared into the risers, his hand shading his eyes, and called Elise's name. Nick, above the lights, glanced out and saw her then ran his eyes down the row to Rita.

"Rita," said Devon again.

THREE

Flood I

1965

WE COULD HAVE BEEN ON AN ISLAND SOMEWHERE, THE RAIN
with that massive tropical weight falling through the headlights
perfectly straight, dense as water poured from a bucket, the trees
on the river bluff sodden and black, leaves twitching overhead
in the warm summer night. The rain on the roof was drumming
so loud I couldn't hear myself think as Aunt Jen lit up a cigarette, smoke drifting past the front seat like a wayward ghost,
like the smell of other people's houses. Always, with the first
hard pop of a match, I anticipated, high in the nose, the whiff
together of sulfur and tobacco, birthday candles. In front was
Uncle Todd's thinning hair and that netted, high-crowned cap
of his, hands playing across the steering wheel, nervous, the
greenish glow of the clock showing five after eight, though it
couldn't be less than a quarter after one, everyone sitting around
in the car after all the big rush to get there, waiting.

"Is it going to let up?" Mother said next to me, her feet propped on the carpeted hump, her tanned knees bent up near her chest as she looked at the sheet of water down the windshield, her glasses reflecting the dashboard lights. Is it going to let up? implied right now, anytime soon, tonight, in my lifetime, all of the above, listen: "Doesn't look like it can't keep this upriver they got ten inches." Hooray for them, even Daddy beside her opening his mouth, compulsive, courteous, everyone suddenly alert and restless. I saw myself poised on the pool's diving block, toes tight, as I watched the painted line, buckling and swaying beneath blue water.

With the heavy thrum of an engine that shifted higher as it climbed the hill came two more headlights, then we could see a cop car pulling up next to us on the rain-flattened grass, a scary sight, windows webbed with water, dark and blank. (This here your car?) It was nothing I'd ever heard in real life, not me, underneath some boy's hammy arm with a beer, none of us old enough to drink, my hair in a curtain smelling of Winstons, the flashlight hopping around inside, catching its eye in the car-door window, catching sin—I'd never been there. Besides, he didn't even look like a cop, jumping out with his thin gray raincoat flapping, the rain plastering his hair to his head as he ducked and ran, which was pretty dumb, like we would open the doors and just let him in. Going to the car from my aunt and uncle's house, I had felt only weight, like a warm massage on my parka-covered head, my hair still flattened and damp on top, sweat starting to make me wet inside the nylon jacket. I knew how intimate water could be, like oil on your fingers, like chlorined silk.

The rush of rain grew louder all at once, drops splattering inside where Uncle Todd had started rolling the window down and was getting water all over the seat, on my leg, letting in a sewery smell and with it a crazy nostalgia for summer, dried sneakers sinking into river water. Then Mother and Aunt Jen yelled at him, pretending to be mad as Uncle Todd rolled the window back up, grinning to himself as he shook his head. It was like the outside air had shot inside them to be sent back out

46

in evangelical tongues, then the rush was gone with a last dancing roar as Uncle Todd opened the door to slide out then
slammed it shut, shoulders lifted up toward his ears.

"Cab Landry" was all that Aunt Jen said, whoever *he* was, but
no one asked. They had stood around in the hallway talking,
just after the skies above the house cracked open, the living
room like a tomb where I lay on the foldaway bed with my eyes
peeled wide, watching the white silhouettes around me. Cab
Cab Bo Bab, Banananana Fo Fab, with his round wet head and
his FBI raincoat. He yelled as he pointed across the bluff, face
close to Uncle Todd's, whose shoulders had darkened all at
once, pale gray to black, water spilling off the bill of his cap.
They shouted at each other over the rain until Uncle Todd
turned and opened the passenger door, the dome light a pasty
yellow on a real cop there behind the wheel in a black slicker,
elbow half along the seat back as he leaned forward, eyebrows
raised into his short blond bangs, his face like a miniature cameo
between the car roof and Uncle Todd's darkening back. Then
Aunt Jen popped the radio on, and when I looked back everybody was gone, water streaking the cop car window and Uncle
Todd disappearing down the bluff next to where both sets of
headlights shot out into the dark, going where I wanted to go,
going to the house, to see the river.

"Can I go with him?" I said and Mother turned to look at me,
patient and a little vague as if she didn't know who on earth I
was. Nana gave me the same look now, but she did it without a
bit of patience, finding nothing funny in a nursing home, wondering what we had gone and done to her house.

"You aren't dressed," Mother said, and my face must have
told her I could not *believe* she had said that (dressed? dressed for
rain?). I was still wearing my shortie pajamas with some old pink
bell-bottoms over them, tight around my thighs, the pajama top
underneath the parka smelling like sleep, like Aunt Jen's pillows, like old spray starch. Who was going to see me out there
in the dark? "It's too late anyway," Mother said and shrugged.

I had made her mad again, the way Nana's stuff made her
mad, the days sultry with the lack of rain, just the brassy-looking

47

blue sky outside and inside Nana's empty rooms, small and tran-
sient with so much gone, her bed and her dresser, in their place
a pile of dated *McCall's* and some cheap china dogs and a
burned-out pan, sewing patterns, an old chenille spread, everything pressed down flat by the air, by Daddy's gaze.

Thunder rolled somewhere above the rain. It had thundered
as we drove the twenty miles back to Uncle Todd's and Aunt
Jen's, raining upriver but not a drop down there, the evening
sky a knubbly blue, thunder rumbling again. Hear that, someone
had suddenly said, so right in the *middle* of the Stones' "I Can't
Get No Satisfaction" Uncle Todd switched to the farm report,
washouts and crests and advisories in this dumb hick voice while
I leaned away, looking out the window at the peanut fields,
green as grass, green as the strip of light that was shooting below
the clouds banked on the horizon.

"—me Rhonda, help—ticket to ri—in the night—" Aunt
Jen was flipping through the Top 40 while I wondered how it
could have grown darker or maybe it just seemed that way looking from the lit radio to where it was raining even harder, no
lightning now. There had been heat lightning all week, vibrating in sheets without sound, throwing in relief the thunderheads
to the north, something we had watched earlier that night with
our lawn chairs set in the unmoving air, little knowing that two
hours later and twenty miles away cop cars would be crawling
through the subdivision at one time my great-granddaddy's land,
the amplified voice of bullhorns warning those in residence to
evacuate, that the river was over its banks, water sliding dark
and dreamy across the lawns. I could hear it under the rain, the
river lapping across the weedy ruts now slick black asphalt, the
tangled scrub turned to shaved Bermuda grass, the expensive
houses, fieldstone and yellow brick, patio doors, even the roofs
now covered with rain-pocked water.

"For chrissakes, don't pout," Mother said, and I jerked my
shoulder up to my ear then froze, hearing only rain now, the
sound of rain by itself. "Lise?" She had that warning edge to her
voice (don't push me, young lady), though I would push her like
any other fifteen-year-old, push back with silence, the only way

48

I had learned how to fight, like cold or roots or water splitting rock. "Stick that lip out any further and we can put a plate on it." Oh sure, funny, the radio fading into crackles and Aunt Jen shooting out smoke in a long sigh as I looked through the window, fingers tight on the armrest, thinking how to do the butterfly stroke, that whipping ankle-locked kick through the water, shoulders lunging.

"How high do you think it'll get?" It was Daddy, loudly, to Mother, to Aunt Jen, to anybody. "What do you think?" Innocence personified, like we were morons or something and wouldn't know what he was doing, Mother looking at him (how high, how *high*), and I was petrified I was going to laugh, lips twitching, like when I was three years old and stood in the hall while she cried, watching Laura crawl around the floor, desperate to keep the smile off my face until I could back in a casual way to the bathroom door where I would slide my head around the corner for a fleeting second to grin hard, helpless to stop. I pressed my head against the car window, pressed my lips together.

"Forget it," she said, familiar and flat, her summer litany, sitting there on the dining-room floor across from Aunt Jen, dividing up Nana's old stuff, half junk, half good. She didn't ever want to look greedy, a glossy pink ceramic bowl held in Aunt Jen's hand . . . just . . . long . . . enough, and Mother would shrug, forget it, eyes half closing in cool dismissal, all my cousins ten years older and married.

"Remember the flood that took out the revival hall?" Aunt Jen said, and I felt Mother tense since they were going to *reminisce* again, which was what Aunt Jen had over her, of course, that she grew up only six blocks away and moved, when she and Uncle Todd married, only one town over. Mother's curved and dipping nose was like Uncle Todd's, he and Daddy having married each other's type, Daddy with Aunt Jen's yeasty skin, her malleable comic face.

First had come two sizzling pops of thunder, then the sudden rush of rain outside the windows, a sound on the roof like sand falling, the thunder cracking and rolling. I could barely see, in the light off the porch, Aunt Jen's impatiens lying flat as could be on the pavement, air-conditioning always twice as cold at night, motel-like against the smell you expected of hot rain and concrete, then the bathroom light down the hall clicked on. I had been dreaming about Nana's kitchen, the way it used to look in the summers I stayed there. I was eating toast, crisp on one side around where the butter and jelly had melted in spots, soft and white on the other.

"—urnh, yet, wah—" Aunt Jen twirled the dial, skipping through static and blurts of noise, then the little red pointer hit the end of the line and she started back. Daddy had scooted up to lean over the front seat, and Mother suddenly twisted around toward me, one elbow up on the back dash with her hand in her hair, looking out my window, looking at nothing. "—hundreds evacuated already, the crest at the local outskirts expected in an hour or less, warning to all motorists, bridges are out at Clemson, Brockhurst—" and Aunt Jen spun it on, bleating and crackling, my cheeks stiff from holding still under Mother's eyes, then music, sweet and easy, big band music, rose out of the front seat. Something about that kind of music meant instant nostalgia, really sad, Ella Fitzgerald crooning out "That Old Black Magic," and very softly next to me I heard Mother singing, *singing,* which I couldn't believe, right in my ear like some kind of prom queen —I mean, come on, give Ella a break. We were reflected like luminous shadows in the windshield, the red tip of Aunt Jen's cigarette, Daddy rubbing his unshaven chin along his arm, my hair frizzing up on top, and Mother singing in that sad stupid voice. Any minute I was going to cry.

"Here, you don't want it," Nana had said. "You don't want to eat it." The awful blueberry tart off her dinner tray last week that she gave to me like I was a kid, when I was tall as Mother, with ugly thighs so I was trying to stay on a diet anyway. The pastry shell, I swear, smelled like the place, but I broke off a tiny piece of crust, and "here," she said, "you don't want to eat it."

"And now back to another swinging set from the beautiful New Orleans Tea Room with lovely Miss Mona Sinclair—" The carpet in the front parlor, flat and hard and prickly with those big mauve flowers and twiny stems, had cracked into pieces when they tried to take it up, split into chunks in their hands, and Mother laughed, coughing on the dust, laughed and laughed as Daddy left. I watched him at the kitchen sink filling up glass after glass of water and pretending to drink it, but he was crying, I knew that even from the bedroom door. Water gushed from the tap, and I closed my eyes to smell the house, smelling the same. How did anyone make out to music that dumb?

"All right, so what is it now?" Mother said. Maybe I had swallowed funny or something (I knew I wasn't crying), but taken by surprise I said the first thing that came to my mind. "Laura." Who was off at riding camp, some place in Virginia, learning how to make a horse dance down a diagonal at the touch of her heel.

"For God's sake, Elise, you could have gone, too." Though she knew I couldn't have gone, too, because I was afraid of horses, hating their big chomping teeth, their shoulders higher than my head. "Try smiling, sweetheart."

I glared out the window instead, crying now, but I didn't care. I hated her. I hated everybody in the car and wished they would let me go out to the house. I knew the spot where Linnie stood on the broken back porch, the planking gone, only the rotting cross-bracing left and the tree roots humped up below like knees. When she walked, her shoes clacked down on air an inch above the exposed supports, the tangle of roots.

"Where's Uncle Todd?" I sounded sullen, and Aunt Jen gave me a sidelong look as she stubbed out her cigarette, the radio starting to fade in and out so she reached across and cut it off, the rain pressing down like a blanket outside.

"Helen's probably got him sandbagging the graves," she said, to lighten things up, Aunt Helen, Daddy's aunt, being good for that. She had been the one to call Uncle Todd just after the storm broke out our way, not to say a thing about the cop cars making the family estate into something out of *The Diary of Anne Frank*, but to worry that the river might get as far as the pink granite slabs where she'd buried the dogs.

"What in God's name did she have on her head?" Mother

51

said. We had driven fast, the big car planing along the water-logged roads, ditches swollen, the night outside curtained in a sheer gray muslin of rain, the blast from the AC vents on my face pressed against the window. Uncle Todd had slowed the car through town then turned down the road by Nana's dark house, Aunt Helen's on the right, where we shot forward under the trees, wet moss whipping the antenna back, soared like we had finned wings on the car, and the river was there, a half a dozen yards or so down the road, just where it dropped below the bluff. The car waggled and swayed as everyone yelled, sliding down the road sideways like something in a dream, then stopped, front wheels a foot from the water, headlights shooting straight out into nothing.

"Her turban." Aunt Jen was deadpan. And that was not to mention the huge rhinestone brooch bobbing in front, Aunt Helen's face below it pale and strange without the false lashes and the lipstick shooting off her mouth, only wrinkled white skin off perfect cheekbones. She ran toward the car as we pulled up, Aunt Jen having laid out Uncle Todd in three barked sentences for nearly drowning us all so he was driving like a blue-haired lady now, grinning to himself. The turban was maroon, splotched to blood black, her fingers on the car door frantic.

"Those wigs of hers," Mother said and laughed. I had shoved the door back all the time as a kid to look into the spare bedroom at the six yellowed Styrofoam heads with the wigs, like so many hooded falcons. Aunt Helen over the phone had paused long enough about the dogs to hoot to Uncle Todd how wasn't *that* a piece of work, Gar's crazy father gunning down that poor old water-power man out of Chicago and the dam didn't even *work* worth a spit in hell.

"Can we give her a rest?" Everyone looked at Daddy, Mother's eyes suddenly as slim as arrowheads behind the glasses, Daddy having these stupid *sensibilities*. When Uncle Todd repeated what Aunt Helen said about the water-power man, Daddy had shifted his eyes real fast to me like I was this security risk for the news, *me*. I mean, come on, he was shot in 1938 (who was I supposed to tell?) and anyway I'd known about it for years.

"What for?" Mother's voice was quiet, the rain clicking down against the windows.

"I'm tired of Helen," Daddy said, but what he meant was he was tired of Mother, we all knew that. It was Uncle Todd who had led Aunt Helen back under the breezeway, her robe blown out and stuck to her legs, the water pouring in a thick silver arc through the broken gutter overhead.

"Oh you are." Mother's voice didn't change. "You are, Martin. Well, do you want to know what *I'm* tired of?" No one did. I didn't. I was just tired of everything, period. I wasn't three years old anymore and could read books on menopause if I wanted or talk to her detestable shrink with his big oily face when she took me in to see that I wasn't arrested in some stage (you like boys?). I could ask him about why she cried so much. "—you moping in some corner about some precious *memory* when there's nothing *there* anymore, if it ever had been." Maybe not, but Linnie was, which was why I had to get to the house, each year always a little closer to collapse. I couldn't be sure if the whole house went that she, that she, you know, that she . . . "—can see your mother *wants* to be in that home, for God's sake; didn't you see her holding onto the door?" Though why wouldn't it worry Nana that, having lost the house, she might lose this linoleumed room as well and the comfortable ice of its air, the door's heavy pneumatic hinge pulling at her arms, her eyes winced against the blast of the afternoon sun off the parking lot just outside. Linnie lost the whole river house to her younger brother when Nana was old enough to figure it out, Linnie, thirty-two years old, in the state asylum before she could say boo, writing those careful and anxious letters home. My great-granddaddy was a scary-looking man, bantamweight with cold blue eyes. "—what kind of hold does she have on you?" Nana? There was a thought. Take Daddy to old oily-face Dr. Do-You-Like-Boys Martinelli so we could find out what exactly Nana *did*, you know, besides keeping him in ringlets those first four years. She wound my hair in old used nylons but the curls always kinked. Linnie kept scrapbooks no one could decipher, why this clipping glued tight up against that, why a full sheet of advertisements for skirts, pages hardened with paste and news-print yellowed stiff as cardboard.

"You can't walk out this time, can you?" Mother's voice lifted. "So how does it feel, huh? Can you tell me that?" Horrible, if she really wanted to know, like the worst. It felt like suffocation, the rain drumming on the roof, air stale inside with our steady breathing, Aunt Jen still as a statue in the front, not looking around. Mother had always been stuck, like Linnie, who had a locked door finally, first the two sets of her father's children and then a locked door. First she had Jack at fifteen, drawing a bead on the young Gaits boy and blasting the world to pieces for the second time in less than a year, their brother Axel already dead, then Jack at twenty-seven, arm around her shoulders, talking soft and fast with the doctor by his side, his face moon pale. Linnie. I read the letters she wrote, copying them out so I would remember. Linnie, in her careful spiky script, behind her locked door: "Just tired I said not *crazy*." I did not want my mother to cry. I did not want any crying in that car, not one tear.

"Would you give it a rest, Grace? Think of Elise." Oh sure, Daddy, what a joke, what a big fat joke *that* was. He clearly had not dried the supper dishes in many a moon. Mother confessed, hands sifting silverware underwater, Mother confided. I knew he didn't sleep with her anymore, and I still thought that I was supposed to do something, that it all depended on something I did. Who do you love (Dr. Martinelli again) the best, Elise, your mother or your father? I sidled my eyes around to Daddy, sitting with his closed-off face, his back to the window, waiting for the fight to blow itself out, with an irritable jump every once in a while in his hand, fingers into a loosened fist and out. He was balding, his eyes a watery blue, and I knew he'd never cared two cents about me.

"What is it exactly you don't want her to hear?" Mother was starting to break, even Aunt Jen sensing it as she eased a cigarette into her mouth, all of us gathering in breath to wait. I personally wanted myself out of it (just leave me out), my fingertips sliding up and down the curved grooves of the door handle.

54

Linnie kept house from the time she was twelve, her daddy off running payroll in Mexico. Not two cents, I would say, not even one cent. "What a worthless father you are?" I thought about the way my hand sliced the water, graceful and cool, clipped as a machine, reach and stroke (the gingham dog and the calico cat, side by side on the table sat). I hated that flat moment in a dive hanging over the water waiting, waiting to hit, to start the stroke (Mother and Daddy sitting in a tree, k-i-s-s-i-n-g). When I tilted my head to the side and the water slapped across my goggled eyes and mouth, it was like the stumbling border of sleep. "What do you think, Jen. Where do you suppose he's getting it?" GeT-Ting iT, the tiny crack of the match and smoke, sweet in the pit of my stomach. On the long patient outbreath, bubbles foamed around my mouth, around my ankles, that strong steady kick like pistons. I closed my eyes and thought about the long wiggling glide down to the silent bottom of the pool where Daddy had thrown the rubber ring, and tears were sliding down like warm water on glass (who do you love the best, who do you love).

"I hope you're finished," Daddy said and he really did hope that, a cautious tendering of unrealistic hope, but he of all people should know nothing was ever finished. She had her head bent forward, one elbow on her knee and the hand in her hair gripped hard and pulling, her face winced up, glasses falling gently down her nose. You could drown by not breathing, drown inside. The silence ticked by. I knew in my heart the rain would not slow, not turn to a patter, to the tentative scattershot of morning, but it would keep drumming in the total darkness, the night outside forever there.

Mother spoke. "You just cannot begin to know how much I hate you." Her mouth barely moved, the words lost in private amazement. You cannot believe. I had already worked my fingers under the handle so pulling up was automatic, easy, everything falling away under my arm as the door swung into a density of water, warm, drenching. It made me stagger, feet slipping on the grass as I tried to slam the door, fading back from my hand, the light inside going out, their turned faces, mouths open like fish, gone, sealed up inside that shiny shell. There was nothing around me, only the pound of rain against my skin and my feet sliding along the grass. I must have been running because my hip suddenly slammed against the front fender of the cop car, knocking me around, and I worked my way across, hands flat on the hood, headlight in a splash across my knees. I had reached the bluff and squatted, starting to scoot over the edge, just as the cop opened his door, that big white door, long and luminous like an archangel's wing raised behind my head.

"Hey!" A shout, muffled, a barely audible warning, but I had already disappeared, slipping downward a few feet then scrambling to my left. Even in the dark I knew where to go. It didn't matter if the river sucked it all away, I would step right in, straight into the water, up to my chest, sweeping my arms through the slowly floating debris, and turn, compass still, then toe myself off. I knew where I had to go.

With a crunching slither the blond cop started down behind me. I moved quickly sideways, catching tree roots, vines, eyes peeled against the rain and dark. He would never have a chance next to me. I knew everything you had to know about quick escapes, about running blind.

FOUR

Hale

2015

Elise came out of the loose bow of the river that lapped a gravel spit at the foot of the pasture, water and grass still lost in the higher slope and windbreak shadow. Hale sat in that same shadow on the deck off the back of the house, his pale chest lightless, the angled plane of wheat-colored hair invisible. It was just past dawn in early spring and he was freezing, made even colder to see Elise break the surface, bobbing for a second through the mist. Her head looked small, hair plastered close and dripping, her shoulders, as she stood, rising in broad curves from the water.

Even urban slang, with its multilingual shorthand for every sexual combination that could be bartered, failed here. That for a year and a half Hale had made it sometimes twice a night in the bed of a woman in her middle sixties, living hundreds of empty miles from the Channel, or any city of size, defied explanation, language itself. He was not there for the romance of communal life on a frontier the fundamentalists thought they had claimed, nor for the practice of austerities in the country quiet, not even for the senseless collison of ostensibly unrelated halves, part of that random comedy of events replacing determinism in the postmillennial public weal. It was simply that the sight of Elise watching him under the sodium lights of the pit had caught Hale by surprise, sucked him in. Old women were a standard surplus of the times, but Elise seemed to transcend the norm, prowling around the Channel alone, half a head taller than most of the raven-haired men. Bent over him later in the rented room, her back wet from the tepid shower, the flat expanse of her forehead trickling as her shoulders turned hard against his thighs, she was not so much like a man as unlike any woman he'd ever had.

The ideas of common social mores, a rational economics, ethical conventions, all had become as empty as the country's prospects for future change. That the year 2000 had dawned and nothing had happened may have reassured the powers that be, but in fact, "nothing" had happened, *nothing* had obtained. The collapse of the cold war in the closing days of the eighties was nothing to the dissolutions north and south that followed, all studiously denied. The underclass had its entrepreneurial market of highly profitable, reality-easing drugs, the upper echelons their own entrenched deceptions of perpetual safety. It was women, though, possessing already an intimate understanding of systems void of meaning, who moved most comfortably through the detritus of the political psyche's breakdown—the aging baby-boom widows by numerical weight but others, too, adept at consensus, at multiple relationships, at lateral movement. In the countryside especially, where they ran what family farms were left, they took hold, growing into a vast subchurch of caustic mysticism beneath the polished veneer of masculine piety. Elise herself kept clear, only observing what passed before her—at the Channel, inside the makeshift lab just beyond the paddock, while asleep when, turning over at night, she lightly shook the bed. Under the threadbare sheets Elise had the untanned skin of a redhead, loosely pliant, a translucent white mottled and veined under Hale's hands, cool as running water.

On the deck in the morning shade Hale flinched as always with the quick shock of seeing Elise: one moment only a milky light above the trees, mist toeing empty gray water, and the next moment Elise, an image in his mind so distinct it was as if she could be cut out and moved. She seemed to float on the dark water like a marble bust, tilting, turning, too far away to read an expression. The sun broke past the trees behind the house to shine high across the river onto the steep bank opposite. Watching Elise, Hale was conscious of how each part of him pressed into the spring air: the curve of arm or knee, the hard sculptured lines of his face. Hale had learned that he was beautiful at nine in the bilge water of a skiff he had helped pole clear, sturdy enough for his age, but the man's weight along his back had pushed him onto his knees, the metal clanking dully underneath, nothing but the swamp to see what beautiful does for you, that and his mother's clairvoyance—she saw. The water stinking of oil and skunkweed, the birds clacking away under the hot silence, his high crying through the man's muddy fingers, all that had fallen away from Hale's memory, leaving only the huge shadow of his mother, chin sunk deep in her own fat, as she listened to spirits he could never hear, tracking the rapist's fleeing heart.

The sun crept down the opposite bank, which lay in a bright ruled edge against the sky that was starting slowly to blue. Far below, Elise sank to her chin in the river then stood again. Hale carefully kept his memories separate. He lived in the now, lightly penciled into the present, detached from the swift ripple of outer impressions that could become in a moment meaningless, fluid events without a history. The grass, now glowing green high above Elise's head, was only that—not to be dislodged, translated backwards into its own absence, a line of shadow falling upward through the trees. Elise was awake and across the room when Hale opened his eyes on the dark to the trailing yelp of a coyote. The mist burning off the river blew around her in curtains, as if she still stood at the window, cigarette cupped to her palm, the water, shifting slightly from gray to green, a barometer of nothing, the way the walls were only a scant degree darker than the windows. The Vietnamerican shrimper had taught him about the endless present at the same time he taught Hale to read the tides. Elise moved her arm across the current, water sliding off her cupped fingers. A river marked nothing temporal except its random disasters and even that with nested debris, not itself. The bone-colored light in the house when he woke up a second time, alone, had drained his heart. Even outside it escaped definition, disappearing into itself except where it turned under the trees into mist.

The sun had started to stream through the trees. Hale would watch Elise listen to the collective's noisy arguments, eyeing the younger ones, the loudest usually, her head turned slightly to smile before moving away. The substance of their incessant talk —the ethical limits to a market economy, decriminalization of private sin, the elasticity of the earth, and always gender, the bedrock of dispute—bored Hale no end, but the sight and sound of them talking was nice. The farmhouse was always a little gritty, unkempt, stuff tracked in on the floor. Downstairs they piled everything on tables that crowded the mismatched furniture, thick cushions sagging. Individual rooms offered surprises —scrubbed wood and weavings done in a delicate milk blue wool, or chintz curtains and select antiques, or the monastic look of Shaker simplicity—but the common rooms were by choice low rent. The collective sitting around at night evaded, as well, easy definition. Old women wearing dungarees yawned with younger women in loose cotton skirts while a middle-aged man flirted with Hale, his antique silk vest lustrous in the lamplight, and one sullen fifteen-year-old, who had shaved the sides of her head, picked at her face as she argued, children in oversized T-shirts racing around the men playing hard-fought poker. Not all of them talked either, but the noise level was high; it seemed to pull the collective close inside the yellow light, linked by the splintered chairs and crummy cushions they sat on, the thin resistance of the farmhouse walls, patched-up wood and glass, keeping them cloistered, keeping them safe. Even when she was sitting in their midst, Elise's idle indifference to their talk set her off from the rest, gave her a curious permanence. Her silent, half-attentive listening suggested to Hale the fable of an ageless witness behind each soul. He looked over the gray hills daubed with chalk, then back to Elise. She would never change. As she moved half lost in the river, he thought of her as reaching straight to bedrock or deeper, past arched white limestone, pockets of dark, down finally into the drop-pocked silence.

Equal vision was all. Hale remembered without any differentiation all the places he had lived—from the salt-damaged swamps of his boyhood to the tepid Gulf to the night trade around the burned-out blocks of the Channel and now here— places neither good nor bad. The others would roll their eyes, even Elise insisting on the objective reality of oppression. She turned, waist-deep in the water, to catch some floating trash and toss it across to the sandbar. "It's the same as believing in the Devil," he had said to her once. "You want to be like those nazi-farmers that come blinking out of their country churches, wired on fear and righteousness?" The stiff, heavyset men with their buzz-cut hair and sunburned necks were, in fact, dwindling in number, possessing more a belief in the outworn myth of their mom-and-apple-pie way of life than one in personalized forces of evil. To the collective they stood in just fine for the Devil, or at least his minions, deputies of the black-coated deacons who traveled, in rotation, from church to church, but even the collective's paranoid fringe knew the outside community was not that simple. The rural regions might well be under the sway of an ad hoc theocracy, but most of the farms from the abandoned conglomerates were owned by women, women far less predictable when it came to the path of righteousness. Old biddies in town might lay down a suffocating moral law from their front porch windows, telephone at hand, but others, rapt with prayer, were known to have distinctly different visions. Hale, confident he could soft-soap the busybodies, had a superstitious fear of the rest, a fear he would adamantly deny even as he pitied the deacons. The few Hale had seen in town or crossing the back roads in their low-slung cars looked dangerous for the most part in their isolation. The pasture along the gravel bar shone bright green, the rest of its upward slope still in shadow, the grass glittering with dew.

Hale glanced over his shoulder at the house, empty that morning with everyone lambing at the Archuleyta camp, not sure himself what prompted that look behind him—wood, glass, paper shades all as they should be, flat and still in the shadows. That crystalline emptiness he felt had less to do with the house than with his own invisibility. Around Elise he felt subtly overtaken, having lost his one certainty, that sweet precision of cheekbones, nose, pale green eyes—the confidence of the beautiful to be seen always exactly the same way. Half the time, Hale knew, Elise saw not him but a lover from her waning youth, or an eerily accurate mirror image of her own solitary self, or no one at all, just one more anonymous manifestation of action in the collective life. Hale's beauty had no separate existence for Elise, while she appropriated the very air around him, all of passing time. She had lifted a thigh clear of the water running in a dull gleam across the downward curves of her stomach, along the breasts sloped against her ribs. She could have been cut from rock, sheeted in an icy sweat for thousands of years, and he watching her from the house for that long.

The sky had deepened to a cloudless blue. His aunt would have been happy there, with room to breathe that the heavy silence of the swamps never gave her, even later his small ten-year-old body in the Toyota truck taking up too much space as they drove into emptier and emptier countrysides. ("I love you, sweetie pie," her tangled hair brushing his cheek, hands busy setting out six cans of stew or ravioli and the tiny stove with its blue jets of compressed gas, all the bare campsites deserted around them; she was going off again.) Hale smiled at the dry hills so unexpectedly green in places. Ramona was like his aunt, who had been so much younger than his mother, impatient, all intense dark-haired motion. Ramona owned the land the commune used but never stayed there for long or involved herself in the collective's decisions. Hale didn't know how to approach Ramona, an elusive woman in her forties always dancing out of touch. Whatever she did away from the ranch, it made her quick-tempered, jumpy. Dangerous. When Hale gave up on Elise and tried arguing with Ramona for the illusory nature of opposition, she had simply asked him whether his mother bought that line of shit, and he had seen again the suffocating dark behind his mother's back in the shanty doorway and coming closer the flaring pockets of fire. Cows usually grazed above the river in the morning, ambling in a slow line toward the abandoned feeder, but they were not there yet. There seemed to be no possibility of them against that slope of green, as flat and empty as the river, now equally void of possibilities in its seamless movement around the bluffs. Standing on the gravel spit, Elise leaned down, one hand gripped on the lower branch of a tree bent near the water, and wiped each foot with a towel.

Hale saw only a tall, slightly paunchy old woman pulling on her boots while she stood in the fly-infested trash of a sandbar. Stuff came down the river, plastic jugs, oil cans, invisible toxins, undermining Hale's faith in the hinterland's ecological superiority, that faith mainly for public consumption, to tweak the collective's holier-than-thou attitude. Sheep ranching was hard on the land, and they had somewhere a growing dump of plastics and metals they couldn't recycle. Elise settled her heel into the boot, stomping it softly against the sand. For Hale the place had a tacky, outer swamplands feel to it, a haphazard ugliness in its outbuildings, the gawky windmill and generator, battered trucks —no Garden of Eden utopia there. The birds sang in the trees, the river chucking across rocks. Hale saw the slight hump at the top of her spine as Elise bent over to dry her hair, the towel flipping around her hands like wings. In the summer there could be a dozen others swimming there and Hale would see only her. When Elise stood, a thin frizz rose up around her head, gray radiating white, the thickness of the vanished river mist.

Of all illusions, Hale found the idea of the commune easiest to subvert. For one thing, it slid precipitously from traditional expectations—of common ownership, say—its raison d'être having less to do with things like universal love than with any of a half a dozen discrete philosophies connected only by their apocalyptic roots. For Ramona it was simple. She owned the ranch. Its profits were there for her own, however suspect, investments. Everyone else had to scramble, and they did, the collision of rationales for the life they lived out there somehow static, formalized. It was as if an event-nonevent as insignificant as the night's shift from one century to another had fifteen years ago locked Ramona and those like her, committed to one ideology or another, into a kind of arrested ferment. Elise slung the towel onto a branch, the bottom edge swaying slightly in the breeze. Whatever didn't move, Hale knew—even words themselves—just wasn't there.

Ramona's dissertation draft was a long dance of numbers and codes, biogenetics, reductions Hale couldn't hope to attain. She had abandoned it in the last years of the twentieth century for a shrill sociopolitical agenda that even the leaders knew wouldn't sate the public lust for apocalypse. Hale at ten had seen them coming, the streaming torches through the trees, his mother and aunt at the kitchen table, and then his mother groaning slightly as she pushed herself up, moved to the door. ("I know a secret path," his aunt leading him by the hand out the back, "but I need you to help me look. A log with a gator smile. A tree like a heron. Do you see a snake made out of green light?") Elise walked the sandbar, toeing the debris without interest, shadows laced and unlaced across her shoulders, and Hale shrugged. Anticipating Armageddon in those years had become a habit, institutionalized now in rituals like those rapt rural meditations. In fact, the apocalypse everyone had supposed would come had petered out, as would the global matriarchy now bruited about in certain circles. It was all half-assed, Ramona waging her private penny-ante war oblivious to the embarrassment of her own property, to her own assumptions about how power worked. Hale shrugged again, flicking a piece of bark off the deck. The ultimate irony was that Hale, who thought the world peopled by too many fanatics already, should find himself faulting Ramona, not for playing at revolution, but for not playing at it seriously enough.

Elise crossed the bottom pasture, the muscled and soft sense of her coming in a shifting series of tiny shocks, registered in afterimages against the scrim of brush along the river. Elise as a collaborator and mentor would be, it seemed to Hale, a devouring presence. He did not know whose work was whose in the lab where he had spent one idle afternoon, but he could recognize how Ramona might have been seduced into a tight hermetic concentration on the art of manipulating unseen entities by a woman with Elise's powers. Hale himself had learned the suck of mystery from watching his mother—a huge woman huddled alone in her yellow house, whispering with spirits in a patois she refused to teach him. Still, Ramona's embrace of pseudorevolution as a way to break free exasperated him. Although he knew on some level that his mother's self-immolation had freed him, the thought was too unbearable, the line between that and abandonment too thin. For all the collective's rolling eyes, his choices at ten, an age less than half of Ramona's when her own separate hell broke loose, still seemed light-years beyond hers, made when she supposedly should have known better, and in her case only a laboratory burned. Hale lifted the foot he had braced against the railing and relaxed his toes. It bothered him that Ramona was still in some exalted part of her mind careening with Elise in a lightless car stinking of explosives along the abandoned streets of the university complex, skirting road blocks and rival mobs as the twentieth century guttered out. The passion was too extreme. Hale stretched his leg. At precisely the same moment, a few hundred miles south, he had been sitting with his aunt in the front seat of the Toyota truck watching the refineries burn, absorbed in the clean aesthetics of boiling flame and night sky framed in the windshield, a perfect view from where they had parked on the cracked asphalt of an old basketball court, the hoops overhead ringing lightly in the cold wind.

Elise was climbing through the fence. As she balanced her weight on one hand against the bottom board and slid her bent leg through then ducked her head to follow, Hale wondered whether she knew he was watching. He could feel the others at the ranch watching him, unsure where safely to place him, so provisionally Elise's lover he became an open possibility. With his sensual, adult, almost feminine beauty, Hale transformed even simple household chores into a sexual act, sometimes haplessly, sometimes with malicious deliberation, creating a minor art form out of the disturbance he caused. Yet for all his apparent distance from debate, Hale depended on their looking. When he noticed Elise watching him in the pit, her eyes had held a shock of recognition, Hale resigned to reminding everyone of old lovers—the ultimate idealization, he was someone people would clearly die for. Except Elise, now starting to pull her leg through the fence. Hale wondered how she did it, how she transcended *his* watching as well, even while climbing through the middle of a fence or pushing up in awkward jerks below him in bed. When he saw her later across the pit, she was laughing, her hands stuck in her back pockets, eyes shifted sideways, a look that Hale now knew she used to evade the boredom of company. Hale didn't know who the lover was she saw in him, whom she pointedly would not die for. The glance she gave him was sometimes half angry, despairing, as if toward something that had never happened.

Hale took a breath and let it out. The birds had stopped singing, the sun up past the garden where Elise had stopped to finger the soil. Hale breathed. Elise was overwhelmingly seductive, that mix of soft and hard, skin loosened and silky around the graceful edges of collarbone, spine, hollowed temples, the stiff reach and turn giving way unexpectedly to a coiling power. She swayed slightly, her back to Hale, and moved onto one knee then the other, slowly lowering her ass to her boots. When she rocked forward, Hale moved his feet apart on the porch railing to watch. He saw her broad, flaring back, the scratched heels of her boots, the halo of her hair bent over the filmy green line of carrots—he saw Elise. A breeze brought the elusive smell of stagnant water, saturated and skunky. ("She was pretty, you know," said his aunt about his mother as a girl. "Looked to me, toddling after her when she had turned eighteen, like a princess, like some beautiful fairy queen.") The salt had leached into the delicate water of the swamps from the oil driller channels so nothing finally could grow; the land got lean as his mother got fat, opulent and burdened. His mother may have talked to ghosts rather than move genes around like Elise, but the careless power was the same, the easy familiarity with the invisible, their impression of permanence. Hale had told the shrimp crew about

66

her, an obese swamp queen with psychic gifts dangerously acute, but he gave her a different name, a different fate. When Elise moved down the row, Hale edged his feet wider on the railing.

Hale thought he alone saw Elise for herself. The others, out of a need to invent some kind of history for themselves, vested her with a heroism that made him impatient. Their need to valorize Elise was to Hale part of their equally irrational idealization of the abortive student revolution that took place back in the 1960s. They may have had in Ramona someone who at twenty-six actually built a bomb, set it in a lab, and tripped the explosion, pausing with Elise, before they ran, to watch the fireball bloom from the window grids, but what they wanted was Elise. And they wanted Elise as a veteran of mythic battles, not as the aging lookout for a dead-end gesture from which even Ramona's exotic looks could not alleviate the boredom, bomb or no bomb. Half the country anyway was at that time under potential arrest. Hale personally knew that Elise had avoided radical politics when she was young. He knew that she had married once and divorced, had no children, owned part of a house still under surveillance by a Bureau clearly as fixated on her revolutionary persona as the people at the ranch. None of it was romantic. The stories Elise on rare occasions told would only hint at old-fashioned mystery—a rich grandmother and her trigger-happy father, river houses, racehorses, the heat and dust of a nineteenth-century southern town.

Elise came up the deck steps. She had a long face, the lines etched in skin as tough as porcelain, a faint scatter of reddish blotches crossing the ridge of her cheeks and along her hairline. Wrinkles ran out from her eyes. She glanced at Hale, her mouth its customary line of wry patience, no one guessing how, when she smiled, the lines lifted in curves around her mouth, cheeks tight, the skin drawn smooth along her jaw, Hale finding it each time a jolting transformation—light, explosive, consuming.

"You're up." Elise stopped beside him.

"Yeah."

"Had breakfast?" She separated out a two-inch string of carrot from the seedlings she held and slid it between his teeth. The

67

taste was crisp and sweet. Still eyeing Hale from the side, she picked up a crumpled pack from the ledge and one-handed shook a cigarette out.

"How was the water?"

"Wet."

Hale squinted toward the river. The sun was up to the edge of the porch, warm against his bare feet still propped on the railing.

"Here." Elise tossed the seedlings into his lap. "A gift."

Touching the damp tops in a bright green spray across his leg, Hale thought of nothing to say. The reality of Elise was always more searing than her imagined presence. The real Elise looked older and did not engage in repartee. The real Elise erased all past possibility. Even with her standing naked beside him, knee bent, one boot on the bottom rail as she considered smoking the cigarette in her hand, he could not visualize rolling with her in bed. The cows had started across the ridge and were wandering single file down the slope. Elise held the cigarette up to her lips as she watched. Where she stood, the sun laid a white band along her shoulders and down her side, turning the hair in the angle of her thigh and groin a molten silver. She took a match from the box on the ledge and popped it against the railing.

"You got plans for the day?" Hale said.

Elise shrugged. "That black horse needs work." Smoke shot out in a brisk stream, and she picked a fleck of tobacco off her tongue. Hale could assume a meditative silence as well as anyone, but Elise up close, even mentally so removed she qualified as absent, was disturbing. He could imagine her voiceless thinking as a subtle rearrangement of himself, of anyone who came near enough to be affected. In the pit the biker fish propositioning Elise had talked fast, her fingers dancing on her bare thigh where the pants split away. Elise flicked ashes, watching the river, and her silence formed a space as big as the pit inside its broken walls, metal clanging on metal as the trucks, queuing up for black-market gasoline, ground their gears, the air under the warm sodium lights stinking of fumes.

Smoke curled in the air. In the sun Elise smelled like cedar, a hot musty scent under the tobacco, stirring as she shifted her weight. The old Vietnamerican had rocked all night with the swells and looked into the stasis between his thoughts, Hale watching across the boat in the dark. Elise was no bubbling release of anything but rather a compacted force somewhere deep inside him. Hale had joined the biker and Elise as sirens wailed in the distance, the two men on the tanker shouting something, then engines revved. Elise had stared at him, the deal momentarily forgotten, people starting to run around them. Hale closed his eyes, buoyed briefly on the updrafts of desire, sexual, murderous. He felt his skin pressed into the metal arms of the chair, but when he opened his eyes, there was only her hot marble back, that face without expression. Following Elise's gaze, the fish had looked over at Hale and rolled her eyes, gum popping in one cheek, then she leaned out, snatched the loot back from Elise, and was gone. She'd had a tattoo on her thigh, Hale suddenly realized, a small blue rose. He looked back out at the river, constantly changing from green to an ivory kind of light to pewter, water cold or cool depending on where it ran, eroding out of its channel to a different configuration each spring, moving outside of lunar cycles. Elise stood on the edge of sight, a white silhouette smoothing the back of one arm along her forehead. "Look in your heart," the shrimper told him. The water of the Gulf, plump with mauve jellyfish, Hale knew was everywhere blood warm, and the thick air of the Gulf always saturated, toxic.

All Hale remembered was Elise suddenly smiling at him with that luminous difference, sirens screaming now at the end of the street, and saying, "Oh shit," so quietly he almost missed the words, "look at you." Elise pointed with the half-smoked butt then stubbed it out. "The river's trashed up this morning." Look at you, she had said, the one thing he was most used to doing, but when he looked as she said to, standing there in the rapidly emptying pit, men floating like blown leaves over the chain-link fence, he was gone. He brought himself back in the eyes of others again and again, but Elise could still by her presence reduce him to nothing; she did not see who he was. *Caro*, she had called him in bed that first night, the room's walls like sheets of paper, the word escaping her slurred and half spoken, *caro—*

Hale translating, dear one. Elise stretched a little, laced her fingers behind her neck, and sighed. After a minute, Hale moved his hand. Lifting it slowly, he laid it down along the swell of her hip, with care, as if she were made of something as cold and dry as ice. As if the skin of his palm might freeze with that one brief touch and stick there against her, hard and burning.

Sometime after lunch Elise took the black horse into the paddock, kicking the gate back with her heel. Standing outside, Hale put the loop of wire over the gate post then waited with his arms folded along the top of the fence. The horse was a chesty little mare, half wild from wintering in the hills, its coat patchy and dull. It eyed Elise and pretended to spook, spinning lightly around the axis of Elise's hand on the lead. Dust puffed in the air.

"Come on," Elise said.

Hale didn't move. Horses weren't anything he cared for—unpredictable, heavy with a thoughtless malevolence—but Elise took no notice. The long drag of her back was like a wind drawing him forward, then she turned, her eyes shifting sideways, and the mare backed. Hale shrugged. "I won't be any good."

"Just hold this." Elise didn't like horses either, but she hid her distaste in a fierce efficiency, irritated by their obstinacy, their dull cunning. The flung lead curled and dropped, and the mare flattened its ears.

Hale picked furiously at the wood under his thumb. The place was still empty around them, the house silent off in the trees. Ten times a day she made him wish he were dead. He had learned how to avoid, with a sliding grace, work he didn't want, danger, the sexual insistence of strangers. Even at the ranch he eased around the ethos of communal labor, immune like Ramona but for different reasons, owning nothing but the tangled half of Elise's bed. That was not, however, why he came slowly into the paddock, latching the gate. Hale was not a whore. And while Elise may have had her colossal expectations, it was actually Ramona who warped Hale to them, Ramona who would already be in the paddock bantering across the mare's back, making obscene suggestions to the horse in that same crooning singsong while Elise laughed, Elise with the sun in her hair above the blowing collar of her red shirt. The squared end of the lead felt warm under Hale's thumb, gritty with dirt.

His aunt had taught him to drive the truck, a rolled-up blanket in the small of his back, toes punching the pedals, the clutch. ("You should know how to move, sweet patootie, times I won't be there"; the county park was so empty he could almost taste it.) Ramona came and went in the big four-wheel drive, tinkered on for unholy speeds, her unaccountability a needling fact in this place Hale couldn't hope to leave on his own. He did not envy her the demons that drove her, but he would have liked that easy mobility. The horse reached down to pluck at a clump of grass, the lead dragging at his hand, then sidled its long nose toward Elise. In a sound muffled as if by distance, Hale heard the blanket landing on its back.

Elise had brought him here but it was always Ramona's place, nowhere land. The hills started up as they crossed the fault line, driving north and west, a bristling of scrubby trees taking over the pastures and farmland, sudden gullies opening up so they dipped and rose and dipped again, the sun sinking down a sky as big as what he had known on the coast but drier, without the buffeting wind. The horizon had darkened into a sharp undulating line by the time Elise turned the small truck onto the commune road. They twisted along, dropping into shadowed culverts and shooting back up into the reddish light, until they bounced over the cracked concrete causeway of a small dam, the gleam of water in a still pool along one side, frogs croaking, and curved up toward the dark line of trees massed at the top of a slope, the lit windows of the house in dim yellow squares below. Hale, stepping out on the deck after he and Elise had finished a cold supper in the kitchen, played the ironic urban gallant while his eyes raked the darkness for something, anything, terrified by the utter blackness out there, no city glow, nothing to leap and flame on the horizon. Ramona sat on the deck railing next to Elise. Inside people laughed, water drumming in a sink, but outside, beyond the lights, there was only a blowing darkness

71

and the sluggish ripple of the river, low at the end of the summer. Ramona saw his fear through her own anger. "The simple life," she finally said. "You looking to get centered or something, lover boy?" Elise had rolled her eyes while Hale warily smiled.

The horse thudded one hoof into the dirt, taking the slow weight of Elise's arm, and Hale turned the lead in his hand. Hale could hear the veiled edge of a threat floating up under her half-sung nonsense. Ramona was the only person he had ever seen engage the flexible edge of Elise's temper. They fought with a deceptive quiet, their argument on the night of his arrival never rising above the low shorthand of surgeons in an operating theater, the hallway dark and airless where he listened.

" 'Looking to get centered'?" Elise had stripped the words of possible amusement, her voice pitched slightly higher, flat. Hale earlier had insisted on sex and could feel a light stickiness now when he shifted his feet.

"He's a prick." Ramona had been harder to see, behind the lamplight at the end of the table, a blur with a glint of tortoise shell, then one long arm moving into the light to tip the book closed.

"How would you know." Elise shrugged.

When Ramona leaned into the light, it startled Hale, her Latino face made incongruously elfin by the flaring line of her eyebrows, her mouth wide and thin, a southern mouth, southern cracker, dark hair dragged in a clumsy loop from the low forehead. Her eyes were narrow and angular, a lot—Hale stared from the dark hallway—like his, the mouth too, the idea filling him with dismay. "Intuition," she said, voice low.

Only later did it occur to Hale that people were sleeping around them, but at the time their quietness made the skin at the back of his neck prickle. There was something foreboding about two women together in a room at night, the unnerving intimacy of women who could be mother and daughter or not sitting alone. Doing nothing—Hale wondered if that was it—no ailing child, no one to wait up for, no work at hand. Elise had seated herself heavily at the table, Ramona leaning back to tuck one foot under her leg. His mother had sat that way with his aunt a million times. Hale had always thought that the combined potency of his mother and his aunt, doing nothing in the kitchen, would have stopped the mob from coming in if his mother hadn't swayed to her feet, enormous in her orange robe, and opened the door.

"Don't tell me." Elise reached for and lit a cigarette. "He has nasty karma."

"Your karma is more the point," Ramona said. "I've got eyes."

Elise blew out smoke impatiently.

Ramona glanced past her at the shadowed door. "You want to take bets he isn't in the hall right now listening in?"

Hale froze. He could have sworn her eyes met his, mocking, that she could see through walls, and what frightened him even more was the lack of genuine malice there, the conviction that she played the game for everyone's entertainment, even his.

"No bets." Elise touched her ash to the china plate. "You would do the same."

"Now why might that be?"

"This is extremely boring."

"Don't play dumb, Elise."

Hale despaired. Ramona had advantages he would never have, a universal and blanket permission to take liberties, plus the information necessary to predict all probabilities, even the random placement of Hale himself in space, while she stayed safely in motion. Shadowed by Elise who leaned forward alongside the lamp, Ramona seemed to flicker and fade in the dark.

"You didn't really know him."

Ramona's face appeared briefly, registering incredulity, resignation, before dissolving back into the shadows. To Hale in the hallway, their voices seemed to have shrunk even smaller. A warm breeze smelling of grass drifted in behind him. "Face it," Ramona might have said, "half of me is Nick."

Elise clucked at the horse, edging it around gently with one elbow as she eased the saddle across its back. Some sort of flying bug ricocheted through the grass near Hale's feet, tiny and bright green. The mare dropped its head and shook the mane down its neck, forcing Hale to move closer. He knew he wasn't like

Ramona at all. He had blond hair, for one thing, and a thinner nose. The skin along his arms freckled, unlike Ramona's, when he tanned. Elise groped under the horse's belly for the cinch.

Ramona had gone the next day and continued to come and go for the year and a half he'd been there. She either ignored him or argued in a desultory way with what she called his pacification—the old saw of blaming the victim. Irritable, moody, changeable, Ramona was at rest, it seemed, only with Elise. When Hale turned to Elise with aggrieved complaints, she shrugged him off. The others left both of them alone. Standing in the empty house before a mottled mirror hung on the back of a door, Hale would study his naked reflection, the blurred lines, greenish tints. He looked dead in the mirror, which amused him, drowned underwater. He would trail one hand gently up past his lips and think himself Ophelia to Ramona's Hamlet.

Hale took a juvenile delight in what he could make Elise feel. Her head tilted back in the pillows, jaw tensed hard, made him exult, his face, he knew, stupid with pleasure—this was what he was good for. Kaboom, he whispered, lowering himself onto her, laughing into the cool skin of her neck and shoulder. After she fell asleep, he would pad around the room, noiselessly opening drawers the contents of which he knew by heart, cracking the curtains on the emptiness outside. The rare safety Hale felt when Elise was asleep brought out a kind of tenderness in him. He crouched alongside the bed and watched her, turned on her side, the high curve of her hip sloping to her waist, stomach slumped to one side. Once when she rolled heavily half onto her back, Hale had flinched, convinced for a sharp second if she opened her eyes and saw him that he would turn to stone.

Elise smacked the mare on its belly and, when it snorted out the air it was holding, pulled the cinch tight. The mare's head came around sharply and Hale jerked back on the lead as Elise dodged clear of its teeth. The horse shook its head and shifted its hind feet, snorting a second time. Hale duly sacrificed himself for her, not the least by staying in the hinterlands with a group of political naïfs. The Channel had been a microcosm in its own way as claustrophobic, but at least things happened there, games went down. Out there Ramona ran the only information worth

74

buying and Hale was a one-man market—no zing. Two weeks ago he had lain on the deck just beyond the sliding glass door while Ramona inside conferred with Elise. The door was open an inch to let a trickle of cold air inside, and the night around him smelled of cedar and water. Ramona's voice rose but Hale could hear only a handful of words. His feet were cold, and he bent one leg slowly and steathily up to cover the toes with his hand; an upstairs light went on.

"He's got to go." Hale laid his cheek against the cushion under his head and looked. Elise, just out of view, was saying something that made Ramona shrug. "I know what to do." Hale felt his mouth twitch and he hugged his knee to his chest to force himself to be still. Chances were rare enough to see Ramona fail, and she, all out of character, was hard up now against the implacable fact of his place with Elise, his duly protected status.

Ramona, who was pacing the room behind him, stopped near the door, her voice lifting: "They've started to empty the base." Elise said something and Ramona snapped her fingers nervously. "He insists on staying and they'll let him. We both know what he's got there."

It was someone else. After the first blank second, Hale found himself smiling as he slowly pressed his teeth to his knee. Above the river he spotted Orion and looked for the three dim stars of his sword. A base, to be emptied or not, outside this black circle of hills was not possible. The Gulf perhaps, slushing and guttering its incessant garbage, or the doorless hole of the breezeway that cut through Elise's fabled house, or even the pink granite block after block of a university he had never seen, but not Ramona's supposed base. When Ramona left the ranch, for Hale, she walked straight off the face of the earth.

The river, still high from the last rain, sounded loud in the cold air. The dead leaves of the live oaks were rustling in the breeze, and a shutter banged. Asked, Hale would have disputed still his vortical attraction to Elise, to what she was in the scheme of things. He would have protested that he lay there in the early spring of a country night for lack of a better place to be, for fate, for the game, for whim, not for the seductive association with Elise's indifferent power. I am love, he thought, listening to Elise start to talk. I love the world.

Elise's voice stopped. Rolling onto his stomach, Hale looked inside. He could see Elise's chair now and Ramona crouched beside it. Her head was bent toward Elise's shoulder, her elbow braced on the chair back, fingers straying in and out of Elise's hair. Hale pushed against the damp wood of the deck with his toes. Ramona turned her head to say something and Elise laughed. Pulling himself up suddenly, Hale stood, hand already on the latch, then he was dragging the glass door open in a bumpy path along its track.

Walking in, Hale felt graceful, oddly tender, as if he came rosy and warm from a run across the moonless roads, only his hair still holding the late winter chill. The outside air followed him in with the delicate flurry of milkweed, or snow, gusts curling all at once to random corners with a sudden foxlike efficiency. Ramona was turning, had turned, swiveled on her heels. Watching her, Hale felt only sensation, the shirt smooth against his belly but loose in a cold line down his back, floor peppered with dirt and bark. He remembered only the door bumping under his palm and how, when he looked from Ramona to Elise, he had smiled.

The lead jerked stinging along his palm, and Hale instinctively closed his fingers, then the horse hit the end and pulled him half to his knees. Elise swore. The stirrups flipped in the air as the mare spun in a tight arc and bucked. Scrambling back, Hale took up the slack too fast, and the mare's head came around hard. Biting at the lead, the horse saw Hale and in the next moment had rocketed forward. Elise hauled on its head, one hand on the bridle, the other wrapped in its mane, but even with all her weight braced on her heels, the horse dragged her across the yard. Hale stood on numb legs, bloody fingers still pressed against the lead, watching Elise's shirt billow behind her, the muscles stand in her bare forearms as dirt scudded around her feet. He could see the grass blow behind her in long cool sheets, then the horse came in between, neck snaking out, forelock drifted sideways above one eye so it looked unkempt, de-

76

mented. Its head snapped down, and Elise's gray frizz showed over the top of its neck, then Elise's face, the mouth shouting, eyes narrowed to black slits. They turned together. Then as suddenly as it had erupted, the horse stopped.

The breeze trickled along the back of Hale's neck, bobbed the new yellow flowers at the edge of the paddock. He could hear the low rush of the river far down to the right. Elise's fingers moved in the black mane, parting and dividing the coarse hair. Her head was close to the mare's ear. The horse blew through its nostrils and shook its head, metal jingling. Hale took a step forward then put his raw palm up to his mouth. The sun beat down on the woman and the black horse, pressed tight together, Elise leaning hard into the mare's shoulder. Hale came closer. "Shit," Elise was saying into the horse's ear, "you got shit for brains." Then she turned her head and pressed her lips to the wet neck.

Late in the afternoon they brought the children back from the lambing. Slouched in the big central room, Hale heard the two-year-old screaming in rage at being left behind in the truck, then someone must have boosted her down. Landon came in the front door with the baby across his shoulder. "Hale," he said politely and set the baby on the floor. Lucky came by with a box of staples, elbowed her way through the kitchen door, and was gone. Hale followed Landon back outside where two others were tossing packs and bedrolls out of the truck. When he reached out for a crate of cooking gear, the older woman hesitated before handing it down.

They didn't like him, mistrusting his erratic offers to help. Hale had no instinct for group work, even the play of social politics. The power that shifted around the commune with the dance of a foreign logic failed to pull him in. Only on the shrimping crew had his own adolescence made belonging preferable to anything else. His aunt dickering with the Vietameri-can on the dock, a head taller than the man and wild-looking next to his compact neatness, had seemed nonetheless strangely like him—to Hale watching from the truck—something in their eyes seeing the same world. ("You'll be fine," his aunt said, hugging him awkwardly around the shoulders, "and open up," she tapped his chest, "before it cracks.")

Lucky glanced over her shoulder as Hale came into the kitchen then went back to pouring rice into a plastic bin. He set down the crate and started to lift the pans out. "You know where they go?" she asked without turning around.

"Most of it." Hale looked out the kitchen window as the three kids ran past, shaking the deck. Lucky was in her middle thirties, her hair in two braids down her back, lean hips swallowed up in oversized jeans. He had hit up on her, maybe a month after he got there, finding her alone in the stables and touching her breast inside the open shirt. She had caught his wrist and held him off her. "It's not Elise," she finally said. "I mean, it is, of course, but it's not just that." A hot breeze dense with manure had flicked the straw scattered at their feet. "You're a loose cannon on deck, you know that? You probably like to play with bombs."

"Like Ramona?"

"No, not like Ramona at all." Lucky let go of his wrist and shrugged. "Maybe one of the younger ones will fuck you."

He hadn't tried. The convolutions of their sexual arrangements were too much work; they didn't even play, pure and simple, at the oldest game in the world.

Two men came in behind him and started moving pots onto the stove, running water over beets in the sink, working up masa for the night's tortillas. Hale moved out of his way as the shorter man, his hair a wiry gray-flecked brown, came out of the stores with a jar of home-canned tomatoes. "Down to the last shelf," he said. The black man patting a ball of dough back and forth grunted. On the stove water started to hiss over beans in a pot. Lucky had disappeared.

Hale went back through the big common room crowded with furniture. Out front Lucky was leaning over the truck fiddling with the motor while a bearded man in his forties and one of the little girls watched. Turning her head without shifting her eyes, Lucky asked for something, and the man bent down to rummage in the toolbox; the girl came up under Lucky's elbow to stare

78

into the engine, naming parts. Lucky reached into the engine. The man handed her a cable then ran his hand along her ass and down between her legs. Lucky's protest was muffled, distracted. When the man didn't move, she came out of the truck, flourishing greasy fingers. "Hey, you want a hand job?" she asked and stuck one hand flat on the front of his shirt.

"That's clean."

"Nothing, darling, about you is clean." Lucky planted another handprint on his shoulder. "Least of all your mind."

Hale, watching from the doorway, smiled slightly. He didn't know who Lucky was partnered with these days, but it wasn't the man now sending the girl into sputtered laughter by singing an improbable description of the truck's engine to the tune "Dem Bones." Lucky reached back inside with a wrench. The man leaned against her, his head turning close to hers, and Hale stepped inside the door.

His aunt could fix the Toyota engine, but she took no pleasure in it, seeing little romance in that uncertain coalescence of metal parts. ("Now quantum mechanics is a lovely thing," grunting as she jerked on the wrench, "but you got with internal combustion another ugly mug entirely.") The speed sometimes charmed her, dust in their wake, windows rattling. He hadn't seen her in seven years, but he would not doubt her safety; she might even still be with the steely black woman who swore she could feel the same magnetic fields as whales and was the best sneak thief he had ever seen. The door to his and Elise's room was half open. He slipped inside and lay on the bed. Somewhere the baby was crying.

Hale closed his eyes and felt his breath, the intake a smooth funneling downward with a slightly hollow chill at the back of his nose, his chest rising, the exhalation warm and expansive. Then again. The bed pushed up against his elbows and heels. There were birds, someone calling from another room, then the slow murmur of people talking, a life flickering and humming just below consciousness. Hale fell through into silence and back into that long murmur, fell through again, nothingness coming in and out of focus. "I am you," his mother had said, "you are

79

me," and when he glanced fearfully at her vastness in the chair and his own small body leaning against her knees, she said, "in the eyes, look here, do you see? yourself there, the same looking out." Her face was big too, swaddled in fat, the angled bones of her cheeks barely visible, her nose long and graceful. Her eyes sat deep under puffs of skin, greenish-brown eyes like river water but they never changed, no matter what they saw. There, the thin face of a five-year-old boy like a flower in the dark room, his lips shaking, eyes wide. Shapes stood around him, smiling, then only yellow lights hopping like toads through the night. He felt her knees hard against his stomach.

Elise opened the door. "Sorry," she said, walking lightly to the closet by the bed. She pulled out a clean shirt. "The baby leaked."

Hale watched her unbutton the old shirt and slide it off her shoulders. Her breasts swayed gently when she turned. He sat up and touched her arm. She let him shift her around, and he pressed his hand up against a breast, feeling its mercury weight in his palm. Her breathing had changed, and when he took the other breast in his mouth, she coughed. It felt cool and soft in his mouth, the tip slowly hardening against his tongue. Someone knocked on the door and went on down the hall.

"Supper," Elise said. When Hale didn't move, she pressed back on his shoulders, the shirt in her hand falling along his chest. "Hale," she said.

At the dinner table, Hale tried to start an argument with Landon, who was holding the baby over his arm as he ate.

"This gender role-reversal shit," Hale said. "You've all got to telegraph the moves every minute from your brains."

Landon shrugged. "We just challenge our assumptions."

"But you calcify the duality that way."

"It's an interim step. Would you pass the beans?"

"That you think you need an interim step is a delusion."

"Then we're deluded." Landon took the bowl.

"We are already one self."

Across the table Lucky snorted. "We are manifestations of one political fact maybe."

"Which is?"

"The obliteration of the patriarchy."

Someone two seats down laughed. "Is this the point where we lift our glasses and sing?"

In bed that night Elise rolled away from Hale then moved back toward him, indecisive, half angry. He let her work out what she wanted, patiently waiting as she lay in the dark, moving when she touched him again, stopping when she drew away. "Sorry," she muttered as she finally pulled his head down to kiss him, slipped her tongue inside his mouth. It was not a graceful fuck this time but a staggered, rolling tumble, her arms hard across his back, heels slipping on the sheets. Hale braced himself with his elbows and knees to catch the clumsy shifts of weight, pushing inside always deeper, sliding between the slippery walls of her, their heat a slow lapping, until he felt her jerk up against him, pause and rise again, a soft sound escaping her. He moved his hips harder as he watched her face, already starting to tilt upward. When she came, all expression left it, the skin fallen back and taut, a polished and pearl-like grimace, eyes empty, Elise, he moved, Elise, Elise. Just before he came, Hale closed his eyes. Breathless, jerking, he saw Elise as someone young, running slowly, dancing along the black rim of a small planet, each footfall sending up a splash of colorless light.

Hale opened his eyes on the dark bedroom and lay still, listening, trying to find out what woke him, but Elise was already dropping back. Hale could see her stretched on her back, one hand up to her mouth, eyes squeezed shut. "Christ," she said and fumbled for the cigarettes on the nightstand.

"What is it?" Hale whispered.

She barely glanced at him. "A dream. Go to sleep." Her fingers shook on the match and when the cigarette was lit she flicked the dead match into the room. She shot the first lungful of smoke at the ceiling and watched it vanish.

"Elise," Hale said from the other side of the bed.

Elise still didn't look at him. "It's nothing." She drew on the cigarette, touched the edge of her eye with her thumb. After a long minute, she closed her eyes and sighed. "There was this big stadium," she said, "like a coliseum. And everybody I had ever known and loved was in there, with all these other people. Except me. Because I knew it was going to burn down. I tried to tell them, but no one believed me. They just went on in, with their blankets and picnic baskets, laughing and happy." She swallowed, lifted the cigarette again. "And it did blow up," she said through the smoke, "like I knew it would. Some people survived. The men who had set the bombs were rounding them up and putting them into two groups: men and women. I think they were going to decide who to kill and who to let go. They had machine guns, ammunition belts. And then Laura came in."

Elise stopped again then frowned. "She was leading Nick. He couldn't see. The fire had blinded him somehow. He just stopped when she stopped and stood there, his hair ruffled up, looking at nothing. He was . . . he looked beautiful, but empty, his eyes clear, like holes onto light. Laura was desperate, begging the terrorists for help, but they couldn't do anything. They were genuinely sorry, I think. He looked harmless, blind and beautiful, but all they could offer to do for her was to kill him."

Elise turned her head away, reaching across to the table to stub the cigarette out. When she lay back and said nothing else, Hale pulled the blanket over his shoulder. "What happened?" he said.

"I woke up." Elise looked at him, tired. "Go back to sleep," she said.

Elise was the one, however, to fall asleep first. Hale listened to her breathe, the sticky sound of her mouth moving. Close to an hour had passed when he suddenly saw headlights slant across the trees outside the window then cut off. Tires crunched through the grass. In the night even the small noise of a hand-brake setting, a door clicking open, a tailgate squeaking down, carried like voices across ice. The boxes being moved sounded heavy. A long while later, Hale heard the tailgate clank back up; keys jingled. Her footsteps didn't register in the damp grass, but after the front door shuddered faintly open, he could hear them going down the hall. Hale lay back in the bed and wrapped his arms tight around his ribs. Ramona was home.

FIVE

Linnie

1956

ELISE LIFTED OUT THE PHOTOGRAPH, A HARD PASTEBOARD square, the picture itself a smaller square, either poorly taken or cropped so that the top of the lady's head was missing. The photograph had been glued down on buff-colored cardboard embossed with a lacy border. The lady in the picture stood in front of a rock that rose from below her hips and curved around her shoulders. Canted forward, hovering behind her, the rock looked as if it were floating in the air. They both could have been floating in the air; they shared the same remote disquiet. Although the lady's legs and hands were also cropped, Elise could tell she was sitting, or half sitting, slouched forward across her waist, tipping her head back slightly. The shirt she wore had delicate stripes and two wide ruffles, and she had wrapped several times around her neck a checkered scarf. The hat put a shadow across most of her face. She had shut her eyes just as the camera clicked, dark oval lids under long eyebrows that made a flattened arch from nose to temple. Her hair was bunched forward in fuzzy curls above her ears. The smile seemed strained, as if she had just started to smile and stopped, her lips big and closed up over her teeth. She might have been crying—Elise looked closer.

Nana said, "You'll ruin your eyes," wondering what the girl wanted with all those faded pictures of relatives long dead. Gar must have been talking to her again. Her brother's preoccupation with the past struck Nana as unhealthy. Gar could stand to do without a captive audience for once, and besides, there were things six-year-olds needn't know. She sat stiffly in the chair by the dresser. "Put that stuff away, darlin', and come let me see if this fits."

Elise walked over, holding out the picture. "Is she crying?"

Nana turned her by the shoulders and laid the basted blouse across her back. "Sun's in her eyes."

"She has a hat." Elise put the photograph up to her nose, frowning. She had sounded out the name in neat block letters on the back: "a-yoont lin-eye-ee," which would be the Aunt Linny Uncle Gar talked about, spelled here -i-e for some reason or other. He would twirl his finger around his ear in a circle when he said her name, which Elise knew meant crazy.

Nana was slipping pins in and out, moving the sleeve down a quarter inch; the child had broad shoulders to be as frail and spindly looking as she was, that dark red hair down her back a mess of tangles. Children had jointed bones so light they reminded her of birds. The fan pulling air from the sitting room rippled the bottom of the bedspread next to her feet.

Elise looked over her shoulder. "Uncle Gar says the kinfolk in Virginia threw your grandmother out on her behind because she was going to have a baby and she wasn't married and that's why you don't live on a big plantation, but what's a plantation?"

"Just a big farm." Nana stood up. Typical, Gar blaming his feckless cash-poor situation on some poor woman who had died two decades before he was born, with not even a photograph left behind.

"How can you throw a *grandmother* out?"

"Well, she wasn't a grandmother then." Nana looked down at Elise's head, wondering how much her granddaughter knew and how much she just repeated Gar. In fact, anyone could get thrown out. "When she moved out here, she was maybe seventeen years old." Elise squatted and picked out another photograph, already thinking about something else.

Nana struck two pins in the cushion on her wrist. She knew next to nothing about her grandmother beyond that pitiful letter she had written to her family back home, no more than a child herself, hastily married and sent away out west as if she had died (I have not received the first line from one of my relations, we have been here some 7 weeks, I have written 8 or 10 letters to Virginia. It can't be the distance). It was the only letter of her mother's Aunt Linnie could find (it seems tis hard for me to get rid of my burthern. Addison says it will be 2 or three, otherwise a gang of *puppys*). "Go play," Nana said.

Elise wondered what had made Nana mad and why whenever some grown-up got mad it meant *she* had to stop what *she* was doing, which wasn't bothering anybody. She sighed and put the pictures back in the box. When she stood up and looked out the window, the sun on the gravel driveway hurt her eyes, the trees in the yard heavy with heat. Elise licked her upper lip and went out the back door by Nana's bed.

Sitting at the sewing machine, Nana pressed her thigh against the lever and fed material under the needle. The machine whirred. Stopping to pull the sleeve around, she looked up and out the window. Down in the yard Elise was climbing through the loose branches of the back hedge. Nana shook her head. Nothing she said or did could keep Elise away from that broken-down house by the river. Now the hedge was waving behind her, a shimmering fountain of sunlit branches. Nana looked at the sleeve stuck under the needle. The light cotton printed with daisies and bees felt like air under her fingers.

Standing at the end of the overgrown drive, Elise peered toward the house. She wasn't supposed to go in there. Nana had told her that the floors inside had rotted out with only weeds

85

left, growing in the dark, and water moccasins. The thought of things growing inside a house gave Elise the creeps. The trees stood so thick with their branches tangled overhead along the drive that the sun barely filtered through, while a few feet away it blazed on the head-high grass in the field behind Nana's back hedge. Around the house the live oaks pressed against the sagging roof, hanks of Spanish moss caught on the two chimneys. The narrow front porch was in shadow. Webs hung down the square columns, and the floor of the porch went without a break from the overgrown beds to the open front door.

The lady didn't see her, the one who was watching the house, too. Elise saw her from the back, standing under the trees with her hair falling down. She looked funny in her big fat sleeves and long dress. The dress, Elise could see as she moved closer, was actually a skirt, dirty at the bottom where it touched the heels of her boots, the shirtwaist coming untucked. There were circles of sweat under the arms. Elise cleared her throat, but the lady didn't turn around. Elise had no idea how grown-ups stood so still.

Linnie didn't hear anything—she never did—except birds and sometimes mosquitoes whining near her face. The colors didn't waver as much when she was quiet, olive green and black in the trees, some pink-looking pansies sprawled onto the grass, that whited-out blue of the sky. Only when she turned her head did everything swim together. She remembered a pill that once would do that, but she was home now, without the drugs. This was her home. The trees along the driveway steadied, green and yellow in the sunlight. She didn't know who the little girl was. With skin pale like that, her momma should make her wear more clothes and certainly tie on a hat in the sun. Linnie touched her own head, the thick bun dragging down. She used to have a hat. The sight of the child made her tired, certain she would have to do something, she just didn't know what. The trees swam across her eyes.

When the lady turned back, Elise tiptoed closer. The sun was baking down on the field, and way back behind them, on Nana's street, a car started up with a roar then droned off. Elise stood at the lady's side. "I'm Linnie," the lady said suddenly, running a snippet of fern around her lips as she looked at the house. Her face was old and bony, the skin around her eyes red. "Melinda Jocelyn Wallace," she said. "This *house* . . . well, I could tell you."

Tell what Linnie didn't altogether know. About getting the blues, worse and worse, like an ache in her throat while she watched the river in the summer twilight. About seeing her brother swung across the doorstep stiff as a board, the wind pouring around him in a silent scream. About Nellie, warm and solid as a pudding in Linnie's lap where she rocked her the night her mother, Linnie's stepmother, died. About Jack and the hot stink of cordite Linnie always smelled around him after that July revival meeting. Linnie frowned. He must be rotting in everlasting hell, so long as it wasn't this one—this hell. It was all right here.

Elise could tell that Linnie had remembered something she didn't like, a wince drawing the brows together over her eyes. They weren't very pretty eyes, all washed out below that puff of hair. The fern brushed her mouth, and her face changed, emptied in a moment of all but a dull duty. Her mouth opened over big teeth. "I wrote architectural histories," she said just before she disappeared. Elise couldn't have said exactly how Linnie vanished. Simply where Linnie had been there was now only the humming afternoon: a hot line of sun on Elise's arm, weeds under her feet, the dusty smell of cedar in the air.

Elise followed the drive around to the barns, pushing open the first big door onto a dusty space that streamed at one end with sunlight. She walked inside. A half dozen bales of hay were still stacked in the loft even though the boards had fallen away down the barn's back wall. Flies buzzed over something in the corner. Kicking through the straw, Elise bent down to pick something off the floor. When the door behind her chunked against the floor, bolts rattling, she jerked around to see Uncle Gar looking through the dust as he rubbed his arm across his face.

"I saw you heading this way," he said. He glanced around the barn. Damn place would collapse in the next big storm, a sight to break his poor daddy's heart. The racehorses had once been stabled there, all that walnut trim and polished tack making the place look like a damn bordello. Gar walked over to inspect a rusted mower with some nasty-looking edges in a corner stall. Sis was crazy letting the kid run around loose. "You shouldn't play here by yourself, sweetheart."

"Nana says it's okay."

"Yeah, well, your Nana's got a trusting soul." Gar swung the gate.

"I'm not by myself anyway. A lady's there, too."

"What lady?"

"The ghost lady." Elise eyed her great-uncle, wondering whether he would just give her one of those looks. You never knew with him.

Gar grunted, staring into the stall. A lady ghost haunting his daddy's old place—wouldn't that be something. Swinging the gate again, he laughed. "The old rooster would probably like that. It just better not be Linnie, though." Gar stopped the gate. "Nosiree, he'd want poor Linnie to stay good and buried."

"Why?" Elise waited, but Uncle Gar had stopped listening. He stopped listening at the worst times. The afternoon sun burned even brighter on the boards, and the air inside the barn felt hot. She watched him slowly wipe his hands on a wadded-up bandana he had taken out of his pocket. He looked old and tired. Turning, he gave the stall gate one last shove. As it crashed against the post, a cloud of doves burst from the loft.

That night, standing on a chair to dry the dishes, Elise asked Nana who Linnie was.

"My aunt, on Papa's side. His oldest sister."

For a minute Elise worked at shoving the dishtowel into the last glass, packing it all the way down then pulling on one end to draw it slowly out. "Why would your daddy not want her to haunt the old house?"

"Where on earth do you get these ideas of yours?" Nana could guess. She wrung out the dishcloth then slapped it over the edge of the sink.

"Uncle Gar. He called her poor Linnie."

"Well, Gar has a soft heart. You can let the pots drain."

The book had "Melinda Wallace" written in ink on the outside flap. When Elise opened it to the first page, she saw something else written in a big ornate hand just below where Linnie's name appeared again. Elise flipped a few more pages filled with lists and numbers then turned back to the first page. She traced the hard curl of the J with one finger.

Standing on the porch, hands wet from watering the plants, Nana looked at the book Elise was holding open for her. When she recognized her papa's writing, she paused. It had always infuriated her, that fancy-pants way he wrote, almost like a girl. And besides, it was a spiteful thing to write in his sister's diary. The book was an old pocket account that had once belonged to their brother Axel.

"What's it say?" Elise glanced at her grandmother, who had bent down to pick up the tin pitcher. She hated having to wait. "Nana?"

"It says, 'At your death this book is mine, J. M. Wallace.' " Nana tipped out the last of the water, watching the drops catch on the potted geraniums. Always mine, mine, mine, with Jack. Nana had heard them fight over Nellie, Aunt Linnie's voice suddenly shooting up high, spitting out words ("you seem to think you are better than God Himself"). After it happened, even though she wasn't supposed to go up to the river house, Nana did, peeking through the window to see Aunt Linnie in the front room, hands twisted up in her lap as she cried. Watching Elise frown at the words, Nana sat in the swing. "Papa was telling everyone he wanted the book after Linnie died," she said mildly.

"Oh." Elise had turned more pages and found the beginning of the diary, the tightly penciled words bumping together, running with dashed lines. "Why?" The words got looser the more Linnie wrote and then stopped and started up tight again. She had crossed out and erased a few times, the paper nearly worn through. Elise glanced at Nana, who was pushing the swing back slightly with her feet.

"Oh, I don't know, darlin'." Nana squinted, wondering whether to move the sprinkler from that patch of lawn by the street. Closing her eyes for a minute, she listened to the swing creak. The smell of wet dirt and geraniums had always made her feel sad and just a little desperate, as if everything in the world were frittering by her.

Elise knew how to read words in print but not the spiky handwriting in Linnie's book. Nana wouldn't have the patience to read it to her, but Roberta, who lived in the front bedroom, might. Roberta kept an antique shop downtown and had dull black hair and pointy glasses.

When Roberta got home, she flipped the book in her hand, automatically checking the binding, the leather, the paper condition. Next to worthless on the market except as a curiosity, unless Linnie was, mirabile dictu, a southern Emily Dickinson. (Yesterday Julius R made me a present of a large picture of Axel there is no gift I could appreciate any more, the dear face seems to have a saddened look I gaze at it longingly.) Roberta turned the page; well, she wasn't that. The child was being excruciatingly patient. "You want me to read you the whole thing?"

"Yes, please." Elise looked over Roberta's arm. The muscles made long slack curves under her pale skin that was dusted all over with black freckles, like pepper.

Roberta peered at the tiny handwriting and thumbed her glasses up her nose. " 'Another diary! Which I am afraid will all too soon follow the fate of the others, and be consigned to oblivion.' " She stopped and skipped down the page, looking for simpler words. "Okay, try this, 'Bert is eight today, baked her a cake which I gave into her full possession to dispose of'—well, hell." Roberta looked up. Seeing Elise's jaw tense slightly, she snorted to herself and turned the page. " 'Can scarcely write for the noise, but quiet only reigns when the children are at school, Fan is playing Frolic of the Frogs.' " Roberta blinked deadpan at Elise, who smiled.

Scanning a few more pages, Roberta grimaced. All that tedious churchgoing, the daily visits with their plodding weight of names—no wonder those women were all hysterics. She skipped forward: had the blues this evening and went over to, across my heart little flashes of sadness come and go, why I cannot, another blue one too, far far more so than the last, thoughts go trooping out like phantoms, I'm feeling very bad, death is nothing. Good lord. Roberta could feel Elise itching at her elbow. What could the child possibly want with this? "Sounds like she was sad a lot," Roberta said brightly. "She called it getting the blues."

Elise reached for the book. She wanted it back if Roberta wasn't going to read it.

"All right, all right. 'Perhaps gazing down the pathway of life, I see far beyond my reach, the unrealized ideals of the Beautiful and True, I stretch forth my hands to grasp them but they rush past like bubbles down a dark stream, O the sad incomprehensible yearnings of the human heart, O the incompleteness of life, the unconquerable emotions that beset us.' " Roberta groaned and flipped pages. "The gods save us, a poem; are you ready? 'Fold the snow white cloth, From his pallid form away, He was my darling yesterday, He is God's today.' " Roberta stopped. Nana was in the doorway.

"You'll give the child nightmares," she said.

Elise was fuming. "Why are you making fun of it?"

"Because it's silly."

"But who's the ghost?"

"What ghost?"

"The one in the sheet."

"Axel." Nana finished drying the spoons in her hand. "He was her brother, maybe a year older. He was killed by a man who wanted the girl Axel was courting. And now it's time to set the table."

Nana looked in on Roberta before going to bed and found her lying on top of the sheets reading Linnie's book. Roberta smiled and snapped the diary shut. "There was a woman in need of lithium if I ever saw one."

Nana wasn't going to ask what lithium was. "She got headaches."

"Well, I guess. They kept dumping motherless children on her. Where was this Pa of hers she gets letters from?"

"Mexico. He ran payroll accounts for the railroad."

"Hmmph." Roberta tipped some lotion in her palm and rubbed her elbows. "You got those scrapbooks she talks about?"

Nana gazed out the screened window by the bed. The scrapbooks looked crazy, a pasted jumble of magazine pictures and homilies, everything packed edge to edge so tight that, looking at them, you found yourself trying to breathe. "No," Nana said.

Roberta gave her a narrow-eyed look then unstuck the night-gown from her chest and blew down the front. Under all the rote religion and awful poetry and strangely flirtatious fussiness, Linnie had a sort of sad, stoic resolution. Roberta could spit the feeling out, dirty as tar. "I thought little girls played with dolls," she said, thinking of Elise.

Elise stood the next day on the trashy concrete slab of the porch and looked inside the house. One of the front doors was gone and the other had swung halfway out and stuck. The draft that came from inside smelled like the river and she could see trees flickering green at the other end of the breezeway. Linnie was inside. Elise had seen her go in just minutes before.

Elise edged her toe over the flat sill. The rooms that opened into the breezeway were dark, their windows caked with dirt. She touched her foot carefully to the wood, afraid to step on the floorboards inside. What if it was like the soft cottony stuff in the attic at home that would mush underneath if you stepped on it, swallowing you up. Her little sister Laura once almost went through. Something rustled through the leaves. Looking up, Elise saw Linnie standing silently in the hall, all the fingers of one hand playing along her lips as she stared out over Elise's head.

The front door was still a thing of horror, how it slowly opened to show her Axel slung between two men like a piece of meat with nothing behind them but a freezing black. Axel, dead, looked stiff and waxy with dirt in his mouth and the back of his head all caved in. Only his hair along the forehead was the same, a brown silk between her fingers, curling at his temples. Linnie looked down for a second and frowned. Someone should send that child to bed. A child had no business here, seeing a man stretched out dead, his head at the back all beaten to a jelly. Could be she was the child whose momma had consumption, bedded down at Alice Saunders' to die. Linnie studied her a moment. Funny how she looked a little like Myra. Axel had been so in love with that girl, that devil smile of his splitting his cheeks. Axel. She wondered how long it took, falling under the first stinging blow of the branch, stumbling up to half turn, falling again.

Elise didn't know why Linnie was pressing the fingers against her mouth so hard, as if she wanted to keep from screaming. There was nothing funny about it either, not like the way ladies tied to the railroad tracks put their hands over their mouths. Linnie had a nightgown on and her face looked different than before, maybe not as old. Her hair was thinner, too, and her skin dripped with sweat.

The doorways blurred by Linnie's eyes like tunnels, spoking off into nowhere, except for the one behind the parlor, where the door was always shut. As it wavered for a moment, she saw a dirty window, the walls stained green, then it was just a door again, hard as you please, with walnut inlay and a glass knob. The door to Jack's room. Jack had hardly believed someone could take his brother away from him like that. It made his eyes turn bright, perfectly round. Linnie bit at her fingers. He could rot, he could rot, walking right by Axel on the floor without a glance, taking Cal Hunnicutt's arm and hauling him around to the front door where the wind was pouring through the house, talking to him in a low voice, firing one hard question after the other, while Axel lay stiff and cold at his feet, Jack scheming already to get his own back.

It took some time. Linnie looked down the breezeway to the square of green light at the end, jerking and winking against the dark. It was July out that way, hot and sultry, the kind of weather they always had for camp meetings by the river. The revival that night had attracted a lot of people, maybe six or seven hundred, though Linnie didn't go. They said later it was a blessing. A half dozen people saw Jack point the pistol a foot from Franklin Gaits's head where he stood listening under a lamp-hung tree. They saw him blow the Gaits boy's brains over three other people sitting nearby, but no one afterwards officially would put a name or description to the killer.

Linnie wasn't sure it was such a blessing. She could see everything twice as big in her mind, how hot it was, all the benches packed, people praying and crying at the front, and the men, especially the men, standing in the little clearing at the back, standing still as trees while her brother walked through them, shoulders cocked, with a "measured tread," as the newspapers said. "Stepping backward two or three steps with pistol in hand with all the grace of a finished tragedian . . ."

Elise was scooting her feet along the floor. In the room just behind Linnie, a window glimmered for a second. Linnie was holding her elbows in her hands. "Why are you wearing your nightie?" said Elise. She stepped around to see her face, Linnie's mouth now closed tight. "In the middle of the day," Elise added. There wasn't a breeze where they were standing, and Elise felt her hair sticking down along her back. "You'll get splinters in your feet," she said at last. Which was when she looked down and saw the white-mouthed snake gliding slowly in and out around Linnie's ankles.

Linnie gazed down at Myra's head. "No use in screaming," she said. Alice Saunders told her that when they rode out to the ranch where Myra had gone six months ago, after Axel had died, to tell her in the stifling parlor that Franklin Gaits had been shot the night before in cold blood, Myra just stood there, taking the back of the sofa in her two hands, and screamed. Back arched like a fit. The air in the room so hot you could burn your lungs breathing it. "No use in that a-tall."

That evening Roberta put a clump of mashed potatoes on Elise's plate and looked at her closely. "You feeling sick?"

Elise shook her head.

Ice clinked in the glasses. It was still daylight out. Roberta put the edge of her fork on a piece of ham and cut down. "Well, guess what, Elisalee," she said. "Your Linnie once turned down a marriage proposal. She says she laughed in his face, just laughed out loud." Not that Linnie would have looked at anyone anyway, by that time surely in love with her dead brother Axel of the soft hair and gamin grin. Small men in that family but pretty to look at, Roberta gave them that, something sexy even in the photographed light along their skin.

94

In the dreams it seemed to Elise the noise was always there, voices her age raised in argument, tearful or in the high-pitched hammer of negotiation, footsteps hard across the floor, doors slamming; sometimes they sang. Elise walked, pushing open doors until she reached the kitchen, the floor dark and sticky with hardened spills, a haze of grease behind the stove, crumbs on the counter. The voices ran laughing through the yard. The sun outside the window was gray. She had the cabbages and brine and the old stone crock, but it was getting altogether too dark to see. She swept the counter clean, a crescent of dirt from little finger to wrist, then swept it again and again. Elise blinked. She was staring at the yellow tile of Nana's kitchen.

"They tell me not to wake you." Nana leaned her hip against the table, arms crossed on her light nightgown, shoulders drawn in. Pouches of skin stood under her eyes. Elise suddenly felt her feet, bare against the warm linoleum. The night was blissfully quiet, punctuated by crickets and the soft brush of a curtain flattening against the screen.

Standing at the top of the lawn the next afternoon, Elise saw Uncle Gar clearing leaves off the goldfish pond. He inched around the edge, bent at a stiff angle to reach the skimmer as far toward the center as it would go. The lily pads rocked at one end, water winking.

Aunt Helen had been getting into the Chevy when Elise came up, the heat rushing out of the open door. Helen certainly didn't know why Gar insisted on parking the car right where the sun was sure to hit it. She flapped at the air with her skirt. There was that grandniece of hers, a pretty little thing, but she'd have to tell her when she got back that the green beans were done for. All right, maybe a half bushel left on the poles but she and Gar had to eat too and there was the canning to do. The child had the most peculiar fascination with garden vegetables.

Elise thought her great-aunt looked pretty for being that old. Aunt Helen sat and bent her sleek legs, shiny with hose, before swinging them into the car. Her hair was especially beautiful, a pile of golden curls visible over the steering wheel as with one limp-looking arm she dragged the door shut. The engine roared.

Before jerking backwards, Aunt Helen waved out the window to Elise, mouthing the word "bank" over the noise.

Gar knocked the flat basket against the grass, grunting a little. Damn elms dying one after the other, littering everything around them. The grass at the edge of the pond was slick. He should have just worn the waders even if they made his legs swell; he was damn sure killing his back this way. When he stopped moving, the gnats settled around his shoulders. He looked behind him and saw Elise.

"Aunt Helen's gone to the bank," she said.

"So I hear." Gar dropped the skimmer with a grunt. "She likes to get out her lockbox and browse. It keeps old Davenport hopping. If he weren't kin, she'd probably give it a rest."

"What's kin?"

"Just a manner of speaking. My aunt married his uncle."

Elise was trying to lift the skimmer but it was top heavy, the basket tangled with weeds. She walked to the end, squatted, and started to pick the wet leaves off.

Gar rubbed his back then slowly sat down on the bench. "Married him for money is what people said. A widower without any heirs. Ed Davenport owned the bank back then, so it caused quite a stir, Aunt Nellie barely out of pinafores and all." Gar had always found Nellie a shade plump for his liking, too pigeon-like by half, but she had a sweet, open-lipped smile. Uncle Ed, for his part, was a cold old coot, collars so stiff they cut an ugly rash all around his neck. Sleeping one week at his aunt's with the measles, Gar had heard him choking and crying in their bedroom late at night, then Nellie doing something to make him stop.

"Linnie once told someone she wouldn't marry him."

"That so?" Gar bent over and yanked some weeds out from under the day lilies. It must have been before his time. The Aunt Linnie he remembered was worn-out-looking, not a woman somebody proposed marriage to. He grunted, shaking dirt off the weeds. Sis thought Aunt Linnie had it hard, but it was Nellie who really had the long row to hoe. He hadn't been much more than four, but he distinctly remembered that night, his papa coming home, every inch of him crackling like static with his satisfaction at what he had done. Giving the doctor till sundown was a rare touch. You could hardly blame the man for not taking a threat like that serious until, seeing Jack suddenly standing there in the dusk, he had no choice but to reach up under the buggy seat for his gun. Self-defense, Papa had said, self-defense plain and simple, his footsteps jerking across the floor.

Elise trailed a piece of stick in the water. The goldfish hung under the lily pads. From the looks of them they should have been bumpy to touch but they weren't. Uncle Gar had seined one out with the skimmer once, and it had flipped in her hand like water come to life, then it wiggled through her fingers and was gone.

"Aunt Nellie shouldn't have been fooling around with that doctor anyway."

"Why not?" Elise fooled around all the time.

"She was married already. Uncle Ed may have been no prize, but he kept her good and gave Aunt Linnie money for the children. Most of them were grown by then, I'll grant you, so maybe Nellie felt her duty less. He was a real looker though, that doctor of hers."

So Sis said. She remembered the catlike way he moved almost more than his gold-rimmed glasses or his smooth baby face or his coal black hair and how it curled around at the back of his neck. She had come in Aunt Nellie's back door and seen the doctor pad across the doorway to the sitting room in his shirtsleeves and suspenders. The kitchen was a little dark room at the back of the house so neither one saw her watching. They had swayed together in the middle of the rug. Sis said Aunt Nellie let him hitch her leg up around him like he was some kind of pole she would climb, her fingers wrapped tight in the curls at his neck.

Gar scratched at a bit of dried mud on his knee and cocked one eye at Elise. "She called in a lawyer, you see. Papa said he wasn't going to stand for it a minute."

"Stand for what?"

"Her dragging the family name in the dirt."

97

"Because she didn't want to get married?" Elise was back to thinking about Linnie.

"Hell, because she didn't want to *stay* married."

"Uncle *Gar.*" Elise stood with her hands on her hips. "But *Linnie* wasn't married."

"Linnie?" Gar pressed his hand down to the small of his back. The kid seemed awfully fussed. "Hell, Linnie didn't matter. What she said didn't matter. Papa just showed poor Aunt Linnie the door." Gar remembered that, too. Jack had kept his hand tight around his sister's upper arm, walking her briskly down the hall, her false braid half unpinned. When she turned in his papa's grip at the door, Gar could see the red mark angled across her cheek. Her mouth was closed tight. Stopping, Jack had leaned close to her face and whispered, "Are you crazy, girl? You come in *my house* and call me your stinking names? I think you might be losing what little ol' sense you got left, Miss Melinda Jocelyn." He had put his lips next to her ear. "No way I'd let a sister of mine make a public whore of herself."

Elise, who knew better, could have even shown him now, if Uncle Gar were there with her in front of the house: there was no door. Which meant his daddy couldn't have shown Linnie a thing. Elise hopped along the walk, her arms held out for balance. From the walk a line of stepping-stones went down the shadowed side of the house.

When she came around the corner, the sun was flooding the bluff at the back of the old house, making the grid of the porch look so white it hurt her eyes. Down at the bottom of a ditch shaded with trees, she could hear the river cluck at its banks. It smelled ripe and septic, the grass along the bluff hot, heady. Happy for some reason, Elise started to spin in lopsided circles across the grass, her shadow running behind her.

Linnie steadied her head with one hand and tried to keep the shadows still. That wouldn't be Nellie anyway. No one like Nellie came here. Love had made Nellie sleek, so when she danced alone across the summer lawn it had been like a marmoset waltzing, like a mink taking a graceful turn. Plump arms lifted in the air, she had laughed to herself until she stopped by the porch, letting her head fall slowly back against the balustrade.

Leaning out, Linnie gazed down into her face. She loved her baby half-sister, grown into a woman, a woman in love. The evening was absolutely still, right at that light-filled moment just before the sunset starts to fade. Nellie's eyes below looked dark and sleepy, then her smile looped slowly out. "Well, I want him and I don't care," she said as if Linnie had already voiced a reproof.

Linnie never said a word. She tried instead to imagine how Nellie's mouth moved on the doctor's mouth, her own lips touching and opening, and the eyes, her eyes, how they would slowly close. The light lay across Nellie's cheeks, erasing the tiny lines at her eyes. It made her skin blaze until she became like a fat wax candle, glowing steadily at the bottom of a well.

Head tilted, Elise stared straight up into Linnie's face, awkward, self-conscious, even though she felt Linnie starting to fade. Wait, she thought, trying to will her to stay by not blinking her eyes. Wait. The river spun and chuckled below them. The breeze had fallen. Without warning, Linnie smiled, and something shot through Elise like a piece of the sun. She reached one hand toward the porch.

"Elise!"

Jerking around, Elise saw Roberta at the end of the drive where it widened just past the house. Something tense in the way Roberta waited, her face in shadow with the sun at her back, made Elise hesitate before she turned to look back at the porch. She ran her eyes along the empty struts; Linnie, of course, had gone. The doors and windows stared blankly under sagging eaves.

"Supper!" Roberta waved. When Elise turned, Roberta relaxed, her wrist resting on top of her head, then she dragged her fingers through her hair. She kept it stylishly short, dyed black. Her heart was still beating like a broken pump in her chest. She must have walked down the old drive too fast. Jesus, she thought, smoothing the blunt ends of her hair down her neck, Elise had given her a start, staring up at the house that way, so tense she looked about to shatter. Roberta pushed her glasses up and looked again, frowning. There had been someone on the porch.

"Hey, didn't you know how late it was getting?" Roberta touched Elise on the shoulder. They were walking on the drive under the trees, their arms pale in the shadows. When Elise didn't answer, she tried again. "What's so interesting back there anyway?"

Elise gave Roberta a wary glance, not wanting to be on her bad side. "I don't know."

"You ever see anyone?"

"Uncle Gar."

"Anybody else?"

Elise shrugged. She looked down and picked up a rock. "I was just fooling around," she said. The rock had a black band around it like a ring. Laura liked rocks.

"Nothing the matter with that."

"Then why does Uncle Gar say you can't?"

Roberta looked at her. "Who was he talking about?"

"His Aunt Nellie. I think."

"What did he say?"

"He said his daddy wouldn't stand for it." Elise hopped back and forth over the ruts. "Well, I know one thing," she said. They were almost at Nana's back hedge; she could smell frying grease and corn bread. "I sure wouldn't fool around with Uncle Gar's and Nana's daddy."

Late that night Roberta propped her feet on a kitchen chair and lit the one cigarette she allowed herself a day. It was long and slender, brown like a ladies' cheroot. Nana set her chin in her hand and watched. "I wish you wouldn't smoke in the kitchen," she said.

Roberta exhaled in lazy bliss. "It's going straight out the window. You can see it."

"Still."

The clock ticked above the stove, blending into the noisy cricking outside the windows. Nana had turned off all the lights except one lamp, but the room still felt hot from cooking supper.

Roberta rolled the cigarette against the lip of an old coaster she used for an ashtray. "Gar saw fit to tell Elise about your free-loving Aunt Nellie," she said, "but it beats me what she made of it."

Nana sighed. "I'll have to talk to him. He doesn't have the sense God gave him."

"I suppose not." Roberta looked over the cigarette at Nana. "Why don't you talk about it?"

"It's things over and done with. Nothing to talk about." Nana turned the cut-glass vase of teaspoons sitting on the table. Nellie had refused to have a thing to do with her half-brother until the day she died. When Nana was older and after all the to-do with Linnie, she had seen Aunt Nellie coming out of the dry-goods store and stopped, but Nellie only smiled. "Your daddy thinks he can get away with anything," she said. "But you know what? Someday he's going to burn in hell." She had touched Nana's cheek. "Your daddy's a shit, sweetheart."

The tip of the cigarette glowed. "Maybe," Roberta said. Someone *had* been up on the porch. It wasn't just light flashing off broken window glass. Hell, that porch wouldn't hold a flea.

"Aunt Linnie took it so hard. I could never understand why she took it that way, like it was personal or something." Nana crossed her arms. "I mean, it wasn't her lover that Papa killed."

But it was. By then every man laying with his head split open at Jack's boot tips was Axel. Roberta didn't have any trouble seeing this. Linnie always too late, always not there when she should be there. Everything had died when Axel died. Roberta glanced at the butt and ground it out.

"I didn't know what to do." Nana felt tired.

Roberta stretched, scraping her chair back along the floor. "How could you?" she said. She reached an arm across the table and took one of Nana's fingers in her hand, rubbing the tip gently. "How old were you? Eight? Nine?"

Nana wasn't listening, her head turned. Elise was standing in the door. "Could I get a drink of water?" she said.

The next morning Elise stood next to Nana's elbow watching her peel peaches for cobbler. She picked a peeling out of the sink and played with it on her tongue, first the fuzzy side down, then the slick sweet one. Nana glanced at her. "Get that out of your mouth," she said.

Elise put the peeling back in the sink. Flies had started buzzing up against the screen. She pinched a tiny bit of dough off the ball sitting on waxed paper by the cobbler dish and put it in her mouth before Nana saw. Her teeth gritted on sugar. "Did you find out what to do?" she said.

"About what?" Nana picked up another peach, wishing vaguely that she could be alone for a minute in her own kitchen.

"Linnie."

"I don't know what you mean, darlin'."

"Last night. You said you didn't know what to do."

"I said that? Scoot over a little, would you please."

"Well." Elise moved her stool an inch.

"Well what? A little *more*, Elise, I need to get to the sugar."

"Did you?" Elise dragged the stool to the end of the counter.

"Papa did what he thought best at the time." Even he had been a little subdued, coming back from putting Linnie inside that place. She had heard him talking to her momma—you wouldn't believe some of those loonies, excuse me, inmates; you couldn't put a comb through half their heads.

"What was best?"

"Elise . . ." Nana flattened the ball of dough with a light roll of the pin.

But Elise was suddenly sick and tired of being fobbed off by everyone. She hit her palms on the counter. "But what *happened?*" she said. What *happened* to Linnie with her eyes all puffy from crying, the way Laura always cried, getting left behind, Elise feeling the hot tears now, her breath sucked up into big hard sobs, feeling that minute like her heart would break. "It's all I want and I ask and I ask you," she cried, "and you just *ignore*, ignore me, and my mommy lets me, my mommy would, but you just, you just go and do—"

"Shh, shh, sit down." Nana pressed her hands on Elise's shoulders until she sat on the stool. "All right," she said, rubbing her hand softly down the child's back. "All right, just slow down now. Slow down. You'll make yourself sick."

The gulping sobs were the worst, but Elise finally managed to stop, head on Nana's knees. Her chest hurt and her nose was starting to run over onto her lip. She felt awful.

"Here, blow." Nana held the Kleenex over Elise's nose. She didn't know why the sight of a child dutifully blowing snot into her hand always made her heart sink with sadness. "Again," she said. Her back ached from all the bending over.

Elise blew and took another Kleenex to wipe her eyes. Nana pulled a kitchen chair around and, wincing a little, sat down. She stared off across the room for a minute, her fingers moving idly along the table, then looked at Elise. The outburst had upset her. The child might be homesick and not telling her, or lonely, too much time by herself. The smell of peaches was overpowering. "What's wrong, Elisalee," she said. "Do you want to go home?"

Elise shook her head.

"Do you miss your mother?"

"No."

"Well, what is it then?" Nana never had any patience.

"Tell me about Linnie," Elise whispered.

Nana looked at her. The fear was ridiculous, Nellie's fingers against her cheek like ice. Elise had pulled her elbows into her lap and was looking at the floor. Her hair fanned out down her back. "All right," Nana said.

Elise looked up. "What did your daddy do?"

"He took her to a place where she could rest."

"Was she tired?"

"Yes."

"Did she like the place?"

Nana hesitated. "I don't think so."

"After a while did she get to go home?"

"No." Papa had moved them up to the old river house within a month of Linnie's leaving. They didn't tell Linnie for a year. The doctors informed Nellie, on Jack's advice, that she couldn't see or write Linnie until enough time had passed for her to settle in.

"*Never?*"

"She would just cry, darlin'. Day after day, up there in that old house of her papa's. She just sat in a chair and cried."

"Why?"

103

"I guess because people she loved had been hurt."

"Who hurt them?"

Nana didn't say anything. He had a quick-talking charm; people liked him. When she remembered him it was always in a crowd, his head moving from group to group, sometimes disappearing behind taller men but always surfacing, a beer high in one hand, collar a flash of white below his face.

Elise smoothed her hands down over her knees. "Did she die in that other place?"

"Yes."

"How long did she stay?"

Nana touched the table lightly with her fingertips. "About thirty years," she said.

Elise let out her breath in a small sigh. Well, now she knew. They should have just let poor Aunt Linnie go home. The sun was flooding the kitchen with a peach-colored light. Even her dirty feet on the linoleum were a warm gold. Picking at her toes, Elise glanced up at her grandmother. "When you're finished, can I poke the holes in the crust?" she said.

That night Roberta handed Nana a glass of sherry and went back to pour her own. She set the bottle down, thinking that Nana looked old tonight; you could see the shape of her head through her hair.

"I got the third degree from a kid once." Roberta sat on the sofa. "He wanted to know just what I had been doing in his mother's bed. I said sleeping, and he gave me this look. When I bounce around like that, he said, Mommy makes me go back to my own bed."

Nana's eyes shifted automatically to the door and back. "Hush," she said.

Rolling her eyes, Roberta took a sip. "So Elise now knows her great-granddaddy is a mean, self-righteous son of a bitch. We've all got feet of clay. Though your father may have set a whole new standard in clay feet, which, I imagine, would please him no end."

"Shut up, Roberta." Nana didn't know what set Roberta off worse—Jack himself or the fact that Nana was still, at sixty-six, her father's daughter.

"If you made him look good," Roberta's eyes glittered above her glass, her voice steady, "as I am sure you did, then why are you so worried?"

Nana leaned her head back into the chair. It was pointless to protest that it was Elise's explosion of tears that weighed on her, the way Elise's face had flattened, eyes trapped in a furious misery. "I'm not," she said.

"The hell you're not. This man destroyed every single thing he ever touched. You going to let him get between you and what you feel for that little girl—"

"He's not, Roberta."

Roberta made a spitting gesture and put down her empty glass. "Why you persist in defending—"

"Stop it." Nana looked a warning across the space between them.

But Roberta was past caring. "Why should I? He's loving it, you know. He watches all the time. He's there even when it's just you and me alone in bed, under the goddam sheets—"

"Stop it!" Nana glared. "I didn't ask for that, Roberta. I don't need a single thing from you, all right?"

Elise woke up to their voices, quiet and angry, then the sight of Roberta and Nana swaying together as if they were dancing in the next room, but it was terrible somehow, dark and scary. A door banged and Elise was running outside in the night, then down the road, her nightgown a cloud around her knees, not stopping until she came out into the moonlight by the river behind the house. The house was a jumble of black, crumbling into the spiky silhouettes of trees, except where the moon had turned the exposed boards of the porch into tarnished silver. Elise could see Linnie walking there, turning to look down at the river, walking back to the door, then around again, stopping at the edge to listen. Elise watched her. Linnie turned and paced back to the house.

They were coming. Linnie peered through the door. She could hear their voices, low rumbles of concerned inquiry and answer, footsteps solemn as a church. It was taking too long this time. She turned and walked the broad planks back to the edge of the porch. The updraft from the river was cool, a pleasant stirring in the lilac-scented night. She loved it there, the *nuances* in any given breath at any time of day or night, each tilt of memory in a different melancholy key, a thing to keep. For all her blues, it was a kind of a life, a good enough life. The breeze lifted her hair off her face as she turned.

The house behind her was lovely, with its sloping wing of three rooms added on later to the square cabin. The wing offset the long open hallway with a delicate asymmetry that was emphasized by the narrow pillars along the front porch. Linnie had long ago written it up. She knew which paneling and inside joists were walnut and how the second chimney was rocked in. She had studied out the best way to add the porch she was standing on to least spoil the lines. Even now, every angle and curve behind her was as intimately there as her own skin. She forgot none of it.

The voices were at the door—Jack's light one a rapid flow of saddened pragmatism, the doctor's deeper, phlegmatic and watchful. They would be here in only a minute or two. Linnie closed her eyes. The river guttered in the shallows just before the bend that she could see, when it was light, from where she stood. They always came after dark. She was tired; she was at her tiredest now. She knew, when Jack took her arm and put his cool appraising face next to hers, she would do whatever he said.

Elise put her hands on the edge of the porch. "Linnie," she whispered. Linnie, watching the house, shrank back a little, turned her head. The long flat lines of her eyebrows dipped then rose into points above her nose, and her eyes curved downward, squeezing closed. When her mouth widened, the skin along her nose stretched flat, and the knobby bones of her face were lost in the swelling ridge of her cheek. The tears dripped off her jaw.

"Shh," Elise said, hopelessly patting the air between them with her hand. There was nothing but the quiet night around them. "Shh," she whispered to the woman on the porch, her hand heavy. "Don't cry."

SIX

Fire I

1996

MOTHERHOOD SEEMED PROBLEMATIC, PRIMARILY BECAUSE IT required a sperm. From habit I checked the predictable elements, circled blots on plastic film, the darkest smear my legal ex, hair in a slant across his eyes, his shoulder warm against my chin, then after Michael the good old boys, transparency for the absence of Nick. Lucy filled the car with silence; I glanced at her then looked away. Motherhood seemed to entail a passion much like science did, multiple and all-consuming, a cell flush with redundancies for every possible cause and effect. Laura found a million things to worry about her daughter doing, while Lucy to me seemed self-contained, something you could hold in your palm. I studied her the way I did the spiraled, jewel-like inner cell, the desert-prairie interface, bubble trails of family ghosts. I was obsessed enough already, too self-absorbed for motherhood—like now, needing concrete data to keep the early research up and stuck with deeply phobic laws against field tests of labmade bugs. If taking the test across the border should push a thinning ethical line, I couldn't help it, only sure the gene-spliced microbe stayed in place, the parameters themselves were pure. I couldn't do that and motherhood too. Swerving around the potholed ruts, I was going just a fraction fast. When I looked up from the open car, I saw in the dull, polluted sky a hawk slowly banking as it rode the heated updrafts higher.

Flight and its erasure of minute distinctions sapped the soul. The seamless overview of orbiting astronauts, or God, made everything more mysterious, obliterating the little we knew. The car creeping by slow degrees through a vacancy of drying land was like a loose receptor, and the test site fifty miles behind was where it poked the surface skin, kneading the phospholipids there, triggering changes inside the cell. All was hubris, a modest microbe hardly having that kind of punch. The latest blip in the field-test data floated at the edge of thought. Lucy, yelling back at me, had looked that way when she was two, the look that Laura said she liked, angry, upper lip flared forward, safer somehow hitting back. We were somehow safer, too.

The safety of the road I drove remained in doubt the last two months, even on return trips when I moved without the payroll cash. Since no one wanted a paper trail, with each trip south I hauled a box of duly exchanged devalued bills, the car a target in the dusty air, a robin's egg on a piece of wire. My head felt light, the hair along my temples stiff with sweat and dirt. In time the dark maroon had crisped with gray, like veins in certain rocks, the skin spotted along the upper curves from too much sun. Aging was of passing interest, the body on its steady course of certain programmed obsolescence. Aging felt a little dumb. Maybe some ten years ago I wouldn't have agreed to run the test, back when I believed in truth and what was due the exploited poor, but I did it without question now. In the glass office tower, I made the deal, leaning across the polished table, the air inside there freezing cold and the men a dozen shadowed suits, two dozen folded manicured hands.

Carlos' hands were something else, young and elastic, muscled taut. I had watched them raise an M-16, play across the laptop computer's keys. An average student with a colonel father stationed somewhere farther south, Carlos was useful for other things, like speaking the native dialect, knowing the local politics. He had his own crazy ideas about the militant violence of radical change. You couldn't control that sort of change, hot-wired enzymes banging around, molecules in a fast slamdance down any one of twenty pathways from which you never duplicated results. "What about a point mutation, if you're going to go with metaphors?" he said, playing devil's advocate as we looked through the autoradiographs. Lucy, slouching at his side, had hung around with him before, leaning against the plywood walls with their tacky rose-colored insulation to muffle the neighboring generator roar. I personally preferred to work alone. Carlos, who in the biology lab could be subdued, even self-effacing, became in the test field something else, a sweaty force blooming outside those medieval walls of cloistered gray—the hallowed university. Undercredentialed, I stayed beneath the notice of the megastars, my work so odd no one thought to take their pound of published flesh. In the lab at night off the empty halls I always felt absurdly clean, cleaner than at the test-field site, studying films in the stifling heat, or worse, en route to make my report. The politics of the choice didn't matter. I simply wanted to see it work—bacteria binding water into any number of staple crops. Nothing grew in the alkaline soil we were driving through except patchy brush. The car threw up a plume of dust as it crossed that hot and empty space, blown as much by my own ambition as by the plateau's restless air.

In college Rita had pointed out how ambition, even ambition denied, was at the root of my fuming impatience. Now my friend and one-time lover was saying I chose to have no choice, talking about this field test that I had told her I flatly couldn't not do. She found out all those corporate backers were really Bolivian businessmen, pegged by Rita as cocaine kings, telling me this while she crouched on the grid savagely wrenching a Leko loose, the shutters rattling as a gel drifted and petaled gently toward my face. So what if they were. Everything came to selling something, dishwashing soap or coke or clones. I wasn't exactly the slickest con. My hands holding the steering wheel would never pass in the sixties' commercial for those of the daughter I didn't have. Without a government willing to buck the gadflies and fund a legitimate test, deals like this were the only way, though Rita held to different truths. She'd leave the world doing agit-prop plays while I went testing altered microbes in a country lacking laws to forbid it. "If it's self-destruction we're after," she said, "I'll take polemic over homemade plague, not to mention staying clear of the border where things, I hear, go up in flames."

Fire was the medium of popular choice, the traditional end for the Christian world denied the effluence of a second flood. Lucy beside me could mimic the preachers with flawless cant, my vibrant niece, at twelve years old the queen of sarcasm, narrow glasses wrapping her head in a smoothly darkened ridge of plastic, her reddish hair whipped into spikes by the air's hot rush around the windshield. Even the leftist take on events had biblical nuances, overtones. Carlos trusted in his sexual instincts to thread the ideological maze, in that oddly androgynous macho-charisma, in love—if Laura only knew.

My sister let her daughter rage, joking to me as she twirled a lock of hair around and around her finger, the same sarcastic edge as Lucy's, maybe bleaker with Milos gone. She made the war between them sound both comical and lunatic, all at the same time touched with terror, her child, like liquid mercury, slipping away between her fingers. The times were bad and getting worse, the catherine wheel of the century in its final fiery revolutions, Armageddon everyone's drug. There were worse things now to worry about than your all-American libidinous boy or the tiny dots of acid on a given edible porous surface. Lucy was like a buoyant chip threading an ever-growing torrent, her cropped hair brushed into stylized fright. That guileless smile was half embarrassed, Lucy master of little more than a graceless fury, yelling at Laura, "Sure, oh *sure*, maybe I should just be a nun, like maybe you want to brick up my *room*." She shifted around from mood to mood. I thought of her as a traumatized cell under pressure of events to replicate, meriting caution, a gingerly patience, every molecule afloat inside snapped asunder and madly dancing.

Though the slamming force had gone from their dances with their stark expression of overt hate, something of that nihilism, Laura insisted, stayed behind. The music, pounding day and night from Lucy's room, with its plodding bass and depressive lyrics, was cloaking something not quite sane. Wistful women in their middle forties, we danced around the kitchen to the Rolling Stones at three one morning, swaying barefoot, a little drunk. What we'd done ourselves looked playful, nothing causing permanent harm. Despite the rabid propaganda, our brain cells all survived intact. Laura switched, with Milos gone, to full-time work in the AI lab, while I had practiced my small-scale science on gene expression in simple forms. That it had led outside the law to a low-rent lab on foreign soil was not the fault of my blighted youth but of the climate, political and real. The outside air had a brassy taste, the car shaking as I followed ruts calcified by months of drought into scalloped, shell-like marble.

Lucy could be cut from stone, still not speaking to me in the car, her profile smooth below the shadowed glasses and the blowing hair. Last night her face had changed for me like one of those plastic hologram disks—see a view, tilt it, see another— now the hard bones of a hooker, next a child in a weepy rage. We never thought it would be this way, watching as the times turned mean, turned crazy. What you had in the outside world was hundreds of enzymes crashing together, nothing as simple as the austere mix of one plus another in a glass-walled tube— though certain doomsayers would have it that way. The hard-line religious and ecology wings were saving the world for its natural demise, everyone to rise in rapture from a desertification preordained. I sometimes thought that stakes were raised whenever generations aged.

"Peaked," said Rita, defying age. She promised us all a post-forty peak if we bought the pig-in-a-python theory, the next renaissance being long overdue. It was hot enough today to feel the rest of North America burn, a blistering drought in the

111

middle of spring. The cluster of shacks and canvas tents, with the greening fields aglow in the heat, was like a ragtag Indian oasis grown up around a swami's hut. I felt sometimes extremely happy, though it didn't feel earned, what I carried away from that plywood lab, playing with nothing I really touched, invisible chains of amino acids, while outside in the sultry heat a field grew something never grown before. That joy was as tangential as my wayward approach to biotech, the man in the hotel conference bar coming up to me and hissing "rogue." A lightness pushed against my chest. I would work in the deafening generator noise, in the nighttime heat, and fall in love with something as dumb as my fingers moving, the strangely deft opposable thumb, the practiced dance of repeated motion, cue chained to cue chained to cue chained to cue. Under the lamplight the finger bones made shadows that gave the illusion of length, of beauty. I had watched my hands as I talked to Carlos, the cigarette turning, cocked and rolled, tapped unsmoked between my fingers. During the day my hands at the bench would stop at the stutter of machine-gun fire. The guards shot at snakes, at rabbits, hawks. They shot every day at moving shadows.

Our shadow traveled beneath the car, brush pooled in black, cracks erased. Driving between them, I wasn't sure which of the two bugged me the most, a narco-mafia on the right that looked for respectable corporate cover or Carlos and his revolutionary schemes. The border was like the skin of a cell, waiting only for a protein to wiggle through from the south and start things up, triggering change, cataclysm, pockets of calcium spraying out like a nervous line of friendly fire. Power for men was always something imposed from outside on something else, nothing consensual or empathetic; everyone had to be some kind of hero. What on earth did they do with their kids, women and children dying daily under IMF austerity plans? Lucy as a one-year-old, riding next to me in the car, would softly pat the cushioned bar, matching her cool observation to mine. The sun beating against our heads was like a hammer, phosphorescent. Tension hummed along the border, poverty pressed up hard against the north's shrinking conspicuous wealth, pungent Catholic superstition infiltrating puritan guilt, markets meshed, dope and labor, by the imposition of capitalist debt. Twice a month I paid out pesos brought from merchants of a shadow trade to a variable group of sullen men to wave their guns over greening fields while women invisibly farmed or foraged. A half a dozen tiny wars across the world were spreading famine. The fields behind their shiny nets could be an ammunitions dump and Lucy with her sulking and her legs a whitely moving torch.

The barn went up with a muffled clap ten years ago. That whump of air imploding to flame was followed by a thin-edged crackle, fire pale in the sun behind Nick's head. I couldn't remember now her name, that girl in class who looked like him, not his blondness but the shape of his eyes, something in how she closed the door. The way her shoulders squared themselves looked just like Nick and maybe the jaw, the shape of her head under all that hair, and the eyes, her eyes looking Mayan, old. Rita had smiled. "A fox," she said, and I shook my head. She had to be a wolf at least, a predator in the bigger leagues. I had never sought out students before, though someone always came around. Carlos had showed up, technically good but somehow lacking that careless passion I sensed in her, whoever she was. Everybody in class was young. Whenever I was away too long, I would start to wish for my putative peers, Rita and Laura and even Hollis, all of them alive somewhere when I was yelling at my own poor mother, who had rested her arm along the seat on family trips when Daddy drove, her hand, loosely clenched, moving slightly with the moving car. Laura said I sounded like our mother when I hadn't slept.

Perchance to dream—Hollis had made a brilliant Hamlet. Everyone was happy that year, Rita like a lioness on the day she cut her waist-length hair, the tawny stuff a bristling velvet smoothed down flat along her head. I'd run my hand from brow to nape, fingers never ready for the soft surprise at the back of her neck. We lasted as lovers less than a year. Hollis made her phallus jokes, but Rita raged, grabbing my arm in a fit one night and throwing me down the front porch steps, Sloan behind her, the dog in its own contagious hysteria feinting and barking at my head. Sloan and I smoked that winter together, for solace, in the frost-killed yard; stoned enough, Sloan would do his imitation of Marlon Brando, bellowing "Rita" to the neighborhood. Rita, who had left me first beside some bleak Minnesota lake, now bitched about Bolivian thugs with never a word on who had bought the theater that she nominally owned. The winter cold in eastern Oregon was blue and empty and never let up, Michael shrugging without surprise the night I told him I planned to go then closing the door and leaving me there. I had listened to the cooler hum, my eyes on the hoods of the microscopes. I hardly thought of him anymore, Michael, the cattle rancher I married who loved cloning cells as much as the land.

The flats stretched still and hot beyond the buffeted block of air in the car. I had a stake in the earth's survival but didn't waste thought on its imminent ruin; I had never been very romantic that way. Lucy, shrugging my questions off, was the real romantic, with her loose, free-floating sense of love, still half playing at grown-up games, all at the moment for the sake of Carlos with his sexy eyes and crooked teeth. I hired him for the test because he had the citizenship I needed and because his bench work seemed okay—"and because he was easy," Rita said, watching me smile, "and because he might actually bomb a train." She was wrong about the last part, though. I didn't like simply dangerous men or just anyone on the lunatic fringe. They had to have a little substance. With Carlos, I wondered what that was, the layers of the man so paper-thin, each one gaudier than the next, student-rebel-middleman-whore. I think if I let myself really see how good he was at guerrilla games, it would overcomplicate my life. He didn't move at all when he heard my voice, but Lucy jumped. Seeing the two of them standing there had shocked me as if a dream had turned and said my name, but he was real and I knew it, having pressed a leg across and down that narrow ass.

I pumped the clutch and shifted down to second as the road gave way, crumbling into washboard ruts. My great-great-grandfather crossed this country back and forth a little farther west, when the land was greener, thick with grass. Addison was a slender man with a springy beard that fanned straight out across his chest in a stiffened spray; it looked glued on in the photograph, a newspaper falling in languid folds across his neatly positioned legs. He worked for the railroad rolling south, keeping the books and doling out pay, gone sometimes for months on end. Nick knew nothing about his past; he could have been born from an ostrich egg. The Method had nothing to work with when it came to actors made like Nick, everything rising straight out of chaos. Lucy looked across at me through those asinine glasses then looked away. That Addison might have taken along his oldest girl was worth a laugh, though they must have made a gallant pair at the open door of the river house, Linnie in lieu of his two dead wives, a hospitable front to domestic loss.

Nick at his house in the country had studied the line of window screens laid flat and covered with psilocybin mushrooms, his fingers touching one then another as gnats hovered around the grass. Nick's charm was hard to quantify, that sexual undertow of his almost easier for pinning him down, but something about his blithely wry acceptance of strange events appealed. His home was on the outer edge. In the country with Nick, I felt I was watching a visitor from another planet approximating domestic life, the empty farmhouse looming around us, filled with early summer dusk. Plus he was always good in bed, his long body moving between my legs as light as a kite of balsam wood. "Have you ever," he asked as we walked the hills, "seen something really big go up?" the barn in the sun a rustic wreck. Something about the emptiness of all that land made Nick uneasy. Addison, too, must have hated the stiffing he got from every ranchero that sold him beef, the endless wind, glad for each hot mile of track hammered home across the land as fiercely as he'd hammered himself that honeysuckled Virginia night into the adolescent girl he would later find he had to marry.

Which was a nicety Nick ignored. I never saw Tila, though she often came around, knowing somehow when he scored, their daughter maybe nine or ten. I knew she was young, or had been younger by a dozen years, seventeen, dark and demure and Catholic and sweet. Nick had lovers everywhere, but Tila was the one who bothered me. "A fool for love," I said one time, and Hollis shrugged. "As are we all." She had just that month had her first abortion. I'd never wanted to have a baby but now that I couldn't I wondered why, the essential thing a man can't do and now I couldn't do it either. How to define a basic condition you suddenly were not but could have been, a primitive power slowly slackened. I felt sometimes geologically old. "That kid of Nick's," Laura said to me once, "will be a knockout, with her daddy's bones and all that hair." I tried to imagine what I would have done, in my mother's house at seventeen with a child of his, a sodden weight of baby warmth, Nick long gone on heavy wings. Maybe just what anyone would, promising the baby in a whispered vow that one day she would inherit the earth.

Recent scholars said that Jesus never promised the meek a thing; it drove the fundamentalists up a wall. Who would want the earth anyway, a place now more or less exhausted, my niece flirting with its upstart heir. Goddam Carlos. She was twelve years old. I had made a point to be carefully calm but her arm felt empty under my hand, my fingers helplessly gripping harder. When Milos left, I thought the rest of us could make a collective father, Sloan and Rita and Hollis and me, but Milos left a clumsy breach. Lucy missed him, turned inside. The more she grew into her gawky legs, the more I feared she would disappear, much more there as a nine-year-old. She still came back, childishly solid, eating with us at three o'clock in the otherwise empty catfish place, pushing at her temples to make the hair stand higher, laughing, freckles sandy across her nose. "She calls me 'moth-er,'" Laura said, laughing one day with me in my office. "They should put an anguished chorus of adolescents saying 'moth-er' on those records they keep shooting out into space," her eyes suddenly rimmed with red. Lucy tilted back the seat and stuck one foot outside the window. When Laura cried, I could feel the ghost of Addison's prim unease float down, his backbone sheathing my own with glass, his milky eyes as pale as marble rolling deep inside my sockets.

All four of them had those light blue eyes, father to son to daughter to son, but there it stopped, recessive genes, the father's son a three-time killer, the myth of all that easy to see but not the actual physical act. Given the imagined crack of bullet crashing into human bone, my gut turns cold then liquifies. Some of the men in the office tower had barrel chests and muscled necks, different each time I cycled through, patient souls. If I proved the drought resistance worked, they still had the FDA to sell, though Rita said they would peddle it to the oligarchies owning Third World land and screw the States. I'd signed a paper not to publish. It put me further beyond the pale from other molecular biologists doing similar research in similar fields. Bench work had a medieval feel of artists' guilds, a brotherhood. Whenever I poked a rod into the agglutinated DNA of plant cells, coming out of solution in a viscous mass of bouncy light, I felt like a priest, an alchemist. Letting the Bolivians own the discourse changed that feeling to something else, alchemist to bureaucrat, a busy Mephistopheles. When I showed Carlos what I meant, the field tests called the devil's work, he laughed and held my hand against him. "That's the devil's work," he said. My great-grandfather Jack M. Wallace would have seduced the corporate thugs and murdered Carlos for touching his niece, while I would do the opposite, lacking only his chilly ease.

Even doing her silent act, Lucy was sweet, her hair red in the lowering sun. The road abruptly switched to asphalt, paving the last twenty miles or so, and the car, freed of the gravel ruts, took off, everything flattened and smooth. Leaving had always been that way, a sudden slippery rushing forth. I'd seen Lucy born like that, Milos wide-eyed behind the mask, Laura's face gray with strain. Rita left on the St. Paul bus, her headbanded hair braided down her back, everyone thinking hippie-freak, while I stood on the street in the freezing wind, the sky like a red pane of ice behind me. Now ten years later I hardly cared, how much like me Nick had seemed to be, how simple that reflective falling in love. The slipstream that poured across the windshield smelled of dust and a whisper of sage. Lucy yawned and lifted her chin. When I drove out of the Oregon desert, the world had been all pink and blue, snow in shallow drifts through the brush, the distant rim of mountains showing a pale skim-milk like glacier ice. The sun had hugged the horizon, pink, nothing but sky and the empty plate of snowy plains and telephone poles.

The memory of Carlos, his hands down Lucy's track shorts, telescoped in jerks. So much of what happened didn't matter. In human cells maybe ninety percent of the RNA is thrown away, looped and clipped and spliced back together. I wanted that field of profligacy, omnipotent flux, multiple truths. The warm room where I worked with my simple bacterium stank of sweat, while in the cold room across the lab they chopped up RNA from mouse cells, huddled in jackets at four degrees. I wanted that. I touched the air, cooler now, shooting around the Fiat's windows. Loss was at the heart of things. I took what comfort I could in a substance so intent on life that only a fraction of its finely chained codons served a purpose at all.

SEVEN

Hollis

1984

People had sentimental notions about public life on a summer evening, but no one had any business doing Shakespeare in a city park, the sky still full of evening light, the actors so many costumed dolls miked inside a plaster bandshell, Hollis more than happy to ditch the role of Lady Anne in *Richard III* for a play in a theater with decent dark. The alley to the parking lot was shadowed by the walls on each side, but she could see sun still on the cracked concrete at the far end. Crunching through broken glass, Hollis saw first the squat blue shape of Elise's Fiat Spider, then Milos' car and Rita's bike. Hollis was early, bored to death with watching water lap the dock and arguing whether to ski back out, a whine of mosquitoes around her head. Who knew what the guy with the car keys thought when she stood up suddenly and said let's go, but Hollis figured it wasn't to drop her on a dirty street of renovated bars, barely pulsing at 6:15 with the cars and music that later would keep the not-so-sentimental up all night. Hollis stretched, her chest stinging with what looked to be a bitch of a burn. He had pressed his dripping bottle of beer up between her breasts to "cool the fire," confirming a lifelong disappointment, the tiresome predictability of any guy who had drunk too much, presenting that beery cave of a mouth, the arm like a forty-pound weight in your lap. Hollis yawned. She had this theory that narcolepsy could be a sexual response.

Rita had painted Stage Door on the back in drippy letters with fat-looking stars. Now there was a woman with a sick sense of humor. The play could use a touch of that, more of the things that Nick suggested, but Milos, their own enfant-terrible director and amateur actor, had other ideas. There was something deeply weird about a Serbo-Croatian, or whatever the hell he was, playing this mythic American rocker. "So what," he was always saying (like "what the fuck is this?") about the slang. Hollis, who still found Milos endearing, especially out of bed when he flashed that half-cocked smile of his, had made him a scrapbook of all your basic extremely macho American icons: phallic cars, the Marlboro man, black leather jackets, cowboy boots. It had been a stretch to find the good stuff, swamped by trenchcoats and flashy suspenders, and completely forget the music rags with their punk postapocalypse mutants. Still, for all the gaping holes in the myth, Milos had been happy as hell. "Hey," he said, turning the pages, "I want to go out and pillage and burn, I want to fuck, I want to kill."

The band was waiting inside the greenroom. Wadded-up paper shot through the air, the lead guitarist swatting it back. The drummer talked, weaving his gaze around Hollis as she picked her way through, "—so, like, I went to hear the dude play, all right, an investment of time on my humble part—" Hollis felt, as always, canceled out by their clubby and total disregard, swinging her arms and hips in a pantomime of sexy toughness, grinning to herself, a short, black-haired woman flaunting her drop-dead looks for these pasty-faced boys. A loose paper wad bounced off her shoulder with snatches of talk "—da de da de da dum DUM dum, like a fucking cardiac arrest, whachamacallit, tachycardia, yeah well the man didn't show after all—" as the bass player slowly moved his legs to let her by. They all had flattened addict eyes, pants low on their hips, patchy hair like cancer victims. They composed mutated rock and roll like she'd never heard, eerie junk, everyone with eyes for Nick. Lots of women singers hung out with gays, but something about Hollis, her attitude, pissed the band members off. A wad of paper clipped the keyboardist's ear and he stood, slapping his chair over backwards.

The dressing rooms were empty. Hollis checked her sunburn in the mirror, thinking how dumb it had been to go out on the lake. As she reached for a jar of body makeup, she remembered fleetingly all those freaked-out southern girls when she peeled down in the locker room after the first day of gym and walked toward the showers, looping a towel around her hips and wondering what the hell her mother figured, hauling her out of L.A. to here, virgin territory, country of God. The burn was starting to disappear under creamy beige as she layered on the character of Becky Lou, rocker moll, Marilyn-momma, bitchin' lady, queen of the hop. Milos as Hoss had a random energy, with all the finesse of a shot-apart snake, untrained actors a pain in the butt. Even after a month's run, Hollis still had to go onstage ready to reblock, ad lib, cue. Milos' methods were hard to fathom. She frowned. Her nipples looked funny in the greenish mirror, long and full like she might be pregnant, something not to be thought. She shrugged, going over her lines. That mythic boring Maserati. Hollis figured she had to be the only woman with L.A. blood who didn't drive, all that easy living in the south, every boyfriend with some kind of car.

Milos opened the door, standing in the mirror as Hollis dipped two fingers back in the jar. She could hear the band now out onstage blasting through "The Way Things Are," atonal, bluesy, ominous, then the door smacked shut, the noise muffled. Since Laura had popped the baby, he had been a completely different man. "Jesus Marie, what did you do to yourself?"

121

"Sun." Hollis was almost through, thankful at least she'd worn that visor someone had brought, life's little mercies. After a long curious look, Milos started whistling softly with the band, declining for now to scramble the words, which drove Hollis nuts, convinced the garbled lyrics would stick in his head like crossed eyes or something. Smoothing the cream along her jaw, Hollis wondered just how men, even the nice ones, managed to take up all the space in a room. Milos turned her shoulder to show her a place she had missed.

"I can get it." His hands were careful, fingers light. Milos had a wild streak she secretly liked, reeling out half drunk last spring to find a bum to teach him to street fight, something he needed to know to play Hoss. The black ex-con, when she and Elise caught up with them, had schizy eyes, muscled arms outreaching Milos by a good three inches, his face impassive, the knife moving like a flame in his fist. Standing together in the shadows, Elise and Hollis had waited, afraid to jar the balance, shoulders barely touching as they breathed and Milos feinted, turned, his face in the moonlight stupid with joy. "You shit," Elise said later, dropping him back by the car he had left twelve blocks away, Hollis unfolding from the Fiat's cramped back seat. "You don't want us around, then don't go and tell Laura what you plan to do. She loves you, you stupid piece of shit. You want her to lose that baby over you?" Milos shouted something and kicked the car but Elise had shot off, Hollis barely into the front seat, laughing as they floored it down the empty street, Elise wild, whooping when they took the bridge, the girders whipping above their heads.

"Got it." Milos handed her back the jar. "No, wait." Reaching from behind, he moved her arm up and across then rubbed a streak of the cream out smooth along the place right where her breast began to curve, sliding his fingers under, his thumb slowly working. The ache between her legs was familiar and annoying and sad all at once, Hollis wondering wearily why they always had to try as she felt him press closer around her, his leg pushing against her ass. She gave him a look in the mirror and he laughed, backing off. " 'I'm too old-fashioned,' " he drawled.

" 'That's it. Gotta kick out the scruples. Go against the code. That's what they used to do. The big ones. Dylan, Jagger, Townshend. All them cats broke codes.' "

" 'Time can't change that,' " Hollis finished for him. "God, Milos, you *always* drop that line." She leaned away from his hands, the band through the thin partition wailing into "Cold Killer," Hendrix pyrotechnics. She had turned into a really incredible nag the last few weeks as the play settled into its run, the opening adrenaline bleeding off. "Sorry," she said, picking up a half-empty pack of cigarettes and pulling one out. Staring at it for a minute, she groaned gently and put it between her lips. She was trying to quit, the smell of tobacco almost making her cry. "How's the infanta, the baby czarina?"

"Very, very small." Milos held his hands apart ten inches. "We have conversations."

"You do." Hollis put the cigarette back.

"I talk to her about the liberation of the Ukraine and she thinks about Laura's breast; we are sympathetic."

Milos these days was hovering around Laura like she was the blessed madonna, the same Laura who when she got with Elise was as wild as her sister, hitting the chilly water at dawn last spring with a wallop (pregnant, she couldn't ride). Hollis, nursing a hangover, watched them swim, their rising arms exactly the same. "Forget it," Laura had said a week later, watching Hollis take one nervous swallow after another of her beer, the summer haze hanging over Rita's garden, everyone suddenly scattered to phone or bathroom or kitchen, leaving the two of them in the battered lawn chairs waving at flies. A lousy moment. Laura's T-shirt had been tight across her stomach.

People were talking outside in the greenroom, Hollis reaching for the sleeveless leather vest, the black miniskirt that seemed to be shrinking by the minute—maybe all that beer after gigs at the club. She got the last snap and breathed, still room. "What is it?" Milos was smiling at her with pity. "The PMS?"

"Yeah, I wish." Hollis opened the door. The room seemed suddenly loud and full, Cheyenne showing off his racing gear, the shiny clinging purple pants, low-cut shoes, his shoulders muscled under the top. "Hey, hey." Hollis waltzed out. "Look at this shit. I'll go you two for the purple shorts."

"Uh-huh, not a chance." He gave her a glance. "What about it, Holl. You chubbing up?"

"Sorry, sweetie, you'll never see *me* working out. I'll take my lousy liver and lungs over greeting the day at 5 A.M. with major physical pain."

Nick was the only one not in, as Gale, stretching out on the sofa, observed. "Well lookee here. There's movement all around but no numero uno. That's what they're backin' their chips on you for."

Hollis patted his cheek and glanced around the room. "I thought we'd got him back to putative normal."

Cheyenne looked down on him and shook his head. "He's regressed."

Leaning over the tall black man now smiling blissfully, eyes closed, Hollis spoke carefully in his ear. "Gale, you're popping flies again."

"So are you," he said. "Solo's the payola."

"Pretty amazing."

Cheyenne shrugged and went to change. Doc/Star-man pushed off from the wall where he'd been leaning. "I caught your Wednesday gig," he said.

Hollis, who liked them, had often tried to figure out what made beautiful men so much more circumscribed by their beauty than women. Maybe the obvious, nothing really ambiguous in gender ever allowed. To take him for gay just came at the trap from another direction, and he wasn't that. The parking lot outside the club last spring had been empty but for the bartender's car and Doc/Star-man's silver Porsche, everything slick with early dew. His come-on had been expert and somehow oblique, not so much uncertain as weirdly disinterested, any one gesture immediately retractable. Even liking him, Hollis had found their sex to be much like visiting a small, empty planet, a system without much complexity. It was often that way, if not the sex itself then the aftermath, those simple, emptied conversations. "I didn't see you," she said.

"You sounded good. That a new bass player?"

"Friend of a friend, just sitting in."

It had been Sloan, sitting in for an errant pianist, who had talked her into doing *The Tooth of Crime*. Even stoned on his ass, Sloan could play, a rippling blues, Hollis in mid song two-stepping into and out of surprise as he played, voice and piano dancing together. She had heard of Rita and her shoestring theater, though never tried out for those sorts of plays—absurd-ist, political, avant-garde. Still, beneath those droopy eyelids of Sloan's there lurked a knack for making uncanny connections, linking two seemingly disparate thoughts, for instance, Hollis and Becky Lou. "It's because I'm close to God," he had told her, "like infants and functional imbeciles."

Hollis went back in to finish her makeup. Rita was something, so possessive about Elise it fenced them off from other friend-ships, though Hollis liked them anyway, perfectly happy to dodge around the reflective eroticism that made the two of them practically glow: Rita with that long braid the color of honey, not really tall but muscled, and Elise wild and vulnerable, all mouth and widening then narrowing eyes. Leaning forward, Hollis peered at her own reflection, wryly noting the heart-shaped face, languid eyes—she picked up the lip brush—a per-fect mouth for being such a bitch. She smiled at the mirror as she wiped her hands, wondering why she felt like crying, but Milos was already opening the door behind her in Hoss's black leathers. "Showtime," he said.

Hollis could read a house from the first moments she swung out onstage, this one moderately full, minds in the ozone. She strode off and stretched briefly as Doc/Star-man cleared his throat, then Milos yelled and they walked on together.

" 'O.K., slick face, what's the scoop. Can we move now?' "

" 'Pretty risky, Hoss.' "

Watching Milos act, Hollis noted for the umpteenth time how he simply camped up what were for him normal fits of passion, all that physical punching through air that he did, slap-ping the walls, hip hitched slightly on the turns. Hollis, on the other hand, had to play against type to get Becky Lou, that edgy mollification of hers. " 'You can't go against the code, Hoss. Once a Marker strikes and sets up colors, that's his turf. . . .' " Hollis' affection for Becky was like what you would feel for a mortal saint, for the woman she knew who would talk in sixties' slang for hours, vaguely passing the joint as she charted the ups and downs of her mission as soul mate and Christian bulwark for a rock-and-roll singer both of them knew, hers a selfless, platonic passion.

" 'But they were playin' pussy, Hoss . . .' " Milos had paced Hollis' loft, making her do the lines again—I mean, you gotta *carry* the fuck, and it's a royal pain. " 'Why do you wanna throw everything away . . .' " Slinging his arms around her shoulders, he had let his weight drop, legs sagging, as he fed her the cues until he heard her start to go crazy, voice filling with contempt. " 'Whatsa matter, you can't take fame no more?' " Onstage, Milos whipped around and started to scream as she backed up-stage, holding out her hands. " 'O.K., O.K. I'm your friend. Remember?' " Afterwards he had asked about love, panting on his back on her floor. When she stared at him, he had grinned and swallowed. "What do you think?" he said. "Are you in love with me?"

Hollis went off, stopping inside the heavy curtain to listen to Milos' monologue. The band began their electric wail that would slowly build to the killer song, the mix of drums and low guitar as ominous as a growing storm. The curtain smelled of camphor and paint. She should really go out to tell Gale that he was up but she felt too tired to move. Even a place as big as her loft shrank to nothing around the likes of Milos. Men would rarely if ever talk about love or ask Hollis if she was in love with them, as if this weren't expected of her, as if it would be maybe asking too much. The spring night was hot, the blinds barely moving, and this charming catlike man sprawled on her floor was asking her the hell about love, a married Serbo-something-or-other with a pregnant wife and a play to direct. "You making a pass?"

"I'm curious." He propped his head up on his hand.

Hollis had long thought love had to do with finding the fa-miliar in someone else, or making it up and putting it there, the problem being to keep it small but not too small. A nameless bang in the back hall of some yahoo's house may have a share of prurient interest but it wasn't love, and that soul-completing-soul stuff never happened. So, what the hell, she probably loved him, if it meant that she loved the strutting pleasure of easy flirtation, the sweet tension in her calves, the fluttery kick of lust, all reason enough to climb into bed. "Yes," she had said, and she did, in fact, love him lying there relaxed on her floor, one hand reaching to touch her ankle, thumb easing under the arch, the same way she loved the animal warmth of affectionate sex and the half-mocking falderal of intelligent sex and the raucous melodrama of beery sex, but not necessarily the affectionate, intelligent, beery individuals, the difference surfacing usually somewhere other than in the sack.

"Hey, baby," Gale bent down and whispered in her ear, cocking his hat over one eye, "in like a stone winner." The last note of the song reverberated into the dark house. Hollis waited two beats then stepped out, Gale sliding cool behind.

Gale was a trip, better in the classical roles that kept him under a little control, something perverse in him liking to play to a liberal white crowd's buried expectations even if only the actors onstage could catch it—that deadpan eye, the fleeting second's frozen smile. Hollis came off a minute later and this time didn't stop. Elise was playing poker with Cheyenne in the greenroom, getting him to run through all the variants he knew, her dark red hair shoved into a barrette on top of her head. "They're dead meat tonight," she said to Hollis.

"A little slow." Hollis sat down. "It's hard to stay focused. All I want to do is go to sleep."

"Eat liver." Elise folded. "It's full of iron."

"Oh boy, now I feel like puking." And she did, the wave of nausea rising like an ocean swell.

"Stanislavski on vomiting—" Elise looked up and her broad smile faded. "Whoops, sorry. Here, put your head down or, that's right, lie down, okay, okay, there you go. Shit, did you eat? How long till Gale's off?" She looked at Cheyenne as she was shoving pillows under Hollis' feet. Just as suddenly Hollis

127

felt fine, Elise's fingers cool on her ankles, like wings, she thought in a cheerful reversion to summer-camp hymns, veiling my feet.

"Couple of minutes," Hollis said and felt Elise's weight shift against her legs, wishing for a bizarre moment that Elise would cover everything, legs, stomach, breasts, arms, with her own cool whiteness, lying across her to keep her safe. "It's okay. It's gone, whatever it was."

"You're sure?" Elise looked down, half smiling. "I'm a great nurse, huh." She had braced one hand on the back of the couch. Hollis loved Elise's face, flexible and transparent, dropping now into those austere lines, almost plain in their severity. Very actresslike, reflecting now rueful dismay, then a glint of evil humor. "You'd still knock them dead, even blowing beets."

"That's the litmus test?"

"Next to being in labor."

"I'll pass." Hollis had held Elise's head a time or two. Once they had an incoherent fight in the upstairs hall of somebody's house about the ethical limits to screwing around, the ostensible subject being the incest taboo in Melanesian society and possibly Byron, Hollis couldn't remember, except that divorced uncles by marriage they decided were fair game, and the estranged lovers of professional colleagues, and second cousins.

"Me, too. I think it's those shower caps they make you wear." Elise started to yawn then stopped herself.

Helplessly yawning in response, Hollis noticed for the first time the faint shadows under Elise's eyes. "You losing Laura's sleep for her, too?"

Elise shook her head. "Nick's."

Cheyenne was saying the vowels to loosen up his mouth as he gently stretched out his triceps. "Gale's coming off." He stood on one foot, pulling the other leg bent behind him with his hand.

Milos looked tired when Hollis hit the lights, a little unfocused. She liked the facilitation the least, Becky's purely mechanical function, moving people on and off the stage. The lines flicked back and forth between them, weaving a net to steady him, always bored by then with holding the stage. Then Hollis was backstage, touching Cheyenne's shoulder as she passed him in the dark. Doc/Star-man, in Doc's red suspenders now, was drinking a Coke, waiting his cue. Jesus, she wanted a cigarette, the backstage hall lined with Fresnels and broken flats, voices small onstage. Acting was not as transcendent as singing. To hear Elise talk, science was the best. She had taken Hollis once to a party for her brokerage boss, a downtown hall full of old-boy breeders with here and there the biologists, passionate sorts, one woman describing the cloning process as a kind of liturgical sleight of hand, her eyes filled with the certainty of God.

Hollis moved lightly, ducked under the platform, and came onstage, watching Milos turn around on one heel, asking about Willard, spitting need. " 'He's dead, Hoss. Shot himself in the mouth.' " People that she needed had left Hollis all her life, making Becky's hardness easy to do, the practical analysis, steady cool. Where she stood stage left she could see Doc watching and looked away, Milos swinging out on her words: " 'Shivs! I ain't used a blade for over ten years.' " The big ex-con had shaved his head so the scars showed bumpy under the streetlight, Elise watching silent beside her.

Offstage, Doc/Star-man handed her the dummy, the two switchblades in their greasy plastic. He smiled a little, licking his lips. Milos had never heard her sing in public, too impatient to sit in a roadhouse bar with its crowded dance floor and yellow lights. The occasional blues she sang would curl like smoke through the beery air. Milos had leaned up on one elbow and pulled until she slid toward him, the rug underneath bunching up against the table leg, his hand on her foot warm and hard, shifting its grip.

Hooking the dummy by its strap to the metal coatrack, Hollis waited, backlit, for Doc/Star-man to finish, the monologue folksy, the band rocking a sleazy C&W guitar lick way out behind. "I am falling in love with you," Milos had said, breaking into this weird courtly diction, an East European formality, his mouth on her knee making her shiver. The shirt on the dummy felt baby-soft under her hand, the plastic mask eerily vacant, safety-pinned to the foam-stuffed sack that was its head, a translucent mold emptier even than a mannequin face. Milos' cue came suddenly loud. She said, " 'It ain't revolution, man.' "

Doc/Star-man was gone, and Hollis crouched by the chair, looking up for a second to find her light, then Milos' hand combed back her hair, his fingers hard at the nape of her neck. He hated the next bit they did, the snatches of song, the stupid laugh, Hoss and Becky never that tender. The rest of the scene always made Hollis sad, Becky showing Hoss the trap already sprung, reciting the myth to make it all go away. " 'All those losers out there barkin' at the moon,' " Milos pulling her closer, kissing her thigh, her leg pressed under his turning weight. " 'Power,' " she whispered. " 'That's all there is. The power of the machine. The killer Machine. That's what you live and die for. That's what you wake up for. Every breath you take you breathe the power. You live the power. You are the power.' "

The chair inched backwards as Milos kicked his weight into it. He had blocked the scene to look like the cover of a trash romance, Hollis kneeling against his leg, but instead of the tumbling locks and Victorian dress you got a fringe of damp hair spiking her neck, legs bared practically up to the crotch. Elise out in the empty house said it looked great, gutted romance. "But do I look like an asshole?" Hollis had asked. "I mean, come on, it is porn or is it farce?"

" 'You're a mover, Hoss. Some people, all they do is wait.' " He had folded the short skirt up above her waist and run a finger lightly around the edge of her underwear, catching one corner and pulling it down. A cushion off the sofa had fallen against her cheek and she pushed it under her head, leaned her face slowly into it, reaching at the last minute to stop his hand but the elastic was across her thighs, sliding away into empty space. Then he was against her again, tucking her foot back between his legs. He rubbed his head on her naked hip.

They were both filmed with sweat under the lights. " 'Are you crazy?' " She always played the lines quieter than they seemed written. Milos' line sounded muffled and she felt his leg tensed under her arm. " 'Do you know what it's like out there,

130

outside the game?' " Careful, totally academic. Her knee felt like it was grinding into the stage and she moved it slightly, taking some weight on her bent foot. " 'There ain't no Second Avenue.' "

The world changed, when your back was turned, suddenly adopted different rules—all the social codes of the southern town she and her mother never figured out because of that silence getting in the way, like the cold blue water in the strip mines over places where veins had been ripped away. " 'All that's gone. That's old time boogie.' "

His leg moved again and the chair scraped back another inch. Milos had run his tongue along the skin hollowed by her hip and teased the groin muscles above her thigh so that she jumped and instinctively pulled her other leg over. Half turning, he put his palm up against her inner knee and pushed lightly. She could feel his cock curved against her ankle, rubbing along her foot. He kissed her stomach and a sound came out of her throat, the blinds clicking as they swayed against the open window.

" 'And what about the kill? You don't need that?' " Hollis sank back a little, letting up on her legs. " 'You're talkin' loser now, baby.' " Hammering away at her investment, ol' Becky Lou. Hollis wanted to close her eyes and go to sleep. " 'What about the gold record.' " A lot of Shepard was basically dumb.

She had to sing from the floor, which always felt weird when she was so used to moving around a mike. Her breathing was never quite the same, the phrasing altered, bouncier maybe. Her tailbone hurt no matter how she sat, tensed with her back to Milos' silence, but the song was nice with those loopy wail-'em-out country riffs. The other lights dimmed around the Leko beating amber against her face, hot across her sunburned chest. The band came up softly behind.

She had finally touched his head, trying to pull him all the way up, the length of her turning body, but he wouldn't budge, moving closer around her leg. The hand against her knee pushed harder, her heel slipping on the bunched-up rug. She suddenly didn't *want* that, half sitting up, elbows jarred, his breath then his tongue touching her. Jesus, she slid, her knee falling open, and he squeezed himself higher, pumping against her. His finger danced up to the crease at her hip, his tongue moving carefully around. It was crazy maybe, but she really didn't want that, her hips lifting anyway, face turned hard into the cotton pillow, closing her eyes. She pulled her arms across her head, gripping the table leg as his tongue slid deep inside her. No, she had thought hopelessly as he moved against her. No.

" 'Isn't it some magic that the night-time brings,' " Hollis bluesed it up a little, briefly happy with the music, doing what she did best. God, she loved belting it out, those deep throaty dips down, becoming nothing but the beat of the song. Coming hard, hips moving, with Milos pressed below, had been endless, strangely loose, as if her head stretched away like the Tenniel drawing of Alice into another room. He had moved up immediately after that, belt clinking as he undid it, ran the zipper, her eyes squeezed shut, head still turned, scarcely noticing when he worked himself in, his breath beating against her cheek.

That they had kept on sleeping together was a bit of a surprise. Hollis had gone along, easy and unthinking, happy with the long slow sex after rehearsal. Milos was the one to call it love, to let the pleasure light up his face when he saw her walk in, his irritating naïveté, as if a little discretion couldn't matter. Laura had studied the middle distance in the half-empty bar, her face quiet, without interest, while Hollis, still sweating a little from the last set, had sipped her drink and told Laura she wanted nothing at all from Milos, not love, not attention, not married bliss. Then it stopped, the week Laura was overdue, just stopped, like water turned off by a tap. Her voice caressed the last note, the band buoyantly letting her down, putting her back, Milos coming silently into place with the chair behind her, the floor shaking under Cheyenne's step as he crossed stage right. " 'Say, Hoss. We just got tapped that the Gypsy's made it through zone five. He's headed this way.' "

Hollis stood in the greenroom stretching out her legs, bent at the waist and rocking heel to toe. She had never been thin, her legs on the short side, but she liked her body's compact warmth. She watched upside down as Elise walked through. "Nick here?" she asked and Elise shook her head.

Doc/Star-man was sitting on the couch. "He's a jerk," he said softly and Hollis stood up and shrugged.

"He hasn't missed it yet." She listened for a minute over the PA to where Milos had got in the scene then glanced across the room. "You ready to go?"

Waiting onstage through the monologue was tiresome, the Bob's-Big-Boy-in-Pasadena riff hard to believe. Hollis cracked her jaw gently around an invisible yawn. Those dumb-ass boys and their stupid cars and their illegal beer and their nervous erections like some kind of obstacle course for girls, some better at that stuff than others. Hollis had thought she knew the rules. She thought she had known a lot of things. The wind had riffled the water's reflection, a pretty place with the trees leafing out. Class war, hell—Shepard knew better. Hollis swallowed so she wouldn't yawn again. It was all libido, raging hormones, but with boys it was all the goddam time.

It was probably just as well her mother bailed them out of L.A. Tinseltown would have devoured them both, her mother scrounging for character parts at a time when women in their forties were practically invisible, so instead she moved them south and east, took a typing class, did the eight-to-five. Hollis still deeply missed her mother, dead now two years from cancer.

Hollis moved and spoke, gliding around Milos' blast of words, Doc and Becky dancing their lazy exit, exchanging glances, faces blank. She flinched under the half-screamed exit cue, Doc's mouth quirking in response, then they were off, shoulders bumping, his voice musing in her ear, for once without its arch defense, "He's good—some of those lines are really awful," as she nodded and went to find a place where she could lie down in peace and quiet.

Sloan was in the greenroom, lighting a joint. "How'd the act go?" he said, and she shrugged, wagged her hand back and forth. Elise was talking in the dressing rooms and Hollis raised her eyebrows at Sloan as she sat. "He came by the house five minutes ago." He let out his breath then dabbed spit on the end of the joint. "Said he didn't know what time it was."

"He's got about three minutes." Hollis closed her eyes. Elise needed to unload Nick, who was walking death as far as she was concerned, stuck, it seemed, at a tricky stage. Rita would barely speak to him. Nick had weirded out as the play went on, dealing big time now was Hollis' guess. Cheyenne padded through the door saying vowels, listened for a moment to Elise talking, then left. A minute later they heard his voice crackling across the PA. "One minute." Hollis sighed.

The door slammed open and Nick was crossing the room, the three-inch heels on his platform shoes smacking the carpet, his legs scissoring endlessly long in the narrow jeans, tank top ribbing his skinny chest, looking beautiful, there was no other word, the makeup tilting his narrowed eyes to pale green flames, freckles faint on his burnished cheeks, gracefully angled, his mouth with its thin lips sweet and curving, hair moussed into a pale blond crest that ruffled drying as he strode by. They listened to the light ring of his shoes as he climbed the steel backstage ladder, the band already launched into the opening bars, the guitar starting its eerie climb higher and higher, then the drums slammed into the beat and seconds later Nick's voice boomed out, low and dark, edged with menace.

Hollis let out her breath and watched everybody in the green-room not watching Elise, who leaned in the dressing-room doorway and rubbed the back of her neck, eyes on the floor. Nick's voice rose. Hollis had seen that heavy metal singing of his, head flung back, even audiences as brain-dead as this one kneed in the gut.

Sloan nudged her leg, offering the joint, and she shook her head, smiling suddenly, basically fond of Sloan with his affable stare behind the glasses, his rounded shoulders. He had got her stoned after the gig, the two of them sitting in the big front seat punching classical tapes into the deck as rain trickled across the windows, Bach, a cello suite, mournful as hell, making their laughter wind down, though she couldn't stop grinning as he slid down the seat to tuck her hair behind her ear. He had a sweet touch, his mouth curled a little at the corners as he brushed her hair lightly again and the rain rattled on the roof.

Rita was sitting down by Hollis' feet, her eyes hard with exasperation as she took the joint. "Hey," she said to Sloan, smiling a little. She was so damn tough, was Rita, so goddam tough and good at her job, her slightly flattened face without expression. Hollis could never figure out what to say to Rita even though they should have been able to talk, about plays and playwrights if nothing else, which they did sometimes, arguing, Hollis always breathless or something afterwards, as if she had run the six-mile loop around the park without stopping. Nick was finishing, reaching that Jim Morrison shriek, the band bam, bam, bamming behind. The silence lasted a split second, then the applause began.

Hollis really didn't want to be there when Nick came in the room. He and Rita were like deeply combustible elements, though Hollis had never seen them fight, the closest that night in June when he came by for the dope. Sitting with the front door open, they had been waiting so they could go out drinking, Rita making the deal for Sloan. Who knew what the hell set him off, maybe just seeing the three of them there, men always freaked out by women in groups. Whatever the reason, he had taken his time until Rita started making little wisecracks, leaning forward on the sofa, no one ready for when he was up on his feet, one hand suddenly tight around Rita's hair, forcing her head down against his hip. He had moved his knee to block her fist coming up, then Elise was walking behind him, Hollis wondering what the hell, standing. He had let Rita go with a twisting jerk and backed off, smiling at Elise. "Sweet," he had said to her, or "Touching," or something like that, beginning to laugh. Rita had just sat there, not looking up when the screen door slammed, just starting after a long moment slowly to count the money again. From Elise, Hollis had looked down at the sofa back, running her thumb over one corner, pressing in a little, then letting up.

Milos came through the door, laughing behind his shoulder at something Nick was saying, blotting his face on a dirty towel. The ladder clanged backstage as the band climbed down, starting to drift through the room. Hollis could feel the faint ring of a headache approaching. Elise was kissing Milos quickly on the lips ("You're looking fabulous out there") and working around

135

to congratulate the band, teasing them out of their Act One shell shock. Leaning forward, Rita talked softly to Sloan, ice rattling and churning in the cooler as people dug out cans and let the lid crash back. Nick lit a cigarette, listening to the guitarist explain something as he fingered the air, his eyes lifting suddenly to meet Hollis' across the room. Something acid licked at the back of her throat and then she was on her feet, ducking between backs and elbows, stepping over junk to get to the bathrooms, waiting for the drummer to come out, then the door had blessedly closed behind her.

After a while she scooped some water from the tap into her mouth, swizzled it around, and spat. If she cried, she would have to do her eyes again. Under the single bare bulb in the mirror, she looked like hell, pale and sweaty. She pulled some toilet paper off the roll and patted her face then closed her eyes. Nick, on some speedy high, had once recited for Elise all the parts in Pinter's *The Caretaker*, including the pauses ("Pause," he had said, without expression, eyes empty), until Hollis noticed she was laughing so she wouldn't panic. Someone knocked on the door. She tossed the wad of paper into the toilet and flushed it then went outside, edging her way to the relative quiet of a dressing room.

The sound of the door clicking shut made her open her eyes. "Sorry. Go back to sleep." Sloan sat down at the dressing table and carefully pulled the scales out of his pack, then the baggie of powder. "Don't look," he said. "Rita will kill me, but delivering Nick has set me back. I was going to do this at home." Sloan rarely did coke but he sold it because it was easy bucks, doing political atonement by folding the quarter grams inside squares cut from *Mother Jones*.

"I didn't plan on falling asleep." Hollis blinked then remembered the scene she still had to play, a bitch to do even when she was ready. She started to sit up.

"Relax." Sloan didn't look around. "You've got a lot of time yet. They just went back on a few minutes ago." He was a nice guy, Sloan, one hell of a mindreader. "Relax," he had said to her in the plush front seat of the Oldsmobile, the grave alle-

136

mande beginning, all that luxurious sadness tumbling and falling around them. His hand moved her hair off her forehead. "You are incredibly beautiful, you know that?" then carefully meeting her lips with his, drawing away, coming back.

Hollis stared at the ceiling webbed with pipes. "I hate myself," she said.

"Yeah? How come?" The scales clinked and he creaked back in the chair, starting again. Outside Nick and Milos came thinly across the PA and Hollis thought she heard Rita laughing. Rita and that ridiculous dog, the two of them like a comic routine, Rita talking and the dog flicking his ears every time he heard something close to a word he knew.

"I don't know." She had seen Rita and Elise catch Max one night with his head in the garbage, skidding madly backwards as they came down and shoved him onto his back, Rita laughing too hard to yell along with Elise, who had her mouth inches from his flattened ear. Hollis, grinning in the door, had really needed to pee as Max did just that, upside down, a miniature bidet. Elise dodged too late, colliding with Rita, then she was laughing too, both of them hooting, her head bent into Rita's hair, their legs tangled, Rita's arm across her waist.

Sloan didn't say anything. Hollis watched him work. He had a comfortable body, soft and hairy, and a slow, easygoing mouth. He was also skilled at getting off clothes. He had lain back in the car and pulled her up on top of him, easing her hips down and over, then rocked her gently forward. She moved, leaning up on their clasped hands, still happy as hell, listening to the quicksilver courante, looking down at him, looking down at herself, and he had laughed, panting, then pulled her fingers up to his mouth. He had said he wanted to look at her doing it, the rain streaking the neon.

Sighing, Hollis sat up then walked over to another table and turned on the lights. She started cleaning up around her eyes, the creases of her mouth. The slinky blue dress she wore in Act Two was hanging behind the door. Sloan folded the paper over and tucked in the flap then dipped into the bag again. "Don't hate yourself," he said.

"All right, I won't." Hollis peered into the mirror. Sloan was a weird one. She had seen him once in that biker bar up from Rita's house, looking just like everybody else in there, a simple hunch of the shoulders or something, in a bizarre way maybe the best actor she'd ever met.

"Nobody gives a shit who you sleep with." Sloan squinted at the scale.

Hollis was sorry she had started this, suddenly wanting to prove him wrong, to be the predatory stereotype. She wasn't some sexy heart-of-gold whore. She just didn't care; she didn't see how it mattered.

"You do what you want," said Sloan.

"So does Rita."

He picked up another square of paper, his glasses catching the light. "No, she doesn't."

Hollis thought about Milos, that Old World romance, the flirting, the charm, the overwhelming *excess* of him, doing exactly what the hell he wanted, all for love. It had sometimes made her feel hollow inside, stretched too far, too thin, always trying to swallow an empty place in her throat. She had just wanted to fuck him, for crying out loud, because it felt good, because she liked it, because he was easy, because he had been directing her scenes, because, because, because, but definitely not for something like love. "Milos wasn't my idea," she said.

Sloan was finishing up. "He's not one to take no—"

"I didn't say no." Hollis yawned suddenly then smiled at her reflection. Jesus, learning to street fight—Milos should have just talked to his friends. Hollis had been over the night Sloan moved on a kid who had ripped him off, a nervous boy with bad skin who thought no one was going to know, sitting there on the sofa watching Letterman and double-hitting on the joint when Rita casually got up to lean against the door. Max had looked up as she moved, then yawned, spilling out of the armchair to stretch each hind leg before sitting beside her, nosing her elbow. Sloan was talking quiet, too low to hear, but Hollis saw the kid stiffen all at once then duck forward, hitting out with his elbows, Sloan moving with him, one hand fisted in the boy's shirt as he stood and then slammed him up against the wall. Turning her head maybe an inch, Hollis watched Rita, who had gently pulled her hair forward over one shoulder and was playing with the soft ends that curled below the rubber band, brushing them back and forth across her palm. The blows sounded flat, wet, like punched Naugahyde. Max watched, tensed with Rita, ears pricked forward like dark flames above his head.

Hollis dragged the leather vest off over her head, unsnapping the skirt as she walked and letting it fall down her legs, stepping out, then taking the blue number off its hanger. Bared, her skin felt cool and she waved the dress in front to make a draft, blowing down between her breasts. She looked up to see Sloan watching, his eyes noncommittal, in his biker-bar hunch. "Every judge in the state," he said, "would say you were asking for it."

Hollis turned her back on pure instinct then lightly touched the wall, the dress loose in her fist. Jesus, he could still surprise her, that particular piece of shit coming out of left field, unbelievably crass when she was always so damn careful, even drunk, and Sloan had no reason to say, no *reason*. Hollis closed her eyes. "So what?" she finally said, turning around. "Like I owe you a quickie or something? To change my fucking clothes?"

"Nope. Don't owe me a thing." Sloan zipped the pack and looped it across one shoulder. Glaring, Hollis watched him for a minute; when his face didn't change, she gave up and shrugged. She put her arms in the sleeves then pulled the dress over her head.

The greenroom was empty but for Elise and Rita sitting together, feet propped on the coffee table, laughing about something, Elise smiling as she angled her arm across her eyes. Rita said something else, tearing another piece off a Styrofoam cup and tossing it toward the table, and Elise laughed harder, her shoulders shaking. Rita smiled, looking across the room at Hollis and Sloan.

Sloan was heading out, waving, as Hollis listened to the PA. She turned in disbelief to Elise. "Gale's doing the ref?" The other actor had quit last week.

"Yeah. We are rapt with respectful amazement."

"What about his total immersion theory of acting? I haven't heard any ref stuff out of him."

"He says it's all in the body language, went to the Y every night this week. Nick calls him the human rubber band."

"Jocks know how to get blown away?"

"Well, that." Elise shrugged a little. "Gale says he got that part talking to Nick."

They had all watched Nick take out the three guns from his pockets, one a crummy-looking Saturday-night Special, the others more serious, a Magnum like a goddam cannon, a sleek .48, then he expertly checked that each one was empty, snapping the pieces, his eyes unmoving. Sure, prop guns, right, Milos reaching with a weird sort of reverential eagerness to pick one up, no one else saying anything, Rita watching Elise. "No one'll bust you," Elise finally said. "It's like everything else. They look so real they've gotta be fakes, right? That's the way people think."

Rita popped the cup between her hands. Hollis half listened to the PA. She had dreamed about Rita once, a weird end-of-the-world kind of dream, where Rita was running across the fields, just running, her eyes white with ice, Max bounding along like a shadow beside her. Rita had pulled one knee up and was now drawing designs with her fingernail in the worn denim. She had beautiful arms, tanned and muscled. Imperceptibly the mood had changed. Hollis knew anyone on the planet talking to the two of them would have changed it, but even a month ago she had still fit in, drinking into cheery oblivion while Elise drove to the next party and the next or watching deeply bad sci-fi movies, Rita crying she laughed so hard, until that friendly back-and-forth stopped too, before Milos ended the affair but with that same kind of finality, a code rejigged without telling her.

Hollis listened to the lines coming from the stage, trying to see how long she had. Half the time the scene made no sense at all, and other times it was sort of vaguely to the point, Becky as the ravaged anima or something, Hollis didn't know what the hell else, a thing performed in Hoss's mind. That theatrical stuff, the actress's hands molesting herself, was hard to take, but Milos had told her to just do the damn hands, even though he and Elise had cut the other sophomoric junk written to be mimed behind the Hoss-Crow fight. Milos, as he directed the scene, had made them both miserable, so now every time when she went on it was the rehearsal she remembered. "I never knew you were that kind of guy." The blanks had gone off a while back, Gale presumably taking a Nickesian hit. She should be getting herself together.

Waiting backstage, Hollis always felt cold, maybe just because she was standing there in some kind of sleazy pseudosilk instead of leather or because she was standing there all alone or because the play was almost over and the night slowly dying inside, people ready to go home. She looked at the big hollow parabola shape of the Fresnel by her foot and stretched her fingers out stiff then relaxed them. Nick was crooning Crow's lines, careful as a lullaby (" 'The floor. The space around you. The sound of your heart' "). She counted, then she was moving noiselessly out downstage, the lights dimmed except for a reddish glint around Nick curved over the big chair, the tape marking her spot a pale green, her knees gritting against the stage just as Milos' voice drifted out to her right, small and lonely (" 'You won't let nobody hurt me will ya'?' "), Nick answering, the light coming up in her eyes.

" 'I never knew you were that kind of guy,' " Hollis said and touched herself. So give me a minute, she had finally yelled at Milos, all right? all right? Still doing Lady Anne in *Richard III* while rehearsing this play, mixing Shakespeare's rhythms with Becky's twang (" 'Come on. I just wanna talk. I wanna have a conversation' "), remembering herself at fourteen when for a time she had stopped talking at all. A really bright idea, Milos full of them, to bring up this long-dead ghost and learn all an actress need know to turn totally mute, a rape (she had asked for it) and Hollis remembering how she had just lain there while he worked. A boy, a car, booze, strip mines rippling water blue as the sky, no one to hear a scream, teeth bloodied by the slap

141

across the face, fingers digging in her lap, then the hips yanked around, the awful chewing sound of a zipper, head angled hard along a door, legs cold, then the pain, eyes hating her, pain, breath hammered down, pain, what he whispered as he moved, saying die, saying cunt. Hear it, Milos (she was twisting on the stage, talking fast, in a rush), so hear it and weep. God damn his fucking pretty-boy looks, God damn his pathological need, God damn every last foul-gened sperm dying in the slick between her legs. She had used Lady Anne's high-flown rage, Milos watching in the empty house, arms crossed, behind rows of folded chairs—she had used her mother's answering rage. If he speaks his name to announce himself, turn the sound in his throat to vomited pause so there may float in the air behind the sweet stale echo *rapist*. If he marries, may his wife find out over time all the infinite ways to hate. Hollis had finally run out of words, looking down at Milos, wanting just to go. This wasn't quite what he had in mind for Becky, who only talked harder in fear, but there was fear. Look closer, she had wanted to tell him. She had tapped a veritable fount of terror. Voilà! see Hollis' long dead wounds "open their congealed mouths and bleed afresh." And all for Milos—a different kind of rape, but it came to the same damn thing in the end. (Hollis scrambled back in the follow spot, her voice rising higher, " 'I'm not that kind of a girl.' ") Jesus, she wished the boy were dead, impaled in some putrid and burning hell, wished more that she had the power to make the whole thing not to have happened at all. She had bled for days. Listen, she said to Milos later, I would do it cold every damn time if it meant I could take out his grunting face.

Hollis made it through the curtain call then went to the bathroom and started throwing up. She flushed the toilet, felt her stomach relax a minute them come up again, her head bent low, dizzy, flushing again, the handle cold and slippery under her fingers. After a while she started crying, the act of puking your guts possibly the scariest and saddest in human experience, crouched by the bowl and crying, hearing as if from miles away the silence in the greenroom, everyone gone. She rocked, crying finally because Nick that night three weeks ago had raped her

142

and there was nothing she was ever going to be able to do about it. She had not even seen it coming, walking out the stage door into the empty alley with him, going home, the street blaring music and car exhaust a hundred feet away and Rita still working inside behind two doors and a fan. Hollis cried, leaning against a wall, tired to death, palming away snot. No one knowing her would believe it, but she had never had to have an abortion before.

Gale looked up when she finally opened the door, turning out the light. He was lying on the sofa, his feet hanging off the end, Galactic Jack's hat tilted over his eyes. "Thought you might have floated away," he said.

Hollis shrugged and carefully sat down. "Something I ate."

"Uh huh." Gale studied her face then looked at the ceiling. "Laura's got people over. Said if Lucy wasn't going to sleep, she might as well party."

"I can't, Gale."

"Sure you can." Gale started to pull his legs in, sitting up. "You alone all the time, you know that? It's like singing, but Hollis, baby, you doing it all the *time.*"

She and Gale walked up the sidewalk to Milos and Laura's house, music beating from the open windows, some demo tape from a local band, raw-edged and jarring. The night was breezy, not as warm as before, her skin feeling weird and tight from hanging her head out the window as Gale drove, letting the wind dry her face. Doc/Star-man opened the door, looked her over curiously as he let them in, then finished off his beer, the music louder inside. Guys were lying around the dark living room talking in those strange shorthand bursts they used. Hollis found a place to stand against the wall, braced on a window sill, near the drummer and bass player in private conversation. A lot of the food, she could see, was already gone.

Nick was straddling a chair across the room, smiling at Milos around his tilted beer, his hair still tufted in parts from the mousse. Hollis looked away. She had seen him with the girl so completely like him she had to be his daughter. They were in the park one evening as Hollis walked toward the bandshell to do one more Lady Anne. The sun was still going down, the grass striped with dark green shadows, and Nick was dancing with her, half singing some tune under his breath as he swung her out the length of his arm then pulled her back ducking under their hands, swayed quickly and spun her away again. She was laughing, nine, maybe ten years old, her thick hair in pigtails, body just starting to lengthen out, but a really good dancer—they had done this before. Then they stopped as quickly as they must have begun and walked on, the girl talking, dropping his hand after a few steps.

Milos waved from across the room then started over. Hollis shook her head to tell him to stay but he kept on. "You okay?" He raised his voice over the music.

"Some kind of stomach bug. I'm fine."

"Can I get you something?"

"No, that's okay. I'm fine." Hollis smiled at him, that really nice jaw of his and those hollowed cheeks, his eyes checking out to either side of her then back. He caught her staring and shrugged a little then laughed. "You did good tonight," she said.

A light was on in the dining alcove before the kitchen, a dim overhead, Rita coming out from the kitchen with a glass, talking to Laura behind her. They stood next to the table, leaning close then stepping back to laugh, set off from the dark living room as if the alcove had been draped behind a scrim. As Hollis watched, Elise came out of the back hall and said something, touching Laura on the shoulder. The three of them swayed and turned, talking under the light, graceful as dancers, Elise the tallest with the big gestures while Laura bent forward to laugh, Rita eating bits of cheese and talking around her fingers. Milos was patting Hollis on the shoulder then turning to go back, a breeze trickling in the window.

Hollis started all at once around the room, stepping over an occasional pair of legs, the music shifting to this reggae thing, someone hiking the volume. Elise had just lightly punched Rita, eyes wide with incredulity, and Laura was dragging her hair up off her neck when Hollis stepped up and stood around, half looking at the plates. "Hey, Hol." Elise turned to widen the group. "Whatcha need?"

"Something not too exciting. Maybe a Saltine."

"I've got some in the pantry." Laura was turning but Hollis waved at the air.

"No problem. This will do." She took a handful of oyster crackers. They were looking at her, Rita slouched with her hip against the table and Laura lifting her hair again, tucking it behind one ear. Elise hummed to the music, dancing her fingers along her side, then reached behind to pick up her drink. Hollis wanted to put the crackers down, to make this chart for them explaining her life and the reasons she did what she did, but she couldn't do anything but stand there, picking one cracker carefully out of her palm. "So what do you know," she finally said, putting the cracker back. "I think I'm pregnant."

Elise looked around with a strange flash of hesitancy, then her face went still, her eyes moving quickly down then up. "Shit, Hollis," she said, and Laura moved after pausing briefly, her hand flipping back her hair, Rita asking casually whose it was. "Some guy," Hollis lied, "hangs out at the club, it doesn't matter."

"Shit," said Elise again.

They had bent in around her and now stopped, waiting to see what she wanted them to do. The difference between her and them was suddenly like something almost completely unbearable. Looking up from the crackers in her hand, Hollis flashed a grin, then she danced two steps to the left, holding out her arms. "Ta-dum," she said.

EIGHT

Roberta

1956

ROBERTA, AFTER SHE GOT HOME, STOOD IN THE BACK HALLWAY sometimes and watched Elise, who always wondered why Roberta was half smiling that way, what she was waiting for her to do, what was *required* of her to make Roberta stop standing there watching, one hand rubbing the opposite elbow. Roberta's glasses, with their clear pointed frames, pressed against her nose so hard they made red dents on either side, and her dense black hair fell from a side part around her face. Elise looked stubbornly down and shrugged. Even when Nana said something to Roberta from the kitchen over the squeak of the oven door, the clank of pots, Roberta answered without moving her head. Picking at the sofa, Elise sent a hard, furtive glare back toward Roberta. She wasn't afraid of *her*.

Roberta wondered absently what on earth the child was

thinking, leaning there against the sofa, her mouth pursed a little, jaw edged forward. Half coquette, half tomboy, girls were so peculiar, J.'s granddaughters even odder than most: little Laura talking all the time with her goofy, wide-mouthed grin, while Elise was complacent, secretive. Even with all that Pre-Raphaelite hair, Elise was no beauty, especially when she pouted that way. Roberta twitched her mouth, amused. J. sounded as if she were getting tired of the solitude she professed to like in her own kitchen on a late afternoon, the pans hitting the burners with a tinny clatter. Roberta turned around, brushing her cupped hand lightly across her elbow as she walked back. "You want some help?"

"Not really." Nana wiped her hands and reached for the tomatoes to start cutting off the overripe parts, the thick yellow caps.

Roberta pulled around a chair. "Those Helen's?"

"You have to ask?"

Roberta grinned. J.'s sister-in-law next door gave them garden trash, the culls just short of compost fodder, massive wooden zucchini and seedy lettuce, pole beans with strings tough as zippers. She was your classic bitch, though Roberta admired in an academic way Helen's flamboyance, that collision of Czech accent and southern drawl, her Dietrich beauty. Roberta had regularly fallen for tall, thin blondes like Helen until she met J. some seven years ago, gray-headed but solid in the hips, capable of a certain wryness even while hocking her cut-glass coasters in Roberta's discreetly situated shop. Roberta turned the crystal vase of spoons on the kitchen table. Falling in love with an Episcopalian widow nearly ten years her senior had been rather reckless even for her, especially in a town that small. "Sold that Dutch dresser today."

"The painted one?"

"The pine with country carving. Buttery looking."

"Nice people?"

"I guess." Roberta reached across the table for a sweet pickle slice. J.'s hands were lovely, flat across the nails like a man's and spotted the color of café au lait. The knife zigzagged down the

147

face of the tomato, and a slice flopped over like a cut of ham. Roberta had given J. the ring she was wearing for their fifth anniversary, gold and tawny opal, from the eighteenth century. With Elise in the house for the summer, they made their dangerous and hurried love in Roberta's front bedroom, half their clothes on, always listening. "Couple in their thirties. Looking for bargains."

Nana laid the tomato slices in a circle around a plate. Running water over the thin blade of the knife, she looked out the window and saw Elise walking the length of the side hedge, one hand out to riffle the clipped branches. Not much to play on out there, but Nana wouldn't let Roberta hang a swing from the tree in the middle of the yard. Her husband had fallen doing that for their Todd's first boy and broken his neck. She had heard the fall all the way inside at the other end of the house, soft as a leaf on grass, then silence—in her heart, she had thought later, a quiet like a white lawn pillow turned cool side up in her heart. Elise had Frederick's hair, same as her daddy did, that funny purpled-up red without, so far, a temper to match; none of Frederick's failings had showed up in either two boys or their children. Nana had gleaned from childhood and marriage what she could of leftover rage only to find there was no place to put it, both husband and father dead within a few short years of each other. "Come from around here?"

"I didn't get the entire genealogy." Roberta never did, lucky to finesse even the maternal surname, while J. could quadrant a passing stranger's family tree with the brisk efficiency of a bird dog, all without thinking, as if she couldn't *not* do it, helpless to an instinct overtrained. "McClelland?" Roberta frowned. "Wait, that might be their street address. Hell, I don't know."

"Doesn't matter. You want to set the table?" Nana's mother had hung on like death to her everyday sterling after Jack put the company silver down as collateral on a horse that pulled up lame, all about the time that Nana made plans to marry. She had sat in the stables rubbing the velvety nose of her lost silver dowry and trading nips of peach brandy with her brother, Gar, until they both felt sick, the stupid horse too beautiful to hate. "Then give Elise a yell. I just saw her out back."

Nana sprinkled some flour in the pan for gravy. Roberta wasn't worth a lick in the kitchen, which kept them from fighting about food at least. When the roux thickened, Nana tilted in some milk, stirring. Roberta's arm came into sight as she scooped up the salt and pepper. "I'm going to need those in a minute," Nana said. She had long bones, Roberta did, and white skin that freckled in a minute though it didn't bother her enough to cover up outside. Standing behind her in the closed shop years ago, Roberta had wrapped her arms around Nana like they were the big curved ribs of a whale, one arm tight to Nana's waist and the other angled up across her drooping breasts, hand cupping her shoulder. "I want you," Roberta whispered, Nana's legs too weak to walk her away. She rapped the spoon against the pan. They fought about any number of things, but food wasn't one of them, or clothes (though Roberta dressed like a gardener), or the antiques she sold, or even the house—nothing touching on their physical survival. The gravy bubbled along the lip of the pan.

Elise heard Roberta calling and crouched lower under the hedge. The doodlebug had uncurled as she paused to look up and was starting to crawl away. She moved the twig. Roberta at least waited until she was at a decent stopping place while Nana always made her jump—I said now, not in a minute, not next week. Letting the doodlebug go, Elise crawled out backwards, wiping her hands on her shorts. Walking toward her across the yard, Roberta moved fast, faster than Nana or Uncle Gar or Aunt Helen. She was a lot taller, too. "Coming," Elise said politely.

Roberta watched Elise drag her palms up her shorts, bangs stuck to her forehead. She practiced an odd automatic courtesy, adult phrases tossed off and forgotten, forming a thin protective layer around her like oil on a fish. Roberta matched Elise's bland formality for lack of anything better, though it could make the child seem painfully sad. One Christmas visit when Elise was four, her father had offered her a bite of his fudge and, not understanding him, she had taken the entire piece into her mouth. Martin had razzed her way too long in front of everyone. Roberta, watching across the kitchen, had seen Elise's eyes fill, her face flush, and had felt in her own mouth the soft, salt-streaked, unswallowable chocolate, like sin, like a sweet, ungovernable sadness. "Nana wants you to wash up for supper."

Watching Elise run inside, Roberta shook her head. It was a Victorian fantasy, the green summer lawn and white house and a little girl with long red curls—her own mother's fantasy. Roberta never in her life had curls but they wouldn't have mattered, her mother wanting only the picture of a child, an accessory like a wide-brimmed hat. Roberta may have forgiven her mother, but she would never like her; she cherished no memories. J. said it was unnatural not to love your mother or at least have some pity, but life was heavy enough without that kind of burden. The surrounding glue of J.'s past was oppressive, the house in front of her built for J.'s 1910 nuptials and behind it the shuttered ruin of her parents' place and beyond that the river and her brother Gar's overgrown dog track, his oil-drum rafts. Roberta rubbed the hard knob of her elbow. She imagined Helen felt the same suffocation, but Helen had lived with it longer. The small shop downtown was a haven for Roberta, antiques anonymous but for age and maker, sometimes not even that, every object estranged and mercifully voiceless.

That evening, sitting in the porch swing while Roberta inside made bemused headway getting Elise out of the tub, Nana heard the slight pop of someone walking on the drive behind the boxwoods, the insects dropping into a still silence: Gar was strolling his property line. Nana crossed her arms and pushed the swing with her feet. Aunt Linnie haunting the house was a prime idea, she thought. Helen made no difference. She'd have her fool brother hanging on to her skirts the rest of her life, never growing up, taking responsibility. Nana rocked the swing harder, listening to his footsteps recede. They didn't tell you about the nights when you got old, how long the intervals were between sleep, how quiet the house. Roberta warmed up milk for Nana in the winter then licked the milk mustache off her lip, Roberta's tongue hard and gentle, her breath minty. Elise came around the porch corner in her nightgown, barefoot, her hair still clipped in a loop on her head.

"G'night." Elise didn't know why Nana held her hands so

tight, fingers laced hard through her own and tucked down, as if Nana wanted to shake her a little, make sure she was there. Nana's lips felt soft and dry, like a pony's, and Elise drew quickly back. She wasn't the snuggling type, even her mother's chest too hard to lean against. When Nana let her hands go, Elise hopped up onto the swing. "Push it *hard.*" She missed the swing set at home probably the most.

"I can't, sweet pea. It'll break or I'll break, one." Even as she spoke, looking down at her granddaughter, Nana toed the swing slightly higher. Elise stared straight ahead, rapt, trying to drum up flight out of that diminutive arc of movement. It hurt Nana to watch. Was the child happy, staying there alone in the summers, or bored, homesick, and how would she ever know? Elise hid disappointment as fast as she felt it. Nana stopped the swing. "It's past your bedtime," she said.

Running around outside in her nightgown was fun. At home her mother would put her to bed when it was still daylight out, the venetian blinds a soft blue, but Roberta had let her dawdle in the bath the way she always did, trying to get her out at first, then losing interest. Elise didn't mind being left to play with the plastic cups, but it still felt funny. Roberta could have been a million miles away, sitting on the bathroom stool, arms crossed, her knees sticking up under her dress. The porch smelled like geraniums and wet dirt.

At the end of the porch, after turning the corner away from Nana, Elise could see the bedside lamp in Roberta's room behind the scrolly stuff on her screen door. Roberta actually had *two* doors, side by side, one going out to the porch and the other into the stuffy front hall inside. The front door was stuck right between them. So you could go in the front door and in Roberta's door and then in her porch door and be back going in the *front* door all over again, around and around. Nana's bedroom also had a screen door that went out onto the back porch. Going from a bedroom right to the outside made Elise feel funny. Her room, though, didn't have any doors at all, only big empty wall-like spaces into the parlor and Nana's bedroom, with curtains on rings no one ever pulled.

From inside the hall, Roberta saw Elise bend down under the

porch light to check out the June bugs that littered the doormat, flinching a little when they moved. A June bug had gone down Roberta's undershirt when she was younger than Elise, a hard terrifying thing, buzzing against her back. When she wouldn't stop screaming, her mother took her inside to the bathroom and shook her clothes until the bug fell out, spinning in its shell against the bare white tile, dark and scrabbling, evil. They hit against her screens at night like bullets. "Do you want a story or not?" Roberta talked through the screen door, pushing a button to turn on the dim light in the hall so Elise could see her.

"Yes, please." Elise pulled open the door, dancing on her toes in exaggerated fright when a bug buzzed into life and jumping for the sill, giggling as Roberta caught her arm. She was always so much heavier than Roberta expected when the mood took Elise to act ridiculous, like now as she collapsed backwards in Roberta's grip, jerking her slightly sideways. Heavier and clingy. It was aggravating. Once Elise started, she stayed silly past the point of any normal adult's patience.

"Then let's go . . . *okay*, Elise." The child had laid her cheek against Roberta's arm, still giggling. It wasn't affection at all but more of a way to get attention, Elise bullying the two of them with her warm weight, playacted kisses, that attenuated embrace. The insincerity exasperated Roberta and made her uncomfortable, hating the willed stupidity in Elise's closed eyes, the sticky closeness, her own desire to push the child away. "*Elise*—"

Elise heard but she couldn't stop. It was like she turned into somebody else, somebody who laughed too hard, was a little awful, wanting what she wanted way too much. When the voice inside her said me, me, me, me, Elise didn't know what else to do but this. In the hallway Roberta had stiffened and was suddenly pushing her off, frowning like she didn't want to touch her, leaving Elise standing all at once by herself on the big milky-looking flowers of the carpet. Roberta sighed hard. Elise looked at her feet. The hall was dim and ugly and smelled funny, the flowers like awful mouths, the whole house quiet and dark around her, nothing familiar, even the tall bed with the white pillows under the lamp and the rotating fan beside it not really hers. Turning, Elise ran to it anyway, leaving Roberta standing there; her face felt hot, her mother a million miles away.

"I hurt her feelings." Roberta sat in the swing and snatched at mosquitoes with her hand, opening her fingers to stare at her palm.

"She won't remember in the morning," Nana said. The night breeze rustled through the pecan tree in the yard.

Opening her eyes with a gasp on the dark the next night, Roberta lay still, testing the weight of the sheet across her chest, her heels sunk into the mattress, the dream all but vanished except for the hard pounding in her chest. There had been a man, bigger than she, lazy-looking. He had leaned over and flicked a bat out of the cobwebs, a gray powdery mouse, quiescent at first then suddenly flying up into her hair, mothlike, crying. Heart still pounding, Roberta turned on the light, the pocket-sized book that was Linnie's diary falling off the table. She automatically leaned down out of bed to pick it up. It seemed to weigh next to nothing, as much as an empty box for playing cards.

Lying back, Roberta flipped the soft leather inner flap. The light seemed to wax and wane as she looked at the writing on the first page. J. worried too much. Every family had skeletons in the closet, crazy aunts like Linnie, or worse; hell, if she had kept in touch Roberta would probably *be* a family skeleton, may even be one anyway. Elise was fine, which was more than Roberta could say for herself. J. had reminded her too much of a child that night, lying across the pillows underneath Roberta's squirming weight, trying gamely not to cry. It was hard to know exactly where to stop. Before freeing the bat, the man in the dream had asked her for sexual advice, which was stupid, stupid. Roberta tossed the book back onto the bedside table. Linnie had deserved her depressions, as far as Roberta was concerned; J. deserved the winced-up eyes, the red marks of Roberta's fingers on her wrists. The book lay half against the lamp. What really galled Roberta about the dream was that he had wanted her advice and not wanted *her*, a completely absurd irritation.

She rolled onto her side and looked outside, the window screens like velvet, the doubled glass squares above half hidden behind the sheer curtains, crickets only faintly singing at this hour. The air inside was hot as hell. Roberta didn't like the fans on when she slept, the hum absorbing the outside sounds, possible intruders. She pulled her nightgown loose. J.'s grandfather chasing around in Mexico letting one wife after another kill herself making babies and his daughter kill off her own childhood raising them, all that dark horrible business of procreation and nurture in a too-small house crowded by trees. Maybe it *was* Addison's fault that his daughter went mad and his son at fifteen became a killer, or Axel's maybe for dying in the first place, hell, for stupidly falling in love. What this had to do with anything, Roberta didn't know. The sheets were twisted around, and she stuck her foot underneath trying to prod them back into place. Here she was at fifty-six, after a relatively gratifying life with three completely normal women lovers, suddenly lying awake in a house not hers obsessing over someone else's ghosts. She was waiting, Roberta suspected, for the day when love would leave her high and dry yet again, J. smiling goodbye, stiff-lipped, at the kitchen stove. Roberta kicked at the sheets again then finally got out to remake the bed.

Elise, she thought, yanking the bedspread back, had ghosts right under her nose if she would only look. To hell with Linnie. A man like Jack wasn't going to let his own daughter get away, especially one with the mean weight of his name around her neck so that all her life she had made herself satisfied with the single letter she thought she could have. Roberta made a crisp corner with the sheet then smoothed the bedspread back down. He was never out of J.'s mind, and Roberta couldn't force him out. The slaps, the wrestling, the mock rape, the hard forcing of herself down across J.'s loose breasts, her legs weakly kicking below Roberta's nudging weight, hands prying, teeth grating against her upper lip until J. turned her head and moaned, having paid—it was draining Roberta's spirit. Hell, maybe it was time they bought a dog, a wheezing Pomeranian to sleep at their feet. Roberta grinned as she plumped up the pillows again, licking at the tears that curved around her mouth.

154

Nana figured Roberta had had a bad night when she saw her in the morning but didn't ask, trying herself not to remember what they had said in the hot front room, what she had let Roberta do. Nana meant first thing to get that diary of her aunt's away from Roberta and put it up, hoping Elise would then forget about it. "You sure you don't want some eggs?" she said.

"Coffee's fine." Roberta rubbed her eyes, looking at the paper. "You see in here they arrested that old drunk Dr. Carey for doing illegal operations at the back of his house?"

"I don't want to fight."

"Abortion would have saved your grandmother a lot of grief."

Silence sometimes worked. Nana stood up to get the coffee-pot, but Roberta went on.

"What if Axel wasn't *meant* to be born, but they made her get married and have him anyway—not in *Virginia,* of course, not where anybody could see, but born nonetheless. So fate kills him off a little later, right? But now it ruins five lives instead of one."

"Fate." Nana snorted. "A real Christian idea. All I know is that taking life is a sin."

"Tell that to your daddy."

Nana waved her hand and walked away.

"Come on, J." Roberta stood up and followed her to the door. "You want all women to be like your grandmother and have eight children and die before they're thirty?"

"Maybe you'd think different if you'd ever had a child yourself." Nana heard the nasty smugness in the words the instant she said them and regretted it; Roberta just drove her to distraction. She was angry, her hands shaking too hard to undo the knot of the apron. The dresser looked a mess with all those tangled nylons she had got out to do Elise's hair, the bed unmade. Working at the knot while Roberta moved behind her, she could hear the clanking grind of the swing out front where Elise was, as usual, pushing it to its limit.

They yelled a lot, which always surprised Elise, hearing their voices all at once go up then sink back to hissing whispers then nothing. Elise had never figured out what made them mad; it seemed like just talking was enough to do it. She had seen a friend's daddy once yell at a man on TV, which had been pretty

155

funny. She shoved the swing higher. Roberta that morning had looked as though she was "cruising for a bruising." That's what her daddy said about her when she picked on Laura. Elise, you are cruising for a bruising. She looked down, dizzy from the swaying floor.

Roberta brought home rhubarb and strawberries that night, detouring in her ancient station wagon out of town to the farmer's market. Elise at supper looked awfully puny, hardly saying a word, even when Roberta brought up Linnie's marriage proposal and her laughing that old bore out of her house. It was curious to see Elise, so heavy and solid when hanging on her arm, become at a distance evanescent, painfully vulnerable. Roberta watched her push around her peas. Eating that early had become a habit for them, but the daylight outside still gave Roberta a fleeting sense of déjà vu. Each night her mother had laid out for Roberta whatever she found in the icebox then took a bath before her husband came home, the long-standing romance of her life to which Roberta was incidental, an unexpected and quickly smoothed out interruption.

Washing up later, Nana handed Roberta a plate to dry. "Let's not start her up again, all right? About Linnie."

"Fine."

"I'm not telling you what to do."

"Of course you are, but that's all right." Roberta held out her hand for another plate.

There was something about the sight of Roberta waiting patiently by the sink that made Nana's heart stop. She felt at those times as if she had never loved anyone as much as she loved this tall black-headed woman, standing there now with a towel in her hand, one hip cocked up against the drainboard. The plate she held felt like a lead weight, the water burning hot as she lifted her hand, clinking the plate against the faucet. It was always like an ache in the back of her throat, that desire, wanting Roberta to stop her, to hold her still, to keep her head from turning to check where Elise might be, her endless obeisances to proprieties she didn't give a nickel for. The plate wavered heavy under the beating faucet. Roberta gave a sigh, and Nana sud-

156

denly dropped everything back in the sudsy water and walked away, drying her hands on her apron. "Let them soak. I don't care," she said. Shrugging, Roberta flipped the towel over her shoulder and reached into the sink.

That night Roberta was awake as soon as J. at the other end of the house got out of bed. She lay still for a minute then drew back the sheet and walked barefoot into the hall. The light in the parlor glimmered beyond the French doors, where Roberta caught the white flash of Elise's nightgown in the beveled glass as she turned down the short back hall to the kitchen. J. behind her stood out longer, her soft robe lifting for a moment in the light.

Roberta moved silently down the hall. J. had been cross all evening, mad at the pie for not being tart enough, the rhubarb cooked too long, and Elise just like her, restless, out of sorts. Elise's sleepwalking was the damnedest thing; Roberta had seen her once come to the bedroom door, eyes like polished buttons, J. off the bed in a flash even though they had just been lying there talking, well, arguing maybe. Roberta stood at the half-open doors and waited. Sometimes Elise went right back to bed and sometimes it was like trying to turn a mule. A light went on in the kitchen.

Roberta wouldn't go back to childhood for money, where monsters in the closet were real as rain. Maybe her mother wasn't a monster, but the friend they'd told her to call Uncle Danny certainly was, with his careful hands and his fetid breath. He had followed her out to the garden shed, promising to mend her broken wagon. Roberta rubbed her nose sadly. Children just didn't have a chance in hell. Elise came out of the kitchen, looking confused, while J. guided her with a hand at her back. They disappeared, and Roberta leaned her head against the glass, unaccountably depressed. What she wouldn't give to sleep the night through just once, but it never happened in the summertime, not anymore, the rooms too hot, the air too weighted with worry.

When she looked up, Nana was at the door. "Go to bed," she said softly to Roberta.

Roberta smiled. "I seem to be sad all the time."

"That's all right."

"It probably isn't, but there's not a whole lot I can do about it." Roberta crossed her arms and leaned a shoulder against the door. "I promise I won't start writing poetry."

Nana started to laugh. "Hush."

"Except maybe an ode to the bone, right there, that arches up over your eyes." Roberta touched J.'s face. "How it's as graceful a line as any in nature, as elegant, as—"

"Go to bed, Roberta."

"All right." Roberta bent forward slightly, smiling. "I'll go to bed with you." She kissed J., then kissed her again, sliding her hand back behind J.'s head, thinking as always how hard and delicate the bones of her neck were, how easy the older woman moved when she let herself. The clock ticked in the parlor. Taking a breath, Roberta pulled J. closer.

Nana stiffened. It'll hurt, he'd told her, don't you know a thing? It'll hurt like hell, daughter of mine. "No," she said.

"Just once, just *once*," Roberta pleaded, "make it easy, J. You don't know how easy it can be."

"No."

"J.—"

"Don't do this."

Roberta let go so suddenly it made them stumble. The hall was dark and airless, and she could feel sweat running down her ribs. The soft cloud of J.'s hair had curled wet under her hand. "Fine," she said. "I won't. So what the hell *do* we do, J.? You tell me."

"I don't know."

"I don't know either." Roberta smoothed her hands up her sides, rubbing the cotton nightgown under the droop of her breasts, distracted, tired. "I don't know either," she said.

The last person she wanted to see the next day was Helen, who came walking into the shop. She had on one of those wigs she wore, a deep gold-blond color cut in a curly cap, and she was wearing a gray silk shirt. "Bertie," she said, deftly turning over a dozen separate items as she walked to the back, reading the prices and sticker numbers. "Darling, do me a favor."

"What." Roberta had to change her coding system every few months to throw Helen off, who was as passionate to know who was selling what as she was shrewd in what she bought. She knew no greater pleasure than to buy the undervalued family antiques surrendered to Roberta by a personal enemy.

"Talk to J. for me, if you would, about Elise, who is the dearest child, of course, but she is *there*, darling, all the time, and Gar naturally would never say a word, but between you and me he is not a young man at all, and the dogs, you understand, are not happy in the shed or even sleeping in the house, they do need to run."

"I thought you let them out at night."

"But darling, they are not nocturnal by nature, you should know yourself just looking at them."

Roberta didn't care for Helen's dogs, with their heavy blunt heads and overslung jaws. Elise was good enough around them, but they made her nervous, so J. had asked Helen to tie them up when she came over. J. thought the way Helen babied those dogs was criminal. "I thought Elise played out back most of the time," Roberta said.

"People think all the time and it doesn't mean a damn thing, darling." Helen didn't know what that tiresome woman meant by all those clear irrelevancies. She wanted her place to be hers, day or night, all the time, and Gar too, the old fool. He was living back in a time where she wasn't even a trace memory, at least not to him. She remembered herself, of course, her toes like pink petals below the yellowing lace, the mash of strudel cake between her fingers, the looming dome of her forehead pressed to the looking glass, but Gar wouldn't know the difference. He didn't have even half her mental resources. Why, she could see his daddy in front of her right now as clear as day.

Roberta shrugged. Helen was too predictably malicious to bother her, even when bitterness wafted like a poison gas out of nowhere. "So let them out. I'll tell J. to warn Elise is all."

Helen looked in front of her. "He had this strutting little walk, you know, until he got old and then he had this stiff little walk. I was only nineteen at the time, but I looked him right in the eye, blue and cold, like a tiny chip of ice." Helen flicked her fingernail against the cut crystal to make it ring. "So he pinched me on the breast. Right there in the back parlor."

Roberta had never speculated on Helen's love life as a girl, her life now so bound to Gar's it was hard to know if any of those supposed suitors existed except as complicated foils. Gar had blue eyes, but that didn't sound like him.

"This *is* Leila Alice's, now isn't it. Come on, Bertie." Helen bent forward, her curly wig gleaming, to look at the sticker.

Roberta wiped up dust. "Gar pinched you, Helen?"

"Lord, no. Gar's daddy." Helen turned two candlesticks over in each hand. "Shoot, he pushed his tongue right into my mouth the day I was a bride to his only son, though he must have been drunk is all I can say, to do a thing like that. You'd think so anyway, wouldn't you." She put the candlesticks down.

"I guess."

Helen was glad Roberta didn't shock, never sure anymore what she herself might say next, sometimes wondering who it was had said the things that came out. "Listen, darling," she backtracked judiciously. "I don't mind Elise, don't tell J. that, all right? It's not the child."

Roberta watched Helen rub the brass trim on a clock, her painted lips trembling slightly. It was odd how age would alternatively thicken and loosen; the rings hung on Helen's fingers. "I won't tell her," she said.

"Hell, tell her, I don't care." Helen shrugged. "You can laugh at us, you and J., but I thank my lucky stars I don't live with some poor dried-up old maid who never had a proper romance but only that foolish pretending the two of you put on. I know all about that."

"Sure you do." Roberta rubbed her eyes. Helen was like some kind of crazy yo-yo.

"Gar's a fine man, you can see for yourself." He would come inside at eleven, not saying a word. Pudding-shouldered, that was his problem; you just couldn't get the man to stand up straight. "He thought I was beautiful enough to die for."

"I know," Roberta said.

"Maybe that's what he should have done. Over there in France."

160

Roberta sighed and took Helen's arm. "I've got work to do," she said.

"Darling, we all do." Helen pulled away and walked to the door. "I'm afraid, however, the green beans are quite finished, more's the pity. Please tell Elise."

Roberta never told anyone any of the things that Helen requested she convey. That evening as she walked down the overgrown drive looking for Elise, Roberta wondered whether Helen was doing all right, if there might be something wrong with Gar. Beneath those lightning switches of pure meanness, she was saying something, and she had picked, for some reason, Roberta to say them to, but it would take a psychiatrist to figure it out. The drive was like a tunnel, even darker as evening approached. Helen had wanted Gar to make the old house into some kind of showplace, before it got into such bad repair, neither Gar nor J. wanting any part of it. Helen even got an architect out to do some kind of preliminary design until Gar told her he'd set the house on fire if she didn't give up and leave it alone.

And there it was now, backed up onto the river, a neat asymmetrical oblong with its sagging roof under the trees, Helen bent down over the back porch railing—but, of course, that wouldn't be her. The dress was wrong, too clumsy or something for Helen, too old. A rank-smelling breeze came up from the river. The stripped wood that was all that was left of the porch looked like bleached bones, the sun over Roberta's shoulder burning inside the windows. She stopped to squint, still half thinking that it had to be Helen—who else would walk back there—something avid in the stance making Roberta more certain. Moving her eyes down, Roberta suddenly saw that it was Elise Helen watched, Elise with her head tilted back, eyes locked on the woman gazing down who *wasn't Helen*, Roberta realized with a jolt, then Elise was reaching up to her, smiling. Roberta yelled. She didn't remember thinking that she should call out or feeling even a flash of fear. There was only the movement of her throat and then the sound of her voice, laid flat as a plate in the evening air.

Nana moved around the kitchen, irritable, wondering what could be taking Roberta so long to fetch one six-year-old child for supper. She banged the oven shut on biscuits probably hard as rocks by now. The tea bags crowded the top of the teapot like flotsam, stuff washed up on a gravel bar, and Nana poked at them with a butter knife. She needed to get ice in the glasses. The kitchen was warm even with the fan on high in the doorway. She dropped the china top on the teapot and frowned.

The kitchen was hers, she thought. She and Frederick never fought in here, and the boys had always been on good behavior at the kitchen table, even full-grown acting younger than their years. She wasn't much of a cook or even all that good at sewing, but the props of domesticity were things she used, something her mother had taught her. The kitchen smelled to her sometimes like her own skin, salt and yeast with just a trace of heated oil, and now all of it—the yellow tile and worn chairs and painted iron trivets and the loose-weave washrag wrung out and dropped over the faucet and the big tin saltshaker—made her furious. Nana closed her eyes, knowing it was Roberta who made her mad. Just sitting at the kitchen table, reading the mail with a glass of tap water at her elbow, Roberta made Nana mad enough to spit.

You had to be thankful your husband didn't beat you, Nana thought—if that wasn't the limit. "Does he hit you?" Mama had asked her. "Well then, you're all right, for goodness sake, J." Papa stayed out of it once she married. "There's just one thing you've got to know," he had told her. "It's all you're worth, you understand me? Give that away and you're next to nothing. Powerless, girl, carnal relations take it all away, any say-so you got, you understand me? You get one thing straight," he had said to her. "It has nothing to do with love."

She'd seen enough by the age of ten to know that, seen him through the bedroom door crowing down at her mother's face, seen Aunt Nellie's arms locked around the doctor's neck, the bare white bottom of the tinsmith going up and down inside the dark stables. The physical want high in her throat was only another kind of pain, but Papa was wrong. It wasn't carnal relations at all; it was need that took everything away. Nana put the salt and pepper on the table. She wasn't going to ask Roberta for a thing.

162

Elise would wake up at night and hear them talking in the kitchen or in the parlor, rooms close enough for it to seem that they murmured right inside her head, the sound of grown-ups at night always making her think someone was sick or back from a party or up for some special reason. Because they stayed up late all the time, there was always an air of hushed emergency to nights in Nana's house. Listening to their voices tonight from the kitchen, Elise wished that Roberta had remembered to leave her a glass of water. The fan hummed beside the bed, clicking a little at the end of each turn.

The bugs outside were really loud. Elise could see through the windows around the bed a little bit of the driveway and the side of the garage lit up by a yellow light bulb. The hedges were black. She was really pretty thirsty. After a minute of listening to their voices go off and on, Elise slid quietly out of bed. The rug was hard and prickly, changing to sticky wood then back as she walked from hers to Nana's room and then to the kitchen door.

Roberta was smoking, her chair rocked back on two legs the way her mother told Elise not to do. The red tip moved from the table up to her mouth and back, then she said something, just a word, and brought the chair back down. Nana across the table was saying something about Linnie, and Elise held her breath for a moment, listening, but it didn't make any sense to her. Nana looked tired, with her arms flat on the table, then Roberta was putting out the cigarette. "I didn't know what to do," Nana said.

Elise was sorry Nana was so sad. The sadness of grown-ups was a terrible problem she wished she could just make go away. "Nana," she whispered. It was dark and peaceful in the kitchen, Roberta leaning over the table and holding Nana's hand. A moth beat down the window screen behind them. Then Nana looked across the room at her.

Back in bed with a glass half full of water beside the fan, Elise thought about Nana and Roberta, how they sometimes scared her, the times when they gave up trying to "do anything with" her and just stood there, way over on some other side, watching helplessly. Nana loved her but she wouldn't be able to save Elise if something ever happened, though Elise thought that Roberta in her hurried, half-irritated way, at the last possible minute, maybe would. She took the glass up carefully in both hands and sipped. Nana's bed creaked in the next room.

It had been Roberta Elise went looking for the night she had the terrible dream about being left behind in the backyard at home, dangling by her hands as punishment from the top fork of a tall tree, while the sun went down and Mother and Daddy and Laura went inside. She woke up scared, listening to the fan beat the air. Roberta would have been tall enough to get her down. Roberta would have done it, too. The lamp they left on in the parlor for her made crisscrossed shadows in the wicker and big black holes out of the closets and hallway. Down at the end of the hall by the front door, Roberta's light lay in a bright square on the carpet.

Nana's voice inside was laughing and pleading both, the way Laura sounded when Elise tickled her, a kind of high crying laughter that made her squirm. When Elise looked around the edge of the door, she saw Nana lying across the bed clutching a pillow, while Roberta bent over her foot holding a little curved pair of scissors, Nana's leg clamped underneath her elbow. She was cutting Nana's corns. Bessie Mae at home had corns and had split out the sides of her shoes to keep them from hurting, but Elise didn't know you could cut them *off*.

Rolling her face into the sheets, Nana laughed. "Come on, Roberta, be nice," she said. Roberta smiled without looking up and gently worked the scissors around. Bent forward in the light, her black hair sprayed across her cheeks, she looked like a saint in the book about Russian churches Elise would look through sometimes in the front room; her face was skinny like in the pictures, her eyes big shadows. Nana's leg jumped and Roberta tightened her elbow to hold it closer. Their nightgowns were all twisted around. "Ow," Nana said.

"Quiet." Roberta sat up a little and Nana winced, trying to turn over. "Look, no, look, you want it to really hurt?" Roberta shifted her arm and Elise, standing in the hall, frowned. It didn't look like fun. The scissors flashed under the lamp. When Roberta brushed her hair off her forehead with the side of her hand,

164

her face for a second looked tired. "Do you?" she asked, poking her elbow further up, past Nana's knee. Their arms and legs coming out of their nightgowns looked disjointed, ridged with the rounded edges of bones when one or the other tensed to turn. "Do you?" Roberta's voice was soft, her elbow moving. Nana turned her head into the pillow and groaned.

Elise walked backwards without a sound. Roberta was talking some more, too low to hear, then Nana's voice rose. She sounded out of breath, asking something, and Roberta laughed. The bed bumped against the floor. By then Elise was at the glass door, turning her head, watching the light inside wink off the shadowy crystals. Standing there, nose against the glass, she had imagined the doors slamming, one, two, three, around Roberta's room, the porch, the hall, all of the doors slamming closed together.

Elise curled under the sheets, counting to a hundred. The house was dark. Nana was snoring just a little, the way she did sometimes, and the carved wooden knob at the bottom of the bed looked in the light that made its way from the parlor like a smile that was also crying.

Roberta leaned in the doorway and watched J. at the sink idly running her hands through a colander of shelled peas. Her neck showed white and bumpy at the back of her dress. In the movies, Roberta thought dryly, I would press a lingering kiss to the soft loose skin at the side of her neck, half twirl her around, and lay her back gently on the kitchen table. The water made a hushing sound over the peas. The sill creaked as Roberta shifted her weight and Nana looked behind her. "You're early," she said, shutting off the water.

"Not really." Roberta glanced at the mail she'd picked up off the hall table. "What were you thinking about?"

"Nothing." The peas made a slithery rattle into the pan and Nana turned on the water again.

"What's the matter, J."

"What do you mean?" Nana moved the pot out of the sink and across to the stove, arms trembling slightly with the tilting weight of the water.

Roberta shrugged and walked away. Bills and grocery flyers mostly and a postcard from Althea in Maine. She didn't see Elise anywhere, though the gallon jar of buttons was out on the parlor floor, a source of improbably endless amusement. Roberta sat down and put her feet up on the table. Nana had followed her into the hall. "I said, what do you mean." She was drying her hands on a towel.

"I'm having crying jags and you seem to be in a constant foul temper. Hell, you'd think we were going through menopause again." Roberta tossed the mail on the table. "Not that it's something we did together, thank God."

"Gar's getting on my nerves."

"There's not a thing the matter with Gar. Some people get old, they live in the past. He's not the only one."

"If that's some kind of oblique reference to me, I do believe you are sadly mistaken, Roberta, on top of which—"

"If the shoe fits." Roberta wearily leaned her head back. "What did Gar tell her today?"

"He didn't. It's something I told her. Because she asked. She had this fit of crying—"

"I swear, it's like pulling goddam teeth—"

"So I told her about Linnie going to the state asylum. Papa sending her." Nana looked behind her, stopped for a minute, then went back into the kitchen.

The amount of time Linnie had spent locked away until she finally died, a few years before the brother who put her there, had shocked Roberta when J. told her. "She wasn't dangerous, was she?" she had said. Harmless lunatics usually stayed at home. Jack, in fact, seemed the greater menace, with his homicidal rationalizations. J. had walked away that time, too.

Roberta reached up over her head and punched the button to the ceiling fan, its long black blades slowly starting to turn. The air began to move overhead. Closing her eyes, Roberta slid down against the back of the sofa and sighed. She hated him, the pictures of Jack with those smooth pearlescent cheeks, his domed forehead, empty eyes, those endless rants to congressmen and the pompous, wheedling love letters, always self-righteous,

166

always certain. Never a dark night of the soul for Jack. Teaching his daughter barely out of knickers and baby fat that love hurts, that love destroys or takes at least its pound of flesh. He would be the one to take it away, too; J. couldn't have missed that either. Jack was dead more than twenty-five years and J. still believed that wanting someone, just *wanting* someone to touch her, could bring him back.

"If it hurts," she had told Roberta once, "then I've paid somehow, I've made it all right. But do you want to know the real kicker?" She had been drinking hot toddies all night for a cold. "It turned out to be the wanting that hurt," she said. "The sex all by itself was nothing." The fan thumped faintly, vibrating the walls. Roberta had seen bruises stay in her skin for weeks.

Nana poured a glaze over the canned ham she had already stuck with cloves. The kitchen smelled sweet, the oven blasting her face with heat as she pushed the ham in and shut the door. Roberta could have said something, was all. She didn't seem to care a fig for Elise, who was much too quiet for a child, too bottled up. That teary panic of hers just tore Nana up, knifing her afterwards whenever she thought of Elise crying, that face-flattened fury. Nana picked a bay leaf out of a tin and dropped it into the simmering peas. Elise wouldn't let anyone hold her, just like herself; Gar would sit like a butterball in any and every available lap, but Nana never had. She stirred the peas, the spoon sucking the bay leaf down.

She hadn't let Frederick beat the boys, and it irked her to death to see their mother pop Elise and Laura for the slightest things. They were only innocent children. Half of what she had said herself as a child was innocent, but Papa's temper went off like a match. He'd yank her across his knee, the hard of his hand against her bare skin, even when she got to be twelve and was talking back because she couldn't help herself, crazy with the irritant of growing up. Children. Nana ran water into the bowl she'd used for the glaze and watched it curl out foaming then gradually start to clear. She swished the washrag around. Elise was all right; everything was fine. Roberta could lie on her tailbone in the back parlor and not say a word if that was what she wanted. It suited Nana fine. Opening the refrigerator, she got out eggs for the corn bread.

Elise came in the back door by Nana's bed and walked noiselessly around to the parlor beyond, wanting more buttons to play with outside. Roberta was sleeping on the couch with her head crammed against the couch back, her black hair ruffled up behind like feathers. She still had her glasses on. Elise tiptoed in and bent over the jar. A couple of the smaller buttons slipped through her fingers, clicking a little as they fell back on top, and when Elise turned, Roberta had opened her eyes. She jumped.

"The trick is not to look guilty," Roberta said and peered closer. "How'd you get so dirty?"

"Playing." Elise looked down at the buttons.

Roberta had closed her eyes again. "Don't let me keep you," she said faintly.

Elise left, stopping only to trickle some of the buttons into her pocket. As she slipped back through the bedroom, Nana in the kitchen saw her and called her to the door. "Stay in the yard," she said, pouring something in the muffin tins. "All right? Supper in thirty, forty minutes."

The screen door slammed and Elise was on the tall back steps, still hot from the afternoon sun, the dusty scent mixing with supper smells drifting out of the kitchen windows. She started down the steps, fingering the buttons, knowing Roberta would come out to get her just like always, walking fast across the thick green grass. When she woke up later that night to their fighting, the first thing she thought was that everything had been fine at the end of the day.

"I don't ask for a thing. I don't want a single thing from you, Roberta."

"What's *that* supposed to mean? You win some martyr prize? I'm supposed to be *disarmed* by this?"

"You can be whatever you want to be."

"Including gone, J.? How about depressed, can I be that? Or lonely or tired or sick of having to play your tedious take-me, rape-me games."

"Don't you dare. Don't you *dare* say that."

"Be careful, J. I don't know, could be a demand in the making. Could be you have a whole long list of things you want after all."

"Wait just a minute. You really think it's *me*? Look at me, Roberta, no, *look* at me. What happens between us, the things you do—it's nothing you haven't done before. No, you can stop that smiling, Roberta. I've seen your face. You know you can hardly stand to feel it."

Elise slipped out of bed and looked around the corner just as Roberta jerked Nana up, the table beside them jarred so a glass fell over, tinkling. Nana was still talking as Roberta shook her, the two of them stumbling and swaying, their nightgowns sticking out around them. It looked awful. Elise stared. It looked like something in a dream.

When the door slammed, Roberta tightened her grip, feeling a sudden heady emptiness. Nana called after Elise, turning. She was heavier, but Roberta had the extra height and longer arms. As they lurched around together, the table went over, Nana's knees, as always bad, giving way, Roberta there to guide her fall. The sofa cracked lightly under their weight. In the breathless pause they could smell the spilled liquor and the carpet dust it was soaking up, chests jumping against each other. Nana's heel, trying to push off the carpet, skidded flat, and she turned her face up to Roberta's, inches away. "What if something happens to her?" she spat.

Nothing would, Roberta thought, lowering her head to kiss J.'s neck. Nothing bad would happen. Not to Elise, not at night in her Nana's backyard in the middle of the summer. Roberta had already weighed the risks to a six-year-old girl running outside on a cloudless night. It wasn't up to them in the end, anyway, two old women with their different kinds of pain. When all was finally said and done, they wouldn't have been able to save a thing.

Pressed down against J., Roberta knew it was over; they may stay together for ten more years, but this was the end, this night the final night. Even though it was still black as pitch outside, the house to Roberta felt cool and buoyant, as if it were just

169

before dawn on an early spring morning, the beginning of time. J.'s leg jerked again as she tried to lever herself up, the carpet too slick, and Roberta moved her hips slightly then wiggled her knee forward. She could hear J.'s breath change and slipped her fingers down, one hand undoing their buttons now, until she felt skin loose and cool on skin. She worked her hand lower and J., crying, turned her head away. The cushions were rough against her bare knees, and Roberta shifted her weight a little then closed her eyes. Excitement flickered deep in her gut, violence latent, a bead of light, at the core of every sexual act. The lamp burned on the glass-topped table as a pillow, pushed out by their moving bodies, fell slowly over the sofa's edge.

NINE

Lucky

2015

ELISE DID NOT REALLY SEE THE COLLECTIVE. THEY WERE A SOCIAL fabric that she fingered, draped beneath her face to gauge the color, the reflection of light across her skin from them, even though many of the people living there were close enough in age to have similar memories, of a mobility inconceivable now with everyone off to Nairobi or Nepal, of open marriages and bonehead politics, dope-laced philosophy, a dozen lost causes, the one-time company of urban artistes. When Lucky complained, Elise flicked the ash off her cigarette and sighed, staring out across the twilit pasture toward the river. "What," she finally asked, "do you want me to do?" And Lucky didn't know, wanting only that Elise take on some improbable responsibility for everyone's fraught reaction to her. Even those who were younger and had studied her work, and were perhaps more willing to argue with her, deferred to that silence, as did the children, who shouldn't have cared at all. Elise was oddly seductive in her remove, and Lucky, rolling her eyes as she rocked back and forth on the deck railing, started to laugh. She always found hilarious her own rationalizations, wanting not, after all, that Elise see the problem of her exaggerated weight in their communal space but that she see her, Lucky, with her agile thirty-three-year-old body and the long braids down her back and her mechanic's hands and the Indianlike planes of her face. Elise. There was something in her apparent boredom they wanted to ruffle—to make her interested, to make her theirs.

Elise resisted Lucky, as she resisted them all, without visible effort. It was as if some essential enzyme were missing to unlock her particular DNA, no one able to read and replicate an experience whose simplest codes were shielded. They could move under the long bank of clotheslines, shoving the laundry cart with one hip, bag swaying against the metal frame, wheels cattywampus in the short grass, and from that extract themselves or their mothers as children handing *their* mothers clothespins and the bleachy wrung-out knots, all of them familiar with the blowing emptiness to be found in a yard at noon, grass crisscrossed with power lines, some even distilling from that same moment the faint heartbeat of their mothers/grandmothers, who would have watched the green flash in and out of the sheets and remembered dirt yards with no color at all. But Elise was never there. The picture of Elise with a mother was inconceivable to Lucky, and the grandmother Elise admitted to having appeared mostly in stories from the grandmother's youth. Yet even revealed at a slant, in hermetic memoirs so lacking in the personal as to seem like miniature documentaries—on the trade in a backwoods bar in Minnesota, for example, or the sound of helicopters busting a marijuana farm in southern Indiana—Elise was not the cipher Lucky believed her to be. Her conversation was full of ordinary facts the others quickly forgot, vicissitudes in the business of brokering cloned cattle or in molecular biology, cold-shouldered for her sex in the one and for her age in the other, difficulties unconvincing in light of her present standing, as Elise was driven wryly to protest.

Lucky wasn't looking for a mother in Elise, any more than the twelve-year-old girls who started following Elise with their eyes. They, like Lucky, waited not to be noticed but to inventory their own conflicted response when Elise did chance to see them —the dizzy, skin-prickling *there* of embarrassment. Lucky secretly loved it, that blast from her ludicrous adolescent past. She had fallen half her life ago for a woman then twice her age, a radical calling for social change as the clock ticked down on the twentieth century. Meg, a political economist who had written critiques of capitalism and how it created a permanent underclass, was a little short for heroics but with wonderful wide hips, muscled like the haunches of a working horse. Her throat had pulsed when she shouted, her black hair rumpled up where her fingers had raked restlessly through. It was that cool possession of certainty or power that had kept Lucky in thrall all those years and that now kept any number of adolescents in mooning orbit about Elise.

Lucky possessed a distance the younger ones lacked, though the amusement she took in her own fascination with Elise drew on more than simple irony. Meg, or the self-inflicted memory of her, had stayed in Lucky's head, even years after she had moved to the country with the others. The brute costs in public health and social well-being that Meg laid at the capitalists' door were mixed in Lucky's memory with the heavy shortsighted crush of her own passion for Meg's emphatic solidity, how the pale skin of her arms and neck looked always firm and sweatless. Meg had flirted with everyone she met, a goofy comic notorious for having no patience, and Lucky at seventeen—rail-thin, sullen and exasperating, panicked by her own sense of deep insignificance— hadn't had a chance. Lucky slammed the posthole digger into the ground and wiggled it around. The wind had dried the shirt against her back, making her thirsty, the sun breaking in and out of the fast-moving clouds. Living through that time had been absolute hell.

She dropped the fence post in the ground and rocked it down, then stamped the dirt around it. Her gloved hands looked even bigger than they already were; the wire would be a bitch to work alone. She looked out across the countryside running with

173

shadows, a contradictory mix of hills and flatness, the sky pressed down to a straight, seemingly solid horizon filled, in fact, with slopes and gullies. Meg had been a daunting person, all that smooth, compacted energy. "So what's wrong?" she had asked Lucky, sitting down on the floor, arms crossed on her raised knees, the storeroom empty for once of other people. "I hear you're unhappy." Lucky half grinned, remembering—more like suicidal, like major despair. She hadn't known enough to earn Meg's intellectual interest, which was all that mattered, making deliberately humorous in retrospect her fumbling attempt to discuss the claims of the ego versus collective self when what she really had wanted was Meg herself or to *be* Meg, who had shifted her weight and pushed her hand through her hair, already running out of patience. Lucky still wanted that, to be endlessly young and in possession of whatever made one an object of desire. Like everyone there, she wanted to be back where the world and her adolescence ended.

They all ran backwards like water following the tilt of gravity, not so much futureless as balked by it, the absence before them of expectations. The loud boom of babies grown everywhere old was deafening, an elephantine passage nearing its end that had left scarcity behind, scorched bare earth. Nothing would happen. The tepid end of their high hopes for revolution had made them all sober and levelheaded, no one now expecting to make a better life than the one they were already making there. Hale argued that they lacked imagination or vision, a gift for going beyond, when they knew they lived simply to play out variants of the human state, inevitable, nontranscendent. Having vision anyway would presuppose something unseen, a closed book, a future time, but their future had been displaced by a sociological anomaly, populated, colonized, and warped by a statistical mass that drew the light down into the fall of its/their memory. Time in those days was selectively elastic, variable at the end behind them and frozen on the event horizon of the present. They no longer professed opinions about the world's apparent failures, not even about the specific failures of love between Ramona and Elise.

174

Nothing of mother-daughter there either, though Hale disagreed, Lucky only shrugging because he had pissed her off and she didn't want him to know how much. Ramona and Elise were talking down by the garden as Lucky changed the Jeep's points, and when Hale didn't leave she had asked him what he meant by mother-daughter anyway. "Collusion," he said immediately, and then he stopped and said, "not letting go." Lucky said that didn't make any sense and just who the hell did he mean, which one. "Both of them," Hale said, "which is why it's so boring— at least the son gets to kill the father, but a daughter just sort of moves inside." "I fought with my mother," Lucky said as she wiped her hands and glanced at Hale. "But she didn't die," he said to her.

Damn right, and Lucky jerked at the wire, wrapped it doubled around the post, and reached for the pliers. Nobody ever died of love, even when it felt that way. Just thinking about it made her want to laugh. No lover had ever been worth that much loss, but she fell in love just the same and would do it again, Lucky had no doubt, at the moment fresh out of passionate attachments. She clipped off the end of the wire and walked to the tangled coil of the second strand. The obsessing about Elise didn't count, Lucky stopped by Elise's indifference and by the formidable presence of prior claims to her affections. Anyway Lucky had always preferred the zingy feel of impending comedy to something more serious. Landon, a large man who was always serious, had rocked his two-month-old daughter in the curve of one arm and picked through the plates still left on the dinner table for something more to eat while Lucky sipped her cooling coffee. "To me love feels like a molecular change," he had said, "something happening in every cell, an irreversible situation. It's as if it were some biological problem. It's not," he said, "in my head at all."

There was nothing, however, organic about Hale. They professed to tolerate Hale, to make magnanimous allowances for the alien presence he represented, when, in fact, they closed him out. His beauty was part of it, and the sudden way Elise produced him after a two-month absence that had left them ever so slightly adrift, something they resented and so flatly denied. The summer had been making its imperceptible shift to fall, days as hot as before but no longer quite so green or full, when Elise was all at once back in the house with a godlike boy no one had seen before, a boy who made audible love with her in the room at the river end of the hall. They were not children. Still, they hated Hale with such a superstitious fear they had no choice but to bury it, atavistic sibling angst, the conviction that someone had slipped inside and installed in the cradle a goblin child. They could find nothing in Hale they recognized, no reflection of who they were in his eyes.

Through with mending the fence, Lucky carried everything to where Paula had told her to stash the tools if she finished early and decided to walk in. The clouds had blown east, the sky clear, the wind starting to settle as the afternoon waned. Halfway up the second hill, Lucky stripped off her shirt and tied it around her waist, the sun warm on her wet back. She didn't see the all-terrain Jeep until she was almost on top of it and the two men pushing it off a rock. The man in the black suit saw her first. "Jezebel," he spat and the other man, a farmer by his looks, glanced over his shoulder. "Put your clothes on, girl," he said.

Lucky was already backing off, but the deacon had started around the Jeep and was running up through the rocks to stop her. Still moving back, she pulled at the sweaty knot of her shirtsleeves and swore lightly. The deacon came closer, panting, and drew up short then backhanded her hard across the face. The scrub oaks hummed with insects and it seemed that the wind had died altogether. "Whore of Babylon," the deacon said quietly.

"You're trespassing," Lucky answered, the knot coming loose. She pushed her arms through the sleeves then pulled the shirt closed across her chest. "You're a good two miles from the right of way." Her cheek stung and she tasted blood inside her mouth. Even out here without a congregation behind them, the deacons scared her—this one seemed a genuine fanatic. She looked past him to the farmer at the bottom of the slope. "You're trespassing," she said again.

"That right?" He crossed his arms and blinked slowly, the line of his mouth hard.

"Yeah, that's right." Lucky eased back a step. The deacon didn't move and she stepped back again. He followed, slapping down the hand holding her shirt closed. "In sorrow thou shalt bring forth children," he said.

For all the collective's self-mocking bravado, they were secretly afraid of the fundamentalists. Their own lambent spiritual sense seemed to lack the necessary weight to counterbalance that blaze of rectitude, that certainty of salvation for true believers and no one else. They themselves were inarticulate on the subject, which was, to a group as intellectual as theirs, a near fatal failing, the absence of words almost as frightening as the flattened cant of quoted King James. Hale was the only one of them unaffected. Even the children's nightmares had men in black suits clambering up the hillsides after them. The loss of their children was a subliminal anxiety—not that the deacons would do anything that extreme. The fear was more for the slow erosion of perceived humanity on either side, the inexorable creation of monsters.

The possibility of uncontrolled violence had been ever present in that final year, the poor in the new East European democracies fucked by the free market and fucked again, while the Third World continued to cut support for its weakest to keep the international bankers afloat. Even the privileged among those now living by the river had felt the heavy thumb of moneyed interests, along with the harried desire to shake off the rightist demagogues, those faceless, inaccessible players. They later had rationalized the bombing, the alleged bombing, the by now legendary bombing, in a dozen different ways: destruction of mere property, tactical disruption of lethal research, smoke screen, political statement, hysteria. They sometimes had trouble remembering just how fast it all had escalated, how seductive the idea of violence finally became inside all the shouting and adrenalized panic, everyone running that night on foot, in packs, like teenagers out to toilet-paper the trees. None of them saw the lab explode, but they came up with ridiculous re-creations—

Ramona lobbing a bomb like a softball, Elise with one hand on a cartoon plunger, lit gasoline spitting across the grass. What was strange was that they never once doubted the act. They even clung to the thought, the light-edged image of Elise and Ramona detonating a granite building in the windy cold of New Year's Eve, without a shred of proof. It had become a central emblematic notion, a governing myth, a fetish.

And now the only anarchist around was Hale, a mere month after his arrival walking into the redolent dark of the back pasture stables where Lucky sorted through the worn-out tack and sliding his hand around her breast. The sexual play was not a total shock, but the cool experimental interest was. Lucky was seven years older, unfriendly, preoccupied, an intimate part of a collective that wanted little or nothing to do with Hale; he should have been a quantum or two less certain. Instead he watched her. His eyes narrowed slightly in a flutter of green as his fingertips found what it was he wanted, Lucky shoving his hand away, hot all at once up and down but keeping her face as steady as his. She had thought of Elise, his hand on Elise and then on her, with something like sorrow, high up in her throat, tasting of old iron. When she was three and her mother broke the china bowl for the kittens, Lucky had felt the same cool taste of failure, too late to slide the dish of milk away from that bare, descending heel. "It's not Elise," she had lied and then taken the words immediately back—she didn't remember, in fact, what she had said except "it's not Elise," when it was, of course, and Hale had known it already. Lightly tanned, ashen-haired, with his eerie beauty, he was Chaos, itchy-fingered, wild. He had thought she meant he was like Ramona when nothing Ramona might be doing approached this dangerous dispassion of Hale's, Lucky turning her back but not before she saw him smile, still palpably wanting her, the hard, lean weight of her, hair like twin ropes down her back. She had told him to try someone younger—someone seventeen, she had thought, some skinny girl in a rage of muddled emotion who might benefit from being seduced by a god.

They were casual with sex, the way people were casual with

tricky, hazardous jobs they had done a million times before, expert and even a little flip but always keeping one eye on things —always, in one way or another, at ready. They didn't formalize anything or make many rules. Their sexual existence was mutable, if Lucky were to pick one word for it, nothing glitzy or clever, just mutable, a thing that changed. But it could be unwieldy, too, enough of them sufficiently nervous around unintelligible forces to sometimes find the sexual currents rough. They were often, it turned out, surprised by sex, surprised to find themselves without warning within a body irrationally intent on another to the exclusion of all else. Although nothing of that intensity lasted, they never discounted the destructive potential, the almost entirely intellectual violence that would go hand in hand with physical love, as if they could understand its dumb imperatives only by staking their egos to it, their separate personalities. All of that may have been only so much conceit— that whom they slept with mattered at all—though some of them argued for the social veneer, the necessity of social glue.

Ramona was different, or the situation involving Ramona was odd, because of her many absences and because she owned the place but primarily because she was diffident to an unusual degree about whom she loved—in Ramona's case, she was casual with sex the way others were casual with jobs that killed. Even at forty-two, she made them jump, always somehow larger than they remembered her being, her long hair more dense on the pillow, her eyes more narrow, her touch hard. They let her pull them down into the long staggered course of a single night's sex because there was something compelling in a desire that direct and indifferent, in her wanting simply to stretch and move around every possible inch of sensate skin, not caring just which of them arched against her or dragged her head up toward them from the sheets.

Lucky had probably made love with Ramona more than most over the years, the first time in a furious and awkward purging of Meg, Lucky cringing by then to remember herself, not suspecting that someone like Ramona might have ghosts of her own to divest. They had been all day rigging the windmill and its

179

generator, Lucky doing most of the work, telling Ramona what to put where, the two of them comfortable together bent over the greasy metal between them, the big thin blades winging in the air above their heads. When it got too dark to work, they scrounged leftovers from the kitchen and a bottle of wine, the house half empty the first few years as everyone disengaged their lives in stages, drifting out for longer and longer periods of time. They were young back then, Ramona and Lucky, at either end of their twenties, young and in love with impossible women, though Lucky was the only one to confess, a little drunk, making herself sound funny, sound deeply absurd. Ramona didn't laugh. She just lifted her arms and coiled her hair up on top of her head and told Lucky they should take the wine and go swimming. The moon was up, a hard, white, lopsided disk, enough light to see by under the trees, the untanned parts of their bodies surprising, humorous, then the water like silk on their legs.

They were never at any time old enough for the thought of an unending world, for the thought of not having what they knew they wanted, for the thought of going on alone. They were never that old. Ramona and Lucky swam in the circling current of black water under trees faintly lit by the moon, their arms and legs weightless and long, trailing behind, tangling together and apart as they drifted and turned, the branches spinning above. They touched, skin cooler than water, lips warmer, hands slowly moving down, their feet sunk in the silty bottom, brushing gravel as they floated in a slow roll from sandbar to water to the chilled weight of air on their backs to sand, everything slippery and warm in between. They moved together, wet hair stuck to their cheeks, tentative, nervous, clumsy, laughing around the soft weight of their tongues, hands between each other's thighs. In retrospect neither really had expected a new utopia, but they hadn't expected the rightists to have it so easy—that was the shock, how easy it was, how small their mass action and contingency plans and orchestrated or random violence. It had been like some whirlwind romance, those final years, some crazy, exhilarating affair without a future, everyone knowing deep inside there was no future, but it was so sexy just the same. Every action was like desperate sex with the only lover they had ever known to match them unerringly thought for thought. Lucky rolled under Ramona in the water, her elbows grating on sand, and laughed, breathless, then laughed again. The trees moved overhead in a black mass. They had all been just short of adulthood, just past Armageddon, just this side of unbearable grief. No one had wanted to marry the movement, but they had finagled each moment to be there with it, illicit love, they had been drunk on the feeling, and then one day it had suddenly stopped. The water lapped up under Lucky's head, warm as a kiss, crickets drowning the sounds she made.

Lucky climbed up the road, waving at Alex as he drove past on his way out to collect the work crews, one of the children with him, standing up in the back of the truck the way she knew she wasn't supposed to do. There weren't many children, relatively speaking, living out there, Landon's baby the youngest and no one pregnant or no one that Lucky knew about at least. She did not want children of her own even though she liked babies—warm and soft, with that uncontrolled reflex of expression when they looked around, a speeded-up film of absurdly adult looks. She just couldn't imagine for herself a gesture that bold in the direction of the future, one that would lock her so irrevocably into place, into accepting the continuation of the world with its present absence of grace.

It would have been fruitless to fuss about it in the end, this number of children or that number, the way no one had ever come up with a way to calculate the earth's optimal population, the variables too many, too subjective, too culturally predetermined. They were not perhaps ideologically a mothering group, though that seemed a ludicrous characterization, as if they were collectively immune from basic biology, as if there were a maternity gene one could lose or mutate. And they genuinely loved those of them who were young, if not the *idea* of them, the uncertainty they presented, whether children any longer could survive. Every child, from the dark-headed girl in overalls riding the bed of the truck like a circus horse to the boy filling his pockets with river rocks to the baby rolling backwards and upside

181

down as Landon lifted her up by the feet to put the diaper below, was vulnerable—to toxins, to dispossession, to what they might do themselves. It was comically hopeless. They would look at the ruffled hair on the small upper forearm of a three-year-old girl and feel both her sense of compacted self and their own potential loss.

It was as if the churchgoers' stern censure that showed itself whenever a child was taken to town, even the babies, pouched in front with their heads nodding, somehow granted to the collective a dark sliver of reluctant honesty, the realization that children could be vulnerable to the adults who loved them, that the maternal could include unspeakable desires. They wanted assurance that the young among them would survive whatever abuse slipped their traces without those responsible knowing, that they themselves would survive their own shame. And lacking that certainty, they bore the children among them slowly, aware on some level that it made no difference how many were born but seduced by the thought of control, containment. They were intent on reversing their own massive blossoming forth, an explosion already slowing at its outer inertial limits, the postmillennial world having always been one of imminent collapse.

Elise was sitting outside on the deck, smoking, when Lucky came through on her way to the river, a boy swinging on the railing as Elise made up a story for him. "Then what," he would say every time she stopped. "Then what," then the girl found out that her long-lost prince was in that very same town but for only a single night, "then what," she put her baby sister safely in a magic cradle that rocked and sang all by itself and she set out to find the prince, "then what," she looked and looked all over the town, inside and out, until she finally came to a big house that someone had made out of white sugar, sparkling like diamonds in the streetlights, "then what," she quietly tiptoed inside, thinking she could surprise the prince when she finally found him and how happy he would be to see her, "then what," she opened door after door after door until she came to the last door but what she saw inside that door made her blood freeze in her veins, "what was it," it was the prince, her beautiful prince, but he now had the head of a dog with a snarling mouth and bloody teeth and ears pricked up above his head like two black candle flames, "but why," the person who had built the sugar house had put him under a terrible spell, "then what," just as she started to run, crying, to the prince who was now no longer her prince, she heard a noise behind her and, turning, she saw that her baby sister had somehow crawled out of the magic cradle and followed her into this evil house, "then what," the dog-prince turned, too, and saw them both, and with a horrible howl he sprang and caught the baby sister in his mouth and started to swallow her down, "that's too scary," shh, the girl threw her cloak over the dog-prince's head and reached down into the dog-prince's throat and caught her baby sister by the hand just before she fell into the darkness inside, and she pulled and pulled and pulled (the boy said nothing now, only listened), until the baby finally came up and out, just as the girl's cloak burst into great black flames, then white flames as the house too started to burn, and the girl put her baby sister next to her heart and she ran.

The boy waited as Elise fell silent and after a moment ventured an ending. "She got away and they lived happily ever after?"

Elise stubbed out the cigarette and tossed the butt into a coffee can. "She got away," she said, "except for one thing. As the baby tumbled down into the prince's throat, she had opened her mouth to cry and her voice slipped out at that very moment, falling down and down inside the prince to be lost to her forever."

Lucky looked at the little boy, who clearly considered it no great loss. He swung himself around again on the railing. They were starting to cook supper inside, pots clanging on the stove. Elise apparently mourned for nothing. At most there was wistful regret, a sophisticated resignation. Lucky watched Elise looking steadily back at her across the deck and dropped her eyes, swinging the towel in one hand, then Leonard came up behind her, snapping his own towel at her butt. He was a pest but so guileless about just wanting to get laid she reluctantly had found herself liking him. He followed her down the steps, singing a tune from a century ago, making up different words—mice make it, lice make it, even people who aren't nice make it. "Shut up." Lucky was laughing.

This was her favorite time of day, late warm evenings with shadows stretched long but still enough sun left to make the air glow, the grass iridescent green. The river clucked across the rocks at the head of the bar. The shade was deeper under the trees, birds flitting through the branches. Leonard, who had already pulled off his shorts, hit the water with a splash then resurfaced, shaking the wet hair out of his eyes. "Water's fine," he called.

Lucky dove, a shallow arc across the elbow of the bar and then under into the cool, dark green current. She held her breath as long as she could, kicking her feet, then shot upward, the spray of water bright against the tunneled trees. She had traveled a fair distance downstream, Leonard still treading water behind her. Kicking forward, she started to swim hard into the current, her arms reaching, trying to keep her body from turning too much—wasted motion, Elise had said, watching her one evening, just tip your head a little to the side to breathe. When she reached then passed Leonard, he paced her for a dozen yards or so and quit, turning onto his back. She swam up to the fallen tree then stopped too, rolling back in the water with her head upstream, floating, her breath coming in pants. The trees flowed up from her feet and across her face in a ripple of leaves and pink-streaked sky, the water so still around her that it seemed as if she didn't move at all.

Leonard came up beside her, spewing water like a porpoise, then smiled, his hair plastered to his shoulders. When he goosed her underwater, she jackknifed away, kicking him in the chest. Men were different, the seduction and sex with men different, everything much more awkward and obvious, interest communicated either not at all or in big simple letters, primary colors. The excitement was different too, as if the odds were against it, or against matching the real sex to the imagined, Lucky's erotic projections never accounting entirely for the way men's minds worked. That men and women everywhere made love seemed so

184

unlikely to her, so strange and hapless, it made her smile, the way very small miracles—just enough gasoline left in the tank to make it, coughing, to the distribution yard—made people smile, in happy relief, and congratulate themselves.

Leonard came out of the river after Lucky, who was standing on the gravel bar squeezing the water from her hair. His erection stuck out in front of him, bobbing a little as he moved. He tried to hang his towel on it, but the dry weight of the cloth pulled it down, Lucky grinning as she watched. "Bet you wish you had one," he said.

"I don't think so."

"Not even to pee standing up?" He walked toward her, toweling off his back. "Kills flies," he added and whapped it against the side of her hip.

"Get away." Lucky started to laugh—there was something so sweet and weird about him, the long shape of his thighs and his swiveling walk, that unself-conscious pleasure he took in the antic behavior of his own body. "You're crazy."

"Neurotic monkeys, they say, make it." He danced, nudging against her. "Cows too long without a lay make it."

"Leonard."

"Let's make it, unnatural love."

"Not in this lifetime." Lucky pulled on her clothes, keeping him off with her elbows. He looked like every other naked man, wide shoulders padded with muscle and narrow hips padded not at all, generic young man—one reason, she thought, why the fundamentalists hated it. Naked, everyone looked alike.

Carrying his shorts and towel, Leonard followed her across the pasture, now deep in shadow, the sky fading as lights started to come on up at the house. He kept grabbing her from behind between her moving legs, laughing as he tripped on the rocks and her heels. When she got to the fence, she looked over her shoulder before she started to climb through. "Don't even think it," she said.

His eyes were hilarious. "I already have. Six variations, one involving a small sheep. We would have to go get the sheep." The sky was lavender behind his head, wet cowlicks already

185

springing up in three directions. Lucky sighed and reached up to finger one curl. When she touched him with the other hand lightly below, his head swayed back. "Okay," he said. "We'll forget the sheep."

Lucky moved down, kneeling in the grass, and took him a little way in her mouth—his cock felt cool and firm, tasting faintly like the river. His hips jerked and she opened her mouth more, slipped her tongue loosely around, moving her hand higher. She felt him hold his breath, the warmth of his flat stomach inches from her forehead. It all seemed so simple at times, the easy motion of nowhere as steady as a rocking cradle, his thick cool pulse in her mouth, the grass in a bristle around her legs smelling of dust, of endless summer. Falling from the dark, his hands came down on either side of her head like wings.

Those mothers/grandmothers of theirs jamming clothespins onto the wet corners of nylon nightgowns, the wind whipping them into billowing shapes, blousy scrawls against the tract-house roofs, all those women now dead had reached at disparate points in their lives a moment of violent stasis that Lucky and the others as their children, or children of their children, had witnessed, later to replicate—frissons of something powerless, sad. Lucky had watched the blue china dish break, blood and milk, all pretty much beyond her control. "My mother," Elise said once, "would take almost anything painful public. I mean *privately* public. The public was small. She selected her public for maximum effect."

Public events were no longer important, or rather did not define the collective's being, provide an understanding of what they did. Reports of legislators tinkering with an antiquated social machinery, sweatshop wages in the southern hemisphere filtering north, renegade acts by a paranoid military, creeping ecological devastation—these did not pertain to their own particular history, the faceless men in power no longer seen as enablers of objective truth. In a sense the public reality had become transparent, once removed, the long political quarrels invisible, the deal-making done in computer space with phantom wealth, the drug deaths unrecorded, the natural losses on a scale too large to begin to imagine, something they dreamed. History had become simply lived memory, crowding them like a freeway pileup as they stood without moving just past the event threshold. Ramona was the only one of them still to see the transparent men in power, their edges as hard as finely cut crystal. She was the only one of them to count the absent father in memory.

They were not as mechanical as Hale saw them, telegraphing their moves from brain to body like overly intellectual actors, those male pulling off a self-consciously brilliant performance as women, those female working at a somewhat lesser illusion. They did not set out that way, especially the young among them, who saw the extreme limits of the masculine prerogative as something arcane, approaching fable. The difference just mattered less out there. And while that lived memory included fathers and their fathers' own species of violence, the fathers themselves seemed mysteriously absent, either fading to the glassy thinness of public figures or into a loose variant of their mothers' impotence. Gender somehow had ceased to matter, any one of them content to push his palm down into the bread dough, fold it over and shove again, kneading an act both dreamy and physical, producing a kind of slow arousal, the dough toughening under her fists as with each push he rubbed against the table and leaned, all her weight on her palm, simply liking the way the yeasty dough smelled.

They couldn't figure Hale and his endless irritation with them, as if they were constantly failing him—an idea that made them, when they were feeling charitable, laugh. And, in fact, there *was* a curious vaudeville flavor to Hale and Elise, Hale's tense and motionless exasperation fed by Elise's blandly agreeable indifference. Elise sitting sideways at the table, flipping through the sheets of breeding data then leaning forward on one elbow to read, her shirt loose across her low breasts, one boot tapping the air, was haplessly wedged in the corner of their eye with Hale poised in the doorway opposite, hands in the pockets of his oversized pants, cornsilk hair drifting across those weirdly dark-lashed eyes, shoulders tensed against the frame, his toes working the wooden floor. During the lambing season the house would empty of everyone but Hale and Elise, and coming back after a night or two, the others would feel the delicate reorientation, as if alone the two had created a superhard space within the house, brittle, everything ready to snap.

Lucky personally didn't give a hoot about explicating the ten million layers between Hale and Elise, nor the frangible fact of their love-making on God knows how many fraught occasions, but their silence would make her laugh if she were in any kind of mood. Going inside from the breezy dark to a room full of casual, incessant jibing, everyone on chairs and couches or on the floor, conversation noisy or in broken bursts or murmurs, with upstairs the sound of water running, the shouts of children, were enough to put Lucky in a mood. The sight of Hale watching from the doorway made her grin. She didn't care that he was rumored to be a throwback to a fabled lover of Elise's youth—a dealer in any number of illegal drugs, now presumably dead, the dog-prince in flames—or that Hale was one emotional giant step beyond everyone else or that, besides resembling some animus of Elise's, he looked like the younger Ramona as well. None of this ameliorated the difference he presented in the room, that of the unassimilated, the vibrant Ur-suitor, preserved intact, Lucky herself, sitting cheerfully down at the table, a candidate for the fucking corn god and when in a mood at least theoretically willing to tamper with Elise's silence.

The moment before she knew Elise would look up, the split second before she saw Elise's mouth tighten at the soft drumming of Lucky's fingers, Lucky lost her nerve, the brief panic like water gushing inside, laughter starting to bubble when she saw it was too late. Elise had lifted her eyes in a sidelong glance, squinting, the irises gold, her eyelids faintly wrinkled. "What," Elise said.

Lucky opted for guileless. "Nothing," she said, widening her own eyes in spurious innocence and spreading her guilty fingers flat.

Elise sighed. "Say it, whatever it is." She clipped her words when she spoke, a delicate paring away that was part of how she thought, assessed, made final decisions. She waited, watching

Lucky, still at an angle from the side. The vast patience she exuded further paralyzed Lucky, who felt mildly hilarious, abandoned by her own intelligence, the words either lost or impossible to say. "Go on," said Elise.

"I can't." Lucky laughed and went on laughing. "I can't say it, I don't know why. Maybe because *nothing* goes on out here, in case you haven't noticed."

"I haven't." Elise still watched her. "You want me to do something about it?"

"I don't know, I don't know." Still amused at herself, Lucky shrugged, starting a judicious retreat into silence, knowing Hale was watching it all. "Okay, I do," she finally said.

"What?" Elise didn't move.

Lucky smiled then looked down, trying vainly to frown, to get serious. "God, Elise, I don't care. Do whatever you want, all right? You'll do that anyway."

Elise paused for a minute, her eyes narrowed slightly as she thought. The noise in the room eddied around them and supper smells drifted from the kitchen. "Is this about everyone," Elise finally said, "or is it about you?"

"Would it matter?"

"No."

Lucky grinned and tapped her fist against her chin, tired of losing the game. "You're the one who brought him," she said at last and stood up and walked away.

They let Hale carry their disappointment, and they were all on some level disappointed, although no one would have used that word exactly—frustrated, maybe, or stalled or confused, but not *disappointed.* That implied a deeper failure somewhere, in what they had decided to believe about themselves, about Ramona, Elise. They could not risk looking at their disappointment, with all its unspoken criticism of forces and events they wished to be infallible, the shaken faith, the possibility of betrayal. None of it could be examined without a pain too great to be entertained or larger, anyway, than anything else they had yet made themselves carry. That they may have been wrong was inadmissible, "wrong" in the context of fundamental belief.

189

That they may have been wrong to want what they wanted was another question, no one interested in the answer, no one willing yet to let that go, so they put it all on Hale, uneasily and provisionally, convincing themselves that if he left them they would want nothing more.

Lucky lay outside alone on the deck watching the stars come out. More and more the evenings at the house had become open-ended prospects, hollow shells leading into a night that perversely and stubbornly refused to end. The oncoming night had started to spook her, black and moonless, the stars a denser and denser sprinkling of cold lights; the murmur of voices and clinking of plates inside could have come from the other side of the world. Staring up, Lucky pressed her back against the wood of the deck, afflicted with vertigo, as if the slowly wheeling stars could pull her off the ground and send her falling out into space. She had dreams of a horrible lightness, of losing her hold and slipping upward by vast and sudden increments, the earth shooting away below, unclaimable, nothing in all the empty air to touch.

One of the children, a three-year-old girl, came out, scraping the sliding screen door along its rusted gutter and leaving it open behind her. "Close the door," Lucky said automatically and the girl turned just as automatically and tried to get it closed, grunting in frustration when it stuck. She had a piece of ice in her hand. Lucky could remember tea-flavored ice, crusty with sugar, from her mother's glass, who would tell her she had taken ice as a child from *her* mother's glass to suck in the summer evenings. The girl sat down on Lucky's stomach and, giggling, stretched out flat, her head up under Lucky's chin. "Star light," she said, pointing with the ice, water running down to her elbow.

"Star bright," said Lucky, "first star . . ."

"First star I see tonight. I wish I may, I wish I might." The girl stopped.

"Have the wish . . ."

"I know, I know, have-the-wish-I-wish-tonight." The girl squirmed, her head small and hard, rolling along Lucky's collarbone.

Lucky half sat up, braced on her hands, and bounced the girl a few times by lifting her hips off the deck. The girl giggled again, trying to stay on. "So what did you wish?"

"I can't *tell* you, Lucky. It won't come true."

"It won't?"

"No! Do that again."

"What?"

"That."

Lucky bounced her. Like having sex, she thought, pushing up with her hips, just about that real. The pasture was lost in the dark, the river invisible but for the sound it made crossing the rocks. The trees formed a blacker mass against the sky.

When Hale found Lucky sitting on the deck, the girl had fallen asleep in her lap, her head hanging in the crook of Lucky's arm, mouth open slightly to breathe. Lucky didn't move as Hale came closer then squatted by her side. "It's not me," he said.

"Fine." Lucky looked down at the sleeping girl, at the soft blur of hair on her arm, golden in the light from the window. The sudden impulse to laugh was ridiculous. She frowned at the white edge of the deck railing and at the darkness beyond with its sense of restless motion, rivers of air moving around the dense cricking of insects, long streams of cooler breeze.

"I'm not the problem with all of you. It ain't me." He was inches from her knee but he didn't touch her.

Lucky thought for a minute then hummed a few notes. "How's it go?" she said idly. "Da da, da da de dum. 'I saw my face . . .' no, wait, 'You'd find your face in mine,' da dum, 'And all my faces tryin', to bring you back to me.' Rhythm and blues, close harmony, like, I don't know their names, black guys. Elise ever do those songs for you?"

Hale just sighed.

"That play they did, those friends of hers. She used to have a tape of the music. But that was before you were born, and I would have been, let's see, about this one's age." Lucky looked down and yawned. "I went to this strange suburban preschool that had a pen of farm animals, honest to God, right out in the back, and this sheep would butt all the little kids down, knock them flat on their faces in the gravel. Scary as shit, that sheep."

"You don't want to hear it."

"Hear what, Hale—that you are the whore with the heart of gold, that you are the diamond in the rough, or maybe that you are David dancing before the Lord with all your might."

Hale stood, hesitated for a moment, then started to walk away, his bare feet silent on the deck. Lucky watched him go, the springy push of his leg under the trousers, the narrow tendon at the back of his heel, his small ass, and said, "Wait," just as he reached for the sliding door. "Hear what."

"Do you know where Ramona goes?" He walked back to her and stopped. Lucky shrugged and looked down, the girl moving her lips lightly together. "Do you know what she brings back?"

Lucky knew because she had once gone with Ramona, maybe five years ago or ten, those times when she left the ranch and drove out over the battered roads in the early light, fog in the gullies like cotton and birds starting to twitter in the trees, driving hours and hours south and west until the land flattened and the grass started to clump in tufts surrounded by wind-scoured dirt. The towns were bleak little places on the railroad with churches and bars or nothing at all but tumbleweeds and it was always in one of the deserted towns that they stopped and bumped down a side street to some run-down house or beer joint where the men would be sitting inside on tipped-back chairs, waiting. They were all alike—muscled arms like stone and half-grown beards and clear, empty eyes. "Guns," Lucky said.

"Not just your run-of-the-mill Uzis, okay? She's big-time now. She must be one of the high-up dealers—I just don't know where they go after here."

"She doesn't sell them."

"You're dreaming in spades."

"Come on, it's just a game for her. How much volume can one woman do in one lousy Jeep?"

Hale paced to the railing and back, soft as a cat. "Specialty items, sweetie. She's not arming a bunch of cockeyed guerrillas —she's selling to professional killers."

Lucky laughed. Ramona with her even gaze and unruly hair and the flat bones of her arms turning the wheel, wrists like iron —they had raced along the old interstates, weaving around the broken roadbeds, and laughed with the sweet sensation of flying, their lips dry in the wind.

Hale bent close, impatient. "If I've noticed, someone out there will have noticed," he said.

"I'm sure nobody cares except you."

"You are as dumb as your sheep, all of you."

"Tell Elise then. She's the only one Ramona listens to anyway." When Hale didn't say anything, Lucky looked up. He was biting his lip, hands deep in his sagging pockets. "Elise doesn't care either," she said.

"Elise . . . doesn't want to save the world."

"And you do."

"I want to save my own skin."

"Then leave, lover boy."

Hale didn't answer. His toes moved along the deck beside her knee. The breeze riffled their sleeves, smelling of dust and cedar, and Lucky shifted the girl's head slightly down her arm. Elise wouldn't go with him in a million years. The house was growing quiet behind them, lights starting to go out, beds, in her rowdy imagination, starting to creak, springs to moan. The breeze lifted the hair away from her face. Lucky looked at Hale again. She could have laid her head against his thin hip, he stood so close in the dark, if comfort had been something she wanted to give.

TEN

Flood II

1965

I BLINKED. THE LEAVES NEXT TO MY FACE WERE BEING STEADILY flicked by the rain that flattened the top of my hair and fell in a patter across my skin, trickling along my mouth then sliding under to hang in drops off my jaw. I blinked again. This was not a ditch I knew, things having changed since I was a kid, especially now, with the river out of its banks. I stepped gingerly off the side, the water making a line against my thigh, turning the pink cotton there to some kind of gray. Half swimming, half walking across, I couldn't tell what it was I stepped on, silty and soft, maybe mud or something worse, gone rotten, maybe even something dead. A branch was bobbing and swaying around on the other side, not something I would normally choose to drag myself up out of a ditch. I was fat, though Mother said I wasn't ("You're not overweight in the least, Elise"), coming as a big surprise since I hadn't really been fat before. One knee sliding around in the mud, I wallowed up from watery slime, rising out of the river like a water monster, the Creature from the Black Lagoon.

I must have been up near Linnie's house since the weeds and bushes were left untrimmed, too dark now to see the way the drive curved around at the end and widened out, the trees against one side of the house, the long flat field that ran from the back straight down to the bluff above the river, in the rain and dark like a thing I had dreamed or something I might have read in a book. The square white column, glimpsed through the trees, looked like it had grown in the middle of nowhere until I saw just above it the edge of the roof. The blackness behind must be the front porch, which shouldn't have been *there*, the river curving in all the wrong places. I could have circled the whole stupid house without seeing it once, way off there in the pouring dark, the flower beds flooded and overflowing the broken bricks along the borders. Boys on the prowl in the middle of the night would chat with me through the bedroom screen, popping their matches on the front porch brick, cigarette smoke like a sour breeze. One time a boy passed out in the tulips, leaving them flat on their sides in the bed, yellow heads bent, stalks like rubber. Nothing was left in the flower beds there but weeds waving underneath the water, a dust turned to mud. "Nothing" was what I said to Mother when she opened up the bedroom door. "No, it's nothing, I just couldn't sleep."

The trees huddled around the house like the four of them together in the yard last evening, Aunt Jen shaking out a cigarette, and Daddy leaning forward on his elbows as he laughed to himself, and Mother frowning with her eyes closing shut just as she started to speak, and Uncle Todd grinning at his baby brother with two half-grown daughters, Laura and me. On vacations together everyone had been fine until our side of the family moved away and I used to think that must have been it, that was the reason for the stuff that followed. I thought when I was a kid, and even now sometimes, if we just went back to the way it was, summers in old plastic lawn chairs drawn up under

195

the mossy trees, dried sneakers piled by the back screen door, then nothing bad could touch us again.

Water came off the edge of the roof like a glassy sheet, crackling a little as it hit the porch, the concrete everywhere dark and shiny. I could barely hear the sound it made, the rain in the leaves like static around me where I had stopped, nervous, a fairly normal fifteen-year-old but I was afraid to walk onto the porch, of seeing someone I didn't expect, more people dead in the last ten years. Nowadays Uncle Gar could be ghosting around with those dogs of his that had been scary enough alive. The translucent sleeves of my parka stuck to my arms, so wet from the rain it lay against me like a second skin, my arms the only part of me staying thin. They would cut through the water beside my face, rise over my head like platinum shafts of some machine, cool and long. The PE teacher had told me to try out for basketball, but how could I play on someone's *team?* I barely understood what anybody said about ordinary things, much less some game.

The sheet of water across the porch was like glass breaking and flowing together, everything pitch black dark behind. The way the leaves were trembling in the rain seemed sad, the river spinning in a million directions, enough to keep me good and lost, never to find my way back to the car. The driveway drifted underwater with no Roberta to come out from under the trees, squinting at the porch like she saw something move, black hair slipping around her fingers. Nana asked about Roberta sometimes, fretting, but Roberta had said she wouldn't be back, not to take Nana in, not to see me home. "Not for all the tea in China," she said. "I'm not coming back for love or money."

A flashlight wavered around in the trees, the rain shining silver in a needled path going back to whoever was holding it out where I couldn't see around the house, moving the pale beam up and down. The headlights behind us had scared Johnny Hart into letting go of my limp-fingered hand, then the flashlight beam had come bopping in. The boys on the phone were a barrel of laughs when they said, "Do you want to have fun in bed?" and laughed like they were mentally deranged, the dirty words hard for them but not me. I practiced for hours saying "fuck off" to myself in the mirror, not knowing why they should pick on me, feeling the same disbelief each time—do you want, do you want, do you want to have fun. The sheet of water slashed down on my head. Now behind it, I could see the door had fallen all the way off its hinges, leaving a hole straight back through the house.

The floorboards were wet, falling away just inside the door, a crazy patched-up grid of supports rising above the slope of the ground, smelling like rain. I couldn't tell anymore why I had come; the ghost of some weird aunt of Nana's was hardly going to just *appear* because I wanted to see her again, and besides, ghosts could hardly die a second time. I heard at the other end in the dark, below the drumming rain, the river lapping like some kind of cat. Water was dripping wherever I looked. The house was like being inside a cave, inside myself where everything leaked. Even reading the booklets that Mother gave me, the actual blood was still a shock, Laura coming to me when it happened to her. The rain smelled clean even mixed that way with the river junk. No one during those summers when I was five until I was ten had periods ever. Mother should be thrilled with menopause. I dreamed sometimes I looked behind and in the water was a trail of red.

The boards creaked under my weight. I had stepped on Daddy's toes as we danced at the junior debutante thingamajig, nearly as tall as he was then, biting my lip. Aunt Helen showed me pictures of herself, posing, the ones with her Dietrich look, flipping them around like playing cards, while in her own portrait Mother lolled, looking backwards in her wedding dress, her curly hair its own dark red. That would never be me, femme fatale, homecoming queen. "Well, I hated it," I said to Daddy who was driving me home, my long white gloves drawn over my elbows. "Look, I'm sorry, but I really did." He didn't say a thing. The water dripping on my head felt cold.

The dark inside glowed with the effort it took me to see, edging past a doorway that led to a room, the windows gone but the walls still standing, a separate breeze coming out of the dark.

Most of the time Nana wouldn't talk about Jack, who had been her very own father, and though Uncle Gar tried, he couldn't make me like him. Jack sounded like the kind of bully who was always too small to win a real fight so he used a lot of nasty words instead ("Do you want me, you know, to stick it in?"). The rain seemed suddenly far away. I didn't talk much about Daddy myself. I saw Nana watching the nursing-home staff like a hawk, maybe thinking she had joined Aunt Linnie. She wasn't happy anymore and I wasn't happy either. Nobody was.

A light flickered once, not at the front door but right inside the room that I was scooting by, maybe coming through the broken-out window, the flashlight person going back around. I tried to tell Laura about the summers, what about them I had loved, how everything seemed so lazy and old, Nana and Roberta in their sleeveless nighties, like cotton petticoats, at the kitchen table. It was as if the muscles just fell off their arms. Some boys made jokes about the way my shoulders looked, built up from the swimming I did, and before that my breasts, already big by the time I was twelve, always something *about* me for boys to find just hysterically funny. Laura said it didn't sound fun to her.

My eyes were making up like a line of little sparks, right at the farthest edge of vision, that disappeared whenever I turned —sense deprivation. A kid in biology did a report, my favorite class, especially the electron microscopes. The sparks had looked for a second like a face, but there was nothing around except dark wet walls and the sound of rain, an empty space below my feet, the spirit of God on the face of the waters. They all had suddenly appeared like that in the dome-lit car, a flash of everybody's face, eyes blank, before I slammed the door and ran. "You don't know," she had said, "how much . . ."

The rain was really pouring in where a limb must have knocked a hole through the roof. My mother came in even when I'd shut the door, came in to *talk*, to ask a couple of therapeutic questions ("You're just like your father, bottled up inside"). Though I wasn't a man, forty-eight years old, with an office somewhere, but only a girl with a swimming pool at the neighborhood Y. I couldn't walk away. When the boys looked through the window at the bed and all the stuffed animals pushed to the end, at the antique rocker and the junk on the walls, I told them none of it felt like mine.

Water was rippling under my feet as I moved them a little on the creaky boards. The ground kept falling slowly away to a sizable drop from the edge of the porch outside at the back. Linnie had started to cry out there while watching the door, the door at the other end of the breezeway out to the porch, not far from me but lost in the dark. Mother sometimes would cry all day, and I had heard Nana crying at night that summer right after Roberta had gone. Nobody even knew I heard them, looking away, afraid they would change into something crazy, something weird, something about the eyes all wrong, but it never happened. Linnie seen on the porch again would pat her hair and start to smile, the river staying put at the bottom of the gully where it rightly belonged instead of running up inside the house, taking over the rooms in the middle of the night.

The little scatter of lights made a face again with pearly skin and a skinny mustache, then whisked away when I turned to look. It wasn't Linnie, maybe her poor dead brother Axel popping in and out like a bunch of fireflies. I pushed my foot out along the board, wishing suddenly I had never come inside, the house shaking in the dark with the falling rain. Aunt Helen alone dismissed Gar's stories, flapping one hand like she shooed away flies. "A prick," she said about Nana's daddy, when I didn't know what the word really meant, when half their words went over my head. I turned around for a second to look, feet balanced and braced on different boards. This was nothing at all like a book romance, too sweaty, the claustrophobic dark filling my eyes like sticky tar. I wasn't exactly dressed for the part, bell-bottoms stuck like glue to my thighs and a stupid pajama top below a nylon parka, no one likely to come to the rescue except, if he had to, Uncle Todd, whippet-thin with a head like a nut. Hardly romantic. I couldn't feel anything coming from the back, a breeze or the sound of water across the porch. Now who would want to go board the door up? Jeez. I wondered why Mary Stewart never wrote about someone stuck at night in a flooded house, sweating to death in the middle of summer.

Water was suddenly running over my foot, warm and sloppy, like the tongue of a dog. I didn't think I would like being kissed for longer than maybe a minute or two. The first time I knew they put their tongues in your mouth was when Aunt Helen said someone did it to her. I kept seeing Little Red Riding Hood's wolf. Laura scrunged up her face when I told her where Johnny Hart had wanted my hand. I touched wet wood, spongy feeling, both hard and soft, then the molding around the door, which didn't move an inch when I pushed. The river made a shushing noise, running against the side of the house.

The curve of a cheek shone in the dark and an eye like glass, Axel or even Jack himself, the dancing lights getting closer. In the dark I leaned harder against the wood then was pushing my hands at the nailed-up boards. I didn't want to see them again, the faces winking in the empty house like creepy whispers, do you want, do you want. All the boys everywhere, they hated our guts, Johnny Hart's hand holding my wrist. The boards started to bend underneath my palms, nails coming out of rotten wood like toothpicks from the middle of a cake, everything old. My fingers, edging up between, caught at the top to swing the board down. A rush of rain-drenched air came in with the sound of water and pattering trees, but I was still stuck inside. Then another board wavered out, falling with a chunk against the porch, what was left of the porch, the river across it like silky stitching. When I looked out, there was no one waiting, only water where there used to be porch and field and sun and the curve of the drive. I didn't much want to look back behind me, but I couldn't crawl through without looking first. I always, even knowing better, picked up the phone left waiting for me. I didn't know what to say to the boys who sat shooting smoke through the window screen.

There was nothing but water and dark inside, then a light, but that time a regular light, bouncing around against the walls as I started to climb out through the boards. Once through, splashing across the porch grid, I licked my palms where splinters had made them bleed, the rain coming down in a rush on my head. They wouldn't come here. No one came here but me and Linnie, walking on air where the boards used to be, all dreamy, her face raw-skinned and pale, with her big, bony hands touching her mouth. I hadn't seen Linnie since sometime before Roberta left, the river out there like a muddy lake, lost in the black of the tops of the trees, nothing but water and falling rain. I liked the sense of being alone, at the house, in my head, in the pool, in sleep, the foldaway bed in the living room and the smell of butts like a separate shell I moved inside. On the porch in the rain *everywhere* was alone, all the warm dark night in steady motion. Laura said riding could be like that. Laura said she had missed me the summers I was gone.

The struts of the porch like long smooth ribs jerked under my feet at the current's tug, sagged and jerked a fraction of an inch. The phone would ring and Mother would yell that it was for me and there they would be, do you want, do you want. It didn't really matter. Even laughed at, I still went swimming each day, every arm and leg muscle pulled and stretched, the chlorine smell that stayed on my skin. They said that runners' periods stopped, that girls in sports were stuck in some stage, there were always some girls who didn't hit it off. They said do you want to have fun in bed.

Rain ran off the tips of my fingers and I licked the drops at the corners of my mouth. Nana had never wanted boys. She said boys never had a reason for doing the things they did, and Roberta had laughed. They should have just gone on and stayed that way, lying on the bed with the fan in the doorway blowing their hair, talking together in the middle of the night. Mother said I needed my beauty sleep when I sat up late reading Mary Stewart, when she woke up and heard me moving around. The boys outside the window tried to tell me the dirtiest jokes they could, and I laughed because they were dumb but funny. The cigarettes made them seem years older, though sometimes the bourbon would make them sick. They'd finally go on, and I'd flap the curtains just before I heard Mother open the door.

The porch thrummed steadily under my heels. Johnny Hart

had asked me to hold his prick and I had told him no. Aunt Helen's hand, like elegance itself, flicked the air. "Jack was a dangerous man," she said. "People that mean don't deserve to live." She said it calmly, like stating a fact. I couldn't say what I would have done if I'd had as a daddy a dangerous man. In Mary Stewart the romantic leads were all at some point dangerous men, but they weren't really mean, not mean like Jack, not out for blood the way he was.

The house looked farther away than it was, where I stood alone in the middle of the porch, water sliding cool around my feet. Like Linnie, I could be walking on air. When I turned, she was standing at the very edge, looking back with a funny kind of tight-lipped smile, then she wasn't there. As I took a step, the whole porch seemed to sway. Linnie wasn't one to give affection. I'd never seen Nana and Roberta kiss. They were brusque with me, their hands on my shoulders pulling me up to their faces and back, while Aunt Helen always got stuff in my hair, whatever she was making, fruitcake, preserves. I used to think Linnie would be like both—not easy, not with her full attention. Mother's arms were small and strangely hard, her stomach mushy against my side. Water swirled against my ankles, pushing the flaps of my pants around. The rain felt warm. There were times when I came up out of the pool and felt like marble soaked with damp, every bare inch of me cool to the touch. The boys at the window didn't know about love. None of those books had a thing to say.

I couldn't see her eyes where Linnie leaned back at the end of the porch, half sitting down, her hands in front across her stomach, hair a mess she had piled on top. Eyes closed, she was like some kind of Buddha. I heard a voice talking inside, yelling, maybe, across the rain. The water was wrapped around my feet. When I was eight, I'd danced with Daddy by standing on the tops of his shoes, in the summertime to country music, pints inside their paper bags, Aunt Jen with her elbows propped on the table and Uncle Todd waltzing me down the floor, his arm like a board across my back. The porch was empty. I heard in the water a cracking sound.

Small and cold, his eyes without color, Jack was standing at the door, not looking at me, the water pulling at my knees as I almost fell, backing away. The rain coming down was all I could hear, was all there was. Johnny Hart took and put my hand, but I didn't, listening to the radio, not looking down at his unzipped pants. The house was black and still behind him. He didn't move. The radio in the car had been playing a song by the Rolling Stones, but I just heard the rain.

A log rose out of the river then went rolling under. The porch shook, water like cream foaming in a cup, and Jack was gone. I looked around, thinking how I could swim in just about any water, the slap and turn of the current just another kind of rhythm. Laura was starting to learn to jump, to launch those heavy horses she schooled into the insubstantial air, jolting back to earth with a thud. We couldn't believe what the other one did, Laura's whole face wrinkling up when I said that he, that he. The porch was starting weirdly to float, buoyant for a moment below my feet. The smell of smoke was like something old. Mother suddenly opened the door.

Her nightgown was blowing in the rainy air. Linnie had never once looked young, but in that one moment she didn't look as old, girlish even, starting to laugh as the porch wheeled around. The house was moving, everything fluid inside the rain, then Linnie was saying something, I thought to me, but I couldn't quite hear. The boards I stood on jerked to a stop then started pulling apart. She barely moved her lips, hair in a braid across her shoulder, face never pretty, her eyes rimmed with red. The boards slid under my feet. When I moved toward her, Linnie started saying something else. I could almost hear the words, I was two steps away, I could see the slow pulse at her throat, then water was rushing up to my waist.

In his slicker, shiny as a water-bug shell, the cop caught my arm just as the porch went under and we leaned into the current, scrabbling with our feet for wood. The water was pouring around our shoulders so hard I couldn't raise my arms. Blond hair plastered against his face, he was yelling at me as I wiggled around to look for her, for Linnie. I suddenly wanted to go, too. When he yelled again, I turned and glared at him then slid under his arm and rolled onto my back like a good drowning person, so much water on my face I couldn't cry. She was gone. The river foamed past as he pulled, one arm hard up under my chin. I saw Mother with her voice slipping over the edge, the night never ending, the rain falling down, then Roberta packing up the antique shop as newspapers blew across the floor. He shifted his grip to under my arms. The nursing-home smell filled my mouth, the cabbage-rose carpets coming up in chunks. My breasts felt flattened. I kicked down and stood for a second then slipped, trying to get his arm away. Laura touched her knee to the horse's shoulder in a ring on a bright Virginia morning. The broken-out boards banged against the wall, and I tugged at his arm, wanting to cry. Linnie was gone, clumsy Linnie, always too tired, in her head romancing her life to herself. I tugged harder as he moved his arm, gripped, and pulled, then he had swung me up, and we were suddenly both inside, in the quiet, the river pouring behind.

His mouth was mad as he started in, one hand still practically breaking my arm, and I tried to say that I knew how to swim, to tell him to just stop *yelling* at me, to get myself untangled from his lap. When at last I couldn't stand it anymore and started to kick my legs and cry, he suddenly stopped and was patting me on the shoulder, saying shh to me, his mouth against the side of my head, the slicker crackling as he moved one leg up out of the water, the rain hitting the roof overhead with the same kind of sound, shh, shh. Legs all jerky from overburn, I cried harder, curled in his lap, my nose running snot all over his chest.

A flashlight made his hair glow white then switched away and came right back, but he was already getting up. There was another light, the two of them shrinking the space of the house, bouncing like Ping-Pong balls, then pointing out where we should step, his hands behind me impersonal, firm. The cop outside of Johnny Hart's car had said, "You kids got beer inside?" A boy who was letting his hair grow long got slapped around when they caught him drunk. There was no one I wanted to see up there behind the two crossed beams of light. "Yeah, she was standing out there on the porch when the thing gave way. Naw, she's fine, maybe scared is all." I saw the netted crown of Uncle Todd's hat, that raincoat like a limp gray skin, the porch a different kind of dark. I didn't see Daddy standing out there.

The front porch smelled foresty and dank, littered with leaves, bits of bark. Everyone had left but me and Daddy, who wanted a word, he'd said to them. "I'd like a word or two with Elise." His voice was calm. The water was still coming off the roof, but without Linnie it was just another old house, abandoned, full of moving water. So everyone's gone away, I thought, except Aunt Helen, who was crazy now if she wasn't before. Daddy's voice floated down ("Just what in the world did you think you were doing?") and I knew it was going to be one of those. I looked at the trees, flicking and trembling beneath the rain. "Running off like that and worrying your mother half to death." I knew I shouldn't have sighed, but I did, and his hand came flying out of the dark, my slapped face burning, then burning again, and again, until I realized something was different this time, something major was wrong. I started to back a step away, and he hit me again, hard enough so I slipped in the water, scrambling sideways, ducking the blows. Then he was slapping at my arms up around my head, trying for anything there he could hit, the concrete wet and cold on my legs. "I saw the way you looked at him. They all of them saw." He was panting now, kicking at my legs. The porch smelled like the forest floor. As I got my back against the wall, I could feel the rain come down even harder, that Daddy and I were the only ones there.

ELEVEN

Laura

1984

OUTSIDE OF TOWN THE HILLS TOOK OVER, A RURAL RANCH-land not yet developed, much too rocky for steeplechase so the dispossessed southern gentry did show jumping in rodeo rings, the English saddle, jodhpurs, and boots in quaint collision with the kicker crowd. Last fall Laura had sat in the stands with her husband Milos to case the competition, the ring growing bright in the gathering dusk, a month before she turned up pregnant and after the first trimester couldn't ride. That monumental twist of fate was topped only by her sister Elise's surprise return as a divorcée, coming back from the West in the middle of winter. Compared to that, Milos' infidelity of recent months was almost dull. Laura turned the car down the road to the stables, the hills a light-flushed spill of shadows and grass, spotted here and there with trees. There still hovered just above the road a lingering sense of the earlier heat, the wind blowing warm through the open windows.

To be pregnant and a week overdue was maddening. It was hard enough to worry about labor and contractions and dilating and whether Milos was going to get over his attack of East European manhood in time to coach her through what by all reports was truly incredible pain without having to hang fucking fire for six fucking days. Did he really expect her to somehow *sympathize* because the play had not yet, in the delicate way of such things, jelled? You have jelled, Laura said to her stomach, hard up against the steering wheel as she made the last curve, catching a whiff of manure. You are just getting fat. She wasn't supposed to be driving either, certainly not out there, not by herself. It was as if all she *was* anymore was pregnant, the thin, pissed-off, deeply smart person she used to be replaced by a mammal life-form, plausibly fierce only about her home. And the putative nest, a battered rent house near a Vietnamese grocery she stopped frequenting when morning sickness made the weird food look even weirder, had grown as tiresome as Milos' affair. The stables looked peaceful, only a few trucks there. Mac was better at training horses to race than at all the meticulous jumping etiquette, but he was patient, finding Jason to keep her horse Stoly in shape.

More and more money was hemorrhaging out, each of the exquisite computer models she designed for researchers at the university becoming proprietary matter, not for resale. Stoly was a beautiful extravagance she probably wouldn't be able to keep, babies requiring endless outlay and Milos insisting on doing art —Elise maybe shouldn't have backed that play. The tires skidded ever so gently as she stopped. The silence was broken by the sounds of horses moving idly in their box stalls, a pail clinking, farther away the slam of a door, birds starting to settle and crickets to rise, balm to her ears. A breeze drifted through the car window. After a minute Laura unsnapped the seat belt and shoved the car door open, swinging her legs around and starting the slow rock forward to get her out of the car.

Jason, who was watching, she could see, as she slammed the

car door and started to make her way up the slight rise to the paddock, was fifteen years old and numbingly shy, possessed of spectacularly bad skin. He loved, however, to jump. Laura had never been able to get more than six words out of him unless it was to talk about the horse, her ballooning stomach a source of word-stopping alarm. He made his inaudible greeting.

"Isn't it late for you to still be out here?" Laura wasn't sure whether it was a perverse curiosity, affection, or sadism that made her talk to Jason, watching him die a thousand deaths in the course of an idle conversation. "Where's your dad?"

"Town." His smile was frozen in place. Laura thought Jason's father might have a small drinking problem, on the cursory evidence of seeing him once in a bar where Hollis was singing, downing shots with the bleary dedication of a tie-one-on kind of guy. When Jason confessed he was too small to play high-school football, the community Holy Grail, her scattershot sympathy had deepened.

"Stoly doing okay?" She was surprised at the sharp tilt she felt into empathetic misery—fucking adolescence. "She still balking at the third gate?"

As Jason went over Stoly's workout, the smile eased away, his face older and for a second transcending the bad skin, Laura taking an oddly proprietary pleasure in the nice line of his jaw, his neatly shaped ears. She listened as she walked, leaning back, her flip-flops soundless in the sawdust. The rich smell of horses and straw and liniment from Jason's moving hands was as familiar to her as her own adolescence.

If the play were in trouble, Elise or Rita would know what to do, although they might not know how to bring Milos around, the dawning of felt truth for Milos taking its own sweet time. The play itself might be the problem, an anachronism of anachronisms. Sitting late one night with Milos, Elise, and Nick around a table crowded with beer bottles, Laura had leaned over her stomach, the only fully sober participant in their communal exegesis of Shepard's play, and said, "It's male masturbation we've got, no, *American* male masturbation, postadolescence. What we've got here, boys and girls, is the ultimate romance."

Stoly put her head out as Laura walked up, the horse snorting softly then stretching her neck, shaking her head twice. Her breath gusted warm into Laura's palm.

Jason unlatched the gate as Laura rubbed her hand up the horse's nose, thinking about the snobby elegance of thorough-breds, including those less than thoroughly bred, like Stoly, that and the spurious wisdom attributed to wideset eyes, even devious horses dumb as mud. But beautiful, Laura amended, watching Jason slip the halter on. "Let's just walk her out," she said. "I have to be getting back."

Elise probably never once in her life had the thought, un-prompted, that she should get back, that return was basic to every running away, that the speedy rush of escape could only be a temporary theatrical gesture, nothing written in fucking marble, nothing for real. Laura watched Stoly walk, coat such a deep umber it was nearly black, mane lifting in the growing breeze, the hills still preternaturally light against the sky. The place was quiet but for the thump of hooves shedding flies, a radio playing Patsy Cline far away inside the house. The baby swelling Laura's stomach had brought her sister home from Ore-gon and the mysterious man she had married there and divorced, whoever he had been—still presumably was. Laura tried to imag-ine him in a kitchen with a view of dry plains and mountains out the window, but all she saw was Milos and the first tiny kitchen they'd had in Boston, depressing to think how long ago that was.

Laura looked at Stoly, who was getting restless, head tossing. Jason was no doubt wondering what to do with her, Laura, all two thousand pounds of her, looking like hell in one of those embroidered Mexican dresses and rubber thongs. She suddenly started to cry, trying as she did to smile heroic reassurance at poor Jason, who was at once extremely busy with the horse. She wished she liked Hollis less, that Hollis would do her the favor of dropping dead or at least stopping the pretense that it didn't matter, that Milos was not being seduced away. Jason finally cleared his throat. "You want her up?" he asked, and Laura, still crying, nodded.

Actually, it probably didn't matter. The endless fact of her pregnancy, the shifting and kicking and nudging presence that shared her every physical moment, had reduced everything beyond the stretched skin of her stomach to minutiae, secondary players—even Milos, even sex. "Oh sure," she had said, staring through the thin nightgown at breasts she had never had before lying on a stomach ditto, her pubic hair not even in sight, thighs flattening out. "Oh sure, right, Milos, I feel really sexy like this." The air was cool on her wet cheeks as she tucked her hair back behind her ears. Hollis was, in a strange way, likable—her physical easiness, that grin with its hint at an inside joke, not so much seductive as conspiratorial. With her short hair and secondhand vintage clothes, she had the look of an urchin, simple as a cat.

Jason was finding many things to do inside the stables, and Laura laughed, her moods, if intense, at least short-lived. "Hey," she said, rubbing the small of her back, "Jason," thinking for one delicious moment that he wouldn't answer but pretend not to hear, the way the old black men in Redbone's bar blandly ignored her pregnant existence. "Jason, come here a minute."

Watching him walk out of the shadowed archway, Laura was struck again by the odd formality that his shyness gave him, his hands moving in self-conscious arcs almost courtly in their reserve, thinking how adolescents moved from gawky dopes into this strange, paralyzed delicacy. Shepard had it all wrong about American boys, or maybe he wanted to enshrine the prevailing myth; even his nerdy outcasts were made over at the Bob's Big Boy rumble into all-American heroes. The reality was so much more interesting, of course. Jason, with his tense, superficially ugly grace, would take Stoly flying over the red-and-white gates like a leaf riding a darkened cataract of muscle.

Milos, in fact, was more the myth than any adolescent she had ever known. Maybe being a displaced person from the time of his birth in whatever camp that was of Ukrainian refugees made him more ready to shed expectations, to assume a role, preferably heroic, though it could just as easily have been his hopeless Russian sentimentality that made him such an ostensible innocent. Whatever it was, Milos fit the mode of sweetly

210

single-minded sex and athleticism set for the all-American boy, still, in his thirties, looking for romantic love.

"Why don't I enter Stoly in the next show, whatever it is, and let you ride," Laura said. "Even after the baby, I'll be out of shape, so you might as well start. I'll talk to Mac." She eased away before Jason could do more than carefully nod, her back aching from standing so long. "You can use my riding clothes. Believe it or not, I'm usually about your size." The hills were darkening outside as the sky flushed. The breeze had dropped, the air thick with the sound of insects. Lights had come on in the house and she could see a truck pulling around the curve, its headlights pale. "Winning a little money," she added softly, "wouldn't hurt."

Mac was smoking on the porch when she got there, boots crossed on the railing. "When you going to drop that kid?" he said as she carefully lowered herself into a wooden rocker.

"Never," she said. "I'm a medical miracle. I'm going to be pregnant the rest of my life."

"Your sister called." Mac gazed off into the middle distance. Laura heard the truck door slam, then the tires grinding gravel. "Said you were in some kind of a fit and if you tried to go out and get up on a horse I was to knock some common sense into you."

"Elise," Laura said, "is a jewel."

"Then Milos called and said for you to get home, there weren't any hospitals out there."

"You've been busy." There was no position, sitting, lying, or standing, where the baby didn't press on some vital organ, at that moment her bladder. The radio crackled across the sound of western swing coming out through the screen door behind them. Laura sighed and shifted her weight. "Let's enter Stoly in the next show that's up. Jason can ride."

"All right." Mac was the calmest person Laura had ever met, unmarried, getting on past fifty, happy with his work. "Everyone should have a father like that," Elise had said, and when Laura pointed out that Mac was too sexy in those faded jeans for anyone's father, Elise had laughed.

"Got to go to the bathroom." Laura rocked herself up and

went inside. The living room was cluttered with gear, the radio playing under a yellow light, bathroom at the back. Men's bathrooms never looked like bathrooms to Laura but more like way stations, with their dumped clothes, smudged glasses half full of booze, always something alien like a motor part balanced at the back of the sink. While pissing, she had started to cry again. She wished she were back alone in her own body, with its flat freckled stomach and narrow hips, so she could make a plausible play for Mac, who had watched her jump a million times, moving up and down, cheek close to Stoly's neck, like a kind of sex. She wanted nothing so much now as to crawl inside his unmade bed with him. The cramping she felt could have been lust or just another Braxton-Hicks, a sad commentary in itself, and sitting on the toilet, Laura closed her eyes, practiced breathing, until it went away.

When she went back out, Mac was leaning against the side of the porch, flicking the butt out into the yard. The screen door slammed behind her and she went over to stand beside him, looking down toward the dark stables. "What's Milos doing?" he said.

"Dumb stuff." Laura shrugged. "Sleeping with someone." Mac wasn't usually one for personal questions and she looked over at him. "That what you meant?"

"If that's what's bothering you." He gave her a close-lipped smile that was simultaneously reserved and sweet. He had a long nose but a nice, rangy face, skin toughened from the sun, hair thinning along his crown in a springy arc. He reached out and rubbed her shoulder through the light cotton. "Is it?"

"Naw." Laura laughed and flipped her hair behind her ear. It was getting dark. His hand felt warm and hard, moving up to the back of her neck. Still smiling, she looked at him again, her head bent forward under his thumb. "You got a yen for fat ladies, Mac?"

"Got one for this fat lady," he said and bent forward to kiss her gently on the lips, polite, then when she stepped a little toward him more serious, closer, his tongue hard and narrow inside her mouth until she felt her stomach pulling her

212

forward, brushing up against his side, and she stepped back, swaying.

"Wow." She smiled and touched his wrist still up by her cheek. "You're every pregnant woman's dream."

"My pleasure." He let her go then and reached automatically for a cigarette in his front pocket, finding nothing there because he was trying to quit. He scratched his jaw then leaned his arm up along the post at the corner of the porch, still watching her. Laura looked down at the embroidered flowers across her front.

"I've got to get back," she said.

"Sex will bring it on," he said almost at the same time, and Laura stared, wondering if she had heard him.

"What?"

"Labor. Sex is supposed to get it started."

It struck them both funny at the same time, the two of them grinning then starting to laugh, finally turning together to sit against the railing and hoot at the beautifully absurd reductions of sexual passion. Laughing, Laura felt happy for the first time in about a week, wrapped inside the dark porch with light streaming out of the windows, the wafting smell of the stables, knowing she eventually had to drive back to that stifling house in town but not for a moment caring why.

She walked to the car by herself, thongs slapping up against her heels as she crossed the yard and followed the gravel drive to the paddock. The car, when she got inside, felt hot and dirty, the back seat full of trash that she and Milos simply tossed behind them. The engine, just after she started it, had some kind of choking stutter to it before leveling out. Hardly, she thought, trying to turn the wheel, born to run or be wild or whatever James Dean thing we aspired to. Elise genuinely loved to drive, but Laura, after the first tire-skidding rush, was bored, put to sleep, the way dope now hit her, Milos baffled at all this *sleeping* in a woman who once had barely slept at all. Her speed-freak days—Laura climbed the rise and turned onto the empty road, accelerating, the wind smelling of melted asphalt and cedar—finishing high school and going through college in a white, talky, amphetamine haze. She must have fucking been

213

out of her mind, Milos charmed by the pale red hair that fell in curls halfway to her waist, her bone-thin frenzy, wired, staying up most of the night, those winters at school relentlessly cold. Laura flipped her hair back behind her ear as she drove.

The town always came up faster than expected, first the isolated pools of light around a store and two gas pumps slipping back into the dark, next the half-empty strips with their parking lots, then more linked together, a line of sodium streetlights, the hills drifting away, the heat intensified. Hearing the radio chitter where she'd turned it down, Laura cranked it back up and punched the buttons, finding some Joan Armatrading, gutsy singer sounding a little like Hollis, who probably was playing fair or at least up front, by her own standards, Hollis not exactly an open person. Anyone willing to walk onstage and be somebody else was necessarily elusive, not altogether there. Laura had come back from Boston to watch Rita and Elise do their thesis project, the Molinaro one-act, thinking at the time that her sister had taken on a hall of mirrors. Hollis, sitting at the bar between sets, the lacy black sleeve torn under one arm, her hair tousled, had said to Laura it was only sex, it was only for now, it had nothing to do with Milos' marriage, what she did had nothing to do with love. And Laura hadn't argued, not entirely sure why. The conversation was somehow too intimate, sitting shoulder to shoulder at the noisy bar, sex too natural for ultimatums, too variable, erratic even, Mac genteelly bending down, his hand on her neck.

A contraction came as she started working her way through the highway interchange, breathing deep in and deep out, in and out, as she downshifted, turned, blinking away more tears, furious since it was fucking Milos' fault she was out in the car at all, in labor, but then it wasn't labor after all, and she took a right down a darker street, still crying as she drove. Milos used to slide up inside her, standing, her legs wrapped around his hips, back pressed against the door they had closed, barely moving, deeper in and out, only their breath in the silence.

The house was lit up when Laura got there, Sloan's junker and Elise's Fiat blocking the drive, so Laura parked on the street, the engine rattling slightly as it died. She clicked the door open, the street empty but for the shadowy glide of cats. Halfway up the walk, she saw the front door open and Rita came out, jingling keys. "Hey," she said, squinting into the dark, "back in one piece?"

"Yeah." Laura didn't have idea one why Rita should hate her, Elise rolling her eyes when Laura brought it up. It sounded dumb even to her, but Laura was sure, sitting on the cracked bar stool watching Rita shoot pool in the late afternoon. She had asked Redbone, who was counting glasses, what she'd done to put Rita off, Redbone shrugging and pursing his lips. "Just being yo'self, I suppose," he'd said, "being born at all." "I didn't ask," Laura said, "for Elise as a sister. It's not like you get a vote or anything."

"Beer run," Rita said, already past her. "You need anything?"

"Look," Laura suddenly said to Rita's back, "it isn't all that big a deal, having a baby. You don't really have to act like I'm a leper, okay?"

Rita had turned and was looking at her, eyes narrowed for a second then reflective, her face for all its impassive stillness oddly revealing. Surprised, Laura thought she saw her own passing misery in Rita's face, then it was gone, Rita smiling and shrugging, the keys in one hand. "You're not a leper," she agreed.

"Well, I'm glad we got *that* straight," Laura said drily.

Inside, Elise sprawled on the couch talking to Milos, who was prowling the room, still half into character from rehearsal. Bottles were beading water on the coffee table and Laura automatically got paper napkins to push underneath, dumped some pretzels into a bowl, finally sinking back into an armchair and closing her eyes. Apparently scenes had clicked tonight, some mysterious meshing of the ensemble soul, Nick and Milos like a fucking *dream*, man, like a merging of minds, two into one. Nick was scary, cool green eyes and feathery hair, legs stretching to there, an inertial force in an emotional vacuum. Elise may have met her match in Nick, just like her in a dozen ways, Laura certain that Nick was trouble. Everyone in their crowd had at

215

some point felt the baby kick, but it was Nick's careful touch she remembered, maybe because he watched her eyes when everyone else looked at her belly and the flutter of skin as the baby moved.

Milos touched her shoulder, leaning over the back of the chair to kiss the top of her head. "Don't do that," he said, "don't run off that way, scares the shit out of me when you do that." Though he could get drunk and sail out after midnight to find a half-wired junkie good with a knife to teach him what his fucking fictional character had to know to take on a fictional killer, Method acting so much masturbation, a description that seemed to keep coming to mind. When Elise was five and Laura was three, Elise had shown her the spot where to put her finger, their mother would have no doubt been horrified to know. Laura started to laugh, opening her eyes, still surprised sometimes to see Elise actually there, with her plum-rose hair and pale skin, shoulders knobby under the tank top, mouth, nose, eyes familiar and unfamiliar, Laura still not believing the ten years that had gone by. Milos stood reading Elise's notes, snapping his fingers lightly, his hair combed straight back from his forehead, while Elise yawned and stretched her arms over her head, Laura wondering for a moment who on earth these people were.

Sloan came out of the glassed-in porch, his black curls wild, glasses glinting as he ran his finger around his gums, then stopped by Laura. "Come on," he said, "at this point you can't hurt a thing getting coked. I read about it in a book. After the delivery date has come and gone, substance abuse is permissible and even encouraged to prevent acts of unpremeditated violence. Freud called it the talking cure. I am in possession," he said, "of the finest kind."

"I thought you spurned the designer drug."

He sighed and pushed his hair off his face. "I do," he said simply, as if that explained everything to his satisfaction and surely Laura's, which it did, the same way Nick had smoothly argued her clothes off it seemed like a million years ago. Nick had Elise's cool fascination with apparent paradox, her all-embracing amusement, sweet and intimate. "You can hate me and love me both," said Nick, "and believe the next day that you never gave in. I promise, no regrets. Like a moment snipped out of the temporal continuum. You have here all the freedom you'll ever have," he said, one finger lightly on the spot Elise had showed her. Sloan, watching Laura's face change, squatted beside her chair. "Whatever you did," he said to her, "that was in another country and besides, *ma chère*, the wench is dead."

Laura thought Sloan might have smoked his brains out, but it was hard to tell. He had sleepy eyes and looked physically soft next to Nick or Milos, easygoing. "Like a snake," Redbone said once, "lazy like one of those boa constrictors, one of those big fat python dudes." But there was something appealing in that shrugged satisfaction, Sloan waiting patiently for her to decide what she wanted to do, and Laura, tempted, starting to smile, still feeling pissed, still gripped with a rebellious impatience. "Okay," she said, getting up.

The louvered windows on the porch were cranked wide open, the air-conditioning unit defunct, only the faintest breeze coming through. Laura lowered herself into a rocking chair then took the mirrored line from Sloan. He sank back, his arms laid out along the chair arms, fingers moving on imaginary keys. "So what does it feel like?" he said. "Still fluid in there, or is the baby now tamped down like so you're getting pressure buildup or something?"

"It just feels lower." Laura, flipping the hair behind her ear, bent over the mirror. "I can still feel the baby moving around, but way low down. Actually, it's the opposite of pressure, more of a mushy feeling, like the bottom's about to fall out, the baby about to come plopping out. Everything," she added, "looks huge down there. I got labia like fucking elephant ears."

Sloan gazed at her with interest, intent. "Man, I don't know," he said, shaking his head. "You think you're going to believe it? I mean, when it's all over and there's this little baby lying there all cleaned up and in a blanket, you going to believe that it was ever inside, I mean, *in your body*. It's too weird. You got inside and outside as two totally different things."

Sloan had a way of voicing thoughts Laura didn't realize she had until he said them, dropping them from some purely instinc-

217

tual plane. An actual baby was another unknown quantity, no one to tell her what it was going to be like. The cocaine jittered along the fringes, a cool blue flame. She felt suddenly exhausted, as if nothing could get her out of the chair, nothing make her move again.

"You look monumental." Sloan still gazed at her, fingering Bach—or that was what he had told her he mentally played when she asked him once—smiling, his eyes small behind the glasses, all that black hair. "Like a thunderhead on the horizon or this wave swelling up, scary as shit. No wonder people made totems like that. Pick up a rock and there you got it, a totem to mommas everywhere, though I bet you no early man was going to see it. Fertility figure in a rock? Too weird, no way."

Laura buzzed, watching the outline of Sloan take shape in a dark line then shrink into light. The heat felt once removed, sweat slicking her sides. "So women made art," she said.

"Everything." Sloan lifted his hands. "Hey, they made science, religion, everything. They did it all." Elise was laughing in the next room, the air eddying through the darkened porch, Laura unsticking the dress from her skin. "One river rock and a pregnant woman and poof, instant history." Sloan kissed his fingertips as he sprang them apart and shrugged, always patently charmed by his own ideas almost because of their simplistic profundity. Softball was another perennial favorite, the geometry of play and that loopy pitch, like male and female, or better yet the difference between doing speed and smoking dope. Sloan's metaphors tended to calcified sources in the early seventies. Elise was in the doorway.

"Aha, the Ping-Pong bounce of cheap philosophy. I knew you were up to no good." Elise dropped on the couch, pulling her hair up off her neck. "The kid's going to come out talking a mile a minute, saying hey, man, wow, *birth*, it's like, I mean, not *death*, you know."

Sloan smiled, unoffended. "God will get you," he said.

Laura was rocking in quick jerks, still feeling incredibly hot and once removed, as if her stomach were in her lap, the baby there but for that strange layer of skin and water. A bird at the window was moronically repeating the same two notes over and over. High, low. Elise kept on Sloan's case, pissed at him, Laura suspected, for cutting her a line and she had only done half of it anyway, watching her sister wave a hand in the air to shut Sloan up, who was cheerful, imperturbable. Elise had a great face, sort of Egyptian when she set her jaw, her hair still wound in one fist. High, low. "What *is* it with that bird," Laura said.

Elise rolled her head along the back of the couch. "What?"

"That bird, can't you hear it?" Laura stopped rocking and waited, hearing Milos running water in the kitchen, Rita driving up outside and parking, then after another half minute the bird again. High, low. "There."

"A bird?" Sloan half turned in the chair to look out through the plastic louvers. Again the listless two notes. "I met this sax player," he said, turning back, "a black guy, Jamaican maybe, who said birds that sang at night were lost souls, dead souls, I can't remember, looking for souls? Weird shit, anyway."

Elise was listening, the bird suddenly silent for a while, Rita out front opening the door and walking through, rustling bags. After it seemed impossible that the sound had ever existed, the two notes came again, flat and toneless. "A brain-damaged soul," Elise said.

Laura looked at Elise. "Yeah, Aunt Linnie. We're in luck tonight."

"Hey, a little respect." Elise grinned.

Rita came out on the porch with four longnecks and set them on the table. "Respect for what?"

Elise took a beer. "An esteemed great-great-aunt who spent half her life in the loony bin, committed by her brother, who lived his whole long life free as a lark even though he blew away three men on three separate occasions of threatened family honor, which may be stretching it for that last poor soul, a water-power man out of Chicago or Indianapolis or somewhere."

"He killed an Army Corps engineer?"

Laura thought this must be how myths were created, a couple of idle conversations late at night and, presto, myth. All those dead people were Elise's business, Laura doing well to remember things that happened to *her* at Nana's. She did have a distinct memory of those tasteless Episcopalian wafers sticking to the roof of her mouth and some great-uncle leaning across the table after church to ask her if she'd got that wafer down ("like goddam peanut butter, idn't it?"), Elise a skinny angel at his elbow.

Milos blew on the side of her neck, breath cool from the ice cube he had in his mouth, his wet hand on her stomach, fingers moving. "Hey, babe, you're a million miles away."

Milos was driving her crazy with all that pent-up energy of his, which seemed to get worse the more she slowed down. Right now she was too tired to sleep, not just the coke but her own mind clicking over and over, Elise and herself two steps off, always two steps off, always catching up, one or the other, Milos' weight on the chair arm rocking her forward and the brain-dead bird outside tooting flat. *"Christ,"* she said.

"What?" Milos pushed himself up, the chair jerking, and turned, dark hair brushing his movie-star jaw, so physically *there* like fingers drumming on a table top, Milos and Hollis sitting in a tree, k-i-s-s . . .

"Some bird outside."

"Where? Here?"

"Milos."

Milos leaned across Elise and smacked the flat louvers so hard they sagged slightly, the crank shifting. Everyone stopped talking to stare, and in the sudden silence the bird, after a brief hesitation, started again. High, low. Sloan smiled happily and looked at Elise. "If your great-grandfather were here," he said, "he could shoot it."

They decided on exorcism, Laura not clear what was being exorcised from where, but everyone taken by the theater of it, the jagged high of a good rehearsal spilling over into the rest of the night. Rita for some inexplicable reason knew one bona fide Romany spell—she said from her aunt—though she wasn't sure if exorcism was what it actually did, taking the white emergency candle Milos had found, feathers from a sofa pillow, Elise's chalk she used to give the actors their marks. Rita was laughing, tossing her braided hair over her shoulder as she drew a pentacle with the chalk on the carpet, the lines of her muscled arms and legs, bare below the running shorts and T-shirt, flexing as she crouched and reached, her skin tanned. Her face with its straight blond brows and wry mouth was beautiful, iconic, as she sprinkled club soda around the circle and then tied the feathers in a loop of blue thread. Looking up, saying something sarcastic, she changed fluidly to surfer girl, her nose crinkling when she laughed, her wide teeth showing. She trickled a spiral of salt inside the pentacle and balanced a tripod she had made of ballpoint pens at the center. Laura rocked, bemused at how compact and sexy Rita looked in the half-light on the blue carpet, one shoulder inside her raised knee as she carefully hung the bunched feathers by a single thread from the tripod's center.

Milos had stuck the candle in a silver holder on the table, and when Rita stood up he was already in the other room turning out the lights. The full dark seemed to pull the outside in, the bird's two-note call practically inside their heads, then Milos was back, stepping over their feet, the flare of the match catching the angled bones of his face. He sat down with Elise on the couch as Rita, on the other side of the table, started to chant. It was suddenly eerie—the still late-night neighborhood, the flickering candle, Rita's concentration across the room as she chanted, no one laughing anymore or even moving as Laura nervously pushed her toes against the spongy stuff of her thongs. She thought about Mac for no reason and the things in his bathroom and his face coming closer to hers on the dark porch. Rita's voice stopped. At that moment a deadening weight was felt in the room, as if a hot pocket of darkness had been scooped into its center, immensely heavy, then Laura heard a soft tock, like the breaking of a vacuum, and the candle went out.

At first no one moved. Laura tried to see, squinting then widening her eyes, Milos within touch, something ghosting, phosphorescent, at the periphery of vision. Elise's voice came out of the dark. "Rita?"

"Shit." Rita sounded faint and faraway, preoccupied, and Laura heard the club soda bottle thud over on the carpet, the slosh and hiss of its contents against the cap. Across the room a light glimmered and trickled away then slipped back, spreading across the high curve of a forehead, reflected in a crescent of light along a pale eye that vanished under its lid and returned, moving down a delicate nose to the strange frizzed lines that swooped out into points on either side of a rounded chin. Laura frowned.

Sloan's voice across the room was filled with polite inquiry. "Aunt Linnie," he said, "has a mustache?"

"No," Elise said flatly. "It's Jack."

When Rita turned on the lights, Laura was surprised at how solid he seemed, rocking on his heels in the pentacle's center, pleased with himself as he tugged at the bottom of his vest and smirked, his tongue sliding behind his lower lip and away, that small chin jutted forward between the stiff airy trajectories of his mustache—how palpable his presence, not ghostlike at all, not charming. Laura realized she was waiting for him to fade and vanish, and when he didn't, she slid her eyes past him to Rita, standing in the doorway by the light switch. "So send him back," she said levelly.

"Christ, Laura." Rita's voice was impatient. "You really think I know what to do?"

Laura thought, why not, you know everything else, you'd know even her ghosts better than I do; they should be theoretically my ghosts too, my great-grandfather this horrible jaunty man putting his fingers into his vest pockets and waiting for any of us to just try, just try. The rocker creaked as she pushed back. Elise never once said that she had seen him, seen Jack, in the house—only Linnie crying as he came out to get her. Milos had leaned forward and was turning an empty bottle in his hand, tossing it slightly, ready, Laura saw, to flip it in a casual arc toward Jack, just to see what it did. Jack was watching him, too, face sarcastic, then suddenly spoke. "Hell, boy, I was cracked up the side of the head with a marble ashtray by a fellow twice your size and it still took me seven months to die."

Milos smiled and looked at Elise beside him, who shrugged. "Someone in the office hit him right after he shot Steck," she said. "You can see the bandage in the newspaper pictures of when he turned himself in." Elise was sitting forward too, her fingertips pressed on the table as if she had arched her hands to play a chord, and she grinned slightly back at Milos. "It doesn't mean the bottle won't do anything."

Milos saw the mirror by Laura's chair, still marked with white powder, and picked it up, turning it slightly so it bounced light off the wall. "Don't mirrors do something or other," he said. "Ah, wait, that's for vampires, which is too bad," he flashed some light into Jack's face, without effect, "unless you are a vampire also."

Jack sat, crossing one leg neatly over the other at the knee and stretching his neck inside the stiff collar, his hair clipped short, sideburns fanning out below the cheekbones. "I've been called plenty of things by plenty of people," he said, "but I don't recall vampire was one of them." He shifted his eyes to Laura's stomach. "I can tell you right now it's a girl," he said. He wagged his foot. "Fat and sassy but bull-headed too—a mind of her own."

The hate she felt was startling. It was not learning it from him in particular, this self-aggrandizing daddy of all daddies, as much as it was learning it at all—the sex and personality of a baby Laura had until now imagined wholly hers. Nothing that definite, in fact, not even a sex had been clear in her mind, but there had been a warmth, a quixotic presence, a fluty and bubbling spirit. That imagined baby was gone as soon as Jack spoke, the violation unexpected, casually murderous. Laura stared at the hard swell of her stomach as if she had never seen it before and would never recognize it again, the flexible sheath for a bull-headed girl stamped by the flat cadence of Jack's speech, his. She hated him, she hated what he had done, her hands smoothing down the light cotton of her dress.

Jack clearly wanted to talk, to tell more, apparently pleased to have an audience. Laura watched them all thinking the same thing—at what physical point did they touch, where could they exert some palpable pressure and make Jack move, how did it work or was it all simply now Jack's show. "Oh, I could tell you some stories all right," he said. "I could tell you a thing or two."

223

He hitched himself up on his elbows and laughed, cocking his head away from Elise. "Don't know as if some people would like to hear it though."

Sloan glanced around, the only one of them still relaxed, slumped back in his chair, possessed of a purely academic interest. "Is the memory only personal? Or being dead, does he have a collective knowledge? Do you know," he looked at Jack, "who was standing on the grassy knoll in Dallas?" No one took up the question, though Laura saw Rita flash a smile, helplessly, the long habit of affection. Sloan was impervious to the possibility of horror, not so much aligned with Jack's self-satisfaction, Laura thought, as unaffected, undisturbed. Even Sloan's acts of violence were disengaged—not, however, with the moral vacancy of her great-grandfather's irritable murders but with a near-spiritual remove. "What exactly," he asked Jack, "do you remember?"

"Every little thing," Jack said, "every goddam little thing. What did those fools expect? I'd taken it through the courts without a single shred of satisfaction, that idiot dam sucking the river dry, some fatuous suit out of Chicago thinking he could do as he pleased, no sir," Jack's face was bright as metal, "he was sure mistaken about that." Laura stared, Jack's speech slipping out in an uninflected and practiced rush down well-worn channels, the anger aged, Jack in love with the flex and pop of his own rage.

Rita moved slightly, over by the door. "Remember how to get yourself back?"

Jack studied her sideways. "Don't know that I want to. Things are real interesting here."

"No," Elise said suddenly, "they are boring. I'm really sorry to tell you this, but *you* are boring. Superficial. Dull." Laura wondered how many synonyms Elise could go.

"Well, I'll tell you one thing," Jack said softly back. "Try all you like, missy, but I'll always find a way to be meaner than you."

In the short silence that followed, Sloan finally snorted a laugh and leaned toward Elise. "Don't worry. I'll be your manager," he said. "I know three people we can kill with good reason, and I bet we could commit my entire neighborhood."

Rita shifted her feet. "Hell, we could commit ourselves."

Laura tried not to laugh, feeling it coming up in clots, a horrible sensation, like ocean swells floating with stuff, coming up and subsiding then up again. She wasn't sure what the laughter would be for, when it came, maybe in a grotesque way for Linnie, for the black Victorian comedy of her removal to the state asylum, poor dumb Linnie, with this romantic *grief*, this hand-to-brow romantic *depression*, a goddam walking gothic *romance*, and here came Jack popping her into a locked ward, to hell with all that. She could feel her mouth trembling and again the hard rise of laughter, trying to think of something sad, which never worked. She let out the breath she'd been holding in a rush, still trying to keep the corners of her mouth still, afraid to catch anyone's eye or to listen to Elise, whatever it was Elise was saying, her voice level, murderous and sweet.

Jack had leaned forward on one elbow, his other hand palm down on the arm of the chair, elbow in the air, eyes so concentrated on Elise they seemed white, the lids without lashes. When he finally spoke, the lines of his mustache barely moved. "You've got one loose mouth on you for someone who doesn't know what she's talking about."

Milos, who was smiling a little at Elise, ignored Jack. "So," he said carefully, "he shot his brother's killer then he shot his sister's lover then he put his other sister in a jail then he shot a man in the water business, like those American westerns we used to read. But your grandmother did not shoot anyone? And your father is not a violent man?"

Elise looked past Milos at Laura, an oddly guilty look, uneasy. Laura shrugged, not knowing what her sister wanted, wondering whether Milos was seriously worried about the gene pool or just making sure nothing crucial was lost in translation, as he would sometimes do, repeating the steps of an argument until Laura sighed and explained the associative leap she had made in her head from what he had said to what she had heard. Both of them actually were drawn to the snarled logic of those postmortems,

225

arguing in endless dispassionate conversation the semantics of a fight that only hours before had them screaming at each other and slamming doors. Laura rocked, remembering what it had been like with Milos, before the baby took up all the room in and around her, Milos as much a romantic as her great-great-aunt Linnie with her sentimental grief.

Rita was saying something to Elise, and Laura thought briefly about their father, then about Mac and all that southern courtliness, his cupped hands on her knee boosting her up to the saddle, the loose cigarettes slipped inside his shirt pocket. Milos had picked up the bottle again and suddenly tossed it, reversed, into his hand then cocked it back up toward his shoulder to throw. Jack, shifting his weight in the chair, glanced at Milos then waved his hand in disgust. "Get away from me, boy," he said. Milos laughed.

Elise and Hollis had gone after him the night he went out, half drunk, to learn street fighting at the source, Laura following him to the door, arguing then slamming it shut behind him, infuriated as much by their judicious silence, not a little drunk themselves, as by his stubborn flamboyance. Laura felt sometimes surrounded by children, her sister the least reliable of all, there and not there, coming back from her invisible marriage, not in a homesick fit, as Laura once had thought, but because Elise saw Laura's getting pregnant as this separation or something, a *betrayal*, she said, Laura turning herself somehow into their mother. So Elise returned, uprooting Laura's life as completely as when she had written from who knew where in the windswept reaches of Oregon to say she was staying and would not be back, not even years later to see Milos and Laura marry during a riotous party beside the lake just as autumn was coming on.

And now even her fucking ghosts were there, Jack starting to glare around the room. Her father had told Laura once that his grandfather let him ride in the buggy to town and sit outside, holding the reins, while Jack made his stops. Her father had sat hunched up on the seat, stiff with anxiety, hah-ing and pulling back each time the old horse shifted its weight, twitched an ear, Laura laughing as she watched him tuck up his shoulders, imitating his six-year-old self. Mac had let her ride out on a two-year-old colt early one morning, just to feel its speed, like nothing else—sheer, bloody-minded power, fences flashing by the side of her face. When she slid down after cooling the colt off, her legs were still stiff from gripping the saddle, folded high, and she punched Mac in the stomach when he looped an arm around her, *damn*, laughing against him because speed for speed's sake was so completely weird, so very, very, very simple.

They were fighting, Elise and Jack, their voices whipping back and forth. "Never heard a woman scream like that," Jack said, "like a pig squealing, I never saw such a thing."

"Why did she scream?" Elise said, sweat tricking along her jaw. Everyone, Laura realized, was hot out there, her own back drenched, Milos' hair raked back wet.

Jack smiled a little. "Why, we were just talking." The smile lingered as his fingers played with the bottom of his vest. "Talking about a thing or two I had every right in the world to know."

"About what."

"For one thing about that fancy doctor putting it to our married kin."

"*She* told you?" Elise stared. "It was *Linnie* told you about Nellie's lover?" Laura didn't look, rocking the chair with her toes, too exhausted to feel what Elise might be feeling, no longer certain she could. It used to be as easy as breathing, what happened to Elise crossing over to her unfiltered, as porous as the sac around the baby. But Laura was determined, as she rocked, not to feel anything this time. Elise could keep her raging pity for a long-dead woman who wasn't any match for her younger brother, not nearly as smart, tripped into betraying her beloved half-sister. She could keep her sorrow for Linnie, a woman with half her life still ahead in which to suffer the blues.

Jack laughed and uncrossed his legs, shaking out his pants.

Someone should call Nick, Laura thought, fight fire with fire. Milos had met Nick not long after they moved there from Boston, Nick at that time dealing grass to the local hippies. It was hard to think of him as their age or only a little older, a contem-

227

porary, Nick who was never innocent. "He looks like Lucifer," Milos told Laura later. "Only Lucifer had the good luck to stop falling." When Laura first saw him, he had been sitting on the back of a pickup at some horse auction, the afternoon starting to cool off even though there was still a lot of dust, Laura walking along unwrapping a hot dog she had just taken from Milos when behind her she heard him say, "That's Nick." She saw first the green eyes carefully casing the crowd, then his long legs in their tight jeans pulled up, boots braced on the tailgate, then how oddly gentle he looked with a little girl, maybe a year or so old, asleep across his lap.

We should get Nick over here, Laura thought, flipping her hair behind her ear. Jack was talking again, Elise bent forward with her eyes closed. Nick had smiled softly down at her, Laura thin and young, drunk and naked, already angry because he made promises the way Elise did, lightly, provisionally. She knew she could no more cut out the probing work of his fingers, the teasing glide and vanish and, when she groaned, his slow return inside her, than she could cut out her heart, cut out the moon from the sky. Nick made a rueful face then fluttered his fingertips across her stomach and lower until she jerked her hips suddenly away. He smiled and drew his leg over hers, holding her down, open, his fingers playing.

Everyone with their big *ideas*, their philosophies, their theories of life. Milos on the couch, turning to wipe his face on his shoulder, bored a little with Jack's talk and with the stale end of the night, rationalized Hollis to her as part of a larger Ur-performance, a dimension of the play, floating in some quasi-mystical place where Hoss and Milos had equal weight. There was Nick with his crap about freedom and power and Sloan with his woman as creator of civilization. They all had the same cocky self-assurance of Jack taking out a gun and restoring order to the general situation by removing whatever to his mind didn't fit.

"You've thought so much," Laura said suddenly, interrupting Jack, "you've got yourself stuck, thinking. You've got it so you can't do anything anymore *except* think yourself up, over and over. You're fifty years *dead,* you stupid asshole, and you've not caught on yet that everyone else around you is gone?"

Jack tugged his cuffs down and shot her a glance. "They're here," he said. "You don't need to worry about that."

"All I see," Laura said flatly, "is you."

And all I feel, she thought, is the need to pee for the fucking two hundredth time tonight, shifting her weight to move the baby, which still lay somehow wedged up against her side, poking her right below the ribs. Hollis was actually on the right track. After nine months as the leaky, swollen, tired support system for a life not her own but inextricably there, Laura knew for a fact that love was a gloss, the fine-print annotation to what still remained an essentially animal life, everyone encased in bodies that moved and ingested and blindly craved and touched like organisms everywhere, the gross business of life going doggedly on. Jack had no body. He was a piece of fucking ephemera. Laura rocked herself up, sighing. "I've got to go pee," she said.

Whether Jack vanished with the thought, with the sound of her voice, or when her water broke was never clear, but Laura had taken only a step when water was all over her legs, on the floor, and she was saying shit, thinking at first that she had started too late for the bathroom, then thinking how practical it was that she had flip-flops on, then wondering about the horses. The room was inexplicably full of them, Arabians and the larger quarter horses, shouldering for room, skittish, with their lips curling back, hind legs shying, the barrel swell of their sides patchy with sweat. Mac, she had thought, I'll have to call Mac to get them, when all at once they were gone and Milos was standing there looking at her.

Laura had thought that when labor finally started, she would feel relief at last to be moving, the waiting over, but instead it felt awful, like coming to the top of a roller coaster, being pushed off without a chance for second thoughts, really not wanting to do this after all. Lying on the couch in the dark living room, she turned into the pillows and started to cry, harder and harder, hearing Milos on the phone in the hall with the doctor and Rita tossing bottles into the garbage can outside. She cried on hopelessly, wishing she could just see Mac who was calm as water and had helped mares birth, crying because it was going to hurt like hell, crying because she was all alone inside it.

"You'll be okay," Elise said, sitting on the coffee table, Sloan standing behind her.

Turning over, Laura tried to talk through the crying. "How do you know?"

Elise didn't say anything, looking down as she clicked two bottle caps in her hand. Laura put her palms over her eyes, crying.

"That's the worst part," Laura finally said, feeling the first real contraction starting up. "The not knowing."

"I love you," Elise said awkwardly.

Laura closed her eyes, still crying a little, waiting for the contraction to stop. "It's not knowing," she said, "where you are. Elise? That's the worst part of all."

TWELVE

Helen

1956

Helen turned the riding mower at the bottom of the lawn, pleased at the tight spin the machine made, sweat making the inside of her wig itch. She ground steadily up the long slope to the house and shrugged off the pinging sound of rocks. Gar, grousing about how often he had to sharpen the blades, didn't have anything better to do. Walking the property line back for the umpteenth time to stare at that miserable house hardly qualified as useful labor. "Keep it up about the house," he had said, "and I'll burn the goddam thing," slapping the floor plans off the table. The mower crested the hill, clipping the border of day lilies along the driveway. The river house, the one belonging to Gar's daddy, would have given her natural style real expression, or such was her humble opinion. The yard blazed under the afternoon sun, the dense green of the bordering trees not moving a leaf. The loose skin of her arms, hands gripping the wheel as she turned, shook with the mower's vibration.

Gar watched Helen wipe out a couple of day lilies, flattened and sucked up under the blade shield, making a godawful grinding noise and spraying petals out as she turned with a lurch and roared away. That woman was a demon on the mower, drove over whatever the hell was there, branches, rocks, those big ham bones she gave the dogs. It was pure luck nothing had ever ricocheted out and killed someone. She was a stubborn woman, Helen. Gar groaned a little, trying to make the driveway turn-around up by the house without stopping to catch his breath. He shook his head. That Elise was odder than a two-dollar bill, his grandniece probably touched by the sun or just too much congenital imagination. Gar got to the white circle of concrete and squinted, hearing Helen on her way back up.

Helen made a half turn and cut the motor, looking at Gar. The silence was almost as deafening as the racket the mower had been making, the two of them stopped as well by the overpowering familiarity of the sight of each other, Gar slumped a little with his eyes screwed up and Helen elegant even with her feet on the pedals, elbows stuck out in the air. "Well," she said, "any new deterioration to report?"

"That little Elise is a character." Gar had decided early in their courtship just to ignore Helen's sarcasm, talking right past it, by now not even registering what she said in that tone of voice of hers. "Sis ought to keep an eye out."

"J. couldn't look after a dog. Those boys of hers always did run wild and you know it, little hellions."

"You want to know what Elise just said to me?"

"I have never found the sayings of six-year-olds very interesting." Helen preferred a little more efficiency in a conversation, but Gar was never going to oblige. She wouldn't have tolerated a dumb man, and he wasn't that, but he took his own good time getting to the point.

"She said she saw a ghost at the house—a 'ghost lady,' she called it. Now doesn't that beat all? A goddam ghost." Gar scratched the back of his neck. It was just a *place*, just piles of wood falling down with farther out along the river the old dog track, grass sticking up through the cinders and gravel, and hauled up above the flood line a couple of oil-drum rafts. He used to run that park pretty good. He never saw what the place used to be like when he went back there, poking around. The used-to-be came up only those times when he dozed in the long room off the kitchen or sat outside after supper with a glass of bourbon. Then he might remember his mother walking through the rooms turning on lights or the skinny little boys hopping on and off the rafts like frogs.

"Not your sainted mother, I hope." Helen pushed her wig harder down on her head, the thing coming unstuck from its bobby pins. Her fingers smelled a bit like gasoline.

"Hell, you know there aren't any ghosts." Gar looked at his wife of nearly fifty years and wondered what in god's name they had done with all that time. No sex to speak of, no children, no work excepting an oddball string of business ventures or betting sometimes on the ponies or the dogs. His father gave him a job for a while in the pecan trade he had finally set up in *his* old age. When they met, Helen had been a cool blond beauty, a few years older than he was and, Gar didn't mind admitting, smarter, too, knowing Czech and English and some French, reading plays out loud to him at night. Now that porcelain skin and the thin lines of her eyebrows arched high above those deepset eyes, her mouth elegant and wide, lips painted red, had gone, all that taut beauty relaxed into something else. Gar wiped at the sweat on his face with the back of his arm.

"Maybe not, maybe not. We don't know, do we?" Helen fingered the keys, ready to turn the mower back on. He made her crazy with impatience, standing slump-shouldered in the sun, every hair on the man now crisply white as if he'd been dusted all over with sugar, powdery *Pfeffernuesse* for everybody's birthdays. He had never paid J.'s boys any mind, still wrapped up all those years in boyhood himself until the old man died. Helen had told him from the very beginning she would not have children under any circumstances, and he had laughed, not knowing anyone could make that sort of decision. He had been so innocent. "Do you put ideas in that child's head?"

"Nah, she doesn't listen to me." Gar shaded his eyes with his hand. "You going to keep riding that goddam mower until sun-stroke gets you?"

"I'm almost through." Helen smiled at him. "She's a lovely child, Elise. Not a bit like that mother of hers, Grace, working in whatever peculiar office it was where he met her . . . As J. so tactfully puts it, a bit of a diamond in the rough."

"Godalmighty, Helen, you worked before I married you."

"I really don't see the connection at all." Helen turned the key and the motor guttered to life. She revved it slightly then pulled off the brake. Gar was saying something it was clearly impossible for her to hear and she smiled again and waved. Turning the wheel, she set off, heat radiating back from the engine hood.

In the near dark of the evening, Helen let the dogs out of the long canning shed where they liked to sleep. The shelves were lined all the way to the eaves with sealed jars of beans or toma-toes, some of them a decade old, the labels peeling off, brittle and dusty. The dogs shouldered past her, knocking her sideways as she touched in passing the soft gray flaps of their ears. The two of them were getting old, too, their legs cramping up, teeth yellowed. Sweethearts, both of them, they nudged her hand and then were off, ghosting away into the dark. The shed smelled like the earth, like stone foundations.

Dogs were simple, Helen thought as she always did, shoving the door closed and picking her way down to a lawn chair set out by the oleanders. Loving the dogs had always been plausible in ways that loving Gar was not. The difficulty with Gar lay not in remembering the initial fascination with him—that deliber-ate gentleman's drawl and stocky pose, his reckless dilettante spirit. No, it was explaining the hoary persistence of love that had her stumped. She stretched out, sighing. You could cut the night air with a knife, hot and buggy, the whiff of rot up from the pond. Her bare heels slipped down through the webbed plastic, feet crossed at her still trim-looking ankles.

Helen had wanted beauty—lawns like green cut velvet, a desk with slim cherrywood drawers, the sleek chrome flourish of a touring car, dogs high-bellied and graceful—and Gar to see it all, of course. Helen smiled as she chewed on her thumb and watched the dark, the porch light visible just above the hedge over at J.'s. If Gar had not been so impossibly irrational about the house he and J. had let fall to ruin in the glade out back, Helen would have had her one last virtuoso moment. She was prepared, she had told him, to work her own fingers to the bone in restoring the rooms, to take out only the necessary trees allowing pathways of air to move up from the river. "Leave it alone," he had said. The architect rolled his eyes as he rolled up the plans, so she stiffed him a little on his fee, put out by the whole ridiculous business. And now that peculiar little child was making up ghosts out of God knew what. Gar had always been a practical sort of man for all his romantic notions. That *modern* streak in him was what made for his success at the track, although she wasn't sure why. Helen tapped her fingernails against the aluminum arm of the chair, staring into the dark that would have to be thick as soup back there where her husband, ghost or no ghosts, had decided every night to walk.

Gar had stood a few minutes at the hedge just past J.'s house, listening. He was under no illusions whatsoever about what his sister thought of him, Miss Know-It-All, old before her time. He grinned suddenly. Elise saying "Push it *hard*" came as clear as if she stood by his elbow. J. murmured back, he could bet good money, telling the girl to rein it in, tone it down, keep her socks pulled up, hell. Walking on, he could hear the dogs running up back of the goldfish pond. They still made their loose circuit of the grounds even with their hind ends all crapped out, both half deaf.

The night closed up around him whenever he stopped, the crickets slowly coming back, the hot air settling in. He had never sweated enough to get himself cool. Helen told him years ago that she liked a man who didn't sweat, his shirts wafting away from his back, dry as a cast-iron skillet and as hot. She had liked his looks in a dinner jacket so he had put the damn thing on, fans bending the candle flames flat to the wick. She had worn those dresses she made herself that would have caused a riot in some parts of town, at least back then, on her the way she was back then. Gar patted at the sweat on his face.

Coming around to skirt the pond, Gar caught sight of Helen

lying in the old lounge chair they kept out there. Elise reminded him more of Helen than she did of J., something in her a little moody, watchful. Helen looked like a movie star lying in the moonlight, head tilted back, arms limp. Her fake blond curls were gleaming nearly silver in the light off the back of the garage. Gar moved silently toward the trees before Helen saw him, not sure why. Thirty years ago they had danced on the goddam lawn every night, bootleg champagne slopping the rims of their glasses. Not that high spirits alone had ever meant for certain they would make love later.

The old tree-lined drive was as black as pitch. Anybody who had ever seen a dead person laid out knew ghosts were a goddam crock. For the longest time, nobody Gar knew died except that dried-up banker chap of Aunt Nellie's and some cousins in the war in Europe, then you got the Depression and for about ten years blood kin were popping off right and left. They shipped Aunt Linnie down from the state asylum in a plain pine box. Remembering only the wild horsey-looking woman with his daddy's handprint pink across her cheek, he had crossed the parlor to see her laid out. Her wrinkled face was pale as chalk, with bags around the sides of her mouth, a big lower lip; her hands the size of a man's had been folded up neat on her chest.

Gar went on down toward the barns where the moonlight poked through the trees and where maybe a dozen yards out the river came into sight. It was a pretty little place, those pecan trees towering above the rest of the trash scrub. The rustling space out there at night made his mind go blanker than a piece of paper—the sounds of crickets and leaves in the dark and the throat-clearing mutter of low water, the air as hot as his breath. Half his life he had spent tending to women and the other half taking a cold-eyed measure of the overblown claims of men for their dogs or horses or, much more rarely, their whores. His daddy was so all-fired important to just about everyone else around there Gar had scooted by, the womenfolk deep down never expecting him to do a damn thing and the men paying up without plotting how they could kill him later—his daddy, all in all, a powerful convenience. Gar bent forward and rubbed his thighs where the muscles bunched up. The old rooster had known it, too.

Helen pushed the dog's muzzle out of her lap then swung her legs over and stood up, wincing a little at the stiffness in her hip, touching her hair. The dogs floated away in front of her, nails scrabbling as they crossed the concrete driveway. The poor darlings, cooped up during the day so a lily-livered child wouldn't feel constrained to play inside her own backyard. The porch light still burned next door and Helen idled over, her backless slippers getting wet in the grass. When she got to the trees, she stopped, not wanting to risk the ruts of the old drive in the total dark. It would be just her luck to break a leg while snooping on her aggravating sister-in-law. A dog bumped her behind the knees and was gone, the insects drifting back. Over that came the cranking noise of the swing as it barely moved, J. and Roberta talking.

They were so damn self-contained, the two of them; J. hadn't said two words to Helen in as many weeks, Roberta little better. It had griped Helen seeing the two of them at the kitchen table as she looked through the back screen door one evening, over there to borrow a stick of oleo. Just the sight of them for one sharp second so easy together, Roberta tilting back her chair as she smoked and J. laughing at something she'd said, had caused Helen to feel a ridiculous shame. It was nothing she would ever understand, how two women could be so unnaturally satisfied with each other. Their voices stopped and started, the porch light a fat yellow globe in the dark. Helen brushed the bugs off the back of her neck, wondering spitefully who of the two of them played the man and who the woman.

The next morning Gar looked at Helen in the mirror as he dabbed calamine lotion on the poison ivy rash up the side of his neck. She was brushing her hair, then she ran her hands flat back, temples bared, and coiled it in one quick motion before snapping the clip into place. It was going to be strawberry blond today, he could see on the styrofoam head behind her, loose curls with a poufed-up top. "Where'd you go last night?"

"Over toward J.'s. They were out on the porch."

"You talk to them?"

"No, just spied on their boring conversation."

Gar grinned at the mirror, tipping more lotion onto his fingers. Helen couldn't figure his sister out. Maybe J. and Roberta *did* smooch it up between the sheets, like Helen said, though J. was such a buttoned-up old biddy, or used to be. Hell, maybe it had turned out to be men, not sex, she couldn't abide. Even when she was engaged and had surely done more than just *kiss* the man, she had stiffened all over to talk about it, the two of them getting sick drunk out in the stables with that bunged-up quarter horse, J.'s face white from more than just the schnapps they were drinking. Hell, he had told her, it didn't *look* like it hurt them. "Trying to catch them in the act?"

"Don't be ridiculous."

"J.'s done worse."

"The only thing worse is bald-faced adultery and your father would've taken care of that, killing that doctor as good as a chastity belt for J. around these parts."

"I wasn't talking about around here."

"Damn it, you know if it's something J. did, you would have told me long before now."

"You were there, sugar pie." Gar buttoned his collar. "I didn't think I had to tell you."

One of those days she would really kill him, kill them all. Helen set the wig then pulled the blouse over her head, the fake silk slipping along her lifted arms. The whole self-satisfied bunch of them had imaginations coming out of their ears, taking any little thing and blowing it up into life and death but blinking an oh so discreet eye when it came to something that might be real. Like her conceited father-in-law leaning up against her on the empty front porch of the river house, hard as a fist, saying she probably liked it like that, standing up, fast, no mussing her hair any, his hips moving a little with his whispered words. She had been too young to say a thing back, though not so young to show him more than her blank face. Eyes looking over his shoulder and mouth set still, she had waited for him to stop doing all that and go away again.

Helen rubbed her face, her palms pushing up the skin of her cheeks, loose and wrinkled. Her fingertips smoothed the wispy bits of her eyebrows along that high arch of bone. Only the eyes themselves, the iris a starburst of stony gray-blue, were unchanged when she looked in the mirror. Gar was gone, rumbling the sliding door back and going down the hall toward the kitchen. When Helen tried to tell her what happened on the porch, J. had put the baby up on her shoulder and walked, saying finally, "He just wants to scare you, is all." She had looked godawful in the heat and that dress she always wore. "You don't show him anything but that face of yours, like something off a Greek statue, and it makes him mad that you're not scared of what might happen." Helen had smiled a little, adjusting her skirt across her knees, and said, "You think I'm not scared?" And J. laughed as she bounced the baby, her eyes shrewd on Helen's face before she turned and said, "You'd be a fool not to be."

Helen flung the bedcovers up and swiped at the face powder spilled on the bureau, kicking shoes into the closet. Her housework had been reduced to essentials ever since she had come to the brilliant realization that grime unseen wasn't grime but patina, keeping up only a random sort of sterility in the kitchen when she cooked. Sailing in for a cup of Gar's peculiar boiled coffee he made by throwing grounds and water into a pot, Helen saw Elise standing on a chair as she poured cinnamon sugar onto her toast. "Your Nana doesn't feed you, darling?"

"It's my second breakfast." Elise was endlessly matter-of-fact. She took all the pleasure out of Helen's sarcasm without knowing she did it, which made it twice as maddening as Gar's pretending not to hear.

"How nice. Some children in China have no breakfast at all, of course." Helen tipped the pot slowly so the grounds wouldn't swirl up, the coffee spitting at the rim.

Elise had no idea who those children in China were, but it seemed like they never ate or only wanted the food left on her plate. That wasn't very practical, China being at the bottom of the world, wherever that was. Now here she was voluntarily *eating* something and Aunt Helen wanted her to send it to China too. Elise squatted in the chair and patted at the cinnamon sugar, a sticky brown from the melted butter, wondering what she was supposed to do. Uncle Gar reached over her head to cut the toast into crooked triangles and put them on a plate. "Here," he said, giving Aunt Helen a look.

Helen shrugged, sitting down with her coffee and the carton of cream. Elise was not a beautiful child but striking, with those thin shoulders under the T-shirt and the wide jaw, wideset eyes. Her bladelike cheekbones always had a blur of sweat in the hollows right beneath the eyes. Children were so impossibly *miniature*, like horribly mobile toys, miracles of engineering. "How's the pansy?" she said.

Elise chewed her toast. The pansy, troweled up out of the bed and dumped into a plastic pot as if Aunt Helen had been cutting cake without thinking about it, had died or, as Nana said following her out to the porch, drowned. Elise wished Aunt Helen would stop reminding her about it. "Fine," she said after a minute.

Sipping her coffee, Helen certainly didn't know why the child got so quiet. She never would understand what Gar found to say to Elise when they talked outside in the middle of the day. "To get hair curly as yours, I had to wind it up around old stockings and tie them in knots." Helen caught Gar's eye and glared.

Elise looked at Aunt Helen's hair, big floppy-looking curls bright as a penny. "I like your hair," she said and wondered why Uncle Gar was laughing, then he shoved back his chair as Aunt Helen gave *him* a look and went out. The screen door smacked behind him as he picked up the dish off the back stoop to go feed the dogs. It was Nana, really, afraid of the big gray dogs, not her.

"Thank you, darling." Helen smoothed her hand down the back of her neck. Elise. solid enough at the kitchen table, seemed depressingly ephemeral.

"A girl in kindergarten," Elise said, "has hair longer than *mine*. She has the longest hair of anybody."

"Is she stuck-up about it?" Helen folded the cream carton shut.

240

Elise smiled, surprised and giggly that Aunt Helen had said something like a kid, especially because it was what she, Elise, had already been thinking. Still smiling hard, eyes on her plate, Elise nodded. "Sort of stuck-up."

"Everybody except your Uncle Gar thought I was stuck-up." Helen wondered what on earth she was saying, whether senility started like that. "Gar was the only one to like me even though I was beautiful. What do you think of *that?*"

Elise was astonished because the beautiful girls in kindergarten had other little girls following them around and saving the swing for them and the boys running up and hitting them on the back. She didn't know how to politely tell Aunt Helen she was all wrong so she just widened her eyes a little and licked her finger to pick up the sugar spilled on her plate.

"Don't think much, do you." Helen stood up and clattered her cup in the sink then poked her finger into the dirt of an African violet. Getting a little dry. Her kitchen was darker than J.'s, with windows only on one side and ivy-covered to boot. Helen had always liked massive food projects, canning or making fruitcake, better than piddly meals, day in and day out, water torture. Through the screen door out to the yard, she could see Gar with the dogs, already done with eating. He shouldn't let them bolt their food.

Elise swung her legs. Aunt Helen's house was awfully dirty. When Elise was younger, she had played in the front rooms by dusting all the things on the tables, painted china ladies and glass bowls and little spoons. The dust was like gray fur, like the kitten living under Nana's house. She put her elbows on the table.

"You want to leave, leave." Helen slapped the dishrag along the light blue tile and tossed it in the sink. It wasn't up to her to entertain the child, slow as molasses. How J. stood it she'd never know.

Elise slid down from the chair and went to the screen door then stopped. They were still out there. One of them had its tongue out with a long string of drool coming down and she could see the teeth and the ripply flaps of skin beside them.

When Uncle Gar clapped his hands at them, they crouched down on their stiff legs then jumped. She fingered the latch.

"For heaven's sake." Helen moved Elise over and opened the door. "Gar, would you kindly put them in the shed so this child can come outside and play?" He moved so heavy these days. She could remember him wrestling with the dogs when they were half-grown pups, still gangly legged, hoisting them up off the ground with their jaws clamped around an old piece of broom-stick. He wasn't all that tall but pretty well built. "*Gar!* Do you hear me?"

Uncle Gar waved his hand, yeah, yeah, and started to walk away. Elise winced. She didn't want them *fighting* about it. She glanced up at Aunt Helen, who was biting the side of her thumb and stopped when she saw Elise watching.

"He wasn't much to look at until he smiled," Helen said, thinking idly you might say the same thing about Elise, who was looking out the screen door again. "Those eyebrows too straight or something, the chin too narrow. But then all of a sudden there would flash that smart-aleck grin and he looked wonderful. That so-called boyish charm. We partied with people half our age."

"Nana didn't go to parties, she says."

"Well, she had babies." Helen picked dirt out from around the light switch with her fingernail. J. also had had a husband who would drink a thimbleful of whiskey and fall flat on his handsome face, as well as in other places, Helen could only conclude. Gar said J. went home to their mother about six months after she was married but got kicked right back out, no sympathy there. Helen had lain in bed, her head on Gar's shoulder, listening to him talk. "I never felt so sorry for anyone in my life," he said.

"I like birthday parties." Elise thought it seemed like a really long time since she had had a birthday. Laura had wanted some of her presents and had cried when Elise jerked them back. She craned her neck slightly and looked across the bright grass out-side. Well, they *had* been hers.

"I hated them." Helen opened the screen door, waving at the heat already rising off the steps. "There's Gar," she said. One of

242

her young Czech uncles had been a photographer, a portrait-maker. Every birthday he posed her and took pictures, with and without her clothes, allegorical shots. He labeled them *Venus* and *Innocence* and *Ophelia*. Some were even bought years and years later by a New York museum—*Pictorialist* photography, beauty and art. All she remembered was the air on her naked skin, frightened by the terrible space around her as she held one pose and then another. And her uncle not seeing little Helena Haveliček anymore but the Muse of History or Ariel or some insipid Cupid with a cardboard bow.

Elise hopped down the steps, her sandals clacking on the concrete. Aunt Helen made her nervous. She seemed to eat Elise up with her eyes sometimes. Elise ran to catch up with Uncle Gar, who was already halfway across the yard with his pruning shears.

Helen put her hands on her hips and sighed. The freezer needed defrosting, but Gar would have to get the cooler in and got to town for a little dry ice. They had held lawn parties during the twenties and through Prohibition, her homemade beer some of the best in town, an old Czech recipe from another uncle. No one ever drank that much, though, already wild just with being young or as wild as the place would let them be. To think she had felt old *then*, watching those girls cut their hair and then their hemlines—into her thirties, the grande dame, the mysterious and beautiful older woman with the faint Central European accent. Helen walked through the shadowy dining room to the front parlor, the sunlight cut by awnings, forsythia waving just outside the windows and zinnias a flash of color in the big beds bordering the lawn. "We are too old for this," she had said to Gar, but she was the one. She remembered leaning up to the mirror, carefully drawing the thin line of her eyebrows in, her mouth half open, hair swept up, and Gar looking at her from the dark, just looking, not wanting to say again how she was so beautiful it made him want to die.

Helen ran her finger along the carved back of a loveseat and looked at it then went to get a dustcloth. The first time Gar ran his hand down her back and it didn't arouse her, she had not worried, rolling over and lifting her face in a kind of mindless reflex. She noticed, though, how peculiar the sex was, practiced and familiar, obviously *steps*. This was after the war; she was twenty-eight. Automatic reflex carried her along even though she was thinking the whole time *now he will do that and I will turn that way and then and then*. She even found it briefly amusing.

Every time after that, though, made her irritable, wildly put out with Gar. Just the feel of her skin sticking against his was enough to make her want to scream. Helen flicked the cloth at the Dresden china lined up on a shelf then blew from behind them a cloud of dust, jerking her head back. That was the trouble with things. They required attention even when the sight of them bored her to tears. She didn't know how, when she was still fairly young, relations with her own husband had developed that same attenuated boredom.

The most exasperating thing was knowing it had nothing to do with love. She had told Gar that, years later as they sat barefoot in the kitchen, the night feeling old and black outside the open door where not a breath of air was moving. "Darling, it has nothing to do with love," she had said. Looking at him, a man already getting just a little jowly, his stomach loose, had made her atrociously sentimental. He had grinned back suddenly, dragged her out of the chair, and two-stepped her toward the hallway. When he started to kiss her on the neck, she had jerked away, mad enough to spit. He was dumb as dirt, poor Gar. Helen took a layer of dust off the shelf, refolded the cloth, and wiped again.

No one used that tiresome room. Helen moved the china along the shelf, pieces chinking lightly against each other. The cruelest trick was all those years when she felt so wild she would have lain flat on her back for the damn postman or any one of a dozen remembered suitors, but Gar, the sight of Gar for some reason . . . Helen walked to the next table. A goddam charade, marriage. She whipped the dustcloth along the tops of the picture frames, then briskly down, across, and up inside, demarcating her mother, Gar's mother, J.'s boys when they were young, her wedding picture, Gar's grandfather looking like an Old Tes-

244

tament prophet. She heard the sprinkler go on outside, the whistling jet starting to click around.

She and J. had fought like cats those years, after the Crash a bad time for everyone. J. with her holier-than-thou simper nearly drove Helen nuts, knowing J.'s marriage didn't have any love to it and hadn't for a while. Helen didn't quibble. "I love Gar like my dearest friend," she said to J., "but I can't stand him to touch me." J. kept on scrubbing the top of the stove. "You've got a duty," she finally said. "Uh huh," Helen shook her head, turning the glass full of spoons so it caught the light, "not me." J. didn't turn around. "You're unnatural," she had said at the stove.

Unnatural. *Unnatural.* Helen ran the dustcloth over the little secretary stuck in the corner. J. should talk. At least Helen had been hungry for the proper sex, that of the male persuasion. She didn't know why she hadn't had a dozen affairs, still a beautiful woman even at forty, thin, so the inevitable sagging and loss didn't show as much. Standing in the dim parlor, she was ready to scream at the incessant stupidity of dust, motes hanging in the flat little wedge of sunlight at the corner of the window. She looked out across the lawn.

The daydreams for years just wouldn't let up, this man or that man, niggling sort of thoughts. She could be anywhere, putting up tomato relish, driving to town, talking after church, and some damn sexual *thought* would flash, just a thought, and it would be like a knife inside. She'd have to catch her breath, sometimes sit down. Nothing but want, want, want, want, want. Helen rapped her knuckle on the glass and watched the mud dauber clinging to the nest up under the awning zoom off, legs dangling. She'd never imagined such a thing. Wanting beauty was simple and pure compared to the thick knots of that other desire. The Parisian "New Look" had been all the rage, big bouffant swirling skirts and tiny waists, everyone suddenly a southern belle.

Why she didn't just go crazy, she would never know. It was not just the sharp liquid *wanting* but its dull disappearance as soon as Gar rolled over in bed then touched her shoulder. His palm would shift, if he met no resistance, to her breast before he heaved himself up onto one elbow and leaned over her, watchful, smiling. It broke her heart. Nothing she'd done seemed bad enough to merit that swift erasure of all desire. Her life at those moments would shrink to nothing, to worse than nothing. The flowered sheets, the faraway ceiling, the smudged lines of the room's corner, even Gar, all had faded or leached out to a horrible sort of simulacrum. She hadn't wanted to live. At those moments she hadn't been able to imagine even the lubricious daydreams coming back. Cool and remote, her body was no longer her own. It might never have been her own.

She could sneer at J. all she liked, and she no doubt had, but guilt had definitely been there, too. Helen took an embroidered pillow off the loveseat and slapped it lightly against the side, watching dust puff out. Not out of some squenched-up sense of duty but because Gar was who he was—both patient and completely irresponsible, a man who could dance like a dream, the love of her life. Helen held the pillow to her stomach. Still, love hadn't made the detestable performance she would finally put on for Gar's sake anything more than what it was. Sex always turned out to be worse than refusing, which was why she sometimes thought she did it, huffing and bumping away in that abominable bed, paying in spades for whatever sin she must have committed to bring on herself this irreversible impotence. Helen bent forward and ran her thumb over the dimpled wood of the chest where some child had smashed a toy down over and over in the moronic way of children. Pride maybe, daring to *want* something, thinking she deserved to have it. Damned if she could figure it out.

Helen tossed the pillow back on the loveseat. She touched the folds of skin at her neck, oddly like silk, then rubbed her shoulder through the blouse. The incremental slippages into old age had eventually amused her as she played with her new loose face in the mirror. Pulling the skin up at her temples made her cheekbones appear, smooth and radiant, then vanish, or she would lift her forehead higher, eyebrows arched in acute astonishment and eyes suddenly prominent, only to sink back, hooded again, as she moved her hands. Sexual feeling had trickled back the older she got, the less gripped by uncontrollable want. Helen closed her eyes, wondering where Gar could have gone to, wishing he would waltz in with a roll of ten-dollar bills from some wild bet on a schizy horse no one else trusted to run a straight line. Instead it would probably be some other nugget of six-year-old wit or else a story he had just remembered that happened fifty years ago. There were moments when she positively hated Gar.

Later that day, leaving Roberta's shop, Helen blinked in the sudden onslaught of afternoon sun, disorienting after the cool dark inside. She knew Roberta was watching. Squinting a little, she set off walking as if she had someplace to go, thinking maybe she should stop in somewhere for a Coca-Cola, to catch her breath. There was a little coffee shop just opposite the courthouse, part of the old Melrose Hotel, no more than two blocks away.

She hadn't gone in there to fight with Roberta or even to say half the things she said. Words just popped out of her mouth those days. It had to be Gar's fault, dredging up the past like nothing in the present day mattered a twig. He wanted old stories? She could tell a few. Starting with his overbearing father she had heard plenty about, before she met him, enough to know she wouldn't give him an inch of satisfaction. He was so cocksure of his own opinion. "Aren't you a little *old* for that boy?" he had said. "Could be he's getting some used goods, though I'd hate to think it, you know that, don't you." No one else was in the living room, cool and dark at the back of the river house, Gar sent out on some fool's errand. When he pinched her, it hadn't been like what you'd get standing in a crowd of happy drunks. Helen had come to the coffee shop door and pushed it open. Only a few people there, two blue-rinsed ladies eating pie in the back and Cy Hodgens nursing a cup of coffee, a couple of teenagers elbowing each other in a booth. Helen set her purse neatly down and sat on a stool at the counter, crossing her legs. No, he had put his whole palm on her breast and pushed up a little, his fingers drifting around, all the time watching her face. "Anybody done *that* to you, girl?"

"Yes ma'am. What can I get you?"

Helen frowned at the man in the apron and cap. "I guess I would like just a Coca-Cola with ice. Could you maybe put a little squirt of that chocolate you got in the bottom of the glass?"

"Yes ma'am. Coming right up."

It had crossed her mind at the time to say that Gar had done "that," and he had by then, and more, but instead she had just looked at her future father-in-law and said not a damn thing. That was when the pinch came, hard enough to hurt. She could tell Gar about that—wouldn't that be a hoot. Nothing he could pass on to a six-year-old, though Gar might not be making those distinctions. J. was blaming *her* for what Elise was hearing when Helen wasn't there. She didn't have a lock for Gar's fool mouth.

The Coca-Cola came, poured over cracked ice, extra sweet as she pulled on the straw stuck down in the syrup at the bottom. She glanced out the window at the courthouse across the way, the old one they still used for offices and whatnot, whitish-yellow stone. The gossipy old men were all in place on the benches set out under the trees. They had had a field day when Jack got his nose out of joint and went and killed that Chicago businessman. Some old busybody had even called Helen at home. She had strolled out, down the front walk, and across to J.'s, who had changed her dress and was ringing up Martin at college, Todd already driving in from whatever canvassing job he was doing for the state. "You want to find Gar?" she said to Helen, who didn't particularly. She had tried the little old shipping office where he and his daddy brokered pecans and that was about the best she could do. "Momma's by herself," J. said next, still holding the phone.

Helen patted her mouth with the paper napkin. Gar was taking after his momma, that way he had started fading away, sometimes right before her very eyes, damn him. Helen didn't make life as hard as his daddy must have made it for her, the poor thing. Gar was like his momma in a dozen ways. Helen stirred her straw in the slushy ice.

As full of himself as he was, even Jack wasn't going to let slip to his sweet little wife what he had in mind for his daughter-in-law. A sly man, his tongue squirting in between her teeth fast as you please, any six people watching, her bridal veil falling out of its pins so she reached up to catch it and then his tongue was as quickly gone. "Daughter," he had said, grinning away. He hadn't been drunk in the least. The Coca-Cola was maybe too sweet or too cold. Helen pushed it away. She had never once in her life shed a tear in a public place, and she sure as hell wasn't going to start now. Roberta, she knew, wouldn't say a word. He was dead anyhow and had been for years.

Helen looked out the window. The bastard never even went to trial. The lawyer kept talking *senility* defense, then Jack up and died, to everyone's relief. They could see how crazy he was, petulant, strutting around the house. Like it was that poor man's fault he had come down from Chicago at all and ended up dead in a hot little office off the courthouse square of some two-bit town. The newspapers said Jack had struggled when they tried to take the gun then suddenly let it go. "Well," he had said, "you can have it then." Eyes like plastic buttons as he pushed himself back up off of her. The courthouse trees fluttered a little in the afternoon sun then drooped again. When Helen looked back at the counter, everything had darkened a sickly gray. It was obvious she should have worn a hat.

Elise should also watch herself. Helen had seen the tops of her bony shoulders burned red as she squatted down in the vegetable garden, pulling up the little strings of carrots that Helen pointed to, thinning them out. She didn't love the child, but that probably didn't matter. Love was iffy, not a thing you guaranteed, even to children, even children of your own. She had been lavishly admired by her second-generation immigrant family but not really coddled or catered to. Elise was cold-blooded in the same sort of way, standoffish, not demonstrably affectionate. J. and Roberta didn't mind, God knew why, to have a cuckoo appear in their peculiar love nest. Helen rapped on the counter for her check. Gar could hardly be seduced away by a little girl as aloof as Helen herself. She rapped again, knocking the half-full glass so it rocked slightly around. The place was a mausoleum. She'd heard the hotel let prostitutes in.

Roberta treated her sometimes like a child or a lunatic, soothing her down. Helen counted out the change after peering at the check then added a nickel tip. That interminably accepting silence of Roberta's was what made Helen say the things she did. Every minute Gar was over in France, even though he hardly saw a morsel of fighting, she had thought how she would die if he was killed. Maybe it would have been better that way, though she knew that was a bunch of romantic bull. Helen clacked her heels across the tile floor, irritated. If we're going to be *conventional*, she thought, shoving at the door, then why not say love died when I lost my damn looks, whenever that was, twenty years ago. The heat came up from the sidewalk in a wave, and she wondered where she had parked the car.

Still, Gar had been waiting for her at the other side of that endless impotence—a patient man, his father less so or not at all. Walking in her back door, Jack had looked scrawny and old. Still so damn sure of himself, though his chin quavered and his walk was stiff. Gar had gone off that morning to call on some big buyer down in the nearest city. Standing there, Jack had smiled a little, looking around the room. Helen was having trouble seeing in the sunlight, although she had remembered the bank and the big Chevy by then, one tire up on the curb, probably blazing inside, a virtual oven, roof baking unshaded in the street. She stepped off a curb, nearly turning her ankle, and walked across against the red light.

"Let's go," he had said, taking her arm and walking toward the bedrooms, as if there wouldn't be any questions, natural as could be. Hell, he probably *was* as crazy as she called him, snatching at her arms as she pulled back, his fingers tightening, strong for a man who was going on seventy. That smile never changed except when she picked up the candlestick off the table as he hauled her along. His mouth had tightened as he cracked her knuckles against the sliding door and she let it go. Helen stopped in the shade, catching her breath. Her heart was pounding like a drum and her mouth felt sticky sweet. She had let him do it. Twenty years younger, strong from gardening or two-stepping all night across some sawdust floor, she could have not. Helen knew it. Turning to walk on, she caught her reflection in the beauty shop window and looked again. An old woman in an untucked blouse, hair askew, all her dark-reflected features sagging. She touched the square post beside her then walked on and touched the next one.

He had made little satisfied grunts each time he found what he wanted under her clothes, like he was making some damn anatomical inventory or other, and then he had undone his pants. He had felt small and about half soft, scooping himself inside, hardening a little as he worked his hips. He had stared down at her, cocky and triumphant, catching her chin once when she turned her head. It didn't last long—a louder grunt or two and then he was pushing himself off and out. Standing there with his shirttails around his skinny thighs, he held himself for a minute and then bent briskly to pull up his pants. Helen pushed her skirt down as she sat up. Jack had smoothed his hair and mustache in the mirror, glanced at her once, and walked out the door.

Helen was at the corner and there down the street was the bank, granite and glass, a couple of pillars. The Chevy up on the curb looked drunk. She waited for a car to pass then started across the street. She should have stayed home instead of giving herself this grief, the sun hot on her head. She fumbled in her purse for the keys. She had told herself she let him do it so he would finally leave her alone for good and all, but that wasn't why. No, she had let him do whatever it was he wanted because she probably deserved to have it happen. Because she had firm-looking breasts and satinlike skin and a cool, classic, fine-boned face and had spent ten years not sleeping with Gar. Because they could damn well have it, might as well, it wasn't hers. The key was stiff in the door then it clicked open and a tidal wave of heat poured out to hang there beating against her face.

Gar walked up the dark back lawn, the crickets all around him like a high-pitched pulse, intercut by the harsh rattle of two cicadas clinging in the trees. He could barely remember the house he'd been born in, a stark wooden frame house closer in to town with a dusty yard, a little front porch. Sis remembered more. It had been torn down for a gas station, then a conve-

251

nience mart. Moving to the big house back of the river should have been like going to paradise, but everything had got tied up with his daddy and what his daddy had done when Gar was a baby. His mother had been distracted, weepy—he remembered *that*—putting things in boxes as if she didn't care where they fell.

A light was on in the back room off the kitchen, but Gar eased the door open just in case Helen had gone to bed. Looking from the kitchen, he could see the dogs in the dim lamplight, stretched out on their specially built beds, legs sticking in the air half crooked, asleep, too deaf or too used to his step to wake themselves up. Helen was watching him from an armchair and Gar jumped on a guilty reflex then half grinned at his own reaction. She'd been snappish lately, even for Helen, restless, jumping from subject to subject like a flea. "Want a little toddy?" Gar said.

"You know if you drink after eight, it gives you heartburn." Helen pushed her fingers through her hair and looked down the length of her cotton nightgown, her bare feet with their thick blue veins set up on the leather hassock. "We aren't as young as we were."

Getting down glasses in the dark kitchen, Gar sighed and took the bourbon from under the sink. He tipped the bottle expertly so a single glug went into each glass, his stomach twinging slightly in anticipation. She didn't used to nag. The room looked cozy in the yellow light, the dogs asleep, his wife stretched out in her chair. He handed her a glass. "J. and I drank the most godawful stuff. Sweet liqueurs. Anything with mint."

"Shoot, you talk to J. and it's like she never tippled a single ounce." Helen looked at the bourbon in the bottom of her glass. "Told me once I must want to be a man. My bad language or some damn thing. Maybe those trousers I gardened in, who the hell knew."

Gar grunted, sitting on the edge of the sofa, elbows on his spread knees, only half listening. Too bad that racehorse came up lame. Put to stud, he'd sired some good-looking colts and that one black filly Gar thought could have been a serious contender, no one expecting such flat-out speed from a filly. He'd liked the country tracks, the men standing around spitting and talking and the riders like carny workers, small and wiry, but especially the horses, nervous and dumb but gorgeous, rocketing off, haunches bunched, then pounding out of the dust, heads lunged forward as they ran.

". . . go to war to be a man. Instead *we* did it. Those of us who would. Didn't have to kill anybody either."

"Did what." Gar looked at Helen, her breasts slumped sideways loose under the nightgown, elbows winged out across the arms of the chair. He sometimes thought he'd shrunk as he got old while she just got taller and skinnier.

"The things men do. It was like night and day, Gar. The way I was before you went to France and when you came back."

"That right?" Gar had hated the army, France, the war, half the time sick. He didn't think about it. Helen hadn't struck him as any different, still pretty much the young blushing bride. It was odd how that time seemed so far back it might not have ever happened, while the things that took place when he was barely walking came to him clearer than yesterday's conversations. He had talked for a while with Elise, he remembered. About Aunt Nellie. Godalmighty, she had hated his daddy. Gar grinned and sipped his drink. She made no bones about it at all.

Helen grimaced, staring at the pictures on the walls. Gar could be dead and stuffed and propped up on the damn sofa for all he was listening to her. Those hard-drinking parties after the war. She'd never said it to Gar, but she had felt it coming off of them, the men, the ones who went to war and the ones who didn't. They hated her and all the younger women with their brand-new jobs and their bobbed-off hair. It was like a little frenzy of hate no one ever talked about. There weren't so many men after the war, and none of them knew what the hell to do. "I put up with you," Helen said.

"You sure did." Gar hoped she wasn't going to start.

"And it may not seem like much consolation either, but I was faithful, damn it. I never once left you, Gar, never once, you hear me?" Helen didn't even like bourbon, the way it made her head buzz. The lamplight seemed to get bright and dark inside the room. The dogs slept.

253

Gar took a swallow. Faithful, unfaithful, he didn't know. His daddy had no business shooting the man. It was Nellie's concern. As Helen was his, and his daddy should have stayed out of *that* as well. Gar had eyes. He had just left it to Helen, even at nineteen a goddam daunting woman. Could be he had left too much to Helen, but how was anyone to know at the time. You reach a point where everything you say is said too late. Something about her had always scared him but never the thought that she might up and leave. Didn't make any sense but it was true.

"So do me the favor," Helen said from across the room, "of not leaving me now."

Gar glanced at her and rubbed his leg. "I'm not going anywhere."

"You're going somewhere, Gar. Every damn day. Bit by bit."

Gar didn't know what Helen was talking about. He hardly even went to town anymore. It was too hard remembering where little things were, streets and stores and what have you. Even that walk back to the old house was getting longer. He'd forget sometimes what it looked like now, all falling down. Talking to Helen was more and more like talking to little Elise. Hell, he was here, wasn't he. "I'm here," he said.

Helen looked at him. He was a thick old man with white hair and a smile she still could see on occasion break out of his jowly sunburned face with a flash of something, the younger Gar. He could still hold a glass with savoir faire, life's little mercies. She put down her own drink and sat up, reaching one arm around his neck. He felt stiff, shifting around toward her, stiff and unyielding, cut out of wood. "Damn it," she said, "don't you die on me, Gar."

Gar still didn't know what she was talking about. "Nobody's going to die," he said.

Helen touched the bristling ends of his hair. He didn't know the first thing about making a living, but the man definitely had the patience of Job. She let her hand slide around to his cheek. "Everybody dies," she said.

THIRTEEN

Fire II

1996

I WATCHED THE NIGHT TURN SLOWLY TO GRAY, MY FOOT PRESS-
ing the accelerator, dawn starting to light up my hands tensed
on the wheel, slick with sweat. My hand still shook when I
leaned across to touch briefly Lucy's arm, who was pretending to
sleep or maybe by now slept in earnest. I had touched her fifty
times or more since we left the border just after midnight, the
stinking shanties and a long flat road of barking dogs, the hallu-
cinatory smell of smoke in the car, as if we packed charred wood
in the back, smoky and wet, a macabre souvenir. Now that I
was ready to think about it, nothing came, the cursor a patient
blink in the corner, then I suddenly saw Lucy turn again in the
border guard's grip, legs a brief white flash in the lights. Even
the pattern of one random sequence cuing another quickly collapsed, the algorithm much too simple: Elise Loves Nick, or

simpler yet, Elise + Nick, equals nothing, equals *nada*. I had almost lost my sister's child, but my DMV record and passport stamps didn't say anything about Bolivian thugs, about illicit test fields across the border. There was only the lightly pulsing gray of dawn, of thought erased, of nothingness. I hadn't had a thought since I heard the man in the freezing office say Nick's name, and I wondered now if my punishment would be to never link two thoughts again, only to see the separate trees, clumps of black just off the road, stunted, thirsty, bits of data.

Lost in the welter of file names and data I kept in my head was that four-letter word, Nick, a man who had been an anomaly probably from the day he was born, creating himself over and over but never losing his Christian name. I hardly wondered, then or now, why a drug-lord minion should know his name, only why I tried to see him, the elevator with its one glass side falling down an outside shaft, the town below pricking with lights. Even Lucy could be predictable, or Laura could guess what her daughter might do. I had been the one remiss, as if the predictable didn't matter, nor Carlos, laughing back at me with one hand moving her track shorts down her skinny hips, the T-shirt folded up on her chest, rumpling its death-band skinhead logo. I should have known better. I should have expected the predictable, that being all you had, the only determination of deviance.

Masculinity itself was deviance, the genetic gates flubbed or missed. Lucy was born red and waxy, long for her weight, Milos holding her high against his green-gowned chest and Laura laughing. Three weeks later Hollis came off from the curtain call, white as a sheet, and went to change the blood-soaked pad, Milos gripping her by the wrist, yelling at her to see a doctor. The simple one-cell organisms were never that simple to engineer, though cloning the suckers got easier to do. Nick would come to the brokerage lab without invitation, ghosting in at 3 A.M. after circumventing two locked doors, high as a kite, talking away. I was not amused. I was not seduced. Quoting reams and reams of Blake, Nick was a man ahead of his time, and now he was dead, four years before the millennium he had always thought would crack things open, though maybe the worst had come and gone and no one, looking up, had noticed. Driving into the pearly light, I gave up knowing what was true.

Truth and beauty, two pillars of philosophy and modern science had a newborn charm, the thought of something that clear and absent, all the theories with high-tech elegance, built for speed, not like the secondhand Fiats I drove. Lucy already wanted to drive, an expressed desire so patently dumb Laura and I just rolled our eyes, half the time in silent agreement, other times less evenly matched. I remained bemused by my sister's fierce compensatory wish to *do* for Lucy, to make the world implausibly fair, driven by lingering memories from childhood of what Laura deemed deprivations—refrigerated water in a paper cup instead of Kool-Aid, a surrogate Barbie with painted-on shoes. It had all the comic earmarks of a reaction to the Great Depression, except that Laura was a generation off, and none of us had a hope in hell of duplicating our parents' success. "You'd have to quit your research, maybe even for a couple of years," Laura said, trying to impress on me what guardianship of Lucy entailed. I had shrugged and said only it sounded extreme, her self-righteous attitude making me reckless, cooler toward Lucy than I would have been, her head buried in my wadded-up jacket, one arm moving with the bumps of the car. She looked much younger than twelve when she slept, having inherited Laura's hair, her daddy's angled, stubborn jaw.

Milos, in his ineffable way, ten years ago had charmed a grant from some state Russian studies program, gone six months to a postal address somewhere in London, then Leningrad. He showed back up with a suitcase full of smuggled art—Ukranian paintings, a primitive folk art heavily Cubist, wild like Milos, who didn't belong with a cranky two-year-old and a wife. Hollis had climbed out of his car drawn up in the lot behind the bar, already dressed to do her set, her black hair ruffled, mouth in a grin. Lucy, in love with her dashing father, now labored under the mistaken impression that she was in love with Carlos as well. I had never seen the resemblance before between Milos and Carlos but it was there—the mad black eyes, unruly hair, their restless need to make things happen, to stir things up, to make things move.

During the police interrogation, nothing had moved, not even time. I told them I had stopped because I'd heard through the grapevine Nick was around and had seen the fire, it had been ten years, I had taken Lucy across the border looking for birds, the drought's effect on migration paths. I kept on lying help-lessly, glibly, wondering what Lucy was saying to them in the other room, if she was scared. Only later, climbing back into the car, did I learn from her that she had kept saying she didn't know, playing dumb, both of us wondering at the time if what we did would put the other in jail, Lucy with God knew what in her urine, the lights stark white in the tiny room. I was suddenly crying, hands gripped tight on the steering wheel, crying for the very first time that night, and then just as abruptly I stopped. The sun was a bright pink line against the horizon, rising to blue-tinged gray.

The sky had been the same pink and blue but infinitely colder when I drove away from my singular marriage, a marriage be-tween two laconic minds. Once I found myself adrift in the distant reaches of Oregon, I had looked for the same in my choice of companionship, drifting farther still, inertial force in a personal vacuum. Moving from experiments with bacteria to higher cells was more of the same, a disappearance into greater nothing. Michael and I were too much alike. Nick was alike in a different way, but Nick was dead, the likeness gone, an ab-sence palpable as the dawn, and I wiped my hands one by one on my denimed legs, playing the pedal, a coolness pouring into the car. Rita had sat on the beat-up pool table, pushed to the back in Redbone's bar, and said, "Good riddance, it's a minor miracle he even finished the play's full run," as Redbone told her to remove her ass from his fine piece of entertainment equip-ment, Sloan neatly clipping the roach and handing it across the bar to me, the empty air of four o'clock curling through the open leatherette door.

When I opened the interrogation room door, I saw Lucy on the bench in the hall, then the scratched waxy linoleum floor and the outer door with its squares of glass, the heavy, endless dark outside. I couldn't not touch her, the bones of her shoulders, the soft bits of hair at the back of her neck, Lucy shrugging away from my hand. I reached across as I drove and touched her again; she wouldn't tell. That was something I would have to do. It was a mystery to me why Laura was the only one privy to my mistakes, my fleeting fears, the one least able to take the weight, most likely to throw it back at me. I never was able to reconcile the random action of human genes with what I was certain existed as fate, except to assume that fate possessed a complexity equal to that of a cell, a system so immense that even karmic relationships had to seem casual. Laura had cried at Nana's house in a forlorn huddle of arms and legs for reasons I couldn't begin to fathom, the room around us old and musty, smelling of summer and cooking peaches; I had squatted by her side as she said, crying, that she wanted our mother. We weren't in the least alike, the overlap of our mutual friends riven with a dozen hairline faults. I couldn't remember what I thought when I heard her say she was having a baby. I must have thought that becoming our mother was taking absence perhaps too far.

Walking into the grimy stucco bungalow off an unpaved street was going too far, lightless beneath the septic smell, the beery rot of open garbage, radios playing out of the dark. After decades of patrolling a sieve, the border guards ceased to make distinctions. The Uzis and AK-47s they intercepted, according to them, were just more of the same, the likeness to war a passing one—this was not a "real" invasion. In any other country Lucy and I would have been jailed then forced to reveal just how we knew to go to that particular house in time for it to go up in flames. It was Lucy who had said Nick's name, crying as she tried to get away. The older guard standing there, patiently holding the tiny notebook, writing with his hand wrapped in a tight ball around the pen, had looked up then and asked, "Nick who?" I was already thinking up strings of lies. Rita claimed that if everyone saw how fluid ostensible reality was, how radically different the things of this world became in the passing blink of an eye, then everyone would immediately flip. "Hey, look at Nietzsche," she said, while I pointed out that scientists as a rule didn't go insane. "Because," Rita said, "they were crazy already."

My mother was briefly crazy and Nick certainly crazy and I continued to believe against the evidence that something I had done or failed to do ensured their separate insanities. Carlos, doing his meticulous bench work, could turn within moments to armed insurrection, the Bolivian executives equally mad if less flamboyant, Lucy in a separate class altogether. At sweet sixteen the world would end, or so she must have sometimes thought, despite the things we said about religious panic and media hype, the current fashions in music and art, countless explanations for the possibility of suddenly dying. I had told her that she had to stay put, that she was not to get out of the car, the top wrenched up, still makeshift, flimsy. I should have checked her into a room. I should have driven both of us home.

Rita had sounded noncommittal when I called to ask about the house she had promised to share, partly in jest. Rita, more than Laura, had always meant a coming home. She had walked from the marijuana fields, her fingers sticky, the evening hot, and said, "I was thinking of Jell-O for supper with those cute little bitty marshmallows inside," laughing as she held her hair off her neck. That grande-dame house hedged about with cottages, side yard full of weeds, was deserted now that Sloan wasn't dealing, Max on the porch with his rickety hips and the resignation of very large dogs, while Rita sprawled on the couch inside. All that was nothing like Nana's house but still at the same time exactly like it, our ongoing short-tempered conversation lacking only the creak of a swing. That sentimentality I'd now reject, preferring the end of the world as I knew it, sleek and cool and reduced to a kind of subatomic breath, a dance of nothing.

She had said something along those lines, the girl in my office with Nick's kind of eyes, Nick's way of moving, blandly indifferent to the gene-mapping project still going on. She had said it was like the effort to say the thousand upon thousand names of God and that when it was finished the meaning would vanish, the biological purpose cease, blink out, the microreality change imperceptibly into something else. "A mystic," I said, and she shook her head, not smiling, so it was left to me to laugh and take my feet off the desk and say, "Well, I'm a realist, too." I slowed the car, coming into a town, trucks outside a franchise coffee shop, lights for traffic that didn't exist. The churchgoers were trying to turn back the clock, no realists there. I had looked at Laura—they were jailing women whose newborns showed signs of prenatal drug and alcohol use, the infants shipped off to foster homes, and Laura approved—then looked at Milos who didn't care, at Rita who did, again at Laura, and for a brief moment I had wanted to cry. Lucy, awake at the change in speed, peered over the edge of the door and yawned. She shoved the jacket higher and tucked her head down, closing her eyes, Lucy, who was old enough for sex but not enough to know that when you died, you died for good.

Nick was dead. I widened my eyes, pressing the accelerator as I left the speed zone, the empty town, fields looking a shade or so greener but still not enough, the incremental cataclysms of things like drought drifting away, the scale too large. I did not believe in forces of evil, only consequence, the proteins forming that particular gene, not something else. Rita and I, stoned, had stood outside the dorm one college night in the bitter cold of a sudden norther as the windows clicked on lights or darkened. "The live ones and the dead ones," we had said, giggling, mesmerized as much by the icy blackness as by the puerile thought of random existence.

I missed at times those things—like cold, like eerie reaches of rational thought, like Nick—I once had thought I hated. I realized I was crying again and stopped, the air warming up outside, an hour or so away from home. The house hung in my mind like dust, the alleylike streets ungentrified, even all the painfully neat cottages starting at the edges to fray, the rule of old men disappearing, too many unrelated gangs. That sweet Latino strut had been swallowed up in a coming chaos much too dark, something to do with Caribbean voodoo, dealers ruthless to a cold extreme. Sloan said he had watched two crack suppliers no more than boys axe through an apartment wall as casually as

261

if they were opening a door. In the evenings we smelled the new-mown grass, heard Mexican polkas two doors down, everything fragile as a bubble of soap.

A simple cell swam with proteins, no one sure what caused the DNA to shudder and loose a gene for the RNA to replicate, the promoter/enhancer nucleotides less fathomable than the gene itself. Bacterial replication was a much more prosaic process, growing balletic higher up, that baroque beauty a thing I yearned for, the apparent social mutation of a neighborhood at least as strange. Was the mutation in the DNA or the timing/mistiming of synthesis or maybe the biochemical pathways? Was a frill misplaced? Did the replicated gene wander perhaps too far afield? Rita shrugged as she thought about the neighborhood around the house, only half joking when she grinned and said, "Who really knows? It may have been Sloan." The countryside went whipping past, pale brown fields and a dusty scent interlaced with the morning wind. Nick and that old house of his—what had he been doing out there, spooked at night by the country dark, the sex on coke weird and endless, losing any meaning it might have had. Nick would get my personal vote for a point mutation, but I wouldn't know. Genetic oncology wasn't my field.

I was a useless drama major, my parents polite with suppressed disbelief, grateful, I supposed, I hadn't resorted to the even less intellectual PE. Lucy was making a concerted effort to hide all evidence of expertise or intelligence or promise, bored with growing up. "Who is this guy?" she had said as I turned the car off the border town's drag toward the muddy river. "A friend of Daddy's?" "Once," I said, "they were in a play," the smells off the street inside the windows. Not bored enough to stay in the car, she had to go play Nancy Drew. I had fantasized about running away when I was a few years past her age, about joining the Flower Generation, taking part in the Summer of Love, too chickenshit in the end to do it. I had hated seeing Rita leave, the upper United States and Canada flattening out cold around me, the truck keys clinking in one loose hand. The door had creaked behind me as I started quickly backing out, hearing the footsteps behind the house skid in the gravel to an ominous stop, Lucy frozen in the doorway. "Get the hell out," I said.

"Get out," I had said to Carlos, slyly smiling back at me then shrugging as he stooped for the gun. Lucy swayed, her chin stuck out, her spiked hair falling across her eyes. "Get out," Laura had said to Milos, who put his head down onto his arms, shoulders so rigid we knew before it happened that the table would go smashing over, the chair on the floor. "Get out," Rita had said, her hand pulling my wrist then I was falling, sliding on my butt hard up against the front porch rail. "Get out," the histrionic Jack had supposedly said to his sister's doctor-lover, "of town by sundown." Rita was laughing as she threw the last of our stuff into the truck, the helicopters starting to whup-whup-whup out over the Indiana farmland, just like the Hueys in clips from Vietnam. "All *right*, it's time to get the hell out of Dodge." We had careened down the right of way and across a field in the summer night, young and stupid, free from harm. How was Lucy ever going to know that feeling, the bullets now for real, the bombs real bombs.

I had recognized the whispery thud of a silencer in the other room, just like the movies, the sound a different anomaly though I reacted to it exactly the same—with interest, brief exasperation, swiftly surveying the likely cause. Not the cool, loosening rush from throat to gut when imagination brought me the boy's brains flicked out across the dress of the woman sitting beside him, the stain across the doctor's belly, the kicked-back jerk of the suited man down from Chicago, all of them dead but not before my heart had quailed. Instead the fact of death in the trashed-out room had possessed a blank banality, a kind of ordinary tackiness, unremarkable, even vaguely domestic. It could be I needed the story attached, an aesthetic proportion, a balance between Nick's sudden absence and the precise duplication of memory. It might be a matter of making room. I allowed the men my great-grandfather killed to move inside, sexy and morbid and strangely witty, ever-shifting components of the larger Brueghel-like composition, something that could pass for a life, but I didn't let Nick. It was all too hard. Hollis had bent her head to my shoulder, both of us drunk, quietly singing Bessie Smith, the house where the party was out on the lake. "There's a reason," she said, "for everything, even this party, even us." Hollis was someone else left out, too good an actress perhaps to pin down. I could rationalize about her all day, but it would always be Laura keeping her out, blood that was thicker than, thicker than water, thicker than the stuff behind Nick's head. I noticed the car was pushing eighty and brought it back down. We were near the turnoff that led to the stables. Rita had watched with a vast forbearance as Hollis and I came reeling around to the porch, singing the blues to the dark. By taking what I knew about the microbe and making some tentative tests, I could maybe edge into the blinding glare of emptiness, away from the boredom of remembering.

Aunt Helen had twisted down the husks, looking for silks sufficiently brown and sticky to give away to me. "Your Uncle Gar," she said, "is on an eight-lane highway all by himself. Memory *lane*," she snorted. "There's nothing nostalgic about it at all. It's only so much empty concrete inside his damn fool head and yours." I figured I had six more months on the field-test work, wondering how much Carlos could do, how much I risked by driving back now that I was in the police computers, what the Bolivians were going to say, whether I had known what I risked when I nosed the car toward the smelly river. The girl in my office had eyes like Nick's but brown where his were chips of green, staring wide open. Thinking of her, I paused and wondered if she might finish the field test for me. I watched the road without seeing it, the sun in my eyes as it curved around.

"What about her?" I had said to Rita, watching Hollis as Lady Anne ream out Richard, Duke of Gloucester, her voice dripping with detestation, something more than the miked sound, something scary, just this side of murder. I saw the stables turnoff from the corner of my eye and decided to take it, the Fiat skidding then swooping down as it dipped from one flood gorge to another, dusty asphalt, empty of water. Lucy stirred. It was full morning now, the trees bright green in the pouring sunshine. Michael had walked down the narrow canyon as I followed behind, the walls rising above our heads threaded with an improbable green, flowering cacti and fireweed and scrub. In the spring we could even hear water move, slipping down into pools of algae. I had watched the back of Michael's head framed by limbs of juniper. I looked at Lucy looking at me, awake, not asking me where we were going. "Was Daddy there?" she had asked me from the dark of the car, and I shook my head: "He's in L.A." Lucy had turned to look outside. "Would you lie to me?" she asked next and I shook my head lightly again. "No, I promise, I just saw Nick. Nick was the only person there." An hour sooner and I would have seen the play of his smile, cool, appraising. There had been lines around his eyes. Somewhere there had to be a place he wasn't. I was beating my palms against the wheel, lightly at first, then gradually harder. I moved my foot across to the brake. Rita had smiled up at me, her eyes heavy with broken sleep. "Nick thinks he's a weapon of mass destruction." But Nick was gone and the land was empty for miles around with birds singing in the sun-drenched trees, I could hear, as the car went slowly by.

FOURTEEN

Ramona

2015

AFTER TRIPS OF A MONTH OR MORE, THE SIGHT OF ELISE AL-
ways came with a fleeting shock, as if Ramona saw her at a
distance the way a stranger might see her. Returning at night,
Ramona had in mind each time a memory of Elise that became,
as she parked the Jeep, a thought, a registering of Elise's putative
presence, the *idea* of her. Later, as she walked by some physical
trace (a hat slung onto the garden post, a cigarette pack left on
the deck), thought would spin into slight surprise, Ramona
never prepared to believe that Elise should have a life separate
from her, Ramona's, own imagining. Then with the following
morning there would be Elise herself, Elise old, the soft white
skin loose around her jaw, her eyes the same topaz color behind
her squint but her hair maybe a shade more silver. It was always
a distinct jolt, distancing.

266

This discontinuity was nothing new. Ramona had grown accustomed to the sharp distinctions, almost a matter of actual taste—salt, bitter, sour, sweet—between the different places she went. The towns were always hot, somnambulant, the proliferation of metal store signs and drab churches seeming to have more presence than the people filling the sidewalks or not, depending on the time of day. The cities at their outermost sprawl were marked by ghostlike office buildings of gold-colored glass or a smoky black, impossible to tell whether anyone used them. Next came the tight-knit neighborhoods bonded around their respective malls, everything a little shabby, crumbling, garbage-strewn. Finally there were the acutely rich or acutely poor ghettos at the imploded center, linked by a complex of gangs from skinheads up to the money lords—a feudalism at work but much harder to fathom, more easily subverted. At the other extreme were the miles of empty countryside between and around city or town, poisoned, wasted, either leached with salt from the rising oceans or blowing away, the more fragile ecosystems destroyed, the cultivated ones marginal at best, only the isolated places no one had ever much wanted worth a spit anymore.

That her father had bought up the rocky land around a small river and out beyond it would never make sense to Ramona. Country boys who went to Vietnam, and who came back embittered, bought places like that and went to live on them, or gentleman farmers—ex-stockbrokers going back to the land—but not a rootless, feather-voiced dealer in every drug you could name and more. All the other dealers put their money into inner-city real estate that would lend itself to gentrification, no one else buying acres of rock and cedar three hundred miles from the nearest city.

Ramona never knew why her father did anything he did, not least why he insisted on seeing her as she grew up, how he managed somehow to keep track of her and her mother's moves from dingy apartment to housing project to a trailer on the edge of an Army base. He walked into Ramona's life each time like a graceful cat, green eyes at a slant, mouth wide and thin, in his straightcut jeans and hand-tooled boots. He was always tender with her, a figure of clear, ineffable romance. Then came the day in her twenty-third year he was suddenly reported dead. Her mother told her, calling Ramona at the university, Tila's English still and always imperfect, the intelligence file on Nick apparently just as meticulous as he in tracking her mother's elusive whereabouts, the closest thing to next of kin they must have decided he had. The polite visits by interested federal agents had been a royal pain in the ass, but the deeds to the land from the very first had been in Ramona's name.

That Nick had been Elise's lover some ten years before was one of those stupidly implausible Dickensian coincidences that cropped up once in a blue moon—more Oedipal, in Ramona's case, than quaint nineteenth-century. She had been angry at the unconscious betrayal, while Elise had philosophically shrugged. The field work by then had been almost finished, everyone carefully cleaning up on Elise's orders, spraying the site to kill any lingering microbes, slowly drawing the perimeter inward. Half the men had been paid off and sent away, or so Carlos said. He would say anything. Under a harvest moon and in the middle of the first cold snap, coming eerily late by months, Ramona had tried to concentrate on the bookkeeping while Carlos described what screwing Elise had been like and how sexy her niece had been and his deprived existence ever since and how Ramona's fall of dark brown hair moved him to tears, her body so much like his they could be twins, soul mates—all of it heard before. But something about the familiar plywood and batting of the lab combined with the sweetness of the cold outside, smelling of smoke, and her own fury at the thought of Elise and her father in bed made Ramona stop finally and look at Carlos without speaking. Ah, he had said softly. His tent had been cold and the silky lining of the unzipped sleeping bag slick and the cot hard and Carlos, braced up on his arms as he beat against her, young and eager and endlessly erect. Panting, half smiling, he had closed his eyes in the musty-smelling dark as he came.

Ramona thought she remained separate from the hedonistic currents that had started to rise with the end of the century, remained in possession of an icy judgment. The quasi-monastic life of the university lab reinforced the illusion, Elise the only disturbing force with her guarded observation. Embracing the apparent austerities of political activism, a strategist par excellence, Ramona could reduce a dozen social variables to the vibrant space of a single equation, not seeing how outside the crowded apartments of her fellow activists those cool reductions lost their meaning. It was the field test and its guerrilla guards that had given Ramona her first taste of the subliminal, sexual thrill attending imminent obliteration at close range. Carlos, university educated, having an urbane familiarity with the guns of his colonel father's profession, seemed less than authentic, but the guards were a different matter. Ramona, contemplating the alien male prerogative for armed resistance, creative acts of terrorism (read torture), had felt that frisson of difference as she stood in the shrinking fields talking to men who shrugged and grinned at her fluid Spanish and her useless questions. "Why do you do it? What do you feel? Ambivalence? Any compassion?"

Why do you do it? she asked herself, close to twenty years later in the sun-slanted kitchen, mixing milk into the bowl of cereal grains, prodding the stuff with a spoon. The trees outside dappled the far end of the deck, otherwise baking white, planks warm. The counter was new, having been ripped out and regrouted with a stack of old tiles, creamy grays and blues, worn in waves. Her bowl rocked gently. For balance, she thought, moving her spoon. The fat conservative weight of the erstwhile baby boom, a northern gerontocracy, leaned against the rest of the world, and Ramona, in the interest of balance, would shift the fulcrum toward that aging weight. "We'll die soon enough," Elise had told her wryly, but Ramona shook her head. Not soon enough. She squinted outside, listening to the children argue over some game down under the deck, the slow chuck of someone splitting wood. If not balance within the political economy, which Ramona was willing to admit was highly unlikely, then at least a fleeting disturbance. Nothing could really be stuck in time, which, theoretical physics aside, didn't curve anywhere but ran ahead, flat and linear, enough of it to accommodate any atrocity. So it must be for imbalance then. With a fulcrum tight against the heavier weight, even random violence on the other end would be enough to upset that division of power. Balance, imbalance, it didn't really matter. Ramona leaned her hip against the kitchen counter, abandoning theory as she ate her breakfast. Years ago, standing in the patch of brilliant green surrounded by acres of dust, Ramona had stared at the killer by reputation of several men and asked, "So what is the intoxication?"

When she was sixteen her father had given her a gun, a Smith and Wesson .38 redesigned for a woman's smaller grip, her weaker wrist. Ramona had looked at the elegant little revolver, rosewood and frosted stainless steel, both clumsy and comfortable in her hand, in her lap, sliding with the loose stuff of her skirt between her legs, and wondered, as she routinely did, whether Nick and she were breaking a law. The gun had a luxurious heaviness to it. Rain spattered the Jaguar's windshield and stopped, the wind rising as a winter storm blew in. "Where'd you get the car?" she had finally asked him, pushing her hair out of her eyes.

Ramona preferred the oblique response, fishing around for the certainties she remained convinced that others possessed. More and more she came up empty, beginning with the bureaucratic wall around her father's death and continuing with Elise—neither exactly rife with answers. Seduction by anyone, much less Elise, was not a possibility Ramona had ever entertained, the envelope of her angular body something she carried with her, unregarded. Elise had teased Ramona when she complained about the lab technician who kept breaking or dropping things around her bench as if he wanted to sabotage her work, Elise swinging her foot as she sat, eying Ramona sideways, holding a plastic film in one hand. "Come on, the poor guy's fallen in love with you." Elise smiled and glanced at the film. "Which I know you don't believe for a moment, so spare me the eyes rolling up to a higher being." Ramona ignored it until the newspapers began calling her exotic, a Mata Hari. "What the hell is a Mata Hari?" she said to Elise. "Sounds like some Polynesian drink."

The screen of the sliding door leading to the deck bellied out from the kids pushing on it, and the same warm smell of pine came beating off the deck as it had through the kitchen window. The commune nowadays got along without her. Ramona had liked it best in the early years when it was only half there, the house much smaller without the addition, people drifting in for two weeks, six weeks, their tents like so many bright balloons come to rest on the strip of flat land by the river. For a month ten or twenty people would be out there terracing the vegetable garden or hammering up supports for the deck, then as if a wind had scattered them they would all be gone, only Lucky left, crouched under the spindly propellerlike blades of the windmill set at the top of the hill behind the house, her busy fingers black with grease.

Ramona had actually been half crazy, working alone out there as Elise tentatively withdrew her attentions, Ramona descending into a long-delayed depression, high half the time or else coming down, raging at Elise, raging at herself. The abrupt dissolution of the romance they had all linked with the revolution that never came provided a strange sort of freedom, her relaxation into a misery that acute perversely joyful. Ramona had enjoyed the rage, the admitting of emotional extremes and the deeply comic behavior they produced, happiest at the dumb solidity of rock bottom, the trial finished and Armageddon punted, the commune only partially there. It wasn't the dailiness of the place now that set it at one remove for her—the pot of geraniums at the door, flies buzzing, the river marked by the tops of the trees —but the absence of that all-consuming grief.

She could still be disturbed, of course, Hale alone nearly enough for a second vaulting and sustained transcendence. Her first startled look from him to Elise, when he walked outside onto the deck, had conflated in it love and hate, something Ramona would never fully pry apart when considering Hale, Hale and Elise, and inevitably Nick, Nick/Hale/herself and Elise, the one ball of wax. Hale had been afraid of the dark. Years before, Ramona had overheard Elise tell Rita how Nick would hate the nights when they lived out there. "Not enough light for him to see," she said, "to see things coming, phantoms in the dark, both of us wired on coke and paranoia." Elise

271

stopped, Ramona's throat tightening, and after a moment went on. "When I walked into that room, his eyes were open. And I thought, Christ, *Christ*, the poor fucker. He must be scared, not able to see. He must be scared out of his fucking mind." Rita had murmured something. She and Sloan still lived in the house, with two Dobermans now, the neighborhood at the edge of a war zone, bikers keeping the Jamaicans at bay, Rita the guiding spirit of an antiterrorist street-theater group, Sloan slowly dying of cancer.

The social psychosis that took over at the twentieth century's end signaled the democratization of violence, acts of terror no longer the exclusive purview of NSC cowboys, rock-and-roll stars, ghetto gangs, celluloid soldiers, right-to-lifers, preachers of doom. Ramona had built the bomb with a self-conscious artistry, placing it inside the lab like another sleekly elegant machine. Moving out past the dimly lit benches, racks of glass tubes, shielded machines, hot room, cold room, darkroom, centrifuge, dishes of lavender jelly, a dozen angles of black and gray and white as familiar as her own house, she had felt for one exhilarating moment no fear at all—not even of sudden footsteps should they echo without warning along a hall. She made no sound at all running, the quick patter of her track shoes in the empty stairwell like a brief shower of rain.

Elise told Ramona that she was indulging in a male masturbation fantasy. Lying on the floor watching Ramona test the tiny transmitter that shut off the clock, Elise had deconstructed the cult of terrorism, requiring, as it did, a wrathful god, power as dominance, choices as simply kill or be killed, sex as murder and murder as sexual, women as targets, death as ecstacy. Ramona half listened. She had seen the radical lesbians, in storm-trooper boots and ammo clips, hoot at each other, mocking the macho masculine model with pillow pregnancies under their belts. She stared at the transmitter, thinking it could be raining, it could be below zero, and carried the box off to the bathroom as she yelled back at Elise to watch the clocking device. "When everyone," Elise remarked mildly from the other room, "carries little transmitters to shut *off* the bombs, then maybe we'll have a democratized violence." Twenty-four hours later, shivering in

272

the freezing dark outside the lab as they listened to the distant shots, the faint shuddering sound of a helicopter, its search beam like a pencil of light, Ramona had smiled wildly, radiantly, back at Elise—only ten seconds left and no one inside. Dropping the transmitter, she wrapped Elise's head in her arms and kissed her hard, tongue thrust inside, just as the windows blew out on a ball of flame.

Ramona slid open the door and walked outside. Feeling the sun press hot on her head, she moved under the fluttering shade, restless, turning down the long flight of stairs. The children had gone off to play somewhere else, the shadowy underdeck empty, stacked with wood. She walked out into the pasture, kicking through the grass as she followed the slope at an angle down toward the river. Seduction had probably been inevitable; it was only a question of who seduced whom. Elise would profess innocence to the end, irritating Ramona each time she did it, her protestations on technical grounds, in the hair-splitting arena of apparent truth, simple face value—a drink after work is a drink after work is a drink, etc. Ramona fumed. Elise had been at the time an implacable authority, the person in power, still striking enough in a bored sort of way, the marbled red hair a chopped-off mess, her hands flaky and dry, gold-colored eyes, an indifferent new weight in her hips. She professed eclectic interests, perversely insisting they were never sexual, at least not at first, not entirely, the flirtation always a subordinate theme. And she never ever made the first move, instead asking questions, invasive, unanswerable questions that left her interlocutors fumbling through confessions, surprised into a state of emotional undress. Ramona ducked through the fence, wondering why no one had built a stile in all those years the fence had stood between them and the river. Her anger with Elise was old, calcified and chalky. "This is a bad idea," Elise had said one day to Ramona. It was not open to argument.

After the break with Elise, what was outside the commune had looked suddenly simple, exquisitely clean—the big interstates that buckled and broke in simple chunks, the sky an empty scrubbed blue, the towns on the outriding roads surrounded by flat fields blasted dry. The thought made Ramona heady at first with the sheer nothingness of it. Even the network of outlaw gasoline traders and dealers in bootleg arms had big simple lines out there, clean angles, elementary equations. In comparison, lacking the rationale once supplied by Elise, the half-built commune seemed void of meaning. "Hold this," Lucky had said, showing her the wrench. "In a minute I'll want you to let that go and set the socket wrench around the other bolt, no, that one," the two of them rigging the generator to run a lab Ramona no longer saw any reason for. The brute logic of the machine kept her marginally amused, preoccupied. It was only when she looked around her that the oppressive nausea started—the insipid complexity of so many stacks of lumber, mattresses, tomato flats, *things*. When she drove out the first time, following the verbal directions of a friend of a friend of Carlos', the simplicity of it all had blown her mind open, cool and empty.

As Ramona climbed along the river, sweat trickling down her back, a sheep bleated, and another, then a black-and-white dog streaked over the ridge and started down, bark choking back to a growl. Ramona waited, hands in her pockets, and after a minute Leonard sauntered into view. "Slumming?" he said cheerfully, whistling the dog back.

"Surveying the realm," Ramona said. "Handing out gold sovereigns to the peons as I pass."

Leonard laughed as she climbed up to join him, the sheep bunched around him. "I pray every day," he said, "for a deacon to come by and drive the devil out of some harmless hermit and into my sheep so I can watch them hurtle into the river, bleating and wailing and fretting the air."

"I thought they did that anyway."

"Not with wonder dog on duty. I didn't know you had graced us with a return performance. Maybe we'd like you better if you brought us presents—plastic beads, little wind-up toys, candied oranges."

Ramona didn't say anything. Leonard was like a buzzing fly, a harmless wit that no one trusted, anyone that affable and promiscuous certain to be an agent provocateur, old hippie suspicions dying hard. Leonard at least laughed at the perceived difference between the rest of the collective and her, a complete fabrication, of course, but persistent—the lady of the manor, the ironic outsider. It was as if the gingerly way they treated Elise were slowly transferring over to Ramona, not at all like Elise, she was almost sure. Ramona frowned, flapping her shirt away from her skin.

"What are you selling these days anyway?" Leonard said lightly.

"Mutton, alfalfa." Ramona started working her way around the sheep. "Prickly pear preserves, white slaves, absinthe."

"God, the romance, the romance of it all."

"Don't let it," she said, looking at him without smiling, "go to your head." Clever Leonard. At least if someone had to spy from within, it was someone with a little entertainment value. She ducked a limb, deciding to find Elise.

Who was not around, naturally. After looking for a while, Ramona shrugged and gave up. The river was low, as always at that time of year, and warmer than she liked. She waded in anyway, sank briefly down to her chin, then pushed off into the deeper water. She wasn't much of a swimmer, happy at that point just to be a few degrees cooler. She snagged a root on the far side and hung in the water, watching her legs drift in the current. Elise didn't want to hear it. Rumor outside was that the crazed old general, left to decommission the remaining base, had ushered the military into a whole new trading relationship, unimagined by even his handlers back east. Ramona kicked her feet slightly to keep floating. Half her contacts claimed to have seen him, but she doubted anyone had, not for two years anyway, a five-star general sunk into the shadows. She had seen him only once, when she stopped at the office tower to report on Elise's field test for her. A door had opened into the unlit hall where Ramona was standing, briefly lost—on the wrong floor she had just realized, already starting back to the glassed-in elevator. She had seen the uniform, the rank, a soft and oddly rounded chin, glasses reflecting the room's overhead lights then reflecting nothing, looking at her. The man Elise had said owned half the cocaine labs in Bolivia was laughing just beyond his shoulder, dark lips pulled back from his teeth.

"I don't know where she went."

275

Ramona opened her eyes. Hale was wading into the water. Gnats hummed around his head. His resemblance to Nick had faded or maybe she had just grown used to it—used to him, God forbid. Ramona took a mouthful of water and spat it back out in a small jet. "Did you see her leave?"

"Maybe an hour ago. She took a *horse*, if you can believe that."

Ramona grinned underwater, watching the water bugs skip along the surface. That was real desperation for you. She shot out another spurt of water. Hale, for all his assertion of detachment and the basic irrelevance of polarized concepts—good-bad, male-female, self-other, power-oppression—*engaged* himself with her life in a way most others living out there wouldn't presume, seeing himself as some kind of improbable counterweight, possibly their salvation. Ramona couldn't remember at the same age being that convinced of her larger purpose, now reduced to playing the constricted but still enjoyable game of *faux* revolution, passions exhausted, angers old. That, according to Hale, was not "right" either. However much Hale might argue for the primacy of the egoless witness, he remained fixated on Ramona's unspeakable self.

"I have an aunt like you," Hale said. He had sat down on the sandy verge, his feet still in the water.

"And how is that."

"A real joker." Hale leveled his gaze at Ramona, mouth curled just at the corners. "A rolling stone."

Hey, Nick would say, leaning against the school-yard fence, his sharp-boned face clean as a breeze. Her girlfriends, when she had them, had huddled and giggled, bunched behind her, behind their spiked hair, armloads of books. At first sight of him, Ramona always felt as if the sky had widened overhead, as if all visible surfaces could break. She stroked upstream and boosted herself out onto a flat chunk of limestone, her legs dangling in the water. Her wet hair stuck to her back and she lifted it up to wring it out, tanned arms dark in the light under the trees. Flicking the water off her hands, she gazed down at her slumped breasts, the slight pouch of her stomach. Her mother had disappeared in the general confusion of the turning century, her phone disconnected, the apartment empty when Ramona went back. "How is Elise?" Ramona said.

Hale flexed his feet in the water. "The same. Here and not here," he said.

Carlos had had his theories about Elise, declaiming as he worked in the lab, pipette clicking. "Elise wants," he said. "She wants things to the point of defying the gods, *especially* even defying the gods. It is different things at different times, but that is what rules Elise. It's very fierce." Carlos grinned under the generator noise as Ramona shrugged. Who knew, then or now, what Elise wanted? None of Elise's friends ever talked with any candor to Ramona, all those embattled women in their early fifties, preoccupied with themselves, with what it was possible to do to stave off the encroaching bad times. They had looked sometimes like the photographs Ramona had seen of Vietnam vets—grim, afflicted with an angry irony, a reined-in patience. Laura had moved to the country with Mac, Hollis disappearing who knew where. Elise never spoke of them except in passing and always of the time before Nick died.

Ramona wiggled her fingers in the water then waved at the gnats. Elise seemed to be disappearing more and more behind that glassy buffer of silence, an old woman encumbered by her body, by her cough from cigarettes taken up the same time Ramona had been taken up, by the authority of her quasi-revolutionary past. Ramona could still smell the wax on the courthouse floors, see the wooden benches that had looked like pews, recall the strangely idealized prospect of jail. Stupid stuff, youthful stuff. Ramona flicked the water again, watching Hale. That first night back, when they had their fight over Hale, Elise had finally sighed in exasperation. "Who do you think I am?"

Ramona hadn't known, only that it was meshed with who or what Nick had been, as if her father's violence could effect a molecular change in others with a certain predisposition, begin the subtle protein switches that created the female man, the revolutionary lost in the maelstrom, spinning around, as legend had the SLA radicals, pouring bullets up through their burning safe house. Ramona thought Hale was talismanic, a reminder to Elise of what she wasn't yet, that woman guerrilla who does not represent women, that contradiction, that sweet void. "A woman in love," Ramona finally said.

"Not since Nick died," Elise said. The house had creaked and ticked around them, a light wind starting to tap at the shutters, Ramona wondering bleakly where that left her. "It's a stupid question," Elise went on without noticing, stubbing out her cigarette. "Maybe I never got past that six-year-old playing on the porch of a derelict house." Ramona sighed, irritated with nostalgic sentiment. "And Hale?" she said, but Elise was finished with the argument. Orpheus, Ramona thought, still grumbling to herself, the Christ child, Krishna. Fighting with Elise exhausted her.

"She has nightmares," Hale said, standing up and wading out to where the river just touched his cutoff jeans.

"What about?"

"You'll have to ask her."

Ramona looked down, the water around her legs only a little less tepid than the air on her skin, now nearly dry. The sound of the river, mixed with the chittery rhythm of cicadas in the trees up near the house, wrapped their spot on the water in a humming silence. "About me?" Ramona said.

"I don't know." Hale looked at her then scooped up water to splash across his bare chest. "You could easily die, doing what you do. You could easily get in somebody's way. You could bring it back here."

"Jesus." Ramona pulled her legs out of the water and stood up, starting toward her clothes. "Credit me with a little intelligence. I know what I'm doing and I certainly know the risks, to me *and* to others. I doubt anyway that Elise is losing sleep over my imminent demise." The rocks were full of trash, so she splashed back into the river. That Elise had left was beginning to bother her; Elise had never before left the ranch to evade unwanted conversations, even those with Ramona. "What's it to you anyway?" She stood on the gravel bar, looking at him across the coil of water. "Why are you acting like someone fending off the decline of western civilization? I'm not some prince of darkness. I'm not this *revolutionary*. When you get right down to it, I'm just the bastard daughter of a junkie dealer living on a two-bit ranch that has come hard up against the world as we know it."

Hale watched her start to yank on her clothes. "You're dealing big-ticket stuff."

"In your dreams." Ramona snorted, floating the shirt out above her head as she slid her arms through the sleeves. "You should see the shit that's for sale out there. I'm just leveling the playing field for the little people."

"Every terrorist is an elitist."

"Congratulations. You qualify."

Hale scooped up more water and tipped it down his back. "Is it just me or do you hate men in general?" he said.

Surprised, Ramona started to laugh. "Oh, sure, Hale," she said. "You tell me how one hates half the living population of a planet. Correct me if I'm wrong, but it seems to me that is something *your* sex has the most expertise in." She stopped to pull on her pants, still irritated. "Maybe I hate men's certainty," she said, "their lack of ambivalence, if you will."

"And you are less certain?"

Ramona was silent, buckling her belt, watching him still standing in the river. "Yeah," she said, "I am. Probably by the tiniest degree, by an *infinitesimal* degree, but I am. Just enough to save my soul. And no doubt cost me my skin," she added.

"What about Elise?"

"I don't know." Ramona pushed her foot into a boot, rocking her heel down.

"She has nightmares."

"That only means she's afraid. You can lack ambivalence and still at moments be afraid." Ramona looked at Hale again, the unbuttoned shirt hanging loose from her shoulders. Her anger had gone away as suddenly as it came. "I wonder," she said, "why it is when you look at me, and it *is* just me, you don't see that cosmic witness you go on and on about. You know, the eyes of God behind everyone's eyes. But not, for some reason, behind mine."

To her surprise, he flushed, staring down into the current

279

breaking gently around his thighs. He *was* beautiful, the water forming gold beads in the half-light on his tanned shoulders, the silky slant of his hair, the line of his jaw curved taut. And young, Ramona thought, young and fretful, why the hell not. She just wanted out of the loop. Maybe that was what Elise finally wanted as well—to be out of the loop, not liable for blame, not the object of some arrested adolescent's sexually crazed heroine worship. Ramona also knew that what she had felt for Elise had not been that. Annoying as it was to use Hale's half-baked mysticism, that strange sort of *recognition* was at the root of her intense attraction to Elise, maybe his too. Hale shrugged slightly, starting to smile at his own discomfort, as he trailed his fingers in the water. Ramona shrugged too, shaking her wet hair out, and walked away from the river.

The surface differences between Elise in her forties and Ramona in her twenties had been predicated as much on Elise's greater caution in showing her hand as on anything else. Ramona—conscious of the weight of Elise's reputation, of her life as already lived halfway through—refused for her own radical purposes to see how similar they were in their thinking, their restless irritation, their sour humor. She attacked Elise with the same critical fury she bent on herself, dissecting the politics of the university, the data compromised by the deal Elise had cut with the Bolivians, Carlos' hidden agenda. Elise's move to the violence of that single bombing was not as anomalous as others thought, including Elise herself. When, after all the Sturm und Drang, she had glanced sidelong at Ramona in bed, exhaling smoke up toward the ceiling, and said, "I was never as angry as you," Ramona had laughed. "Yes, you were," she said. "Rita told me. You took it out on all those college-age boys pumping gas for the summer or working in the local hardware store. 'Elise was like a cat playing with mice,' she said to me. You were like a bomb ticking."

The shuttered house was empty but for people working in the kitchen, the rooms holding a trace of the morning cool. A breeze moving up from the river trickled through the wooden blinds. Ramona stood over the desk, flipping without reading through the account sheets, and tried to factor in the added risk of Hale's vocal worry. There was a tentative meet set for that night just off the ranch, which now felt hinky to her or maybe Elise's disappearing act had knocked her off balance. She didn't know. She didn't like to link her off-ranch business with Elise, the differences there too thin. She felt with Elise the same unnerving violence she felt running guns, the same sense of being hauled along by some almost comically primitive force. Ramona sat down at the desk and started going through the accounts.

Her own struggle to inch out from Elise's not inconsiderable shadow was sidelined twice, once for the short course of the trial and again as society bent beneath the weight of the passing millennium. Both times she fell back for safety on tighter and tighter circles of control—all thought, all logic, all protocols— as Elise stood on the periphery watching, enormously seductive in that unbreachable silence she affected, observing with something that might have been pleasure Ramona's ill-repressed passion for her, love, whatever it was.

It may have bothered Elise in the end, making love to her, to Nick's daughter. They had lacked time to make the necessary mental separations. There was not room for any divisions as time itself was slowly eclipsed, frozen, turned eerily back on itself. Hale, Ramona thought, must have been terrifying, coming out of the crowd, especially the Channel crowd of pimps and addicts and petty scam artists, Nick's kind of crowd—her father fleetingly back in the flesh. But Hale turned out to be easy, much less quarrelsome than Ramona, the incest taboo less onerous on Elise's guarded sensibilities, that sharp sexual difference simpler. Ramona added up the last numbers and drew a line. He was also beautiful—long, muscled legs vanishing into the water, his fingers flicking the surface.

The afternoon had drifted into a hot stillness. Ramona walked to the sliding door onto the deck, but the river was too thickly shaded by trees for her to see if Hale was still there. She moved restlessly back through the room and finally stretched out on the unsprung sofa. Her father had not been *beautiful* exactly, as she remembered him, too pared down, with too many edges, his piecemeal beauty somehow too flagrant. Most of the time she had never noticed. The thought of Nick having a look, a physical existence separate from that of being her father, was inconceivable. He was just Daddy, and then with a strained sophistication he was Nick, but the flesh-and-blood person never changed. He had hauled her around when she was little like any other father, propped up on his hip with her arms around his neck. He had danced with her in fleeting jitterbugs, hugged her up quick against his side, yelled at her when she did something dumb. He had kissed her in swift goodbye from inside a dozen or more strange cars. The two of them had been comfortable together, making up their private jokes, and then he was gone.

There was always a moment in those towns off the interstate as she stood outside the creaky café or the boarded-up house, listening to the sound of the wind, when she would imagine her father inside—tilted back in a chair with his legs swung wide or up on a counter drinking a beer, watchful and smiling. She would go up the steps and push open the screen door and walk inside the half-lit room, stacked with bad furniture or echoing empty, and pick out of the wide-spaced bodyguards the man in charge by how he sat, stood, or walked, and it was always like Nick but never him. The room would sing, though, with a cold kind of power, a colorless rush. Walking without expression through the grit, the barred light, Ramona would feel each time unbelievably high, omnipotent, joyously crazed. There was no other feeling like it. She would go back endlessly just for that, to walk the cold edge again and again.

Footsteps crossed from the front of the house then stopped at the room where Ramona was lying. "I'm not asleep," she said, opening her eyes.

Lucky dropped a tool belt clanking on the table. She was smaller than she looked, walking in long steps across the floor, braids swinging. She pushed Ramona's feet off, sat down with a sigh, then pulled Ramona's legs back across her own. She rested her head back along the sofa, eyes angled across to Ramona's face. "I've been patching that pitiful shack up at Archuleyta. When'd you get back?"

"Last night."

"Paula tells me Elise up and left."

"Apparently so."

"That's weird." Lucky closed her eyes; she was getting crow's feet from squinting into the sun. The room was warm, growing darker as the sun dropped toward the other side of the house. "God, I'm tired. I think I'm getting old."

Ramona grunted in reply. She liked Lucky, that practical insouciance of hers, something imperturbably optimistic in her that resisted even her fierce depressions. Lucky had driven outside with her the first five years or so, then she stopped. It made her too restless, she said—it made her want to be crazy, feeding her own lousier impulses.

Opening her eyes, Lucky started to tug Ramona's boots off her feet. "Day is done," she said cheerfully, dropping one boot onto the floor and starting on the other. "Let's hope she hasn't taken off in earnest. Last time she did that we ended up with the Halester. A real joy. A *great* addition to the collective life." She dropped the other boot on the floor.

"Hale has a new morbid interest."

"I know." Lucky started massaging Ramona's right foot. "Wild-eyed, spittle-flecked dealers of death, starring yourself. And I've never once seen you spit while speaking, much less roll your eyes."

"Mmm." Lucky's hands felt good. Ramona felt herself relax for the first time since she had been back. "I rolled my eyes at Hale today."

"No." Lucky's own eyes widened in mock disbelief. She lifted the other foot. "Well, he *must* have provoked you."

"He wanted to know why I hated men."

Lucky sputtered a laugh, stopping for a minute to grin in delight across the room. "Why women hate men," she said, shaking her head. "That's an old one."

Ramona laughed too, laying her arm across her eyes. Uncomplicated friendship, no struggles, no blame, or blame so ephemerally present as to be nonexistent—it should all be that way. Lucky had lost her heart to one of those wildly attractive radicals

283

rousing the crowds with a megaphone and then had resolved not to lose it again. That she managed that feat while becoming neither an ascetic nor a shrew had Ramona's respect. Lucky was direct; you could take a core sample of Lucky and find no nasty surprises.

The sofa was wide enough for a daybed, creaking a little as Lucky shifted her weight upward alongside Ramona's legs. She started working the belt out of its buckle. When Ramona, protesting, moved her free hand down to stop her, Lucky shhh-ed her softly. "Lucky . . ." Ramona lifted her arm off her eyes. "Wait, I can't . . ."

"Reciprocate?" Lucky grinned briefly up at her, the belt coming undone. "Life in the business world. Relax, *ma chérie*, it's free. I'm upswept by passion. I'm happy to see you. Close your eyes."

Ramona sank back in the pillows and sighed. Sex had a thousand dimensions, but the slow lovemaking with a friend of ten years had to be one of the very best. There was none of the danger and panting effort and deep incipient violence of sudden lust, of frenzied first-time affairs. She felt her pants loosened around her hips, then Lucky's hand cool on her stomach and sliding down, one finger easing slowly through the tangled curls then deep inside, slick and smooth. Her knees opened and she took a breath. Gently circling her finger, Lucky pushed Ramona's shirt above her breasts and squirmed far enough up to take the tip in her mouth. Ramona touched Lucky's smooth head, running her finger down the part to the delicate bones at the base of her neck. Lucky moved up and over to the other breast, dipping now two fingers curved inside as Ramona arched her hips, pressed her hand harder on Lucky's head. Simple comfort, the simple reminder that things you could do alone didn't always have to be done alone, that someone was there. Lucky was smiling when Ramona opened her eyes and looked down. "Hey," she said softly, moving her own hips, her wet fingers circling harder, flat. Ramona smiled too on an indrawn breath, smiled at themselves, lying together in the shuttered room, barely moving, each small pulse of Lucky's hand opening her wider and wider until she couldn't look into Lucky's eyes anymore, her head dropping back. All right, she thought, all right. Then Lucky's mouth was again moving on her breast, a cool rush suddenly shooting down below, and Ramona groaned, lifting her hips up to meet it, thinking yes, thinking stay, stay, stay, stay, thinking I don't want to be alone anymore.

Lucky lay with her head high on Ramona's bare stomach, idly wiping her hand on Ramona's pants leg. "I can hear your heart beat all the way down here."

Ramona laughed, bouncing Lucky's head, feeling sweat start to slide down her ribs. "That's your bloody fault."

"It is, isn't it?" Lucky sat up, happy, and untangled her legs. She leaned over Ramona, arms braced on either side, and kissed her quickly on the mouth. "Welcome home," she said.

Elise didn't come back for dinner. Ramona sat at the table, ignoring the noisy conversation, her mind drifting to Elise with an annoying frequency, as if thoughts were stones and Elise the green river bottom. A large amount of her thinking was held in imagined exchange with Elise, but never as much as now, while entertaining the possibility, at least, of Elise's permanent absence. No longer there, the polite narrow-eyed wait for response, the oblique view, the outrageous and risible reasoning, the mammoth patience, the dizzying cool distance. Gone. It made her heart stop briefly until she could dismiss the thought, angry with herself and angrier each time it came back, the stone floating down in lazy cradles of motion. Gone. Ramona stood up and carried her plate to the kitchen. Hale and Leonard were talking on the deck in the dusk, Hale tense, Leonard teasing, their voices too low to hear from the window. Dipping her plate in the soapy tub and then in the scalding rinse water, Ramona watched until Hale turned and sauntered inside. Leonard sat down and lit a joint.

They had both left the house when Ramona, jingling the keys, walked through the rocky grass to the Jeep. It was full dark, the bugs making a cricking racket, a few fireflies still out. She slid in the seat, set the key, and then turned—half expecting an explosion, she realized, after the engine started with a clanking rattle, either that or nothing at all. She shifted the gears and launched into reverse. As much as she drove at night, she had never really enjoyed it, not like the days with the sky whipping a high blue overhead and the land stretched out to the edges of nowhere. The space closed in at night to the flash of underlit branches, white clumps of grass, and the oily wavering ribbon of road, shadowed with potholes and angled cracks. The warm wind flicked through the window.

The flames jumped out of the dark when she topped one of the last rises before the ranch road met the right of way, jigging at a spot where something had been propped across, boards or something. Her foot backed off the accelerator, though she knew they would have seen her headlights at the same time she saw the roadblock. The flames vanished as she went into a dip and she hesitated again, wondering whether to cut her lights and turn, though there was scant room, the road dropping off on either side into a dry gully. If she turned, they could follow her back, and there was nothing, at least, in the Jeep tonight. She shrugged and gunned it up the rise, shooting out over the top and down the other side. The flames, she could see as she closed in on the block, were in oil drums, a truck parked off the side, maybe men in the jumping shadows. She braked at the last possible moment, skidding across into the boards, which popped free and clattered down against each other, too many to get around. She throttled the engine down and waited, listening to the twigs snap in the fire.

"Turn your vehicle off." The man, stepping out, showed her his gun, a deer rifle, pretty small potatoes.

"Who the hell are you?" Ramona said, the Jeep running.

"Sheriff's department. Drug interdiction."

"You're on my land. You got a warrant for this roadblock?"

"Don't need one. Turn the vehicle off."

Sighing, Ramona obliged, ready to do her community-outrage number, civil liberties, property rights, whatever the hell would cow these local bozos, playing with peashooters. "Heard of due process?" she said flatly in the silence. "Laws of search and seizure?"

"Get out of the vehicle and keep your hands where I can see them."

286

"Oh, man." Ramona rolled her eyes and thought briefly of Lucky. "Could we skip the hallowed police routine since you are clearly not police and I am clearly not a homicidal maniac?" She didn't move from the Jeep, her arm draped across the steering wheel. It felt bad, the whole thing; it stank to high heaven. She could feel sweat trickling between her breasts. Deep shit, she thought, trying to see which were just shadows jumping and which were men, what they carried, I'm in deep shit now. If it were going to be rape or simple assault, she was better off in the Jeep. The more rabidly puritanical types had not been known ever to kill outright the women they attacked.

"Do what the man says." The other man had a rifle, too, modified somehow, but she couldn't see in the flickering light.

"Look," she started again with what she hoped sounded like hard-held patience, "I don't know what sort of peculiar information you—"

"You say you own this place."

"Right, and you're on it, as far as I can tell, illegally."

"She the one owns this place?" A third man pushed Hale into the light.

Ramona saw him about to lie as if she could see a cloud balloon above his head with the lie inside it and wondered briefly why he would think it necessary to hide her identity and thought past that to know that if they wanted her in particular they would have other ways to confirm it, Hale risking complicity and thus the complicity of everyone else living out there, and even reached the sharp cool rage that anyone should presume to choose for her before Hale could start to speak. "I have ID," she said, unclipping the license from the dash and tossing it through the headlights.

The first man walked over and picked it up. "Ra-mo-na," he said and grinned into the lights shooting up at wolfish angles below his face. "That's the one, all right. We going to have to drag you out of there?"

"Looks like it." Ramona glanced at Hale. "Would you let him go now? It's past his bedtime."

"Well, I just don't know. We found him at that meet site

287

looking for some poor chap now in the brig or whatever it is the army calls its isolation cells these days."

Not religious nuts, then—something the second man was clearly not happy Ramona should know. "You got some fucking mouth on you, Carleton."

"The Army is helping the sheriff interdict drugs? I didn't know we had reached such exalted levels of cooperation." Ramona stuck with mad-as-hell citizen, but her feet felt cold, her stomach cold. She had always thumbed down the consequences —people dead, retaliation, going to jail—and she didn't really know what to do with the alien reality now that it was there. "Christ." She was mad at the mess, mad at Hale. What did he do? "What the hell did you do?" she said to him.

"Leonard told me about the meet. It was a bust. Ramona, it's a setup or something."

The second man was yelling at Hale, but Ramona suddenly couldn't hear. She touched the keys, but Hale was still held by the third guy, damn it, damn it, damn it. She gripped the wheel, but the first man had come around to the side and was grabbing her arm. *Damn* it. She kicked at him, twisting her arm out of his hold. He caught her foot, turned it and yanked, and she was sliding down along the seat, snatching at the wheel again. Someone else was yelling but no one shot off the guns, which was odd, just the yells and the crackling fire and the sound of her breath. Kicking again, she swung for a wild moment half out of the Jeep, hanging by her fingers from the steering wheel, the edge of the door frame, then she let go, curling up as she fell. The man dropped her foot, and she rolled away in a crouch, testing her weight on the ankle, sore and shaky. Where was Hale, she thought, scooting around the Jeep, aware all at once of the quiet. Where was everyone?

The firelight licked at the empty road, the Jeep's headlights bouncing off the scrub at the roadside, the scrawny bits of grass. A car, or something heavier, a truck, was coming from the right of way. She could hear it downshift for the hill, the engine getting louder the closer it got, then it stopped, no lights, just outside the line of dark. Still in a crouch, staring into the blackness, Ramona heard someone running slowly up from behind her, footsteps slapping the sticky asphalt. Run away, she thought, at first imagining it was advice for herself but then realizing she meant that lone runner coming ever closer—run back, run away. "Run away," she said softly and stood.

The sound of the shot came after the bruising blow to her chest, as if someone invisible had thrown a punch, an incredibly hard punch, then the bumper of the Jeep smashed up against her hip, the hood hitting her jaw as a second shot split the dark, with a jolt low in her back. Slipping down, Ramona touched the tar on the road, her hand wet with something, a headlight warm against her cheek. I've been shot, she thought, then, take a breath, and there was one, laced with a liquid sort of pain, curiously cold. Turning her head slightly, she saw Elise at the edge of the road, stumbling on the verge, panting. What was everyone doing here? Ramona wondered, squinting as the dark started to dance, watching Elise half turn, Hale like a shadow briefly behind her, then gone. The first sight of her should have been one of slackening age, but Elise looked young, angry, that white white skin, her swiveling hips—take a breath, Ramona remembered, the air now like fire. Elise was speaking, her hair glowing around her head, those shrewd eyes casing the situation, moving around then down to Ramona's face. It's you, Ramona thought, you watching me, as Elise jerked her arm away from someone, furious, speaking more words. I'm sorry, Ramona thought, I wanted something, then as an afterthought, take a breath, and it came, a shallow sip of air. Touching the sticky asphalt, her fingers wet, she fleetingly remembered something, a sudden bump of recognition—oh yes, this, *this* death—then the wind was lifting her off the ground. Wait, I have to stay, she thought, dismayed, trying to reach back down. Elise came closer, her skin flushed in the firelight, half smiling with disbelief, saying "no," and Ramona nodded, agreeing without knowing why, the wind now freezing cold. I am that, she thought, whoever she is, I once knew her name, then, take a breath, closing her eyes into the rushing dark, and there wasn't one.

FIFTEEN

Epilogue

1986

Flowers began to show along the banks of the road as the car crossed the fault line between the low limestone hills and the flat plains behind, loose pink petals flipped to their mauve undersides in the wind of the tires. The evening air poured along Elise's cheek and arm as she drove. It smelled sweet —there was no other word for it—a subtle dry sweetness laced with cedar. Buckled in the car seat beside her, twenty-two-month-old Lucy solemnly studied the pictures in a board book propped upside down on the padded bar in front of her. Working her fingers along the edge, she turned a page and stared at a row of kittens, mewing and clowning, Elise could see, heads down. When Lucy saw her aunt watching, her eyebrows soared and she let loose a gurgled laugh. Elise smiled back. That Laura's baby should make her feel as if it were possible to die of love she had not expected at all. Behind her Elise could feel the three women relax as they leaned into the curves and swayed forward, ducking their heads to look at the hills with their sudden pockets and ribbons of color. The flowers were incidental, although Rita had brought a camera and was already leaning up against the seat behind Elise, playing with the zoom lens, panning along the first of the narrow ranch roads that led toward Nick's house and property.

The original idea had been to have a weekend to themselves, a giddy reversion to the intimacy of college dorms, fifth-grade slumber parties; the wildflowers were extra. Hollis, sitting at the bar, had run her hand through her hair and laughed, saying, "Oh great, nature, I'll bring the Jack Daniel's," while Rita circled the pool table behind them humming "Where Have All the Flowers Gone?" It was either a brilliant idea, Elise thought, or totally insane. Laura, lifting Lucy into the car seat and brushing her lips along the soft spray of reddish hair at her temple as she pulled the straps over her head, voted for insane. "You have forgotten," she said, "how those slumber parties turned out— everyone mad at everyone else." Sloan, leaning over Elise's shoulder, was explaining how the Olds's steering pulled a little to the left and that the clanking squeak was a normal noise whereas a *grinding* squeak wasn't and when the fuel gauge registered a quarter tank it meant maybe fifteen more miles max, Elise nodding as she yanked the seat forward and back to fit her legs, her visor pulled down low over her eyes. Maneuvering through the traffic out of town, Elise heard only bits of conversation from the back, Laura's hair in the rearview mirror blowing around her face; it was hot even for May and they had got a late start. Now the air outside was full of evening light, streaming in a luminous eddy that rushed through the car and tumbled the women in the back together, shoulders and voices bumping.

Elise liked driving, liked being alone in the front seat with Lucy, who watched her, hands softly patting the bumper bar. Elise would hand her different toys from the assortment scattered between them on the seat, board books and brightly colored plastic. Laura's hair flashed in the mirror, then Hollis' rumpled black as she leaned across to look at Rita's camera, scooting forward, one elbow braced against the front seat. Elise switched her eyes back to the road. Rita was saying something about the lens as Elise punched in another tape, the speakers in the Olds sounding tinny, Aretha Franklin dwarfed by the wind.

They took a break after an hour, Elise slowing the car onto the shoulder of the road. The grass was green from the spring rains, rocks showing in a chalky stubble underneath, while in the creases of the hills a muddle of white-picked pastel turned and flattened under the breeze. Bluebonnets filled a little valley, royal blue deepening to ultramarine. "Flowers," said Hollis, swinging the bottle by the neck then taking a meditative slug as she strolled into the field. Rita stretched by the car, her blond hair in its loose braid gleaming, then swung the camera on its strap around her neck and pointed it at Hollis, turning the lens to focus. "Hey," she said, looking up and following Hollis, "do Rosalind, do some Rosalind lines."

Elise laughed, leaning against the car. "Rita and Shakespeare. The Theater in the Park doesn't know what bizarre competition it's getting."

Laura was changing Lucy's diaper. "Hollis do this, Hollis do that." She snapped up the cotton overalls. "Doesn't the star treatment contradict your collectivist principles?"

Elise handed her a beer. "It's not star treatment." Laura shrugged, flipping her hair back behind her ears and gazing down at Lucy. She looked at the beer in her hand and popped the tab, then set it on the car roof so she could lift Lucy out and stand her up on the road. The baby took off, arms out, running a few steps, then she stopped, squatted, and picked up a rock.

Laura took a swallow and wrinkled her nose. "I drank all that beer to richen my milk—it's lost its illicit zing or something. Especially now I'm not breastfeeding anymore." She watched Lucy stand and start off again only to pull up short, eyes caught by a vanishing lizard. "How can something be both a deeply emotional experience and a deep bore?"

"I thought that was the definition of life." Elise opened a Coke. "Go get a shooter from Hollis then. I'll watch Lucy."

"Naw, I'll take her." Laura grinned fleetingly in her sister's direction. "I trust you, I trust you, I just want Rita to take her picture. Did you ever see so many fucking bluebonnets?" She walked down the road and scooped Lucy up from behind, swinging her around in one arm and nuzzling her neck as she picked her way through the flowers, the beer held out in her other hand.

Elise stayed by the car. Rita was directing the shots, Hollis now improvising with Lucy, tipping her upside down to make her laugh, the baby's breathy chuckle coming back up to Elise where she waited. The road was empty, the only other sounds an occasional twitter from the trees and the clop of hoof against rock where cows grazed on the other side of the road. Elise stretched. The breeze puffed at the loose-headed flowers by the road and she could hear the engine ticking behind her.

" 'A horse, a horse, my kingdom for a horse.' " Hollis said the lines cheerfully and handed the Jack Daniel's across to Laura, her voice coming across the field clear in the evening quiet.

" 'What a piece of work is man, how noble in reason, how infinite in faculty, in something, something, how express and admirable.' " Rita was winding the film. "From *Hair*," she added. "I also know all the words to 'Frank Mills.' "

" 'Is that a dagger I see before me?' " Laura held the bottle up to her eyes. " 'Out, out, damn spot.' "

" 'Something is rotten in the state of Denmark.' " Hollis had her hands in her pockets, laughing, Lucy standing beside her holding onto her leg. "*Hamlet* has all the best lines."

Elise smiled. The cows nearby were pulling mouthfuls of grass out of the dirt with a soft ripping noise. Nick knew odd bits of Shakespeare, Malvolio's lines or chunks from *Timon of Athens*, reciting them in a soft-voiced rush when he was high. He had been gone more than three months. Rita was waiting for Elise to get over it. "So, you'll get over it," she said, waving the spaghetti spoon as the dog, sprawled behind her on the kitchen floor, looked up for flying food. "Everyone gets over it."

Back in the car, Rita and Laura kept drinking, Elise feeling the billow of laughter start to rise and thin out behind her. Rita was taking pictures of everyone, Laura clowning. Elise could see

Hollis half turned against the car door, throwing in a word or two, her mouth tucked into the lightest of passing sarcasms. Okay, totally insane, Elise conceded, having balanced before on those moments when parties at Milos and Laura's gathered up and suddenly heaved forward, a wave hanging on that second when the music's volume seemed to have doubled unnoticed and all the rooms pulsed, shoulder packed, every face in the shadows laughing. Elise privately loved the dangerous throw-weight of those moments, even knowing how long the rest of the night would be. Always Rita would come from dancing, sweaty and laughing, T-shirt knotted up under her breasts, and throw an arm around Elise, who seldom danced, saying, "I love you, you know? Elise? I love you so much," laughing, but with it clear in her face—she wasn't just full of drunken kindness.

Elise braked hard as she topped a rise, the car, as Sloan had warned her, pulling to the left, the treadless tires threatening for a second to skid, while the steer turned the wide bracket of its horns toward them from the middle of the road. Everyone was colliding in the back, yelling, Rita the first to see the steer, already with her camera poked past Elise's shoulder, fiddling with the stops to get enough exposure in the failing light. "Shoot out your own window," Elise said.

"It's stuck, remember?" Rita gripped the back of the seat then leaned out the window to aim the camera. Elbow propped on the door frame so she could steady the camera for the time it would take the shutter to close, Rita pressed the button. Elise waited, feeling both the hard curve of Rita's ribs and the squashy press of her breast, her body warm and damp, as if Rita had materialized in the breath of the steer outside and would stay only as long as the longhorn stayed, turning its head away and shifting its weight on those narrow ankles as delicately as a dancer.

The shutter clicked. Rita jerked as she rebalanced to advance the film and focus again, then she was pulling herself back inside in an explosive confusion of arms and camera, laughing again, her smile shooting past Elise's cheek. "How Greek," she said, "or Cretan or something." Her hand on Elise's shoulder pushed suddenly and vanished. Elise touched the gear shift, thinking of Rita hauling Fresnels one-handed up a ladder or sprawled back on the couch as she groaned, tenting her bent arm over her eyes, her feet crossed on the table. "You'll get over it," Rita said. When they fell together into the harp case at the end of the Molinaro play, Rita had coiled underneath her like a cat, a muscled warmth, breath sharp.

"See the bull?" Laura leaned over the front seat, pointing for Lucy. The baby turned her solemn gaze to the steer still in the road then looked back at her mother. "Longhorn," Laura said, enunciating carefully.

As night fell Elise realized they were lost. Looking at the map, she frowned, the light draining away with inexorable speed, the fuel gauge drifting toward that infamous quarter mark. The road crossing had no signs, so Elise mentally flipped a coin, switched the headlights on, and turned. Lucy sighed, bored with the toys, a chewed apple slice loose in her fingers. Elise had no idea babies could sigh like that, with such an adult weariness. She reached over to take the apple, Lucy watching it go with slightly puckered brows before switching her eyes back.

When Elise slowed the car to bump over a ledge shoring up the road where a creek bed ran, she felt the front tires splash into running water. The conversation in the back had dropped, and Elise could see Laura's head turning in the rearview mirror, her arms stretched along the back seat. "My God," she said in bemusement. "Where the fuck are we?"

"In the heart of the country," Elise said.

Laura didn't hear her. "Hey, Elise," her voice rose, "where the fuck are we?"

"In the heart of the country!" Elise was suddenly mad. "We're deep in the heart of the heart of the goddam country, okay?"

"Hey, you can just listen." Laura's voice slowed.

Looking in the mirror, Elise recognized at once the cold, blurry-eyed deliberation that locked in when Laura had a drunken grievance to express. For such a docile-looking person, with her slight build and closed-in shoulders, Laura could be a mean drunk. The car had sprayed clear of the creek and was topping another rise, Elise wishing that she knew where the hell they were.

"Listen, *Elise.*" Laura had scooted forward. "Hey, listen, you want to yell at everyone, fine, but the fucking *world* doesn't revolve around your nasty little affliction of angst now that the junkie prince is out of the scene, to no one's, I repeat, no one's regret except yours, you alone without even the rudimentary knowledge that Nick is a shit, lacking any redeeming value whatsoever. So don't you fucking *yell* at me because I might be wondering where the hell I am, with my almost-two-year-old child, I might add, which is more responsibility than you may be *accustomed* to, Elise."

"Just let me drive." Elise kept her voice level, the headlights at the grating of another cattle guard. Laura had an unerring instinct for deeply painful, bloodless wounds, all the hidden guilt decoded or otherwise self-confessed, their lifelong intimacy lending Elise to imprudent speech. For some reason she was loath to counterpunch when Laura attacked—residual big-sister qualms, she thought, or latent masochism. She had dreamed once that Laura threw a bare-knuckled punch at her face and she, Elise, had leaned into it, pushed the edge of her cheekbone at Laura's fist, welcomed the blow. Slowing the car, Elise picked up the map, reaching overhead to turn on the light. Laura was still sitting forward, the two others silent, Hollis watching and Rita with her head tilted back against the seat, eyes on the ceiling. The car looked dingy under the light, everyone suddenly old inside.

Laura's face was up close. "You act like God, you've got yourself so well defended, you don't think anything else matters so long as you stay safe and tight, I mean, to fucking hell with anybody else, right? Let them twist in the wind, you got what you want, you go where you want, you do what you want. Hey, it doesn't matter that ten years ago no one knew for I don't know how many months whether you were fucking alive or dead. What makes you so special, Elise? How come your maybe being dead doesn't matter, why do you think nothing about you *affects* anyone? I mean, who elected you goddam God is what I want to know."

"Laura." Elise spoke slowly. "I am nothing, noth-ing. Okay? I am a mote. I am a grain of sand."

Laura smacked her fist against the back of the seat. "Don't give me that crap. You know what that 'I-am-nothing' crap means? It means you don't have to come down to the level of us mortals, us pitiful needy mortals with our fucked-up lives. You get to stay perfect, Elise, Little Miss Perfect, Little Miss 'I Am Nothing' Perfect."

Moving the map, Elise saw Lucy watching. The baby stared, eyebrows tilted slightly in a loose scrawl of surprise but the eyes themselves steady, round and observant. The utter lack of judgment in that silent acceptance of present madness made Elise deeply sad. See your aunt? she thought. See your mother call your aunt funny names? "Stop it," she said to Laura, and Lucy jumped then drew in her lower lip to cry. Elise picked up a blue cloth bunny and handed it to her. Distracted, the baby fingered the toy then looked back toward her mother and laughed. Elise felt the sadness swell.

"Stop what, Elise, stop *what*? You know what you are, deep down? Huh? Elise? You're a victim junkie, that's what. You've got to wrap yourself up in sickos like Nick just to be sure you're living like everybody else, just to convince yourself you're *that* unloved, right? You've got to be that unloved all the time."

Elise turned to start the car but everything suddenly felt too difficult, the light still a dim yellow above them. Laura's voice rose and fell behind her, but Elise's tears, when they came, were unexpected, a thick heat in her nose spilling over, her mouth shaking. She was crying for Nick, she rationalized, for all the time lost among them, Hollis bleeding, Rita getting on that goddam bus, crying for not saving even Laura, whose anger pressed the air out in a tight layer against the car. The night was a black skin just outside, beyond which Elise could imagine nothing.

Elise opened the door, then she was standing outside and almost immediately running, the asphalt pushing up smooth against her feet. The car faded back then disappeared entirely as the road lifted and dropped. Elise squinted into the partial moonlight, the black trees, running hard but effortlessly, as if she had done this before, as if there were some final cataclysm she had to run down this road to meet. She could have run, she thought with a flash of joy, forever.

Out of breath finally, she slowed, jogged a few paces, and stopped. She walked to the top of the next rise, hands on her hips, chest heaving, exhilaration slowly ebbing away. An owl hooted from the dark, a gliding upbeat and two steady echoes, then again. The stars made the sky glow, a pale backdrop against the flattened hills.

Walking back, she saw Hollis come out of the dark, strolling down the middle of the road, hands in her pockets. She stopped when she saw Elise and waited, turning her face slightly into the wind, the light stuff of her pants rippling. "It's so quiet," she said when Elise came up.

The scrub was filled with the faint ringing noise of night insects, but Elise knew what Hollis meant. "Yeah, it is."

Hollis just stood there listening, the wind pushing around her hair. "I love it out here," she said suddenly. "Isn't that weird? I didn't think I would."

"It can be bad." Elise pushed against the stitch still in her side. The owl hooted behind them. "Too much dark, too much nothing." Elise stopped herself.

The wind rustled through the trees, live oaks still with a bristling of dead leaves among the new. Hollis held out her arms and walked backwards, her chin lifted to the wind. "Nothing's okay," she said half to Elise, half to herself. The owl hooted again from the dark.

SIXTEEN

Epilogue

1954

THE BACK PORCH WAS TINY, MORE LIKE A STOOP TACKED HIGH up onto the house, a flight of gray-painted steps going down to the yard. Blistering hot most of the day, it held the sun's heat against the white clapboard wall, the faded mat before the door, the dirt baked to dusty rock in the flower boxes and pots. Elise crouched on the second step and stared into the green-streaked darkness that reached down under the porch; she was looking for cats. A saucer chinked as she moved to a lower step. She couldn't see anything, only an edge of shadow under the lip of the step and a pattern of green below where the sun pushed through the broken lattice. The weeds flickered as she watched.

The dry smell of dirt made her sad. She didn't care much for plants but these were especially boring: potted cacti and planters of strange leathery succulents, soft as the ball of her thumb.

Carefully avoiding the cacti, even the pale lumpish ones dusted with white prickles that looked plush as fur, she touched one of the succulents. She squeezed a leaf then surreptitiously dug her fingernail into its center, trying to pop the thick bubble. Her nail left a dark green half-moon behind.

"Kitty, kitty, kitty," she whispered under the stairs, not so much the separate words as the light stutter of tongue against teeth. "Kitty, kitty, kitty." She scooted down another step.

The stairs ended in a white glare of gravel where the drive spilled into the parched yard, weeds beaten to dirt by the tires of Roberta's station wagon. The garage, one-time carriage-house, never lived up to its promise. Looking through the crack between the sagging doors, Elise had only ever seen gardening clutter. The trunks wedged along the rafters, thick with dust, were out of reach.

Elise glanced at the house next door. Its cracked concrete driveway ran alongside Nana's gravel one, concrete steps leading up to its back door. One afternoon last Easter a man had yelled and beaten up a woman and thrown her down the steps while she and Laura watched from the bedroom window, rigid with appalled delight. Now Elise always saw her when she looked at the stoop, the woman falling, like a painted shadow on the wall.

Elise bumped down the last few steps, the heat stinging the backs of her legs. The siding had pulled away near the bottom and she could see the foundations, the ground sloping up under the house. "Kitty, kitty, kitty."

She had been there two whole days by herself already. Before that had been the long car ride, watching from where she lay on the back seat how the telephone wires dipped together and sprang apart, then the hot still town and finally Nana's house, tucked up a little behind the front yard. Elise had peered through the screen into Nana's front hall before Laura pushed the round button that buzzed deep inside the house and their mother reached over their heads to open the door. Nana, coming out of the dark hall with her arms stretched downward, had been a little flustered, her shoes heavy on the painted wood of the porch. As she took their daddy's arm, patting his sleeve absently over and over, Elise and Laura went inside and down the hall, staying on the cabbage roses that laid their anemic blooms along the carpet. At the end of the hall they stopped all at once and backed up close together to greet Roberta.

Roberta smiled wryly down at them, her suitcase at her feet. A tall, thin woman, she had black hair cut straight below her chin and deepset eyes. Only the sagging lines around those eyes and the fall of loose muscle when she raised her arms made her look old. She gripped each girl's chin to tilt their faces up, appraising with amusement the embarrassed slide of their eyes. Roberta always left so their parents could use her bedroom during their stay. She didn't say where she went, but Elise imagined her at the shop, stretched out on a brass bed or lying smooth and still below the towering cornice of a headboard carved from Indian mahogany.

Running through the rooms later that day, Elise had heard screen doors slam, the gurgle of the toilet's slow flush, the immense black fans groaning into motion until the ceilings shook. In the kitchen her mother and Aunt Jen and Nana crammed pots onto the stove and put a clove-pricked ham in to bake, while jellied salads melted on the drainboard next to slabs of tomato and cucumber, gherkins, the pungent white of sauerkraut. The dining room was dark, the table a big polished pool at its center, while along one wall French shutters lay folded flat into narrow frames for the hedges outside.

When they stood behind their chairs for the blessing, Uncle Gar's elbow grazed Elise's head as he rubbed the back of his neck, then the chairs were bumping over the carpet as everyone sat down and started filling their plates. Hot tea gushed over the crackle of ice, causing the silted sugar to eddy briefly, the glasses to sweat. Everyone talked. Elise, sitting at one side of the table, watched Nana turn finally at the end of the meal and bend her face with its Roman nose and full-lipped mouth toward two-year-old Laura, perched on a set of phone books. Laura huddled her elbows together on the table in front of her plate, ignoring what Nana was whispering at her. Laura hardly ever ate at dinner. Later, when everyone was washing up, Elise found her in the dark backyard, her pants around her feet, pooping in the grass at the edge of the hedge. Without saying a word, Elise picked up handfuls of twiggy dirt to cover it up, Laura standing in the dark after she pulled her pants back on, hitting at the bobbing tips of the hedge.

On the next night, after everyone left for home, leaving Elise behind, she had lain awake in bed and thought about the kittens under the house. Watching the table fan revolve in the dim glow of the parlor light, she heard the crunch of the station wagon's tires turning on the gravel behind the house. Roberta, easing open the screen door at the foot of Nana's bed, whispered something into the dark, then the bedsprings twanged gently. They were always talking together, more than just friends, maybe close like her and Laura. The slow back and forth of their low voices had put Elise to sleep.

"Kitty, kitty, kitty." Elise squinted under the house one last time then stood up, dusting the grass blades off her palms. She looked toward the hedge then walked around and pushed through the thinnest part. The drive was full of weeds, but she could see flowers waving in the gardens on the other side. Aunt Helen's house seemed to Elise like a cottage in an enchanted forest where hidden danger lurked. The huge gardens made the house seem small, the steep angle of the roof like thatch, beetle-browed. It was always quiet, quiet, quiet, the sun beating on the circular drive and a silvery arm of water sweeping high across the lawn. The dogs were what made it dangerous, locked in the gardening shed or inside the house, getting up from their beds and trotting without a sound to the door where Elise stood.

Aunt Helen was a mix of effusive affection and total indifference, the shift back and forth confusing. When Aunt Helen put her arms around Elise in a hard hug, Elise always backed away, not wanting the sticky stuff on Aunt Helen's face to touch her. The house inside was dark, the kitchen gloomy, the back room shuttered and smelling of dogs.

The wooden sliding doors along the hall were hard to push back and forth, but Elise still managed to play with them. She liked how they disappeared into the wall, leaving a big empty square of space and the bedroom beyond until, pulled by the brass handle, they rumbled back, darkly varnished like the floor. When someone eventually told her to stop, Elise would go into the front room to draw in the dust or to pick all the winking glass objects carefully off a table so she could stroke a Kleenex across the top, watching the glossy brown wood reappear.

Once, walking soundlessly back down the dim hall to the kitchen, Elise saw the wide doorway to Aunt Helen's bedroom emptied and open. She had put both hands on the handle to pull when she saw Uncle Gar inside, sitting on a chair like a wooden Indian, his fists on his knees. Aunt Helen was leaning against the bed that was high as a small hill and covered in a dark burgundy bedspread. She was buttoning up the front of her dress. When Uncle Gar made a noise, Elise tiptoed back. The furniture stood in the front room like big cats on clawed feet, the sun shining far away on the green lawn outside the window.

Elise walked down the driveway, skimming the tops of the weeds with her hands. When a breeze blew, it was almost cool under the trees, less along the driveway than beside the cracked concrete porch of the empty house out back, shaded by a sagging roof and more trees so that it was always dark, morning or after-noon. The yard around that house for some reason was always noisy, cicadas shrilling in the trees and birds calling back and forth, raspy croaks or long warbles like someone crying. Branches rattled against the old roof as lizards flicked, rustling, into the grass. Still there was nothing that Elise could really *do* except stand in the shade and scratch her bites. This massive boredom made the empty house even more alluring.

Nana had said she would skin her alive if Elise set even one foot inside, but Elise didn't think that meant the front porch. The concrete was cool and gritty. If she stuck some Spanish moss up around the thorny shrubs at the edge of the porch, it made like an outside wall, and she could mark off rooms with broken brick from around the flower beds. Elise talked to herself under her breath while she played, explaining all the things she did, the rules involved in collecting moss, picking bricks, the reasons for the twig people to be set first there and then there.

Sometimes she heard someone else thinking out loud, too, nearby, like a low conversation going on in another room. The thoughts were methodical, repetitious, sometimes counting silverware or straightening rooms, other times thinking out how to build a porch off the back, up to the tree-hung line of the river, the grass rippling green and silver in the noonday sun. The voice murmured and murmured beside Elise's ear, thinking aloud, sad thoughts, old-fashioned words—how she loved to see the little bright-faced boys and girls in school, how it reminded her of her own childhood, that sweet and happy period of her existence, truly life's sweet and golden springtime.

Elise stood beside the front door. Compared to the cricking and rustling and twittering and thinking she heard outside, the house just past the door was still. The air smelled cool and a little rotten, as if water had seeped up from underneath and was softening the wood. There was nothing to see, not even flashes of green between the boards nailed up over the windows. The blackness seemed to start right at the doorsill, just inside, dark and quiet. Elise stared through a gap in the door, trying to imagine Nana's rose-covered carpet or Aunt Helen's lion chairs crouched on the floors, but she couldn't. It was a house full of nothing at all and she secretly loved it. Standing alone on the shaded, rustling porch, she wanted to go inside.